<u>PRAISE FOR ETHAN CROSS:</u>

"A fast paced, all too real thriller with a villain right out of James Patterson and *Criminal Minds*."
– Andrew Gross, #1 *New York Times* bestselling author of *Reckless* and *Don't Look Twice* on *The Shepherd*

"Cross pushes the boundaries in this sinisterly clever showdown between one shadowy vigilante justice group and three twisted serial killers. The surprises are fast and furious, and will leave you breathless to read more."
– Lisa Gardner, #1 *New York Times* bestselling author of *Catch Me* and *Love You More* on *The Prophet*

"The twists and turns of this intricately plotted novel will keep readers on their toes and flipping pages furiously."
– RT Book Reviews on *The Shepherd*

"This powerful thriller keeps the pace at a rapid fire. Once I started reading, it was difficult to put the book down.... It is a must-have for the action and thriller fan, and a great addition to any library. *The Shepherd* is full of surprises to the very end — you won't be disappointed and you won't see it coming."
– Blogcritics

"*The Prophet* confirms, confidently and vociferously, that Ethan Cross is one of the best damn writers in the genre."
– Anthony J. Franze, bestselling author of *The Last Justice*

FATHER OF FEAR

FATHER OF FEAR

ETHAN CROSS

THE
STORY PLANT

The Story Plant
Studio Digital CT, LLC
PO Box 4331
Stamford, CT 06907

Copyright © 2014 by Aaron Brown
Jacket design by Aaron Brown

Print ISBN-13: 978-1-61188-121-9
E-book ISBN-13: 978-1-61188-122-6

Visit our website at www.TheStoryPlant.com
Visit the author's website at www.EthanCross.com

First Story Plant printing: August 2014
Printed in the United States of America
0 9 8 7 6 5 4 3 2 1

For my daughter Madison...
even though she's too afraid to read my books

ACKNOWLEDGMENTS

First of all, I want to thank my beautiful wife, Gina, and my kids—James, Madison, and Calissa—for their love and support (especially Gina who has to endure a lot craziness in the name of research and put up with me in general).

Next, I wish to thank my parents, Leroy and Emily, for taking me to countless movies as a child and instilling in me a deep love of stories. Also, thank you to my mother, Emily, for always being my first beta reader and my mother-in-law, Karen, for being my best saleswoman.

And, as always, none of this would be possible without the help of my UK editor, Francesca Pathak; my wonderful agents, Danny Baror and Heather Baror-Shapiro; and my incredible mentor, editor, and friend, Lou Aronica. In addition to these, I wouldn't be here without the guidance and friendship of all my fellow authors at the International Thriller Writers organization.

To all of these and my extraordinary readers, thank you so much. I couldn't be living my dream without your support!

PROLOGUE

DONNY JEUNG CONSIDERED REMOVING HIS BADGE BEFORE STICKING THE HYPODERMIC NEEDLE IN HIS ARM. It was a strange and fleeting thought. What difference did it make? He could take off the uniform and the badge and the gun, and he'd still be a cop. And he'd also still be a junkie. Such thoughts floated into the ether as he depressed the plunger and the heroin entered his veins. He leaned back against the toilet bowl, the porcelain cool on his back. Sounds and smells took on exaggerated vibrancy. The aroma of pine-scented air freshener and the acrid tang of urine swirled over the muted conversations and scraping of plates in the restaurant. Euphoria enfolded him, and for a few moments, he forgot the argument he'd had with his father earlier that evening.

His father, Captain Dae-Hyun Jeung of the Kansas City Police Department, was the highest-ranking Korean immigrant in American law enforcement and wanted his son to follow in his footsteps. Donny had never wanted to be a cop and had only agreed to join the academy because it was the best of his limited options.

He jumped as the radio on his shoulder crackled to life. "Donny, get out here. We've got a possible burglary in progress."

"On my way," Donny replied as he tried to clear his head.

He pushed open the door of the bathroom stall, splashed some water on his face, and floated past the throng of restaurant patrons—mostly drunks and college kids at that hour—as he made his way out to the cruiser. He fell into the passenger seat and noticed his partner, a large-framed guy named Neil Wagner, shoot him a suspicious glance before they pulled from the parking lot. Donny wanted to smack the condescending look from the other cop's face.

Wagner's gut hung over his belt, and he stank of cigarette smoke. He had barely passed his last physical-performance exam, and yet Wagner had the nerve to judge Donny for a few harmless extra-curricular activities. Luckily, Wagner knew better than to say anything or report Donny. It was one of the few instances when Donny was glad to have Captain Dae-Hyun Jeung as a father. Not that his father would protect him out of love, but the captain wouldn't want to hurt his own illustrious reputation and his dreams of one day becoming commissioner.

They followed Barry Road into the Jefferson Highlands, onto streets filled with modest but newer homes with large well-maintained yards. The residences sat back from the street, and shadows obscured the house numbers. When they located the source of the call, Wagner pulled to the curb, and they began to check the perimeter. Donny moved to the east side of the house while Neil circled west.

Donny's flashlight beam danced over the red-rock landscaping as he checked the windows for any signs of forced entry. His head felt like it wasn't attached to his body, and he fought to maintain focus on the task at hand. He tripped over a tiny lawn gnome that wore a funny red hat matching its plump cheeks. Donny giggled at the peculiar little figure and then kicked it over on its side.

"I think I heard something out front. I'm going to head back that way," Wagner said over the radio.

"Copy that."

Donny continued around to the home's rear. No swing sets, sandboxes, or toys. No kids in the house. He congratulated himself for the deduction. He could have been a detective. *Take that, Dad.*

"Donny, head back to the car. We're at the wrong—"

"Don't move! I've got a gun!" a voice shrieked behind Donny and startled him into action. Without thinking, he whirled around, dropped to one knee, and fired his Glock at the shadowy figure who had threatened his life.

A small voice cried out in pain, and the figure crumpled to the grass of the backyard. Donny kept his gun trained on the unmoving form of the attacker. He heard running footsteps coming around the side of the house and looked up to see Wagner heading toward him, wide-eyed and winded.

Donny didn't move from his shooting stance as Wagner shone his light on the assailant. Wagner bent down and checked for a pulse. "Dear God ... you stupid ..." Wagner uttered a string of curses and ran his hands through his shaggy brown hair as he paced back and forth across the manicured lawn.

"What is it?" Donny asked. "This guy was gonna shoot me. I was defending myself."

Wagner's face twisted in fury. He stomped over to Donny and grabbed him by the collar, pulling him up to his feet and dragging him toward the body. "Look at her! It's some old woman. I was trying to tell you that we went to the wrong house. She probably thought we were burglars!"

"She had a gun."

"Do you see a gun here? Do you have any idea what you've done?"

Donny searched for answers and replayed the events in his mind. "I was defending myself," he whispered again.

"We're screwed, Donny. All of us. You just killed an innocent woman in her own backyard."

"I ... it was my fault. You didn't do anything wrong. I'll take responsibility."

Wagner jammed a finger against Donny's chest. "You ignorant, naive little prick. You've screwed the whole department on this one. The media's going to eat us alive. You think your drug habit isn't going to come out? Think your father isn't going down for this?"

"I thought ... She ..."

"You don't think, kid. That's the problem. Just shut your mouth and do exactly as I say. I'm calling your father, and we're going to figure a way out of this."

PART ONE

CHAPTER ONE

HER REAL NAME WAS RHONDA HAYNIE, BUT HER CLIENTS CALLED HER
SCARLET. None of them had ever asked her about a last name or
inquired if "Scarlet" actually appeared on her birth certificate. The
kind of men who hired her didn't care about who she was as a person. They paid for the fantasy, and that was what they got. And some
of those fantasies tested the boundaries of what even she would do
for money; they exposed the dark and depraved inner workings of
people who seemed perfectly normal by all outward appearances.

When she opened the door of the motel room, Rhonda knew
that tonight's job would push those boundaries once again.

The paint on the walls had most likely started its lifecycle as a
flat white but had now aged into a dull yellow. Only one lamp lit
the space from the far corner, leaving most of the room in shadow.
No lights overhead. All the better to hide the filth-ridden sheets
and floors that were probably swept once every six months. Generic
prints of babbling brooks and nature scenes had once covered
repairs in the drywall that hid holes placed there by inebriated former occupants. For some reason, the pictures had all been removed
and stacked in the corner. The bed hadn't been slept in or touched,
and a blanket and pillow lay crumpled along the floor against the far
wall. The place smelled like the carpet had been left out in the rain.

It was no surprise that none of the motel's other rooms seemed
to be occupied and that the parking lot was free of cars.

The client had pulled an old wooden desk chair into the center
of the room and handcuffed himself to it. He just sat there, shirtless
and staring at the wall, clothed in darkness. Trepidation clawed at the

18

corners of Rhonda's mind, but the rent needed to be paid, and so she stepped cautiously into the room and closed the door behind her.

"Hello, darling. It looks like you're all ready for me." She stepped toward the dresser and flipped on another small lamp. She gasped at what the light revealed.

Scars covered the man's chest and arms. She had seen plenty in her time on the streets, but never anything like this. Burns, knife wounds, bullet holes. More damaged tissue than healthy skin. His body was a road map of pain and suffering.

"Is something wrong?" he said in a deep and confident voice.

Rhonda forced her gaze up to his face for the first time. It didn't match the rest of the man. Handsome. Youthful. Strong features and bright, intelligent eyes. She often wondered what led her clients to seek her services. With this man, the reasons were self-evident. Anyone would be self-conscious about scars like this.

She offered her best smile. "No, baby. Everything's fine. Just give me a minute to freshen up, and we'll get started."

She moved toward the bathroom, but his next words stopped her. "There's no need for that. We won't be engaging in any sexual activity."

"Then what kind of activities did you have in mind?"

"There's a knife on the dresser. I want you to cut me. Just stick in the tip and run a nice long slice. Along a tricep, to start."

Rhonda had received more than her fair share of crazy requests. Some guys wanted to be beaten or whipped or to dress her up in all manner of crazy outfits and live out their sick fantasies. But she'd never had a client ask her to mutilate his body. The thought of it nearly made her sick.

"I was told that you were the most adventurous companion that the service offered. The money's there on the dresser beside the knife. It's three times the fee that I was quoted."

She looked at the dresser and the money. Judging by the thickness of the wad of bills, he was telling the truth. Still, she knew her limits all too well. She couldn't go through with this, and she didn't want to spend too much time in the company of any man who would make such a request.

Then an idea took shape. "Are these real handcuffs?" Rhonda asked. An edge of fear caused her voice to tremble.

She tried to examine them without raising too much suspicion, running her fingers over the edges of the cuffs and feeling for releases or anything to indicate that they were fakes.

"They're standard police-issue."

"How did you plan on getting those off when our business was completed? Are you a magician?" Rhonda tried to laugh, but it didn't sound convincing even to her own ears.

The man smiled, but the expression didn't reach his eyes. "I assumed you would be kind enough to remove them. The key's also on the dresser."

"Good. That's what I hoped."

She patted him on the shoulder, grabbed the money and the key, and headed for the door. Her fingers wrapped around the knob—but then something struck her from behind. Strong hands squeezed her shoulders and spun her around, slamming her back against the door.

He pressed the edge of the blade against her neck with just enough force to hold her in place without breaking the skin. His breath was hot on her exposed flesh. "I apologize if I gave the impression that I was secured to the chair. Because of all the scarring that runs up my forearms, my wrists are much larger than my hands. It comes in handy when I want to slip out of a pair of cuffs. The restraints were to keep me from lashing out involuntarily when you began to make the incisions. They were for your protection."

Tears ran down Rhonda's cheeks, streaking the layers of make-up. "Please ... don't ..."

The man lowered the knife from her throat and leaned closer. "I suppose that I shouldn't judge you too harshly. I do admire a woman who shows initiative, and you can't blame a girl for trying. But you see, we had a verbal contract, and you've yet to hold up your end of things."

Her fingers clawed at her thigh, pulling up the black fabric of the skirt. She kept a small switchblade concealed there for moments such as this. "You want me to cut you?" She felt the metal handle of the knife, pulled it free, and pushed the button to expose the blade. "How's this for a start?"

Rhonda jammed the knife into his leg and shoved him away. She expected him to drop, but he remained on his feet and fell against the room's door, blocking her escape. Screaming for help, she bolted for the bathroom, nearly falling over the chair resting in the middle of the floor. Once inside, she slammed the door behind her and engaged the lock.

Lime green tile-covered the walls, and the room smelled of mildew and urine. A blow shook the doorframe. "You're trying my patience," the man said calmly from the other side.

Her whole body trembled. She wiped the man's blood from her hand onto her dress as she scanned the room for a way out. The shower curtain was thin and white, and light shone through it. She ripped it back, snapping the rings in the process. They fell to the tile with small metallic clinks.

A window occupied the back wall. She scrambled into the tub and pushed up on the window's frame. It wouldn't move. She checked for a lock. Flipped the latch. Pushed again. But the window still wouldn't budge. It must have been painted shut.

The bathroom door flew open. The wood splintered, and the knob struck the tile on the opposite wall. The old green ceramics cracked and shattered and fell to the floor.

Rhonda screamed, but he was already on top of her. His grip was like a vise. It crushed her airway and cut off her cries. He pressed her against the window and lifted her from the floor of the tub.

She clawed at his hand and kicked at him with her legs, but he was so strong and refused to relent. A wave of dizziness swept over her, and she realized that this was her last moment on Earth. She would never see her baby girl again. She would never have the chance to tell her grandma that she was sorry for running away after her parents died.

She wondered what he would do with her body. Would he mutilate her? Bury her in some shallow grave, a feast for the bugs? She imagined the worms crawling through her veins.

The man raised the knife and admired the blade. Light from the translucent window danced across its surface.

This was it. Rhonda tried not to think of the pain to come. Would he bury the knife in her stomach, stabbing her over and over, savoring each thrust in some twisted sexual way? Or would he slice her throat and let her bleed out quickly? She prayed for a quick death.

The knife came toward her. She wanted to close her eyes, didn't want to see the sight of her own blood. But, for some reason, her eyelids refused to obey the signal that her brain was sending.

She watched as the blade swiped across his forearm just in front of her face, opening three long gashes in his flesh. The blood flowed quickly and dripped down into the bathtub. He closed his eyes as if savoring the moment and licked the blade clean.

Then he relinquished his grip. She dropped to her knees, and he backed away. She gasped in greedy mouthfuls of air, and violent sobbing seized her whole body.

Rhonda looked up to see him sitting on the toilet, watching her. He took a deep breath and said, "I apologize. I lost my head for a moment. I didn't want to hurt you. To tell you the truth, this is the first time that I've contracted with someone of your profession."

Her hands found the edge of the tub, and she pushed herself to her feet, preparing to lunge for the door. He must have sensed her intention and moved forward, blocking her way out.

"What's your name? Your real name."

"Screw you." Her throat felt like she'd swallowed sandpaper.

He stepped closer, and his eyes narrowed. "I've killed a lot of people. Men, women. Knives, guns, fire, my bare hands. I possess an unnatural talent for extinguishing life. But I'm trying to be a good boy here, and I would appreciate it if you showed me at least some small measure of respect. What's your name?"

"Rhonda," she said through the tears.

"Thank you, Rhonda. It's moments such as these when a person must examine their existence and their place in this world. We all have regrets. Some mistakes can be rectified, and some can never be undone. The trick is realizing the difference and acting upon it. In the past, I would have enjoyed killing you. I would have drawn out the process and extracted every exquisite moment of pain possible. But I've come to believe that there are three kinds of people in this world. At our core, we're all either a creator, a maintainer, or a destroyer."

He took another step toward her, reached out, and took her hands in his. She didn't recoil from his touch. She just stood there, oddly transfixed. Hypnotized by the intensity of his gaze.

"Maintainers keep the status quo. They're the worker bees of our little hive, and they enjoy keeping the cosmic wheels turning. It's what they were made for, and without them the walls of our reality would crumble. Then there are creators. Those rare individuals who dare to discover new things and think differently, to break the chains of fear and bring into existence something beautiful and new. I fall into the third group. The destroyers. But I want to be better than that. I need to be more. Unfortunately, I've found that I only feel alive when I'm inflicting pain or experiencing it myself."

The man kept hold of Rhonda's hand as he guided her gently back into the bedroom. "What I'm asking you to do is a kindness to me. I want you to help me be a better person. To transcend my nature as a destroyer and become something more."

He gestured toward the chair and laid the knife in her palm. She stared down at it in confusion. When her gaze returned to his face, he smiled and said, "Now, are you ready to begin?"

CHAPTER TWO

MARCUS WILLIAMS STARED AT HIS OFFICE CEILING, COUNTING THE DOTS IN THE TILES AND TRYING TO IGNORE THE TERRIBLE POUNDING IN HIS SKULL. The throbbing stabs felt like tiny construction workers jackhammering against the backs of his eyeballs. If someone had told him that drilling a hole in his skull would have relieved the pain, he would at that moment have been standing in line at the hardware store, anxiously waiting for the business to open its doors.

He wondered if the headaches would still be happening if he didn't work for the Shepherd Organization. On the surface, the group was a think-tank operating under the auspices of the Department of Justice and the Attorney General's office. In reality, their mandate was to track down serial killers by any means necessary. Even if that meant bending or outright breaking the law to do it.

Marcus gently pulled his arm out from beneath Maggie Carlisle's naked form. She stirred, rolled her shoulders, and said with a moan, "It's time you got a real bed."

"This is a real bed."

"It's a futon. Death Row inmates have nicer beds than this."

"What can I say? I know how to treat a girl right."

He pulled himself up from the futon, the thin metal frame creaking beneath his shifting weight. "Where you going?" Maggie asked, yawning.

"Nowhere. Go back to sleep. I just need some Tylenol."

Maggie rolled over, exposing the long tanned curve of her back and her golden blonde hair.

He stared at her a moment. Their relationship had always been rocky, and they had achieved a sort of stalemate, but he couldn't seem to shake her words and actions after an incident with a serial killer in Chicago. He had asked her to leave the Shepherd Organization, to put all the death and darkness behind them and start new. To be normal. She had turned him down. She had chosen her job over him. That just didn't sit right, and although he had tried to let it go, he knew that resentment had tainted their relationship. He imagined that once upon a time he would have fought to make things right, but these days he just didn't have the energy to fight anymore. What was the point?

Marcus glanced around the office at his collection of movie memorabilia and screen-used props. An Indiana Jones hat. A replica pulse rifle from *Aliens*. Carl Weathers's severed arm from *Predator*. He could have bought a house in the burbs for what he had paid for that one. But he didn't want a house. Once, maybe, but not now. He would never be normal, and the sooner he accepted that, the better off he'd be. Nearly everything he owned was in that room. He ate, slept, and worked there when he wasn't on the road, which wasn't too damn often.

He would have been on the road at the moment—tracking down a murderer known as the Coercion Killer—if he hadn't been recalled to DC for some kind of mandatory psych evaluation. The Director claimed that it was just a routine hoop that the pencil-pushers were making them jump through, but Marcus suspected there was more to it than that. Even he had to admit that his work had began to suffer due to the headaches and insomnia.

His fingertips slid across the dark woodgrain of his desk's surface as he rounded the workspace and pulled open a drawer. He took out his pills and a bottle of eighteen-year-old Glenfiddich. Then he downed the OxyContin with a long swig of Scotch straight from the bottle. His eyes watered, and his face contorted as the dark liquid slid down his throat.

He leaned back and closed his eyes as he waited for the drugs to dull the pain. After a few moments, he started back to the bed, but a vibrating against his leg stopped him in his tracks. Only a handful of people in the world had his cell number, and a call this late at night was never good. It was one of two things. Either they had an urgent situation, and the Director needed them on the road immediately. Or his older brother wanted to chat.

For most people, a call from a sibling at such a late hour would have been a minor annoyance. But when your brother was one of the most wanted men in the country and a notorious serial murderer, a late-night phone call took on a whole new dimension. Still, family was family, and Ackerman was the only family Marcus had left.

Marcus looked at his phone and didn't recognize the number, which almost without fail meant that it was Ackerman calling from a burner cell line.

He and Ackerman shared a set of parents, although they hadn't grown up together and Marcus had only recently learned their true connection. His mother had escaped with him while he was still in the womb, abandoning his brother to a life of torture and sadism at the hands of their biological father. Ackerman Sr. had been a not-so-well-respected psychologist who wanted to explore the mind of a serial killer by creating one from his own young son. What had followed for his brother were years trapped in an undying hell marked with abuse and agony and ultimately a string of corpses from one coast to the next, the true number of which was still unknown.

Marcus couldn't help but sympathize with his brother. Marcus had been raised by a New York City cop in a loving and caring home, at least up until the time when his parents were murdered. And, even then, his aunt had given him the best home she could. Despite all that, his nature was still one of violence, and dark thoughts swirled at the back of his conscious mind. Even blessed with a normal childhood, Marcus was far from normal. Ackerman had never been given a chance.

And then there was a recent revelation that Ackerman might have had even less freewill regarding his murderous tendencies than previously thought.

Answering the call, Marcus said, "Hello?"

"It's good to hear your voice. Have you missed me, brother?"

"What do you want, Frank? I was sleeping."

"No, you weren't. And did you know you're the only person who has ever called me Frank?"

"Fascinating. Can we get on with it?"

"You're in bit of a pissy mood. The headaches are getting worse, aren't they?"

"Yeah, well, you're not helping the situation."

"I'm sorry for that. I don't want to be a burden on you dear brother. But I was calling to tell you that I've been a good boy."

Marcus walked to the window and watched the trees of Northern Virginia sway in shadow as Ackerman described a run-in with a prostitute. Finally, Ackerman said, "You made me promise not to take anyone's life, if you would keep taking my calls, and I have fought very hard to keep that vow. Although I think it's a bit extreme. A little too black and white for my tastes. After all, sometimes the situation warrants—"

"No. Never."

"Agree to disagree. Besides, *you* kill people."

"I'm tired, Frank. I'd like to get at least a little sleep tonight."

"I saw a preview for a movie yesterday that got me thinking. The plot involved an apocalypse of some kind and dealt with the survivors in the aftermath. The details aren't relevant, but it made me realize that, in a world like that, I would be a hero or even a king."

"High monarch of a burned-out wasteland. Good for you. I'm going back to bed."

"That thought spiraled into other revelations. Consider this: in any other period throughout history, our skills would have made us valuable assets instead of the outcasts that we are now. If we'd been born in Ancient Greece, I could have rivaled the great warrior Achilles and you would have been my Hector. During the Spanish Inquisition or the Middle Ages, my talents in the art of inflicting pain would have been in high demand. Even in the not too distant past of the Old West, I would have been a folk hero like Billy the Kid."

"You're a regular man of the people. When you're not murdering them in their sleep."

"I've never killed anyone in their sleep. I always wake them up first. But think about it. Maybe there are so many murderers these days because men with our gifts can't find an honest trade to act as a healthy outlet for the natural predatory hunger in their souls. Anyway, something to think about. Sweet dreams, brother."

Ackerman ended the call. Marcus moved back to his desk, opened the drawer again, and popped two more pills.

CHAPTER THREE

JOSH STEFANSON HAD NEVER THOUGHT OF HIMSELF AS HEROIC, BUT HE HAD
BEEN RELATIVELY CONFIDENT THAT HE WOULD RISE TO THE OCCASION IF
AN EMERGENCY EVER PRESENTED ITSELF. Despite working a desk job at
a local architectural firm—as opposed to something more physical
and dangerous like a firefighter or police officer—he felt that he
could protect his family. Now was his chance to find out.

He had seen the news stories about the killer loose in the Kansas
City area whom the media had dubbed the Coercion Killer. Still, he
hadn't given a second thought to such things. The chances of actually running afoul of a serial killer were astronomical, much too low
to make him question his safety or that of his family. Being the next
victim of the Coercion Killer would be akin to winning the lottery.

But, people did win.

He drove the little blue Nissan into the parking lot and found
a spot next to the entrance. The lot was nearly empty, only three
other cars parked toward the back, suggesting that they belonged to
employees. That was good: no witnesses.

Josh's hands shook, and sweat dripped down his face. He didn't
bother to wipe it away. The gun rested in the glovebox. A .38 special
that had been his father-in-law's. He had never been around guns,
but his wife Nancy had grown up on a farm south of KC. She had
insisted that they have one in the house and that he knew how to use
it. He had gone along with it, not that he ever thought he would have
cause to touch the thing.

Josh opened the glovebox and pulled out the gun and a box of ammunition, spilling some of the cartridges on the floor in the process. The bullets rattled against the revolver's cylinder as he forced his trembling fingers to shove them into place.

Six shots, but hopefully he would only need one.

He kept a photo of Nancy and the kids tucked up beside the odometer. It had been taken the previous summer at Blue Springs Lake. He liked to look at it when he was stuck in traffic and fantasize that he was drinking a beer on the boat instead of heading to work.

As he admired their smiling faces, he knew what had to be done. If he thought about it too long, he would talk himself out of it. He would either go through with this or Nancy and the kids would die. It was as simple as that. There was no room for second-guessing or alternative solutions. It was black and white. Time to man up and protect his family. To be the hero that he hoped he had the guts to be.

Josh slid the gun into the pocket of his khakis and exited the vehicle. The breeze carried the smell of flowers and pollen. He fought the urge to sneeze, failed, and nearly lost his glasses in the process. The asphalt felt sticky beneath his feet. The sun hurt his eyes, which were already irritated from crying.

He could see his target through the bookstore's front window, but a hardback book blocked the man's face. The store was empty apart from the owner.

The whole situation felt so surreal. It didn't seem that he walked to the shop's door, more that he floated there as if it were all a dream. Or a nightmare. The door came open, and a ringing bell announced his presence. The owner lowered his book and greeted his customer with a smile.

Josh's heart jumped and then sank. The man behind the counter looked like such a nice man. Kind eyes and an inviting smile on a wrinkled face. Gray and balding. Someone's grandfather.

He raised the gun, not even realizing that he'd removed it from the pocket of his khakis. The old man's smile disappeared, and fear contorted his kind features.

"I'm so sorry," Josh said through the tears.

The man raised his hands. "Take all the money. I won't give you any trouble."

Josh cocked the revolver's hammer.

The old man shook his head and backed away. "Think about what you're doing, son."

"I'm sorry. There's no other way."

The man shuddered but was relatively calm, considering the situation. "We always have a choice. I haven't done anything to you. I don't even know you. I'm just a normal guy who wants to see his family again."

"So am I," Josh said as he squeezed the trigger.

CHAPTER FOUR

ONE WEEK LATER
KANSAS CITY, MO

MARCUS RAN A HAND THROUGH HIS DARK HAIR AND GAVE AN EXASPER-ATED SIGH AS HE DROPPED THE KANSAS CITY PD'S CASE FILE BACK ONTO THE OAK-LAMINATE TABLE. The last killing involved a man named Josh Stefanson—a husband and father of two who had been drawn into the Coercion Killer's sick game. The killer's tactic was simple. He kidnapped the family of an average person and then forced them to murder another completely innocent individual. If the killer's directions were followed, the kidnapped family was released unharmed. If not, they were returned in pieces.

So far the killer had remained true to his word and the rules of the game. But Marcus knew that there was a lot more to the case than the local police department or FBI realized. Only the Shepherd Organization had all the information. He just didn't know what to do with it yet, and he had been explicitly ordered not to share anything with the local investigators or FBI.

"Anything happening out there?" Marcus asked his partner, Andrew Garrison, as he walked across the tiny second-floor apartment to the window.

Marcus looked down at the record store in the street opposite the apartment. A forty-two-inch computer monitor resting beside Andrew displayed camera signals being sent from miniature high-res extruded plastic cameras positioned inside the shop and along the street. But, trusting his eyes over technology, Andrew had also trained a tripod-mounted Vanguard VSP-61 spotting scope on the store's front entrance.

"Nothing. I think he knows," Andrew replied, leaning back in his chair and placing his hands behind his head.

"He's still accessing the files."

"Yeah, but he's not taking the bait."

Marcus had learned after a previous case that Ackerman had been accessing the Shepherd Organization's servers through a back door on one of their office systems. But upon learning of the intrusion, the Director had decided that instead of closing up the hole they would use it against the killer. At least, that was the plan. So far, they had provided Ackerman with false information three times without him taking the bait. In this case, Marcus had inserted observations into the files that the owner of a specialty shop named Permanent Records might have seen the killer but was unwilling to help for some unknown reason.

Due to his connection with Marcus, Ackerman liked to insert himself into their investigations. On a case in Chicago, he had tortured information out of an uncooperative witness and had ultimately murdered the man, using an execution method popularized during the Spanish Inquisition.

The witness had turned out to be a pedophile linked to the disappearances of several young boys, and the information that Ackerman had forced out of him had led to the resolution of the case. But, as Marcus seemed to be asking himself more and more every day, he wondered if the ends justified the means.

Andrew rubbed his eyes and asked, "How was your psych eval?"

"Painful and counter-productive. I should have been here."

"Believe it or not, the world keeps on turning without you."

"That's a matter of opinion. When do you go in for your own eval?"

Andrew hesitated before saying, "I'm not sure."

Marcus nodded, his suspicions confirmed. "Do you think I'm slipping?"

"I think you're one of the best detectives I've ever worked with."

"That's not what I asked."

"You really want to have this conversation now?"

"You're the one who's always trying to get me talk about things. So talk."

They stared at each other a moment. Marcus had seen that look on Andrew's face many times before. His partner was searching for the most diplomatic way to voice his concerns without hurting anyone's feelings.

"Just say what's on your—"

A knock on the door drew Marcus's attention away from the discussion, his hand straying to the Sig Sauer P220 Equinox on his hip. They turned to the computer monitor in unison to see a group of seven men standing in the hall. Marcus recognized the muscular frame of the lead figure—his boss, a man known only to him as the Director. The Director had recently shaved his head since his hair was starting to thin, but Marcus suspected that the man, who had to be reaching his retirement years, could still take down most men half his age.

Andrew opened the door, and the group filed in. The Director greeted them warmly while five of the others checked the corners and scanned their surroundings with cautious, rapid glances. Their fluid and efficient movements spoke of field training in the military or intelligence communities and experience in covert operations.

Marcus's eyes narrowed as the final member of the group stepped inside and closed the door behind them. He was different from the others. Expensive suit covering a small frame. Designer glasses. Manicured fingernails. A leather briefcase dangling from his left fist. Obviously some kind of bureaucrat. But Marcus wondered what could have drawn one of the elite away from the marble palaces in DC to a stakeout in one of Kansas City's worst neighborhoods. And why would he bring a team of operators along with him? None of the reasons could be good.

The man in the suit smiled and stuck out his hand. His voice was soft and friendly. It possessed a nasal quality overlaid by a New England accent. The intensity in his eyes accompanied an air of confidence. "Special Agent Williams. I've heard a lot about you."

Marcus met the man's gaze, and without returning the greeting, he asked the Director, "What the hell is all this?"

With a look of warning, the Director said, "Marcus, this is Deputy Assistant Attorney General Trevor Fagan. He's our new boss. The Attorney General's office has decided to take a more active role in our operations."

"Really? Then what's with the goon squad?"

"These men are a black-ops team of contractors on loan to us from the CIA."

"Contractors? So they're mercenaries. Like Blackwater?"

"Something like that. They're here to assist in the capture of Francis Ackerman Jr."

"You mean they're here to kill him. We've talked about this. We need Ackerman alive. He has knowledge about—"

The Director raised a hand. "Let's take this in the other room."

The man who had recruited Marcus to be a Shepherd walked into the apartment's small bedroom with Fagan at his heels. Marcus was the last to enter. He shut the door behind them. The room was empty except for some blankets and an air mattress stuffed into one corner.

Fagan opened the briefcase and handed a manilla folder to Marcus. In his soft voice, Fagan said, "That's your psych eval."

Marcus didn't open the folder. The pounding behind his eyeballs grew in intensity. "Why don't you give me the short version?"

Fagan nodded. His demeanor reminded Marcus of an airline rep about to tell him that they had lost his luggage. "Sure. According to the evaluation, we should pull you from active duty. Here are the highlights that I remember." Fagan started counting off points on his fingers as he paced the room. "Paranoid, impulsive, a problem with authority, chronic insomnia, migraines, possible addiction to painkillers for the headaches, patient doesn't seem to care whether he lives or dies to the point of having a death wish, irritability, verging on a nervous breakdown. Did I miss anything important, Director?"

The Director sighed and wouldn't make eye contact. "I think that about sums it up."

An air-conditioning unit rattled annoyingly in the window. Marcus broke the unit down in his mind into each component and examined them—screws, metal, knobs, condenser fan, blower, plastic grille, filter, condenser coil, evaporator coil. He tried to imagine the problem that was causing the rattle. He repeated this with the window and the housing keeping the unit in place. Fagan's leather shoes squeaked on the hardwood floor. The bureaucrat wore some kind of padded inserts and walked with too much pressure on his heels—he most likely suffered from heel spurs. He favored his right leg, sign of an old injury. The Director had missed a small spot when shaving his head just above the left ear, leaving a patch of dark stubble. The five operators in the other room were moving around. Marcus could hear their boots on the linoleum in the kitchen and on the hardwood near the windows. Probably verifying the integrity of the surveillance system. A lemon-colored moth flapped against the light overhead. The high-pitched beep of a car horn sounded outside the window. Probably a compact car. A door opened in the apartment upstairs and footsteps padded across the carpeted floor.

Marcus wasn't ignoring the importance of the current situation or tuning out the Director and Fagan. He simply couldn't filter out the rest of the information as well. It all melted together in his head like watching a thousand television screens at once. He soaked up every detail and filed them away in his mental database for future reference. He tried to focus completely on the conversation, but he couldn't turn off the rest of the world no matter how hard he tried.

He cracked his neck to the side and pressed his thumb and forefinger against the bridge of his nose. He said, "You need me on this case, and you know it. If you want to fire me or put me in a rubber room or whatever you had in mind, that's fine. But not until after this one is finished."

Fagan said, "I'm not here to take you off the case, Agent Williams, and I'm not here to fire you. I'm here to get you back on track. We're on the same team."

Then the Deputy Assistant AG patted Marcus on the shoulder and walked into the other room. The Director started past as well, but Marcus grabbed his arm and whispered, "What's really going on here?"

The Director's gaze traveled from Marcus to Fagan and back again, as if he were debating whether or not to disobey orders. Then he said softly, "The powers that be are thinking of shutting down the Shepherd Organization, and that man is the one who gets to decide our fate. So, for once, please try to play nice."

"What does that look like?"

"When it comes to Fagan, whatever your instincts tell you to do, just do the opposite."

CHAPTER FIVE

THE APPRENTICE NO LONGER THOUGHT OF ITSELF AS A PERSON. It was a thing. A monster. An inanimate object on a mission, like a bullet pointed toward an intended target. No remorse. No guilt. No second-guessing. It had been told what to think and do, and it knew nothing else but to obey.

It wasn't even sure if it was truly alive or if this was hell. It couldn't be sure that it had ever been alive. Although there were vague pictures that floated through its mind on occasion, they seemed like memories of a life that it couldn't remember living.

It would eat when its stomach ached. Not because it understood hunger, but because that was what it had been told to do. It defecated into a bucket when it felt the urge. But if the master's instructions hadn't been specific on that point, it would have just released the waste onto itself. It registered the smell of the feces swimming in the bucket to its right, but it didn't feel anything about the smell one way or another. It felt nothing. It wasn't alive.

It sat in front of the picture window, staring at the house across the street and taking meticulous notes about the family's comings and goings. As it jotted down the time of the light being turned off in the living room, it had an odd thought. It could read and write and tell time and understand concepts like deception and fear and death. It could drive a car and fire a gun and respond when spoken to. But it didn't remember learning of such things, as if it had simply been programmed upon its creation with a default set of knowledge.

The house around it was devoid of furniture or pictures. The space only held the chair in which it sat, the bucket to its right, and the binoculars and notebook on the window ledge. It raised the binoculars and watched as Julie Dunham shut off the light in the hall-way and joined her husband, Brad Dunham, in the bedroom. That room was lit with a bluish tinge indicating that the television was still on. It knew that Julie would soon join her husband in slumber. Then it would start the timer as the master had instructed.

It sat in place for the next two hours, unmoving, unthinking, just a swirling of the fuzzy and strange images and sensations. Then the timer beeped, and it stood up from the chair, covered its face with a black balaclava, and made its way over to the Dunham home. It kept to the shadows to remain unseen, as the master had instructed.

The security system in the home would be armed, but the mas-ter had prepared for that fact. The apprentice removed a small rect-angular device from its pocket and pressed the gray button at the center. With a mechanical whir and a protest of hinges, the garage door slid up.

The apprentice then moved inside and slid beneath Julie's car before closing the garage door with another press of the button. Now it would wait for Brad to leave for work, and once he was gone, it would take the family, just as the master had instructed. It didn't want to hurt the people inside the house, and it had a hazy sense that what it was doing was wrong. But it also knew that to disobey would bring great pain, and that was the one thing it could still feel.

CHAPTER SIX

MARCUS HAD BEEN RESTING ON THE AIR MATTRESS AND TRYING IN VAIN TO FALL ASLEEP FOR TWO HOURS WHEN ANDREW CALLED TO HIM FROM THE ADJACENT ROOM. The Director had taken the night shift and then Andrew had relieved him at eight in the morning. Marcus wasn't supposed to take over until one o'clock that afternoon. Something must have been happening. He leaped to his feet and hurried to Andrew's side. The CIA operators also came to life, preparing their equipment and readying themselves to move out. The room smelled of burned coffee and brimmed with anxious tension.

"I think we have something," Andrew said. He tapped a key on the computer and brought up a full-screen view of a dirty-looking man with long red hair hanging over half of his face and a scraggly red beard. The man moved toward the front of the record store in a stumbling zigzag.

"Is that him, Marcus?" the Director asked.

"The build's right. I can't be sure, but it looks just like the disguise he used when he killed Crowley in Chicago. See the way his hair is masking half of his face? Ackerman likes to use that trick to throw off facial-recognition software. Most of the programs rely on symmetry. Covering half of the face keeps them from getting a read."

"We can't afford to wait until we're a hundred percent," Fagan said in his nasally New England accent. Then he nodded to the leader of the CIA squad, a tall blond with a lined face and deep-set pale blue eyes. "Go get him. We want him alive—but don't take any chances."

None of the operators said a word as they headed for the door. Each man was dressed in plain clothes, but all were armed with tasers and handguns concealed beneath thin jackets and hooded sweatshirts. The government had most likely trained them extensively to blend into a crowd, but there was no crowd out there to blend with. Marcus was relatively sure that Ackerman would spot them from a mile away.

He started after them, but Fagan wrapped a hand around his bicep and said, "I want you to stay here. These guys are the best. They can handle Ackerman."

He ripped his arm free of the politician's grasp. "I'm not taking any chances."

"Marcus, you're too close to this. Stand down," the Director said.

Gritting his teeth, Marcus moved back to the monitors. He'd been reduced to an audience member at his own fight, and there wasn't much he could say about it. At least, not until things went south.

❖

Out of the corner of his eye, Ackerman saw the group of agents exit the apartment building. They tried to act like a group of friends on their way to a bar or a baseball game, but he could tell what they were. They couldn't conceal their animal natures and predatory grace. Not from a man who had also been trained to kill.

Someone had upped the stakes of the game. These men moved with a calm efficiency and practiced ease that spoke of military training and skill. Could be members of the FBI's elite Hostage Rescue Team or, even better, a team of operators from Delta Force or the CIA.

Ackerman felt flattered.

The thought of being hunted by such men and in turn hunting them forced adrenaline into his veins and sent excitement pulsing through all his senses. It had been a long time since he had faced a real challenge, and he had forgotten how good it felt to be in mortal danger. It made him feel truly alive.

Not that his brother wasn't a wonderful opponent. He just knew that Marcus would never be able to pull the trigger. Marcus could try to hide his feelings beneath that hard exterior, but Ackerman knew that at least a part of his brother loved him and wanted to save him.

But the men coming for him now held no such affinity. They wouldn't hesitate to end his life in a gloriously bloody fashion.

This was going to be fun.

◆

Marcus watched the monitors and shook with nervous anticipation as the operators circled their target. The bearded man seemed oblivious to their approach, but if it was Ackerman, Marcus knew that he wouldn't go down without a fight.

The man pushed through the front door of the record shop, the electronic ding of the door's bell ringing out through the speakers of Marcus's computer. He seemed to glance around for a worker, but the store's owner and one customer had already slipped out the back when they received the word that a possible suspect was approaching. Marcus didn't want to take any chances of Ackerman grabbing a hostage, and the owner of the shop—a retired cop—had been more than willing to help.

The target began shuffling through some old Beatles records. Marcus looked toward the approaching CIA team. Two were coming through the front door with one waiting on the street as a second line of defense while the remaining two members of the team had circled around through the alley and were coming in the back. Smooth, efficient, confident. Too confident.

His gaze shifted back to the store's interior. The bearded man with the shaggy red hair still seemed unaware of the presence of the attackers, but Marcus guessed that would be how Ackerman would play it: act like his guard was down, lure his opponents into a false sense of security.

The agents went in hard and fast. The one on the right aimed a big .45 caliber pistol while the one on the left held his taser out at arm's length.

The redhead still didn't turn toward them.

Marcus involuntarily and pointlessly placed his hand over his gun. It wasn't as if he could help them through the computer screen.

"Don't move. Show us your hands," taser-man said.

This finally drew the bearded guy's attention. He wheeled toward them with the look of a scared rabbit on his face.

"Hands up! Now!" the pistol-wielding agent screamed.

The bearded man bolted for the rear of the store but came up against the other two agents. He pulled up short. His eyes darting in every direction before the barbs of one of the tasers penetrated his flesh. He fell to the linoleum floor in a fit of violent convulsions.

The red wig fell from his head to reveal short dark hair.

A split second later a pair of agents were on top of him, securing his hands and feet. The others held back with their weapons still trained on the downed figure, taking no chances.

"This isn't right," Marcus said.

Fagan grinned. "I told you these guys are the best. And you were the one who set up this operation. It doesn't reflect badly on you that they took him down so easily. You put him in that position. Good work all around."

"That's not what I mean. Have them pull off the fake beard and show his face to the cameras."

Fagan relayed the order into his radio, and they all watched as the agents revealed the dirty face of a young man with bloodshot eyes and gaunt features.

"It's not him."

"It's some homeless guy. Ackerman played us," the Director said.

Marcus barely heard his boss. He had shoved Andrew out of the way and was working the controls of the computer. He brought up the video footage of moments before on the street as the bearded man had approached.

"What are you doing?" Andrew asked.

"He would have wanted to watch."

"There!" Marcus jammed a finger against the monitor over the image of a young blond woman pushing a new plastic baby carriage.

Fagan said, "What are you—"

But Marcus was already on the move. He rushed into the bedroom and threw open one of the windows to reveal the fire escape. The rusting old metal protested as his weight dropped onto it.

He took the grated stairs three at a time, grabbing the railing and using it as a pivot to slide around the corners. When he reached the bottom, he kicked the ladder. It dropped to the asphalt of the alleyway with a resounding clang.

Marcus slid down to street level and sprinted down the alley away from the record store. The blond woman had walked straight past the store and then turned away to the left. His only hope was to circle around and cut her off.

The sudden burst of adrenaline and the pounding of his heart combined with the throbbing headache and made him feel dizzy and nauseous. But the adrenaline also made his legs pump hard and fast.

His pounding footfalls echoed off the walls of the alley. Above and to the left, he heard someone calling after him and following him down the fire escape. He ignored them. They wouldn't arrive in time to make any difference.

He came up on the end of the alley as it intersected with another street. Pulling his Sig Sauer semi-automatic, he pivoted around the corner. But neither the blond woman nor anyone else was in sight.

Pistol still in hand, he rushed across the street and into another alley. This one smelled of grease and ginger and sesame oil. A small white man carrying a trash bag and wearing a shirt covered with Chinese symbols pushed open a door on the right.

Marcus didn't say a word as he shoved past the man into the kitchen of a Chinese restaurant. A cook yelled something unintelligible. A waitress pushed through from the dining area carrying a tray of plates piled with food remnants. Her eyes went wide at the sight of the large man barreling down on her. Marcus didn't have time to stop. The pair collided, and the plates crashed to the tile floor. Shards of glass and grains of rice and pieces of orange chicken went everywhere. He spun away, slipping in the mixture of sauces and leftover food, and stumbled into the dining area.

The restaurant's patrons yelped in shock as he pulled his gun. Mothers cowered beneath booths with their children while others fled toward the bathrooms. He ignored them all.

Marcus burst onto the street and sighted down the barrel of his Sig Sauer at the young blonde woman pushing a baby stroller and making her way up the street. She was heading straight for him. Less than fifteen feet away.

Only she wasn't a "she" at all. She was his brother—Francis Ackerman Jr.

❖

Ackerman's face broke into a huge grin at the sight of the man staring at him over the barrel of a gun. Marcus had seen through the ruse, and Ackerman beamed with pride at his baby brother.

Of course, he still wasn't going to let himself be captured. He had considered such a possibility. That was why he had loaded the seat of the hooded infant stroller full of a simple binary explosive made from potassium permanganate and brake fluid. All he needed to do was tilt the carriage at the proper angle or shove it forward at sufficient velocity, and the two chemicals would mix and cause a chemical combustion. Simple, yet effective. It was amazing the things one could learn on the Internet.

He didn't believe that the bomb would be powerful enough to kill or injure anyone—and therefore not violate his promise to Marcus—but it should still serve as a nice distraction.

"Hello, Marcus."

"You make an ugly woman," Marcus replied

"Really? I thought I looked rather alluring. You can put the gun down. I know you wouldn't kill me. We're family, after all."

"Maybe you're right," Marcus said as he pointed the gun down at the lower half of Ackerman's body. "But I won't hesitate to shoot you in the leg."

"As fun as all that sounds—"

Ackerman was about to shove the carriage toward his brother, but Marcus's next move stopped him cold. Marcus lowered the gun and jammed it back in his holster.

Then Marcus said, "I'm sure you've got some backup plan. You always do. You always come prepared. We'll probably still catch you, but someone might get hurt in the process."

"So you're surrendering?"

"No—you are."

Ackerman laughed. "I think you're a bit unclear on the rules of our little game. And I'm not going back into a cage. I spent most of my life in one. I think I'd rather be dead."

"I need your help."

Ackerman heard more sets of running footsteps pounding down the street behind him. The team of agents from the record store were almost there. If he was going to make a move, now was the time.

"That's a new one. So what can I do for you?"

"You can help me catch our father."

Ackerman's smile faded. "He's dead. I killed him myself."

"Apparently not. He's still out there."

"Believe me. I killed him. It's the one thing I'm good at."

"He must be better at surviving than you are at killing."

"What makes you so sure?"

"Surrender, and I'll tell you everything. You'll just have to trust me. I swear on our mother's grave that I'm telling you the truth."

Ackerman thought about that for a long moment. Then he raised his hands and said, "Fine, you win. I'm all yours, brother. But don't touch the stroller. There's a bomb in there."

"Only you would put a bomb in a baby carriage."

Ackerman's smile returned. "At least I took the baby out first."

CHAPTER SEVEN

BRAD DUNHAM WAS A SIMPLE MAN, BUT NOT A STUPID ONE. He enjoyed working with his hands and his strong back, but he also had a good business sense which led him to focus on areas that most other general contractors ignored. Customer service, marketing, public relations, strategic partnerships—these things and a strong work ethic were what had taken Brad from a one-person handy man operation to a full-blown construction firm with five teams of workers handling different projects. His success had brought other perks as well, like being able to come home in the middle of the day and surprise his wife Julie with lunch at a nice restaurant and an afternoon excursion into the city.

But Brad knew that something was wrong the moment he pulled into his garage and stepped out of his truck.

A large white envelope, the same kind he used for mailing contracts, was taped to the door leading into his kitchen. He stood there and stared at it for a moment. It was a little larger than a normal sheet of paper. Maybe nine by twelve inches. Crisp, clean, white, new. *Open Me* was written across its front in large red letters.

His mind reeled with possibilities. Divorce papers? A goodbye note? He and Julie had their problems, just like any other couple. But he hadn't seen anything like this coming. He moved toward the door with hesitant footsteps. The smell of gasoline and engine exhaust still hung in the air, and he listened to the truck's engine pinging and crackling as it cooled down from the drive home.

Taking a deep breath, he forced himself to grab the packet. Maybe he was jumping to conclusions? Maybe it was just a note saying to turn down the crockpot or that she'd be home late? Maybe it was a good thing? A surprise?

The packet bent in half as he pulled it free. He turned it over and undid the fastening. It contained some papers and photos of a man he didn't recognize, but there was also something heavier in the bottom—a silver home-made DVD in a clear jewel case. *Watch Me* was written across the front of the disc in the same red lettering.

Maybe it was a game of some kind? But Julie wasn't the spontaneous or playful type.

He opened the door and called out, "Julie? Are you home? Hello?"

Silence filled his home's corridors. No response came. He repeated himself three more times, but still nothing. Then he realized that Julie's car was still in the garage. But maybe she had left with a friend? He chastised himself for being so indecisive and concluded that he might as well stop speculating and just watch the video.

Brad threw his keys on the gray and black Formica countertop, just as he did every other day. Then he kicked off his boots and placed them next to the door. The kitchen smelled of vinegar. Julie used a vinegar mixture as a natural cleaning fluid. He would have preferred the smell of bleach or other harsh chemicals, but he stayed out of her business.

His son's backpack still sat on the woodgrain surface of the kitchen table.

He swallowed hard. Something wasn't right.

He wasted no more time. He moved to the living room, flicked on the television, booted up the DVD player, and activated the surround-sound system. Then he slid the disc into the tray and sat down on the coffee table as he waited for it to load.

It was a short wait, and then the face that filled the screen made him flinch back and shudder. The visage was horrific. It was that of a man in his mid-thirties with dark features and high cheekbones. The features were twisted in terrible agony, but they were also frozen and dead. The eyes didn't match the rest of the face. They were alive with a sinister glee.

After a second, Brad realized that it was some terrible but realistic mask.

The lips didn't move, but a voice came out from behind the mask and thundered from the surround-sound speakers. Brad grabbed for the remote and adjusted the volume.

The voice inside the grotesque mask was hypnotic, eerily calm, and compelling. Not malevolent, but not friendly.

"Hello, Mr. Dunham. I'm sure you're wondering what's going on, so I'll cut to the heart of the matter. The papers have started calling me the Coercion Killer. It's as good a name as any. But you and your family might as well call me God, because I have your world in my hands. I've studied you. I've watched you. But you can't truly know another human being until you've seen them in crisis. Will you be at your best when things are at their worst? Let's find out."

Brad couldn't believe this was happening. Something like this hadn't even crossed his mind when he'd first seen the packet.

The killer's hypnotic voice continued on. "I know that you own a gun. A 9mm Beretta. You're going to use it to kill someone. Inside the packet is all the information you need to know about your target. A twelve-hour timer starts at five o'clock this evening. If the timer runs out and the man whose details are in the packet is still living, I will return your wife to you in pieces. She will die a very horrible and painful death. When she takes her last breath, I'll start another timer. If your target is still living at the end of that timer, then your son will share his mother's fate, and our experiment will be over. If you've followed my saga in the papers, you'll know that I'm a man of my word. If you follow through at your end, your family will be released unharmed. If you don't, they'll die. They have been sedated the entire time they've been with me. They can come home and wake up in their beds and barely know that anything's even happened. They can't identify me or provide any information to the police. I have no reason beyond the reaches of our little game to kill them. So now you must ask yourself what you'll do for them. Dying for them is easy, but will you *kill* for them? Will you spend the rest of your life in prison to save them? I have my theories about what will happen next. I believe that I know what kind of a man you are ... Do you?"

The grotesque death mask hovered on the big screen of the TV for a moment longer, and then the screen faded to black. As the nightmarish face disappeared, Brad Dunham dropped to his knees and threw up all over the living room's new carpet.

CHAPTER EIGHT

THE CIA CONTRACTORS HAD CLAMPED A PAIR OF FLEX-CUFFS ON THE SUR-
RENDERING ACKERMAN AND HAD DRAGGED HIM BACK TO THE APARTMENT.
They closed around him like a protective detail covering a foreign
diplomat. Except that they had guns that were held low and were
leveled at the person whom they would have been shielding. They
moved with assurance and efficiency but tried not to draw attention
to themselves.

Marcus followed a few steps behind, pushing the explosive-filled
stroller and watching the strange cavalcade. Ackerman didn't resist
at all. He let them almost carry him over the sidewalk, through the
door of the apartment building, up a dimly lit stairwell, and into
their makeshift headquarters.

Andrew's eyes went wide as they entered. "I'll be damned. This
may sound funny, but I actually didn't think we'd catch him. At least,
not alive."

Ackerman said, "Thank you, Andrew, for the vote of confidence."

"He surrendered and has agreed to help us," Marcus added, more
for the ears of the overzealous clandestine operators than for Andrew.

"Good job, men," Fagan said.

The Director walked up and punched Ackerman in the gut. The
killer doubled over and chuckled. "Good to see you as well, Phillip."

Confused, Marcus turned to his brother. "You know his name?"

Ackerman reared back to his full height and looked the Director
squarely in the eyes. "Of course. I know all. See all."

The Director met Ackerman's gaze without flinching, his hands
clenched at his sides.

Marcus shook his head in disbelief. The Director was a bit of a strange man. To Marcus's knowledge, no member of their team had ever called the Director by his real name, nor did they know what it was. He supposed that was one thing about his brother—Ackerman was full of surprises.

The CIA contractors shoved Ackerman down into a chair at the kitchen table and their big blond leader said, "We can't keep him here. My men are bringing the transport van around. You have until then to ask him a few questions. Then we're moving him to an isolated facility we've acquired beyond the city limits."

"An isolated facility," Ackerman said. "That sounds exciting. But first things first. How do you know that our father is alive?"

"We're asking the questions," Fagan said.

Marcus rolled his eyes, knowing that it was pointless to play tough with Ackerman. "A package addressed to me was sent to the Attorney General's office. It contained two items. A missing video from your childhood, and a newspaper clipping from Kansas City about a series of elaborate murders. His fingerprints were all over both. Still, we were worried that they were from you and had been staged somehow. That is, until we ran voice-print analysis comparisons between videos left by the killer in this case—the media call him the Coercion Killer—and the videos of the experiments our father conducted on you when you were a boy. The voice was a match. Since we're playing show-and-tell, what made you sure that he was dead?"

"Typically, when you stab someone six times in the back and shove them into an alligator-infested swamp, they stay dead."

"Why were you in a swamp?"

"This was after the police had caught on to what father was doing to me. And some time after we traveled to New York to kill our mother and your adopted father, Marcus. We were hiding on a stolen houseboat in Louisiana. We were playing one of Father's favorite games. He always forced me to read literature and study random topics, then he would quiz me on the details. If I answered a question incorrectly, he would hurt me in some diabolically clever way. In this case, he stabbed a knife through my hand. Then he made the mistake of turning his back on me. I pulled the knife free, and the rest belongs in a history book."

The Director said, "Okay, but then why have we never seen or heard anything from him for all these years?"

Ackerman ignored the question and asked Marcus, "Are these restraints really necessary?"

Marcus cocked an eyebrow. "I honestly cannot believe you just asked me that. Answer the Director."

"I didn't hear the magic word."

The Director struck Ackerman across the face, a firm open-fisted blow. Marcus put a hand on the Director's chest. "Come on. You know he doesn't even feel it."

"I know that. But I still enjoy it."

Ackerman gave the older man a wink. "It was good for me too, sweetie."

Marcus held the Director back and said, "Please."

"Father trained me how to kill without people even being aware that a murder had occurred. He had all these theories about how someone with our particular tastes could operate without detection for years. He made an art form of it. But that never appealed to me. What's the point in committing the perfect murder if no one knows it? I *wanted* to be infamous. But Father, if he's still alive as you say, then I suspect he's been active all these years, and you didn't even realize he was out there."

Marcus had already considered that possibility. Which was why he had been studying the cases of every missing person in a hundred-mile radius of KC. He had spent hours diving into every detail of those cases, memorizing every face. But, so far, he hadn't discovered any pattern or accomplished anything beyond occupying the time when he should have been sleeping.

"So why show himself now?" Marcus asked. "These killings are very dramatic. The person doing this wants attention and a lot of it. He takes the family of one victim and then forces them to murder someone else in order for the family to be set free."

Ackerman nodded. "That does sound like him. Don't you see? The whole thing is a social experiment. Father's a very inquisitive student of human nature. That's why he chose psychology as a field of expertise. He gets to observe the reactions of people in extreme circumstances and also to study the effects that the killings have on a community and society at large."

To his men, Fagan said, "Bastard sounds jealous that he didn't think of it first."

Ackerman smiled. "Maybe I am."

The Director asked, "What about aliases?"

"I heard him use a few from time to time, but I'd have to think about what they were."

The blond CIA contractor received a message over his radio that their transport had arrived. "We can finish this at the holding facility," he said.

Ackerman looked at Marcus as the goon squad dragged him to his feet. He said, "You asked the right question. Why did Father come out of hiding? And in such a public way? There has to be a reason. An initiating event that made him decide to track you down and to stage this big production. If you can figure out what made him emerge from the shadows, then you can force him the rest of the way into the light."

CHAPTER NINE

THE CIA CONTRACTORS HAD ACQUIRED AN OLD FARMHOUSE NORTH OF HARRISONVILLE, MO TO SERVE AS ACKERMAN'S TEMPORARY DETENTION CENTER. Built in the 1920s, the one-and-a-half-story yellow craftsman-style home sat on forty acres and rested within a small valley. The place came pre-filled with furniture that looked as if it hadn't been moved since the 1960s. Hardwood floors, beautiful wood trim, French doors. Kitchen, back porch, dining room, laundry room, and living room on the main floor, with three bedrooms and a bathroom upstairs. The topography of most of the area was flat, but small hills crowned with sporadic trees surrounded the house and yard. Beyond that was farmland. And beyond that was the highway.

Marcus didn't like the place. Ackerman would have places to run to if he got loose, and the perimeter wasn't easy to defend. He supposed neither factor mattered much. They weren't expecting an attack, and Ackerman wouldn't try to escape—at least, not yet.

The goon squad had set up shop in the living room and converted the dining room into a makeshift prison. That left the upstairs for Marcus, Andrew, Maggie, and the Director, which worked out perfectly since Marcus and Maggie would share a room.

Marcus watched through a second-story window as a gray panel van pulled up and the black-ops team unloaded Ackerman. They were calm and efficient, as though they'd previously carried out the same type of extraction many times. But Marcus knew that they'd never dealt with a prisoner like Ackerman before, and thinking of his brother as just another high-value target could lead to all of their deaths.

The first thing Maggie had done upon entering the room was strip off the bed sheets and replace them with a newly purchased set. Then she had scrubbed the bedroom from top to bottom with a strong-smelling cleaning fluid. She was just starting to organize her clothes in the closet, each garment covered by a layer of plastic, when the van pulled up. She turned away from her organizing and joined Marcus at the window.

She chewed on her fingernails as she watched Ackerman through the pane of dusty glass. She ground her teeth at the sight of him. "I can't believe that we didn't just kill him," she said.

"He surrendered," Marcus replied.

"What difference does that make? He doesn't deserve to be breathing."

"We need him."

"He won't help us. It's not in his nature."

Marcus turned away from the window and leaned back against the old yellowing plaster of the bedroom wall. "My father is out there right now on a killing spree that has this whole state living in terror. And Ackerman is the only one who knows him. We have no good leads. Nothing. We need every bit of help we can get."

"We can't trust him."

"Who said anything about trusting him? Besides, the only person that hates my father more than me is my big brother."

"That's another thing. I don't like how easily you've started referring to him as your brother. He's not your family." Maggie placed a hand on his chest. "We're your family. *He's* a monster."

"If he's a monster, then what does that make me?"

"You're nothing like him."

Marcus sat down on the bed and closed his eyes. The room stank of Maggie's cleaning fluids. "You don't know me," he said. "Not really."

She walked over to him, the hardwood protesting at each step, and leaned down into his face. "How dare you say that! You know how hard I've had to work to crack your shell. And just when I think we're making progress, you start pulling away."

"I start pulling away? That's funny. I believe I was the one who asked you to leave all this behind."

"Marcus, you know I—"

"You know why I can't sleep, Maggie?" Marcus said. "Because when I sleep, I dream of murdering people. And in my dreams, I like it. I'm exactly like him."

"That's just your own fears coming through in your dreams. It doesn't mean anything."

"I don't want to have this conversation right now. I need to talk to my brother."

Marcus walked out and closed the door behind him. He stood there a moment in the hall and heard Maggie start to cry. He reached for the knob and was about to go back in and apologize when the Director called up from the bottom of the stairs.

"Marcus! You need to get back to the city. There's been another abduction. A woman and her young son, and this time we're finally ahead of the game."

"What about Ackerman?"

"He'll be here when you get back. You and Andrew need to check out that scene. The clock's ticking."

Marcus double-timed it down the stairs. Andrew was already waiting by the door, but before Marcus could join him, Fagan stepped in from the living room and said, "And remember, Agent Williams, you're just there to observe. Take the info they give you but keep your conclusions and anything you find to yourself."

"If they don't have all the information, then the locals and the FBI will just be spinning their wheels. I thought we were all on the same team."

"The same team, yes, but with different parts to play. Don't draw attention to yourself or to this organization. That's an order."

Marcus wanted to tell Fagan what he could do with his orders, but remembering his earlier conversation with the Director, he choked back his words and replied, "Yes, sir."

Chapter Ten

Thomas White hummed a tune that he couldn't get out of his head as he descended the stairs from the loft apartment that overlooked his small shop. The piece of music was the String Quartet No. 8 in C minor by composer Dmitri Shostakovich. It was a dark piece of classical music filled with raw emotion and torment. He found it soothing.

His music store, The Thirteenth Fret, was on 4th Street in the heart of the business district of Leavenworth, KS. He had started giving music lessons there many years ago and now ran the store for the late owner's daughter, who had no interest in music but enjoyed getting her monthly percentage. She had tried to sell the business to him on many occasions, but he preferred the property records to be in someone else's name.

Music was his passion—or at least one of them. Guitars lined the walls from floor to ceiling while the center of the store contained speakers, pianos, amplifiers, and various other items such as cords and strings. A glass-fronted and humidity-controlled space occupied half of the back wall and housed many rare and expensive instruments. The other half of the back area was a soundproof space designated solely for music lessons.

The piece by Shostakovich still in his mind, Thomas White removed an Ibanez Tosin Abasi Signature eight-string guitar from the wall and plugged it into a Mesa Boogie Triple Rectifier amp. Cranking up the volume, he played a version of the Shostakovich composition that he had arranged for guitar, incorporating sweep-picking and finger-tapping techniques. His fingers flew over the frets as he lost himself in the music.

After what felt like only a few moments, he put the guitar down and turned to see his new student watching him with awe. Thomas checked his watch. He had lost track of time, and they were already five minutes behind. He hated to be off schedule.

The kid's eyes were wide with wonder, and a goofy grin creased his visage. Long black hair hung over his pimpled face, and he wore a black Metallica T-shirt displaying the cover of *Master of Puppets*. A guitar gig bag hung over one shoulder. "That was amazing," the kid said. "You can shred."

Thomas basked in the praise. He bowed and said in his deep hypnotic voice, "Thank you. You must be Joel. I'm Thomas White. I understand that you want to learn the guitar?"

"I guess, man. I have a buddy that plays drums, and he's been wanting me to jam with him. I got this Yamaha for Christmas two years ago, but I've never really learned anything on it. Just a few things off YouTube. Should I get it out?"

Thomas White gently rested the Ibanez guitar on a stand and replied, "No, we won't actually be playing anything this first lesson. I assume you have an iPod or music on your phone? Most people your age do."

"Sure, I have an iPhone."

"Good. I want you to go through your phone and find your five favorite songs. Any genre. I want to hear the songs that speak to your heart."

"Okay. But we're not going to play anything?"

"Not this time. You see, it's my belief that anyone can learn notes and chords and where to put their fingers. But not everyone can truly play. Music isn't like a sport. It's not a competition. It's not about how good you are. It's about whether or not you can release the music in your heart into the world. It's about passion. It's about emotion. Some of the best songs ever written only contain a few chords, but the composers poured their souls into them. I can teach you the mechanics, but that passion can't be learned. You can fake it to a point, but just like anything else in life, the truth will eventually shine through. That's the difference between most musicians and the true artists. So today I just want to discover your passions. It will help guide our experience together."

The kid smiled a lopsided grin and nodded. "Awesome. Give me a minute."

"Take your time."

Thomas White—a man known as Francis Ackerman Sr. in a former life—watched as the boy tapped around on his iPhone. He admired the strong jaw and handsome features hidden behind the dark and greasy mop of hair. He smelled the boy's cologne in the air. The faint scent of citrus and mint. Then he imagined Joel's features twisted in fear and torment. Joel had the perfect face to be turned into one of his death masks.

Unfortunately, he never killed anyone he knew or even anyone with whom he held a tenuous association. *Don't shit where you eat,* that was his rule. It was a simple yet effective guideline. Just like all his other rules about how to be simultaneously a prolific serial killer and a free man.

CHAPTER ELEVEN

Detective Kaleb Duran helped control the perimeter as he waited for the men from the Governor's office to arrive. He looked toward the victim's home—a greenish-gray ranch-style covered in vertical barn-style siding with red-brick accents. He should have been in there with the other detectives from the task force. This was the first big case he had been involved with, and his mother had stuck him on the sidelines babysitting some bureaucrats.

The Coercion Killer case was a political minefield that had the whole state living in fear, and so it was no surprise that the Governor had requested two representatives to observe the investigation. But it did come as a surprise when Kaleb's mother—Captain Maria Duran, commander of KC's homicide division—assigned him to be their liaison. He should have been in there with the lead detectives and FBI agents, watching and learning how to properly conduct a murder investigation of this magnitude. Instead, he was stuck outside in the drizzling rain waiting for the Governor's two reps to grace him with their presence.

A man from the opposite side of the police cordon called out to him. "Hey, buddy, what's going on in there? Is it that Coercion Killer?"

"You can find out on the news like everybody else."

The man was a biker type covered in tattoos, with a piercing through his nose and huge holes in his ears. Kaleb hated the way that guys like that always seemed to wrongly view him as a kindred spirit instead of a cop. He had considered removing his own tattoos. They would probably never let him into the FBI with the tribal motif that crawled from his chest up his neck.

Through the rain, Kaleb saw two men approaching the barricades. He told the cop to let them through and then shook hands with the pair of glorified errand boys. He had first met the pair two weeks previously when he'd been assigned as their babysitter. The first man, Andrew Garrison, seemed competent enough. He wore a black suit, white shirt, and a black tie and could have blended in with the agents from the FBI's Behavioral Analysis Unit who were conducting their inquiries inside the house. The other guy, Marcus Williams, wore an untucked black button-down shirt, no tie, and a leather jacket. He had two days' worth of beard growth on his face and dark bags beneath bloodshot eyes. He looked as if he hadn't slept in a week.

"Give us the details," Williams said as they walked toward the house.

"I already told Mr. Garrison everything over the phone. You guys didn't really have to come down here."

"Tell us again, kid."

Kaleb bit back a sarcastic comment and replied, "Same as the others. Sometime after Brad Dunham left for work the UNSUB entered the house and abducted Mr. Dunham's wife and son. When Mr. Dunham returned home, he found a packet containing a video message and information about his target. Pretty much everything identical to the past cases. The only difference is that this time we have a head start. Mr. Dunham's best friend is one of our detectives, and so Mr. Dunham called him immediately for advice."

"Signs of a struggle? Witnesses?"

"We're questioning all the neighbors. No signs of forced entry. There's a broken glass in the kitchen, and the milk was left out on the counter with the cap off. We're also checking for a connection between the family and the target or between them and the other victims."

"You won't find any. He chooses them all at random."

"How can you be sure of that?"

"It makes him harder to track and catch. That's what I would do," Williams said as he pushed through the front door.

CHAPTER *TWELVE*

T HE METAL CHAIR RESTED IN THE CENTER OF THE DINING ROOM. They had removed everything else, bolted the chair to the floor, and tied a rope around the chair and the prisoner's midsection. Ackerman's arms were pulled behind his back at an awkward and uncomfortable angle. A thick nylon rope encircled his wrists up to his elbows and had been secured to a two-by-four stud that the CIA contractors had broken through the plaster wall to expose. Another rope bound his feet in the same manner. They had even knocked out a portion of the ceiling and fixed a rope to a beam and then around his neck, forming a noose. If he moved his head more than an inch, he would choke himself.

Two of the dire-looking contractors sat in separate corners of the room, each with a Benelli M1014 shotgun on his lap. They worked in short two-hour shifts to keep them vigilant.

Ackerman had to admit it. These guys weren't playing around, and they knew their jobs.

The door of the dining room swung open and the black-clad leader and small suited man entered the room. The big man had sandy blond hair, a thickly lined and tanned face, and narrowed eyes that indicated an extended stay in a desert climate. He had a smug look of satisfaction on his face. The smaller man looked as though he belonged on Wall Street. His shoes squeaked on the hardwood floor, and he stank of expensive cologne. The big man pulled in a chair from the living room for the small man to sit down on.

"I'm Deputy Assistant Attorney General Trevor Fagan," the small man said.

Ackerman said, "That's a mouthful. Are you here to offer me a deal for my cooperation?"

Fagan laughed. "No deals. Not for you."

"Then why would I want to help you?"

"The satisfaction of finishing what you started. Your father's still out there. You failed to finish the job the first time. I'm offering you a second chance."

"Where's Marcus?"

"There's been another abduction. He's gone to the scene."

"I'll only speak to my brother."

Fagan leaned forward on his chair as if he were going to share a secret. "I need to know everything about your father. Any aliases that he's used? Places he might be hiding? Anything that could help us."

Ackerman smiled. "How long has your wife been cheating on you?"

"What? How did ..." Fagan caught himself and gritted his teeth. "Answer the questions."

"I don't blame her. I would cheat on you too. I bet you're all rules and regulations in bed. And she probably has more of an emotional connection with the washing machine."

Fagan stood and headed for the door. "I'm not playing your game. My associate here, Mr. Craig, is a very skilled interrogator. It's his specialty. In fact, he probably enjoys it a little too much."

A throaty laugh came from the killer's throat. He felt the noose tighten as he chuckled. "You're threatening me with torture? That's hilarious."

Fagan ignored him. He kept going and shut the door behind him. The big blond man sat in the chair vacated by the bureaucrat. He cracked his knuckles and pulled a KA-BAR combat knife from his boot. "How many?" Mr. Craig asked.

"How many what?"

"Men have you killed?"

"That's sort of a sexist thing to say. Don't the women I've killed count as well?"

Mr. Craig punched Ackerman hard across the bridge of his nose. His head whipped back, but the noose kept it from moving very far. The sweet pain shot down his spine. "How many people have *you* murdered, Mr. Craig? I can still smell their blood on you."

"I'm a patriot."

"Oscar Wilde said that patriotism is a virtue of the vicious. But no, I won't even give you that much credit. You're just a psychopath with a government pension. You joined up because you wanted an excuse to hurt people. The recruiters didn't see talent and potential. They saw a predatory hunger and a sadistic need that they could bend to their will. Tell me about the things you've done to prisoners and enemy combatants when you knew you could get away with it."

Craig punched him again. Ackerman laughed. "Do you know anything about me? My father is second in the art of torture only to Satan himself. And God truly molded human beings into amazing creatures. I find it laughable when people argue about evolution and creationism as if they're two mutually exclusive concepts. God made us to adapt to our environments in order to overcome adversity. I'm sure the creator had climate change and food shortages in mind when he programmed our ability to refashion ourselves, but that potential for adjustment also served me quite well. I endured so much pain as a boy that my mind rewired itself to the point that pain for me is an almost pleasurable experience."

"I've read your file, but I don't know if I buy that you're as immune to pain as you think."

"Feel free to try, but I may like it."

"I think I can come up with some things that even you won't enjoy."

"Pictures of puppies and little children sometimes give me a headache and make my teeth hurt. If that helps."

Craig raised the knife. "I like a challenge."

Ackerman grinned. "We have that in common."

CHAPTER THIRTEEN

THE DUNHAMS' LIVING ROOM WAS AN OPEN SPACE WITH A FLAT-SCREEN TV ON ONE WALL AND A MASSIVE FIREPLACE CONSTRUCTED OF GRAY AND WHITE BRICKS BUILT INTO THE OTHER. White walls. Eggshell carpet. White leather couch. Marcus grimaced as he looked around. He said to Andrew, "This place seem weird to you? Kind of bleached-out?"

Andrew looked around as if he hadn't noticed. "Not really. Remind me, what color did you paint your office last month?"

"Black."

"You're not normal. You realize that, right?"

Marcus scowled. "Well, I do now."

The crime-scene techs and officers were still hard at work, gathering evidence. He didn't expect them to find any. He took in every detail of the scene. He closed his eyes and put himself into the killer's mind.

His process differed from those of the FBI profilers. In fact, he really didn't have a process. He just remembered everything that he saw, and he could relate to the men whom he hunted. His method was more like old-school detective work. Examine the scene. Put yourself in the bad guy's shoes. Notice something out of place. And be smart enough to connect that piece of evidence with something that could lead you to the killer's doorstep or at least to another clue.

The keypad to a security system rested beside the front door. Marcus wondered how the killer had bypassed it.

He walked through to the kitchen. Saw the milk jug on the counter and the broken glass on the floor. A half-eaten grapefruit and a bowl of sugary cereal that had turned to mush sat on the kitchen table. The mother's purse rested on the counter. The mother and son had both been having breakfast. The father had already left for work. Marcus wondered how the killer knew their routine so well. He must have been watching them for an extended period of time.

Marcus floated through the scene in a daze, ignoring all the other people. Kaleb was saying something, but Marcus barely registered the words. Then Kaleb abandoned them as he went to speak with some of the other detectives, and Marcus and Andrew moved into the garage.

The father's truck—a big black utilitarian work vehicle covered in a layer of rock dust—was in its space now, but it wouldn't have been when the killer took the family, and so Marcus ignored it. The kitchen connected directly with the garage, and Marcus suspected that the killer had come in through that entrance. There were several devices on the market that could clone a garage-door opener. When the family was out one day, the killer could have followed them, broken into their car, and cloned the garage-door opener, which would have given him full access to the house through the garage.

But the mother and son would have heard the big mechanical door open while they were having breakfast. It would have alerted them. But the bedrooms were at the opposite end of the house. If the killer had opened the door in the night, he could have entered without being heard at all.

Marcus checked beneath the wife's car, a light blue Ford Taurus. The concrete floor of the garage was relatively clean, but nearly every garage floor had a layer of dirt tracked in from the cars. This one was no exception. And beneath the Taurus, the dirt had been disturbed. The signs were barely visible, but they were there—the signs of a person sliding beneath the vehicle and out again.

"He waited here for them all night, didn't he?" Andrew asked.

"I think so. Then, after the father left for work, he waited a bit longer. Until they were both in the same place, having breakfast. After that, he took them both down fast and hard. Probably two tasers, one for each of them. Shoot the mom. Drop the taser. Shoot the son. Then drug them both while they're incapacitated."

"But how did he get two unconscious people out of the house in broad daylight without anyone seeing a thing? I could see it happening, but not at every scene. And this is a fairly busy street."

Marcus said, "He's using some technique to blend in. Someone's seen him, but they didn't register him as out of place. Hours later, they didn't remember seeing anything at all. You dress up like a mailman or a meter reader, and you're as good as invisible to most people."

"Yeah, but a mailman dragging two bodies behind him would raise some suspicion. Plus he knows their routine. He's been watching them."

"Exactly."

"But a car or van parked on a suburban street like this for an extended period of time or some guy just hanging around would be noticed."

"I've got a theory about that, which means that we have another scene to check that the locals haven't got to yet."

"What do you mean?"

Marcus moved out of the garage and back toward the front door. "Tell the kid we're leaving. I think I know how the killer was watching them."

CHAPTER FOURTEEN

WHEN THEY HAD FIRST PULLED UP TO THE SCENE, MARCUS HAD NOTICED THE FOR-SALE SIGN IN THE YARD OF A BIG YELLOW BUNGALOW ACROSS THE STREET. The sign was blue with white letters. It sat at a lopsided angle, and a layer of grime covered it, as if it had weathered more than its share of storms in the same spot. As he considered how the killer had watched his victims, Marcus remembered pictures from the other abduction scenes. The KCPD had been thorough in their jobs and had photographed the view up and down each block for context. It was a smart move. He remembered other homes for sale sitting opposite the other scenes. It might even have been the reason why those families were chosen—homes opposite properties that had been vacant for an extended amount of time. Although that knowledge wouldn't help them find future victims, it was still another piece to the puzzle, another question answered.

Marcus picked the lock while Andrew stood guard in the alley. A big oak tree shaded the backyard, and a faded white privacy fence provided some cover. He smelled burning leaves and barbecue in the air. The door had a simple deadbolt mechanism. A bit of maneuvering and a few seconds' time, and they were inside as easily as if they owned the place.

"What are we going to tell the locals if we find something?" Andrew asked.

"We're not supposed to tell them anything."

"Does that mean you're actually going to follow orders?"

Marcus didn't reply. He was focused on the scene. The back door opened into a kitchen. Tan linoleum covered the floors, and the cabinets looked like they were straight from the 1950s, with a flat pale yellow finish. A layer of dust covered everything, and the house smelled faintly of excrement.

They walked through a dining room and past a set of pocket doors into a front room that had been remodeled. The carpet had been pulled up and the hardwood refinished. The old plaster had been replaced with drywall. It was like stepping from the past into the present. He supposed that the owner had started updating the house one room at a time and then decided it was easiest to buy new.

The entire house was empty of furniture except for a folding chair leaning against the wall beside the front bay window. Marcus unfolded the chair and sat down, facing the Dunham house. From here, he could see the entire property. He could see the bedroom windows, the garage, and even a portion of the backyard. It was a perfect spot for surveillance.

Andrew bent down and examined a spot on the floor. "Look at these scratches. Could be from the legs of a tripod."

Marcus noticed another spot near where Andrew was pointing. The dust had been disturbed, and a circular object had left a ring. It was maybe a foot in diameter. Andrew noticed it too. "Wonder what was sitting there?" he said.

"A bucket," Marcus replied, sighing and rubbing the bridge of his nose.

"Why would he have a bucket?"

"When I was a kid, my dad ..." Marcus hesitated. Thinking of the New York city cop who had raised him brought back thoughts about how he had always thought of himself as being a second-generation police officer. The realization still stung as he thought of his true heritage. "John Williams, my adopted father, liked to go camping. We'd get away from the city and spend a weekend out in the woods. Just the two of us. He would take a bucket along to use as a mobile toilet."

"So you think Ackerman Sr. didn't even take time off from his surveillance to use the bathroom? That's some pretty serious dedication. Robots aren't that committed."

"You know the word 'robot' comes from the Czech word 'robotnik,' which means 'slave,' and that description might not be far from the truth. I don't think my father took them."

"We know he did."

"We know he's involved. I'm starting to think that he has an apprentice. Which also means that the FBI's profile is going to be all wrong. They're looking for one killer and building their assessment from that. Two killers means a totally different profile. And we can't tell them a thing."

CHAPTER FIFTEEN

K ALEB STEPPED OUT THROUGH THE FRONT DOOR OF THE DUNHAM HOUSE
AND EXAMINED THE FACES OF THE PEOPLE IN THE CROWD OF ONLOOKERS
STANDING BEHIND THE POLICE CAUTION TAPE. A crime scene always drew
a crowd. And criminals often liked to stand in the crowd and bask
in the aftermath of their deeds. He knew that officers would be dis-
creetly taking pictures of the crowd and comparing them with photos from past scenes, but a part of him hoped that he would be the
one to notice that person who was enjoying himself just a bit too
much.

His encounter with the governor's reps had been relatively pain-
less, and he had even had a chance to discuss the case with one of
the FBI agents assigned to the task force. Kaleb had invited the agent
to dinner with the hope of picking his brain about applying to the
FBI academy. The sooner he could get out from beneath his mother's command the better.

As he surveyed the crowd, his gaze strayed across the street to
two old men sitting on a blacktop driveway in a pair of rusty lawn
chairs. They were both white-haired. One in a sweater, even though
it wasn't sweater weather. The other in a tan and white striped shirt
and blue polyester pants. They each had a beer in their hand and a
cigar in their mouth.

Kaleb stepped beneath the police tape and approached the two
men. "Good afternoon, gentlemen. Have any of the officers talked to
you?"

The man in the polyester pants puffed his cigar and said, "They
came by earlier. I'm glad to tell you what I told them. Which was
pretty much nothing. We'd love to help, but we didn't see anyone or

anything out of the ordinary. Just the usual folks leaving for work, mailmen, deliveries and such."

"Deliveries? What kind of deliveries?"

"Hell, I don't know. The usual. That big brown truck."

"UPS," the other man added in a soft and frail voice.

Kaleb's pulsed quickened. His father had liked to take him deer hunting before he died. Kaleb recognized the same sensation now as when he had sat in the tree-stand, heard the breaking of branches, and seen a twelve-point buck poke its head through the foliage. "Did this truck deliver to the Dunham house?"

The two men exchanged glances. Polyester pants said, "I can't say for sure, son."

"Just think back. Take your time. Did you see the delivery person? Did you see what kind of packages they were carrying?"

Polyester pants shook his head, but his soft-spoken friend said, "I didn't see the delivery man, but it must have been a big package, now that you mention it."

"Why do you say that?"

"They usually park out by the curb, walk the parcels up to the door, and ring the bell. But today the truck backed into a driveway like they were delivering a big icebox or stove or something."

"At the Dunham house?"

"I couldn't say for sure."

"And you didn't see the driver?"

"No, sorry. Everybody has stuff delivered nowadays. Nobody goes to the store to interact with their neighbors like they used to. You see those damn trucks everywhere. They blend right in."

Kaleb suppressed a grin—that would be exactly why the killer would choose to drive one. "Yes, they do. Thanks for your help, gentlemen."

"Anytime, kid," polyester pants said as he sipped his can of Pabst beer as though it were a fine wine.

Kaleb trotted across the street, excitement quickening his pace. He couldn't wait to tell the lead detective and the FBI agents what he had learned. This could be the best real lead they had uncovered. Before entering the house, as an afterthought, he pulled out his phone and sent a text message to the governor's rep, Garrison. That way no one could say that he had neglected to keep them in the loop.

Chapter Sixteen

T HE OLD HOUSE CREAKED AND GROANED AS THE AUTUMN WIND POUNDED AGAINST ITS WOODEN SIDING. The air was cold and smelled of bleach and varnish. Thomas White checked the vitals and fluids connected to the mother and her son. They rested on two old gurneys, the kind used in earlier twentieth-century mental institutions. Bags of chemicals hung from hooks, and the liquids ran into their arms through intravenous needles. White had put them into chemically-induced comas, just as he had the others. If the patriarch of their family chose to kill in their name, they would be released with little memory of the encounter. If the father failed, he would wake them from their drugged stupor just in time to see death coming.

They had set up shop in the old home's parlor, which White found humorous—the room was still being used to entertain guests. He moved to the son's side and stroked the boy's face. The young man's face would make a nice addition to his collection, if it came to that. Looking at the boy, he couldn't help but think of his own son—his only son—Marcus.

He had first noticed Marcus during a national news broadcast out of Colorado. Thomas had set up a Google alert to notify him of any news stories or pages mentioning the term *Francis Ackerman*. One article that popped up described a fire at a hospital in Colorado Springs. He had watched the video of the broadcast online and saw a man being taken from the scene who looked eerily like himself—minus thirty years, fifty pounds, and the balding head. Under normal circumstances, he would have dismissed this as a coincidence, but in a story that involved the name Ackerman, there had to be a connection.

His research into the young man from the broadcast yielded wonderful results. He learned all he could about Marcus Williams, things that even Marcus himself didn't know. His heart had ached to find his true son for years, and now he had. That information, coupled with the loss of the only woman he had loved since Marcus's mother, had forced Thomas to consider his legacy and what he would leave behind for the world. He didn't want to be merely a footnote to the exploits of the monster that shared his name. And his plans were coming together nicely.

Returning to the mother's side, he leaned down and kissed her cheek. "I've been doing this for a long time, Mrs. Dunham. I know people. I know them better than they know themselves. Your husband is going to fail. And when he does ... well, we don't want to spoil the surprise."

He stroked her cheek and imagined what her now serene features would look like when they were twisted in agony.

Chapter Seventeen

MARCUS AND ANDREW WERE ON THEIR WAY BACK TO THE FARMHOUSE WHEN ANDREW RECEIVED THE TEXT FROM KALEB ABOUT THE DELIVERY TRUCK. Marcus pulled their black Suburban over at a gas station and initiated a video call with the team's technical guru, Stan Macallan. Stan didn't look like a typical MIT graduate and former owner of a major dot com company; he looked more like the bass player from a ska band or some kid from a skate park if you added twenty years, ten inches, and a hundred pounds.

Stan's face and chest filled the screen of Marcus's iPhone. A long beard covered the face. Nothing covered the chest, exposing a tattoo of Popeye on one pectoral and Super Mario smashing through a block on the other. Marcus said, "Stan, what have I told you about wearing clothes in the office?"

"Hey, this might be your office, but it's my home. And why the hell are you video chatting with me anyway? Video calls are so stupid. They're only good for parents to check that their kids aren't at a party or for long-distance couples to get naked and—"

"Fascinating, Stan. Write a blog post about it. But before you do that, I've got some work for you to do." Marcus explained about the brown delivery truck possibly being spotted at the abduction scene and told Stan to run a check on any trucks within a hundred-mile radius that had been stolen or sold.

After a few moments of clicking keys and Stan humming the *Battle Hymn of the Republic*, the technical genius said, "Okay, brown trucks mean UPS. I found one case of some UPS trucks being stolen in Topeka, but the police think that it's insurance fraud. But I got to thinking about it, and someone could just as easily paint any truck brown to look like a UPS truck. So I checked on that and found a few possibles with the most interesting being a FedEx employee that went missing with his truck six months ago and neither he nor his truck has been seen since. The police think that he stole the vehicle. The dude's name is Joe Colwell, and he has a record a mile long, including several violent offenses. Bounced around foster homes at a young age, but his mother kept regaining custody. She had been in and out of prison, rehab, and mental institutions for drugs and increasingly erratic behavior. Colwell only got the job at FedEx because a friend's father was a manager at the distribution center."

From the passenger seat, Andrew said, "Sounds like Colwell could be your father's apprentice. He fits the mold."

"It's the best lead we have right now," Marcus said. "Do you have a last-known for him, Stan?"

"Yeah, it's his mother's house, but it's the address he used on his FedEx application. Cops have questioned her, and she claims that she has no idea what happened to him. I'm sending the details to your phone."

"Good work. Thanks, Stan," Marcus said as he killed the call. A second later, his phone dinged with the address, and he put the car into drive and pulled out into traffic.

❖

Marcus rang the bell three times before they heard movement inside the house. The place was more of a shack, with brown shingle siding and a front yard piled with junk and two-foot-tall grass. The woman who answered the door was blonde and surprisingly pretty. She looked like a former model, except for the T-shirt yellowed from sweat and teeth the same color. When she opened the door, he could see stacks of old newspapers and piles of trash covering the floor behind her.

"Hello, ma'am," Marcus said, flashing his ID. "We're from the Hetfield and Ulrich Detective Agency. We've been hired to find your son Joe because he's come into a large sum of money."

"Money? How?" she asked.

Marcus expected her voice to sound harsh like that of a long-time smoker, but it was high and sweet with a slight Southern drawl.

"I'm not at liberty to say, ma'am. But I can tell you this, it is a substantial amount. We've also been told that if we make every reasonable effort to find Joe and are unable to locate him, then the money will default to his closest living relative."

Her eyes narrowed in suspicion, and she looked both of the men up and down. She glanced to the street at the SUV sitting by the curb. She seemed hesitant but must have decided that even the slight prospect of the money outweighed any loyalty she had to her son. She said, "I haven't seen him in months. But I know the last place he was living."

CHAPTER EIGHTEEN

THE OPPOSITE SIDE OF THE GLASS IN THE INTERROGATION ROOM WAS A SPACE THAT FEW PEOPLE EVER SAW. It reminded Kaleb of a walk-in closet. The interrogation room itself was fifteen by fifteen foot square with off-white walls, a gray metal table, three chairs, and fluorescent lighting humming overhead. The viewing room matched the interrogation room's length but was only a third of the width. Along one wall, it held a small table supporting a computer monitor and some recording equipment. The rest of the space was dedicated to observation.

Kaleb leaned against the back wall. Two senior homicide detectives stood with their noses to the glass as an FBI agent questioned Brad Dunham in the interrogation room. Brad, of course, wasn't a suspect of any kind, but he might have possessed information about why his family had been chosen or he might have seen something that he didn't even realize was pertinent. The FBI agent handled Brad with skill and consideration, not pushing too hard but deep enough to get the information they needed. Brad was being helpful but was also growing visibly anxious and agitated. Time was running out, and he knew it.

The door to the observation room opened, and the light stung Kaleb's eyes. Captain Maria Duran, Kaleb's mother, walked into the darkness and shut the door behind her. She squinted as her eyes adjusted, and she noticed him in the corner. "What the hell are you doing in here?" she said.

"He wanted to observe the questioning, boss," one of the lead detectives said.

Her gaze didn't leave Kaleb. "I would think that Detective Duran would have better things to do than stand around. We do have two people about to be killed out there somewhere."

Kaleb resisted the urge to rise to her challenge. Instead, he maintained his composure and said, "I'm glad you're here, Captain. I have an idea that might buy those people some time."

"The best way to help them is to do your job."

"Fine, but I was thinking that—"

A commotion in the interrogation room drew the attention of the group. Brad Dunham knocked over his chair and screamed, "I should never have gone to the police! I hope you're doing more than asking me a bunch of pointless questions!"

The FBI agent tried to calm him down, but fear had overcome Brad's sensibilities, and he stormed from the room.

"Go after him," Captain Duran said to one of the detectives.

The detective hurried from the room, and Maria Duran said, "Okay, Kaleb, what's your big idea?"

Chapter Nineteen

THE ADDRESS THAT COLWELL'S MOTHER HAD GIVEN THEM LED TO A TWO-
STORY WHITE COLONIAL. It was the kind of place that would have
made a nice home fifty years ago and with a little help from someone
who enjoyed working with their hands could be nice again. In its
current state, it was the perfect place for someone like Joe Colwell
to hide.

Marcus pulled the Suburban up to the curb across the street and
two houses down. Then they watched the property for a half-hour,
searching for any signs of life. Unfortunately, time wouldn't permit
a stakeout.

"Go around to the back. I'll come at him from the front. We'll go
in fast and hard on my signal," Marcus said.

They each stuck small flesh-colored radio receivers in their ears,
and Andrew said, "Do you read me?"

Marcus nodded, and Andrew stepped away from the vehicle,
winding his way around to the back of the house from a neighboring
alleyway. Marcus checked his Sig Sauer pistol and then waited for
Andrew to take up position. He cracked his neck to the side, getting
in fight mode, and took a deep breath before opening the driver's
door. Situations like this never seemed to get any easier. No matter
how good he was, one meth-head with a shotgun could put a real
damper on his day. Death was always there waiting in the corner of
his eye. He wondered where the Reaper would send him when that
moment came. A part of him longed for the release. A part of him
feared it.

The boards of the front porch were rotten and sagging. Marcus stepped onto them with care for fear of falling through. Two large windows occupied the house's face, looking onto the porch, and the front door contained a diamond-shaped window of its own. He tried to watch them all at the same time with his peripheral vision for any signs of movement.

"I'm in position," Andrew said in his ear through the small receiver.

Marcus pulled the Sig from its holster and said, "Go."

Some doors were made cheaply and burst easily. This wasn't one of them. It was a fifty-year-old solid wood door manufactured in a time when people cared about craftsmanship. The latch would be a couple of inches under the knob, and so that was where Marcus focused his kick. He turned sideways with his dominant leg closest to the door. When he kicked, he leaned forward as if he were falling against the door and put all his weight into the blow. His shoe's sole connected with wood, and the frame shattered under the impact.

The door opened into a foyer with a staircase winding up to Marcus's left. He glanced at the stairs, but the immediate danger would come from the living room to his right. He pivoted, using the entryway for cover, and scanned the room. It contained a floor lamp, an old brown floral couch, and a couple of side tables topped with smaller lamps. The wind from the open front door kicked up smells of musty fabric and body odor.

He repeated the procedure on the next three rooms—a parlor, a dining room, and a bathroom. All empty. He and Andrew met in the home's kitchen. A bag of moldy bread sat on the counter, and the space stank of dirty dishes and rotting food. Some would have concluded that no one had lived there for some time, but Marcus had seen people live in much worse conditions.

"Upstairs," he said to Andrew.

Andrew nodded, and they moved cautiously back through the house to the front staircase. Andrew went up first, the old stairs groaning beneath his weight. They met on the landing at the top, and then Marcus focused on the room to the right while Andrew went left.

Inside the room on the right, Marcus saw a mattress on the floor and some clothes scattered on top of an old dresser. He checked behind the door, looked in the closet. Nothing.

Andrew must have found more of the same because they quickly met back in the hall. The solid oak door of the next room was shut, but there was a bathroom on the left that was open. Marcus slid along the right wall while Andrew checked it. Then Andrew joined Marcus on the opposite of the closed door. With a nod, Andrew turned the knob, and Marcus swung into the room with his pistol at the ready.

This room contained no furniture, clothing, or anything else that one would expect to find in someone's residence. A metal gurney, the kind you would find in an old hospital, sat in the room's center. Beside it rested bags of fluids hanging from rusty metal rods. Tubes dangled from the bags and were connected to a woman's arm. Dirty-looking clothes covered her thin, bruised frame. Leather straps wound around her wrists and ankles. A black hood covered her face.

Andrew checked the closet and then asked, "Is it the Dunham woman?"

"Can't be. She looks like she's been here longer than that."

Marcus pulled off the hood, and the face beneath made him feel as though the floor had dropped out from under him. His heart pounded, and he shook his head in disbelief.

Her skin was ashen, her face gaunt, and her blond hair had been cut short, but he recognized the woman on the gurney. Hers was a face he would never forget.

CHAPTER TWENTY

BRAD DUNHAM PULLED HIS TRUCK UP TO THE CAR DEALERSHIP AND RIPPED THE 9MM BERETTA PISTOL FROM THE POCKET OF HIS HOODED SWEAT-SHIRT. It caught on the fabric and came out at an awkward angle. He checked the magazine. Fully loaded.

He wasn't sure that this was going to work, but he would do anything to save his family. The loved ones of those who had complied with the madman's demands in the past had been released. There was no reason to think that the same thing wouldn't happen this time.

All he had to do was murder a stranger.

He could see his target through the front window of the dealership's show room. The man was heavyset and wore a blue polo shirt displaying the dealership's logo on the breast pocket.

It was time.

Brad stepped from the vehicle, the Beretta dangling from his left fist. Then he pushed his way through the glass front doors of the dealership, raised the gun, and fired.

Chapter Twenty-One

Maggie Carlisle stepped into the dining room of the old farm-house and looked at Ackerman with great satisfaction. Bruises and bloody gashes covered the left half of the killer's face, and blood had soaked through his shirt from the fresh wounds that the man they called Mr. Craig had inflicted. Her satisfaction drained away as she saw the look in Ackerman's eyes. It wasn't a look of defeat and brokenness. It was an almost gleeful look of triumph.

"What the hell are you smiling at?" she said.

"It's good to see you, Maggie. After all, we're practically family. I've never had a sister before. It's a nice thought."

She resisted the urge to punch him. He would just enjoy it. "If it were up to me, you'd be dead already. And if you don't watch yourself, I may kill you myself."

"Maggie, that's hurtful. I thought we could put the past behind us. We're on the same team now."

She leaned in close. "Make no mistake. We will *never* be on the same team. We're barely the same species."

"I understand. It'll take time. But I'll win you over. We both want what's best for Marcus."

This time Maggie couldn't resist the impulse to strike him. She slapped him hard across the face, his head jerking to the side from the impact. He laughed and spat blood onto the floor. "That's the spirit, little sister."

"You remember the first time we met, you bastard. You killed a good friend of mine. Alexai. He was a good man. I was the one who had to tell his grandkids that they'd never see him again."

"I remember him, but I'm afraid we didn't have time to get properly acquainted. I'm sorry for taking your friend from you. There's nothing I can do to make that right. All I can do now is attempt to atone for my sins and ask for your forgiveness."

"That's really the card you want to play with me? The role of the repentant sinner? I don't buy it. People don't change. You're a murderer. As long as you're breathing, you're a danger to anyone around you. And I'm not going to stand by while you cozy up to Marcus and convince him that you're different now. Besides, even if you have changed, you still have to pay for what you've done. Blood for blood."

"I could tell you that an eye for an eye makes the whole world blind or let he *or she* without sin cast the first stone. But I can see the hatred in your eyes. You should be careful about staring into that abyss, Maggie. It will stare back at you. Hatred has a way of corrupting your soul and poisoning everything good in it. There's nothing I can say or do, but you don't have to like me, my dear. That doesn't change the fact that you need me."

Maggie's hand strayed toward the Glock 19 on her belt. She could do it right here and now. He was defenseless. She could pull the gun before the guards in the room could stop her and put two bullets in his brain. He would be feeling the fires of hell before he even realized what had happened. His reign of blood and terror would be over. She had the power to end it, to make it right for all those victims.

But a voice in the back of her mind told her that would make her as bad as him. Another voice said that it was justice, not vengeance.

Maggie was still wrestling with whether or not to end his life when she heard a commotion in the front room and Marcus's voice yelling for help.

Chapter Twenty-Two

A S THE PARAMEDICS RUSHED IN WITH THE MAN FROM THE CAR DEALER-SHIP, KALEB SAT IN THE HOSPITAL'S FRONT WAITING ROOM, PLAYING THE ROLE OF A VISITOR. No one seemed to give much more than a curious glance toward the paramedics or the nurses that took the patient from them. No one seemed suspicious or out of place.

They had plain-clothes officers stationed at every entrance. One of the questions in the case had always been how the Coercion Killer confirmed that the target had actually been killed. Some felt that he watched the victim's home or place of business, but they had found no signs of that. Kaleb's theory was that he came to the hospital to be sure.

"I'm going back to the operating room," he said into his radio.

The antiseptic white hallways bustled with life. Nurses, order-lies, doctors, visitors. Any one of them could be their killer, but they had no description of the madman. Everyone was a possible suspect.

The nurses and a doctor had brought the target into one of the operating rooms and had shut the door behind them. Kaleb couldn't see what was happening inside, which meant that neither could anyone else.

A nurse's station sat directly across from the operating room. The nurse at the desk had been briefed on the situation. She gave Kaleb a nod as he walked past and took a seat. She handed him a white coat. He pulled it over his shoulders and tried to look as if he belonged there.

The nurse said, "This is kind of exciting."

She was a cute brunette with dimples and full lips. Kaleb gave her a wink. "All in a day's work."

He sat there for the next half-hour, watching each person who passed carefully. The loudspeaker called out from time to time, sending doctors and nurses to and fro. The fluorescent lights pulsed and hummed overhead to the point of giving him a headache. No one seemed to pay much attention to the operating room or asked about the patient inside. Some nurses, a few orderlies, a few maintenance people, visitors, doctors, volunteers. They all passed by or stopped and asked for directions or checked on the status of a patient. No one seemed suspicious or out of place.

Still, Kaleb had a feeling that the killer was close.

❖

It entered the hospital through the parking garage and passed men it recognized as police officers. The master had forced it to memorize the faces of all the city's police officers and the FBI agents that would be working the case. It saw familiar faces near the entrances and in the halls.

But it knew what to do. Its instructions had been very clear. The master was very thorough and planned for every contingency. The master knew everything, saw everything. There was no escape from him or his wrath. He had proven that to it on many occasions. It no longer doubted his infallibility or questioned his will.

It had studied the layout of the hospital. It passed by the operating room that would contain the target. One of the detectives sat at the nurse's station, pretending to work at the hospital. It knew better. It wasn't fooled by the ruse.

As it moved past the desk, it saw a mother and a young boy in the hallway ahead. The mother was short, with graying hair and a kind face. Her arm was in a sling. The boy held her good hand. His steps were excited bounces, and his shaggy brown hair flopped up and down with each movement. He wore a blue Spider-Man T-shirt. The boy smiled up at it as he bounced by. It experienced a brief flash of memory. Another vague ghost of a past lived by someone else. Its mind couldn't make a connection between the memory and reality. Just some emotion that it couldn't classify or name.

The next corridor veered to the right and contained its desti-nation—a storage closet containing linens for the beds and general cleaning supplies. Nothing valuable. Nothing dangerous. Nothing that would call for the closet to be locked up. The master also said that the security cameras did not have a clear view of this room. It didn't realize why that was important, but it also didn't care. The master had his reasons and motivations, and they weren't to be ques-tioned.

Once inside the tight space, it unslung the small duffel bag from its shoulder and removed the items contained within. Its movements were practiced and mechanical. The master's instructions were pre-cise and left no room for interpretation or confusion. To disobey them or deviate from them would bring great pain.

It assembled the H&K MP7 A1 machine pistol and attached a long sound suppressor to the muzzle. Then it pulled a black bala-clava mask over its face and re-entered the hall.

The master had said that the next part would be the most diffi-cult, and that it should proceed swiftly with no hesitation. It didn't know why it would hesitate. It wasn't afraid. It felt nothing, or at least its brain didn't connect what it felt with anything relevant. There was only the master's voice in its head. His instructions, and his wrath if it failed.

It pulled the red fire-alarm handle down and then tossed the smoke grenades into the adjacent corridor. They clattered down the hall and came to rest in front of the nurse's station.

❖

To the nurse, Kaleb said, "So you've lived in KC for a year and haven't been to Oklahoma Joe's Barbecue?"

She shrugged and smiled. "I don't get out much."

"We're going to have to change that. Maybe we can—"

A loud ringing noise burst into life and filled the hall. The sound battered his ears. The nurse said, "It's the fire alarm."

She began to stand, but Kaleb pulled her back down. "Don't move."

He heard the metal *ting* of something striking the floor and rolling toward them. A second later, smoke billowed up from in front
of the desk and started to fill the corridor. He leaned over the desk's
laminate surface and saw two canisters spewing out white gas.

Kaleb pulled his Beretta pistol from its holster and aimed down
the hall. But within a few seconds, he couldn't see anything, and
a mass of people were moving down the corridor, heading for the
exits. He heard their coughs and footfalls and saw their vague forms
moving through the smoke. He heard shouted directions from hospital staff, a child's cry of fear, a mother's assurances, the rasping of
heavy and anxious breathing.

And then he heard a series of muffled thumps from across the
hall. It sounded like a roofer hammering on a row of shingles in
quick succession. The sounds came in a rapid rhythm and died away
as quickly as they began.

"Follow them out," Kaleb said to the nurse.

"What about you?"

"I have to check on our decoy."

The gentleman from the dealership whom the Coercion Killer
had chosen to be Brad Dunham's target should have been perfectly
safe in the operating room. Kaleb's job was to watch for someone
checking on the man's status, not to protect him. The three officers
who had posed as the two nurses and the doctor had drawn that
duty. It was their job to sell the ruse and protect the man who had
agreed to be their bait.

Still, if they were in trouble, he needed to help. He radioed to the
rest of the team that he had heard something within the operating
room, and then he moved toward the door.

Kaleb pushed his way through the escaping mob that filled the
hallway and groped his way along the wall until he found the door.
He knocked four times with loud, clear taps. But no response came
from the other side.

He repeated the procedure. Nothing.

Slowly, he pushed the door inward just a crack. He didn't want
any friendly-fire incidents. He said, "It's Detective Duran. Is everything okay in there?"

Still no response.

Kaleb felt on the verge of a heart attack, and his breathing was quick and shallow. Forcing his shaking hands to come under control, he steadied himself and then pushed into the room with his gun at the ready.

The smell of burned gunpowder and hot gun oil was strong in the air. The three cops and the man from the car dealership were dead. Each had been shot multiple times. Some bullets to the torso, and some to the head. All their dead eyes stared at Kaleb accusingly.

This had been his operation. It had been his idea to stage an attack by Brad Dunham on the target and fake the man's death. He had thought it to be a sound plan, and his mother had surprisingly agreed and had gone along with it. Faking the attack, he had argued, would not only buy time for the Dunham family and hopefully get them released, but it would also give them the chance to watch for the killer at the hospital.

It had seemed like a good plan. No one would lose and everyone, except for the killer, would win.

This was his fault. Not only had he not saved anyone, he had caused more people to lose their lives.

Kaleb nearly vomited up his lunch. But he quickly recovered, grabbed for his radio, and said, "Lock down the hospital. The killer's inside!"

❖

It had followed the master's instructions to the letter. Pull the alarm handle. Throw the smoke grenades. Wait for the people to panic. Join the crowd and slip into the operating room or the morgue, depending on where they took the target. Shoot everyone inside. Ditch the gun and the duffel bag. Stuff the balaclava into its pants, so as to avoid the possibility of leaving behind a hair or skin sample. Slip out among the crowd.

And it had nearly carried out its final instruction—walk out the front door and keep going.

Ahead were two police officers. They were checking each person as they left the hospital, watching everyone closely, checking the pockets of some, questioning others. Still, they couldn't keep them in the hospital with a possible fire blazing; the master had said so.

And if it was stopped, the master had provided instructions for that as well. It was to fight. To fight until it could no longer move its arms and legs. Until it could truly see and feel nothing. The master had said to "fight to the death." But it wasn't sure that it was alive, and so it couldn't tell if the master had meant the death of the police officers or if that was merely a figure of speech.

In this instance, the meaning didn't matter. No fighting was necessary. It passed by four police officers without any of them giving it more than a passing glance.

Then it was in the open air and on its way home to the master.

CHAPTER TWENTY-THREE

MAGGIE HAD WATCHED IN CONFUSION AS MARCUS CARRIED AN UNCON-SCIOUS WOMAN FROM THE SUBURBAN UP TO ONE OF THE SECOND-STORY BEDROOMS. The Director had called for a doctor he could trust, but the woman looked to Maggie as though she needed to be in a hospital. She couldn't figure out why Marcus would have brought her to the farmhouse instead. The mysterious blonde kept mumbling, saying the name *Dylan*, but she had obviously been under some serious sedation and had yet to recover.

Marcus hadn't said a word to Maggie since coming in. He had simply pulled a chair up next to the woman's bed and held her hand. Maggie knew him well enough to see that there was no point in trying to get him to talk, at least not at the moment.

It took the doctor whom the Director had phoned a little over an hour to arrive. He was mid-thirties and handsome but with a tired, world-weary downturn to his features. He immediately ushered Marcus from the bedroom and shut the door as he began his work.

Marcus stood in the hall beside the door, leaning his head back against the plaster.

Maggie joined him and said, "What happened out there? Where did she come from?"

Marcus didn't meet her gaze. "We followed a lead on the killer and found her instead. Andrew stayed behind to see if anyone comes back to the house where we found her."

"Why didn't you take her to the hospital?"

"Too many questions from the doctors. And when she comes out of this stupor, I want her close."

"Is she another of Ackerman Sr.'s victims?"

"I think so."

Marcus's eyes were focused on the floor, and he seemed much too upset about the whole situation. This was a good thing. They had rescued a woman from the clutches of a killer, and hopefully, she could provide them with information that would lead back to the man they were hunting.

Maggie said, "What aren't you telling me?"

Marcus rubbed the bridge of his nose and breathed deeply. "I know that woman. She was taken by my father because of me."

"What do you mean? Who is she?"

"Her name is Claire Cassidy, and once upon a time back when I was a cop in New York, Claire and I were engaged."

Maggie felt her stomach spin and her pulse quicken. "You were going to get married?"

"It was a long time ago."

"I don't care how long ago it was. Why didn't you ever tell me about her?"

"You didn't ask."

"Don't give me that crap. I've told you everything about my past. I assumed you might mention the fact that you nearly married another woman."

"It was nine years ago. I never thought I'd see her again."

"It doesn't matter."

"Maggie, I don't want to fight. We have enough going on right now."

"Why did you break up?"

"Do we have to get into this now?"

"Considering that you were apparently never going to tell me anything about her, yeah, I think now would be good."

"She worked at the DA's office. Our paths crossed. We ended up dating for about a year. She got a better job offer in Idaho. I was too wrapped up in my own career and refused to go with her. She refused to stay. That was the end of it. Not much more to tell."

"And you haven't seen or spoken with her since?"

"She came back to the city once. Maybe six months after we broke up. She stayed the weekend with me. After that, we both decided it would be too hard to ever do anything like that again. It just opened up old wounds. We completely lost touch."

"Why would your Ackerman Sr. kidnap your old fiancée?"

"I don't know, but I intend to find out."

CHAPTER TWENTY-FOUR

THOMAS WHITE PLACED THE LAST OF THE CAMERAS ON TRIPODS POSITIONED STRATEGICALLY AROUND THE ROOM. Videography had become another of his passions. He had always recorded his experiments, but that had been more for future scientific use and for his own reliving of those special moments. Now it had become an art form. Technology was truly amazing. With a few clicks of a mouse, he could research and order the most sophisticated equipment, and with a few more clicks, he could learn how to use it.

The cameras pumped their data into a Macbook Pro computer and then backed it up onto a firewire hard drive. Later, White could edit the video and cut between the different angles separately or arrange them together in a collage.

Today's procedure would eventually make it onto the Internet, but for right now, he had a specific audience in mind—the KCPD, Brad Dunham, and most importantly, his son.

Julie Dunham lay stretched out on an operating table in the center of the room, her arms splayed out at her sides and secured with thick leather bonds. A sheet of plastic rested beneath the table, covering the hardwood floor. No reason to ruin the flooring with all that blood.

A large mirror hung from the ceiling above her body. The kind purchased at hardcore sex shops and meant to be placed above one's bed. White didn't want her to miss a single exquisite moment of what was to come. The spectators for the camera show might have been the husband and the police, but Julie was also part of the audience. In fact, she had the best seat in the house.

She had just started to wake up and fight against her bonds. He could smell her fear, and it was glorious. Her final death throes would make for a wonderful mask—another of his passions.

His father had been a renowned mask maker in New Orleans. He had tried to pass his trade onto his son, but Thomas had never truly shown an interest. He had absorbed the knowledge, but he hadn't invested the hours necessary to master the craft. At least, not until later in his life.

Then he had realized that the medium was perfect for capturing a person's final moments. Not just the pain of their death, but the fear. He could, of course, review the videos. But the masks were different. He could reach out and feel them. It brought him back to the moment. He could taste their fear over and over again, and wearing the grotesque masks of death heightened the fear of the next victim. It was as though the fear grew and spread and expanded from person to person like a cancer of the soul that could be transferred from victim to victim.

He approached Julie Dunham wearing the mask of another woman about her age. He had forgotten the woman's name, but not her fear. Julie cowered and shrieked and wet herself, the urine drizzling down onto the plastic sheet. It was glorious. White wanted to clap and giggle like a child, but instead, he said, "Are you afraid to die, Julie?"

"Please, I'll—"

He hushed her with a finger to the lips. "I've heard it all, my dear. Nothing can save you now. Don't waste your final moments blubbering."

He circled the operating table as he spoke, like a shark sensing blood in the water. "I've applied a local anesthetic to your limbs, and so you should feel a minimal amount of pain considering what's about to be done to you. I'm going to slice off each of your fingers. Then your hands. Don't worry—I'll cauterize the wounds, so that you don't bleed out too quickly. Then I'll start with your feet and toes and repeat the procedure. When we're done with that, I'll decide whether or not I want to force you to live like that or end your suffering and cut off your head."

Terror spread across Julie's beautiful features, and she screamed at the top of her lungs. She called for help, but there was no one to hear her. White drank in her fear and then began his work.

CHAPTER TWENTY-FIVE

IN ORDER FOR THEIR RUSE TO BE SUCCESSFUL, BRAD DUNHAM NEEDED TO SELL HIS ROLE AS WELL. After pretending to kill the target, he ran from the dealership, jumped into his truck, and raced out of the lot. He immediately returned home and waited for contact from the abductor. In the past cases where the target had been killed, the person or the police had received a call, telling them where to find the person's loved ones.

Two FBI agents were already waiting in the house when he returned home, with more police officers ready to move in from down the street. When the abductor called, they would trace the call back and track the madman down.

At least, that was the plan.

But it seemed to Brad that the call should have come in hours ago. What was taking the abductor so long to release his family? He had asked the agents if everything had gone well at the hospital, but they had told him to focus on his end of things.

He had nearly worn a hole in the floor from pacing by the time the phone rang. He waited for the agents to give him the go-ahead, then he answered. "Hello?"

"Do you think that I'm a fool, Mr. Dunham?"

"No, I—"

"It was a rhetorical question. I'm not a fool. I can't be cheated. I can't be tricked. I am five steps ahead of your friends in the FBI. I assume they're listening and tracing this, so I'll be brief." The killer gave an address on the south side of Kansas City. "You'll find a box in an alleyway there containing the remaining pieces of your wife. Check your work e-mail, and you'll find an address linking to a video of her last moments. It's now midnight. You have twenty-four hours to eliminate your next target or your son will share her fate. Shoot him in the head and make sure that it's done right this time."

Brad's voice shook as sobs racked his body, but he managed to say, "Wait! What next target?"

"That's for your ears only."

The killer ended the call, but Brad heard another phone ringing. He stood dazed for a moment, his mind unable to process the information bombarding it. Then he ran into the kitchen to locate the source of the ringing. The FBI agent was at his back telling him to wait, but Brad ignored the big man in the dark suit.

The sound was coming from his wife's purse. It was Julie's cell phone.

He fumbled through the contents of the purse, shoving aside her wallet and make-up and a thousand other miscellaneous items that he couldn't identify, until he finally found the source of the ringing. He pulled it free and slid his finger across the display to answer the call.

The killer's familiar voice gave Brad the name and description of the next target.

Then the phone clicked dead, and Brad stared at the strange object in his hand as if he could no longer recognize it. The FBI agent asked urgently what the killer had said, but Brad barely registered the words. He was thinking of his wife and his son and trying to make sense of events that seemed to exist only in nightmares. This couldn't be real. It couldn't be happening. He prayed to wake up.

But he didn't wake up. This wasn't a dream.

The tears came first. Then the anger. He shattered the phone against the wall, tossed a chair from the kitchen table through the sliding glass door, and lashed out at the FBI agents. Brad was still screaming his wife's name when they tackled him to the floor and placed the cuffs on his wrists.

CHAPTER TWENTY-SIX

MARCUS AND ANDREW REACHED THE BRIEFING ROOM AT THE KCPD METRO POLICE STATION A HALF-HOUR AFTER RECEIVING A TEXT FROM KALEB TELLING THEM ABOUT THE MURDERS AT THE HOSPITAL AND THAT THEY HAD RECEIVED A NEW VIDEO. It was six in the morning. The briefing room looked like a classroom pulled from a community college. Block walls painted white. Speckled linoleum. Bars of fluorescent lighting shining out from behind translucent tiles in the recessed ceiling. Rows of gray tables filled the space, with two whiteboards and a podium occupying the front of the room.

Marcus found new police stations strangely disturbing. His old station house at the 77th Precinct in Brooklyn with its crumbling red brick and worn wood gave a feeling that the same rooms had been used by cops a hundred years ago and that the men and women inside were upholding a proud legacy. The new constructions were cold and institutional. No sense of history or heritage.

Kaleb led them inside. An FBI agent and Captain Duran looked over some case files at the podium. Most of the other tables were empty. Only the front two rows were in use by detectives from the task force who were waiting for the briefing to begin. Each of the detectives had a cup of coffee resting in front of them. The smell wafted up from their cups and made Marcus crave one.

As if reading his mind, Kaleb said, "Coffee?"

"Please," Marcus said, even though he suspected it would be cheap and weak.

"None for me," Andrew said.

Kaleb moved to the back of the room and filled two styrofoam cups while Marcus and Andrew sat down two rows behind the other men and women. Kaleb didn't ask if Marcus wanted cream and sugar. He just delivered back a steaming cup of black caffeine.

"Thanks," Marcus said to Kaleb. "So I heard that the deal at the hospital and the car dealership was your idea?"

Kaleb nodded and replied, "Unfortunately."

"It was a good idea. The fact that it didn't work doesn't diminish that."

"Tell that to Captain Duran."

"Your mother?"

"Again, unfortunately."

"Has to be tough working for her."

"You have no idea. The only reason I'm still on the case after the fiasco at the hospital is because I've already been working with the two of you. And the funny thing is that I get it from both sides. She's harder on me than any of the other guys, but they act like I get special treatment. Last Christmas, someone hung pacifiers on a miniature Christmas tree and left it on my desk. The star read *Mama's Boy*."

Andrew said, "It could be worse."

"How's that?"

Marcus answered, "Your parents could be serial killers."

From the front of the room, Captain Duran announced, "Let's get started, people."

The detectives immediately quieted down. Captain Duran was a woman who commanded immediate attention. Marcus analyzed her. Not for any particular reason, just out of habit. Maria Duran seemed to him a woman of contradictions. Her demeanor was stern and all business, but her hair and make-up looked as if they had been done by a team of beauticians. Her curly black hair cascaded over her shoulders, instead of being pulled back or put up into a more professional style. She wore a conservative gray pantsuit and light purple shirt, but the top two buttons were undone, revealing some cleavage. She put out a tough image and demanded respect, but she also wanted no one to forget that she was a woman. She invoked equal parts fear and animal desire, and she seemed to get off on both.

She said, "Normally, we wouldn't show this type of video to everyone. But I feel that you all need to see what's coming for this boy if you fail to find him. Plus, we need as many sets of eyes on this as possible. Let us know if you notice anything that could help." She asked one of the detectives to turn out the lights, and a video filled one of the whiteboards from a projector mounted on the ceiling.

The video was similar to the others that the killer had sent the police previously. Except for the location of the killing and the mask that the madman wore. This time he wore the face of a young woman in great agony.

To Andrew, Marcus whispered, "The masks are different in every video."

Kaleb overheard and said, "We're checking on that. We think they're custom made. Detective Lazaro is questioning custom mask designers with enough skill to have made them or taught someone else how."

Marcus watched as his father's brutal depravity was put on display, but he tried not to focus on what was happening in the video. Instead, he focused on the details. He examined the gurney. The plastic sheeting. The clothes his father wore. Every detail, every frame, every sound. All of it broken down to its basic components and scrutinized.

Before he realized what he was doing, he was on his feet saying, "Hold on."

Captain Duran paused the video, squinted into the dark room, and said, "Who said that?"

Fagan's voice echoed in Marcus's ears, but it was too late to turn back now. He said, "I recognize the house." He walked over and flipped on the lights. Then he approached the podium. Captain Duran eyed him with confusion and suspicion as he grabbed the stack of case files from her hands and sifted through them.

After finding the correct file, he said, "The first target was an old man named Lawrence Goodweather. He was killed in his home. His only daughter lives in California, and she put the house up for sale. But who wants to buy a house where someone was just murdered?"

Marcus flipped through photos of the crime scene and held one up to the image that was paused on the screen. "See the woodwork, the layout of the doors, this crack in the drywall, the water damage on the ceiling here? This video was shot inside Lawrence Good-weather's house."

Maria Duran and the lead FBI agent looked from the photo to the screen. Repeated the process several times. The FBI agent nodded, and Duran said, "I think you're right."

Many of the detectives were already on their feet, ready to mobilize on the house. Duran stopped them. "Okay, we're going to do this right. SWAT's on standby. They'll recon the place first. This may be where he's keeping the Dunham boy, or it may be his base of operations. Or it may just be another crime scene. Either way, SWAT's in charge. We do this by the numbers. Get to it."

Everyone hurried from the room, except for Marcus and Andrew.

Marcus was still staring at the photo with a dour look on his face. Andrew asked, "I thought we were only supposed to observe."

"What can I say? I'm impulsive, and I have a problem with authority. My psych eval says so."

"So what's on your mind now? You have that 'something ain't right' look on your face. I hate it when you get that look."

"I just can't shake the feeling that we're playing his game, reacting exactly how he wants us to. We were obviously meant to find Claire. And someone else would have figured out that this was the Goodweather house if I hadn't. I'm worried that this is part of his plan."

"I don't know if anyone else but you would have noticed those minor details."

"Maybe, maybe not. Either way, he's obviously studied me, and he knew that I'd see the video and figure it out."

"Okay, then what do we do about it?"

"Nothing. We have to play his game. At least for now."

CHAPTER TWENTY-SEVEN

THE MORE THAT MAGGIE STARED AT THE SLEEPING FORM OF CLAIRE CAS-
SIDY, THE MORE SHE FELT THAT THEY RESEMBLED ONE ANOTHER. They
had the same small nose. Same skin tone. Both blonde. Same build.
Claire was suffering from malnutrition and abuse, but in a healthy
state, they could have passed for sisters.

Something about that really pissed Maggie off. As if she was just
a stand-in for Marcus's past love.

She supposed that was irrational. He obviously just had a type.
That wasn't a big deal. But the fact that he hadn't told her that he
had once been engaged, that bothered her. It had been a long time
ago, but why had he kept it secret? Would he have ever told her? She
didn't know what to think.

Maggie had always been insecure in their relationship. A part of
her worried that Marcus would grow tired of dealing with the many
eccentricities that accompanied her obsessive compulsive disorder.
And a part of her wouldn't blame him. It seemed that the list of
her compulsions grew every year, and she worried about what that
would mean for her twenty years down the road.

Her contemplation of future obsessions was broken as Claire's
eyes fluttered open. "Where am I? Who are you? Where's my son?"

Maggie placed a hand on Claire's shoulder. "You're safe." Into
the adjacent room, she called, "Director!"

The Director entered the bedroom and pulled up another chair
beside Claire's bed. "Hello, my dear. Glad to see you're feeling better."

"Where's my son?"

The Director leaned in close. His voice was calm and soothing. "Let's start from the beginning. We work for the Department of Justice. We're a think-tank that helps track down serial killers. During the course of one of our investigations, we found you. You were being fed intravenously and had been drugged. You're going to have to fill in the blanks from there."

Claire sat forward. "We have to go back. My son."

Maggie held her down and said, "There was no one else in that house. We'll help you find your son, but you have to tell us what happened to you."

Claire's gaze darted around the room as if she were considering making a break for it, but she finally said, "Dylan and I were walking to our car after going to a movie one night. Someone must have come up behind us. I'm not sure. I just remember being hit on the head, and when I came to, Dylan was gone and I was in a dungeon."

"A dungeon? Like a basement?" the Director asked.

"Maybe. I can't be sure. It was completely dark. The walls were stone. The floor was dirty and damp. I don't know how long I was down there in the dark. It felt like an eternity."

Maggie said, "We've checked with your work and the local police. It looks like you went missing about a week and a half ago."

"That's it? It felt like much longer."

"Did you ever see the man who took you?" the Director asked.

"No—he slid a tray of food in through a slot. He never even spoke to me. The only time he came into my cell, he beat me and injected something into my arm. That was the last thing I remember. The light blinded me when he came in. I didn't see his face. I'm sorry. Where's Marcus?"

Maggie said, "How did you know that Marcus was here?"

Claire sat forward again. Her focus shifted between the two of them. "I heard his voice when I was drugged up. How's he involved with you?"

The Director answered, "He's the one who found you, and he's a member of our team."

Claire leaned back. "I thought maybe he had found out about Dylan somehow, and then came to find him when we went missing."

Silence hung in the air, and Maggie finally asked, "Why would he come for your son?"

"*Our* son. Marcus is Dylan's father."

CHAPTER TWENTY-EIGHT

THE SUBURBAN CAME TO REST AT THE END OF THE DUSTY OLD FIELD LANE THAT WOUND ITS WAY UP TO THEIR SAFE HOUSE. Marcus and Andrew hopped out of the vehicle, but Maggie met them on the porch.

Marcus said, "So what's the emergency? Something with Ackerman?"

"No," Maggie said. "Let's take a little walk."

Andrew, as if sensing that this had to do with personal matters, said, "Maybe I'll go check on things in the house."

But Maggie stopped him. "No, I think Marcus might need us both there with him on this."

Something in her eyes told Marcus that this was an emergency of a different kind. Not physical, but emotional. He couldn't grasp what that could possibly be, but there was no point in arguing with her.

The three of them stepped down from the porch and started into the yard. They had wound a circuitous path around it to the edge of the field and back to the lane before Maggie spoke.

"I've been debating about how to tell you this," she said. "I guess there's really no easy way to say it. Claire woke up, and the Director and I spoke with her."

Andrew asked, "Did she know anything useful?"

"Not about the man that took her. She was kidnapped about a week and a half ago. She and her son Dylan. He's eight years old."

They kept walking for a few minutes in silence, crossing the lane and following it along the field beside an old split-rail fence. Weeds and tall grass licked their legs, and the air was fresh with pollen and the smell of wet hay. Combines kicked up dust in the distance as farmers harvested their crops.

Marcus stopped and placed his palms on the fence's top rail. He knew where Maggie's story was headed without her speaking the words. "Is she positive that he's mine?" he asked.

"She seems pretty sure."

Marcus started to say something else, but the words wouldn't come. He remembered falling on the playground once as a boy. The blacktop of the elementary school in Brooklyn had hidden a layer of ice. He'd run out onto it, and his feet had slid out from beneath him. He had flown into the air and landed flat on his back. The air had left his lungs, the impact stealing his life's breath. He remembered lying there for what felt like several moments, gasping for air. He had felt in that moment that he was going to die. His child's mind had believed that the end had come.

He felt the same way in that moment leaning against the split-rail fence. He couldn't breathe. He couldn't speak. And he couldn't shake the sensation of life as he knew it coming to an end.

❖

The door to Claire's room stood open. She sat on the bed, staring off into space. Marcus recognized her clothes as belonging to Maggie. The sweatpants and hooded sweatshirt hung loosely on Claire's small frame. Maggie probably had twenty pounds of lean muscle on his ex-fiancée.

She noticed him but didn't speak. He joined her on the bed. It was still unmade, a white floral bedspread bunched up on the floor. They sat in silence for a moment, but then she said, "You look like ten gallons of shit in a five-gallon bucket."

Marcus chuckled in spite of the situation. She did always have a talent for making him laugh. "It's good to see you too, Claire."

"I'm sorry," she said.

"You don't have to be. I'm sorry that you and your son got wrapped up in this mess."

"He's *our* son, and I'm sorry for not telling you. You must hate me."

"I could never hate you. It was a shock, but I understand why you didn't tell me. I can't say that I blame you. Anyone who gets close to me gets hurt. He's better off without me in his life."

"That's not true. You're too hard on yourself."

"Then why didn't you tell me? Even if you didn't want me around him, I could have helped financially."

"We don't need your money, and I thought about calling probably every day for the past eight years. It happened that weekend after we had already broken up. I didn't tell you at the time, but I was seeing someone else then. I didn't tell you because I ..." Tears filled Claire's eyes, and her voice quivered. "I let him think that Dylan was his. I thought it would be easiest for everyone. He was a good man. I knew he'd be a good father."

"And you knew I wouldn't be."

"It wasn't that."

"It's okay. I've never even been good for myself. And I've only gotten worse since you knew me."

"I was sorry to hear about your aunt. One of my old friends from the DA's office told me about it. I thought about coming home for the funeral, but I didn't want to cause you any extra grief."

"So what happened with you and the guy who thought he was Dylan's father? Where's he at now?"

"He died in a car accident when Dylan was three. After that, it seemed like I'd missed my opportunity to tell you." Claire sat there for a moment and added, "Are you really not going to get mad? Where's that smartass hothead I used to know?"

"I'm too tired to be angry or come up with smartass comments anymore."

"You look tired. What happened to the guy that would sit up all night pounding through case files? He was so full of life, so driven."

"He got old."

"You're younger than I am."

"Life happens. All I want to do now is lie down and sleep."

"Sounds like depression."

Marcus changed the subject. "Did they tell you who we think took your son?"

"They said it was your father. Your biological father. That he must have figured out that Dylan was his grandson."

Marcus turned to her, wiped away the tears, and gently guided her chin up until they were eye to eye. "We can't change the past. But I swear that I'll get your son back to you, even if it costs my own life. I owe both of you nothing less." He kissed her on the forehead and added, "And I'll make damn sure that the man who took him doesn't hurt you or Dylan ever again."

CHAPTER TWENTY-NINE

L AWRENCE GOODWEATHER'S FORMER RESIDENCE—AND THE SCENE OF THE LAST MURDER—WAS A LARGE TWO-STORY WHITE HOUSE WITH A PARTIAL STONE FRONT. The big house on Forrest Avenue had sat empty since the time of the Goodweather murder. It was old but well maintained, just as one would expect from a retired gentleman accustomed to working with his hands.

All the teams were in place and ready to enter the house. SWAT had set up an invisible perimeter and was waiting for the *go* signal. Kaleb Duran sat three houses down in the driveway of one of the neighbors. He had requisitioned an old beige Buick Regal from the impound to use during the operation. One of the other detectives sat in the passenger seat, sipping coffee and looking uninterested.

Kaleb drummed his fingers on the steering wheel and tapped his foot on the floorboard in nervous anticipation. "What the hell are we waiting for?" he asked, more to himself than the other man in the car. The other detective just shrugged.

SWAT had already done a cursory recon of the property and hadn't seen anyone inside. They should have been storming the castle. Waiting was a waste of time.

Kaleb growled in disgust, pulled his cell phone from the pocket of his jeans, and dialed his mother's number. "What are we waiting for?" he asked as soon as she picked up.

"We're going to give it some time. If he's using this as a staging area, then we may get lucky and catch the guy. We haven't seen any signs of life inside, and if we go in now, we blow our best shot at him."

"But there's a crime scene in that house. We might find some evidence to lead us to him. And what if the kid's in there?"

"We haven't found any evidence that we could use to locate him at the other crime scenes. No reason to think this one would be any different. And SWAT doesn't think anyone's inside."

"They can't be sure of that."

"I don't have time for this. The call's been made."

Captain Duran hung up. Kaleb said, "Dammit, I don't like this. We're wasting time."

The other detective leaned back and closed his eyes. "Patience, kid. The captain knows what she's doing."

"I hope you're right."

The next hour crawled by with little activity. A few kids. A lady walking a dog. A couple of joggers. No one paid any attention to the house or so much as gave it a second glance. The sun was high in the sky, and the Dunham boy's time was running out.

Then Kaleb's radio buzzed into life. "We got someone suspicious coming up the alley from the east."

Kaleb couldn't see the alley from his position. One of the other cops asked, "Can you see the face?"

"No, the suspect's wearing a dark-hooded sweatshirt with the hood pulled up. He's keeping his head low, like he's trying to conceal his face."

Captain Duran's voice echoed from the tinny speaker. "This could be it, people. Everyone be ready. If the suspect enters the house, we move in."

"Dammit," Kaleb said. "I wish I could see what's happening back there."

"Suspect is approaching the back porch ... Still can't see the face ... He's going in ... I repeat, he's in the house."

Captain Duran said, "SWAT move in. All teams are go. Maintain control of the perimeter. Make sure he doesn't run."

Kaleb stepped out of the Regal and looked across the street at the Goodweather house. The SWAT team poured out of the house next door and converged on the target home. Four black-clad men entered through the front, and four went in the back. Kaleb wanted to be in there with them. Not being part of the action was killing him.

The sound of the first explosion rocked him back on his heels. Screams poured out over the radio. Most of it was unintelligible, but he recognized words like *bomb ... trap ... pull back.*

Kaleb sprinted across the street. The other detective yelled something at his back, but he paid the old pencil-pusher little mind. The men in that house needed help.

The rumble of two more explosions echoed up the quiet suburban block before Kaleb reached the other side of the street.

CHAPTER THIRTY

KALEB LEAPED UP THE FRONT STAIRS OF THE GOODWEATHER HOUSE AND PUSHED OPEN THE HEAVY OAK EXTERIOR DOOR. The scene inside looked like something from a war zone. Plaster dust and debris hung in the air. Men were screaming in agony. A smell that reminded him of fireworks on the Fourth of July clung to his nostrils. His gun was out and at the ready.

Two of the black-clad SWAT officers dragged a fallen brother into the front room. Kaleb ran over to help. The face of the man on the floor was a bloody mess. His helmet had been discarded, and nails jutted out of his face at all angles. He screamed and cursed and spat blood. Kaleb grabbed him by the collar and helped drag him onto the porch.

Kaleb recognized one of the officers trying to stop the bleeding and asked, "What the hell happened in there?"

"We walked right into it. The crazy bastard had rigged up a bunch of nail bombs. We have five down."

"What about the suspect?"

"I don't know."

Kaleb grabbed the radio from his belt and said into the receiver, "This is Detective Duran. Suspect is not in custody. I repeat, suspect is not in custody. Maintain the perimeter. I'm going to search the house."

Someone said over the radio, "Duran, wait for the bomb squad!"

But Kaleb ignored them and re-entered the house. One of the remaining SWAT officers took up position behind Kaleb, his MP4 rifle at the ready. His eyes were wide and angry. He gave Kaleb a nod, and they moved forward into the house.

A stairwell led up on the right. They took the stairs and moved cautiously through the upstairs hall. Watching for any more traps. The upstairs bedrooms were clear. A door at the end of the hall led up to an unfinished attic. They searched for any hiding places among the exposed beams and insulation, but the entire space was open for storage. Nowhere for a person to hide.

They backtracked down the stairs and checked the main floor. The smell of the explosions still hung heavy in the air, and the plaster dust and insulation fibers floating through the house made Kaleb's skin itch. The back kitchen was a shambles. Nails protruded from the cabinets in several spots, and blood smears covered the speckled linoleum. The fallen officers had been pulled out of harm's way. The back door remained open. Kaleb looked out and saw officers maintaining the perimeter.

A set of old concrete steps led down from the utility room. The SWAT officer went first, flipping on a tactical light attached to his MP4. The steps were damp and slick. The house's lowest level was a half-basement with unfinished block walls. Kaleb pulled the chain of an overhead light, and a naked bulb burst to life.

The space contained the water heater and furnace, an old workbench, a sump pump, and some shelves holding old cans of paint and other junk. But nothing else. No suspect. No traps.

The SWAT officer motioned at a wooden access door for the crawlspace. Nodding, Kaleb grabbed the door by its rusty metal handle and yanked it open. The SWAT officer shone his light inside. The access entry was maybe three feet high. He crawled into the tight space and checked all the corners, but the beam of his tactical light only revealed spiderwebs and a dirt floor.

The black-clad officer and Kaleb exchanged confused looks and then went back through the entire house for a second sweep. This time, they were even more careful and methodical.

They found nothing. The suspect had entered the house and then vanished.

CHAPTER THIRTY-ONE

S TILL NOTHING," ANDREW SAID, LOWERING THE PHONE FROM HIS EAR.
Marcus pinched the bridge of his nose. His head hurt so
badly that he was on the verge of throwing up. It had been over four
hours since they had left Kaleb at the police station and local law
enforcement was mobilizing to move on the Goodweather house. In
that time, they had received no updates. "Keep trying him. Try the
station. See if you can get anyone there. I think it's time that I had a
heart-to-heart with my brother."

Marcus moved down the stairs and past the guards from the CIA
to the house's dining room. Ackerman sat restrained in the center of
the room. A black hood covered his face, and his shirt was bloody.
Marcus pulled off the hood to reveal a swollen and beaten face.

Ackerman tried to grin, but his swollen cheeks made it impossible. "It's good to see you, brother. I worried that you'd forgotten
about me."

"Who did this to you?"

"Mr. Craig, the tall blond from the CIA. I told him that he should
at least buy me dinner before moving straight to foreplay, but he
wasn't amused. They tried to force me to talk."

Marcus shot a look of disdain at the two guards seated in opposite corners of the room, but neither of them reacted. "What did you
tell them?"

"Nothing. I told them that I would only speak with you. I can be
a bit of a stubborn asshole at times. I think it runs in the family. You
mentioned before that father sent you a videotape. What was on it?"

Marcus walked over to one of the guards seated in a corner. He
said, "I need your chair."

The guard's eyes narrowed, but he said nothing and vacated the seat. Marcus pulled it over beside Ackerman. "You know that the FBI has the entire collection of the tapes showing you being tortured and experimented on when you were a boy."

"Yes. I understand that they're required viewing for the Behavioral Analysis Unit. Rather flattering."

"They call them the Ackerman Tapes. But there's a two-week period missing from them. Our father documented nearly everything, but then there's a gap with nothing. A bit of a conspiracy theory has even developed about what happened during that time."

"Have you watched the tapes?"

"Yes, and there appears to be a change in you between the time before the gap and after."

"Maybe Father communed with the Devil."

"No, but he did perform brain surgery on you. The tape he sent to me was of the two missing weeks. I think it was his way of authenticating himself. He explains that he wasn't getting the result he wanted from you and had decided to resort to more invasive procedures. He intentionally damaged your amygdala."

Ackerman said, "You can't make an omelette without scrambling a few brains, but I don't remember any of that."

"Video doesn't lie. The amygdala is the part of the brain that controls fear and governs a lot of other primitive instincts that we don't fully understand. I did some research on other people who have experienced similar damage to their brains. In a study published in *Current Biology* by researchers from the University of Iowa, one woman with damage to the amygdala was unable to experience fear like a normal person. But not only can't she feel fear like the rest of us, she's somehow drawn to activities and situations that are dangerous and that she should be afraid of."

Ackerman looked away. "I've heard enough."

"Don't you see what this means? The damage to your brain coupled with the abuse you experienced forced you to be drawn to pain and fear. You couldn't help it. You didn't have a chance. Maybe we can even repair—"

"No! You remember the story from the Bible when Jesus and his disciples came across a blind man, and the disciples asked who had sinned to make this man blind, him or his parents? Jesus replied that it happened so that the work of God might be displayed in his life. That's me. I'm not broken, brother. Well, maybe I am, but I'm broken on purpose. I'm exactly who I'm supposed to be. I'm an instrument of fate. I'm the hand of God himself. I'm not just some lab rat stuck in a maze. I'm part of a grand plan. And so are you."

They stared at each other for a moment until a knock sounded at the dining room door. Andrew came in and said, "Sorry to interrupt, but I was able to reach someone at the police station."

Marcus asked, "So what happened at the Goodweather house?"

"They decided to sit on it for a while, and it paid off. Someone went in."

"There's a suspect in custody? Is it my father?"

"That's the thing. SWAT went in after the guy, and it was a trap. Son of a bitch had set up nail bombs to greet the SWAT team. But then they searched the house, and the suspect was gone. Vanished like a damn ghost."

"How is that possible?"

"Beats the hell out of me."

Ackerman drew the attention of both men when he said, "Was there a crawlspace in the house?"

Andrew answered, "I don't know. Why?"

"You should call the officers at the scene immediately. Father invariably liked to have an escape plan, and he always chose a safe house with a crawlspace for just that reason. He would fashion a coffin-like box that he would conceal in the dirt floor. You could crawl right over his little hideaway and never know it was there, unless you knew what to look for."

"What are you saying?"

"Your killer never left. He's still in the house."

Chapter Thirty-Two

KALEB SAT ACROSS THE STREET FROM THE GOODWEATHER HOUSE ON THE HOOD OF THE OLD BUICK REGAL, SMOKING A CIGARETTE AND THINKING OF THE GOOD MEN WHO HAD DIED INSIDE THE HOME'S WALLS. Two of the SWAT officers had been pronounced DOA, and two others were in critical condition. And to top it all off, their killer had escaped.

Uniformed police officers had evacuated the surrounding homes, blocked off the street, and erected barricades—keeping civilians a safe distance from the house in case any more explosive devices were found. Neighbors and reporters had congregated on the other side of the barriers.

After the bomb squad pronounced the scene safe, the CSI teams went to work. Most of the other members of the task force had headed back to the station to pursue other leads. The Dunham kid's time was almost up. Kaleb chose to stay behind.

Their failure wasn't all his fault. He wasn't even a lead member of the task force. He was just a grunt. Still, he felt responsible.

His phone vibrated against his leg. He checked the caller ID and declined the call. He didn't want to explain anything to the Governor's reps. He didn't want to talk to anyone. His misery didn't need any company.

❖

It checked its watch. The LED display came to life with a hum and lit the interior of the box with an eerie green glow. The box was like a coffin, but it wasn't afraid. It didn't feel claustrophobic or experience any sensation that the walls were closing in on it. Although it felt like it should be scared—it sensed that at one time it would have been very afraid to lie in the small space.

It remembered the face of an old man, lying in a similar box. It walked up to the box and stared at the man inside. Tears were in its eyes, but it didn't understand why. Its mother was there. She was sobbing and being consoled by another older woman.

The memory faded as quickly as it had appeared, but it had brought a strange realization. It had a mother. It had once had family and friends. It had once been alive. It had once been a real person.

Or had it? It couldn't be sure. And even if a person with a soul had once dwelled within this husk, that being had moved on. It was empty. It was just a thing. A monster built to follow instructions or face the consequences of disobedience.

The master's words came back to it. The master's instructions. Words of life. What if the master had sensed its hesitation? The master saw all and knew all. Would it be punished for the memory? Would it endure great pain for questioning its existence?

It wasn't sure, but it knew that if it didn't carry out its task, then the pain would come. With the promise of suffering in mind, it pushed itself out of the coffin carefully. The lid of the box was recessed in the ground and covered with dirt to conceal it from the outside. It pushed the lid up and laid it gently to the side, as it had been told, just in case it needed to go back into its hiding place. Like a cockroach fleeing back to the shadows when the lights came on.

Sliding out into the darkness of the crawlspace, it waited and listened. It heard footsteps on the floor above, but it didn't hear any-one inside the basement. It crawled to the access panel and pushed it open just enough to peer into the rest of basement. The lights were off. There was no sound except for the hum of the furnace and the flickering of the pilot light inside the water heater.

Carefully, it pushed the panel completely open and dropped onto the concrete floor. The master's instructions had been clear at every step. They left no room for interpretation. It counted to thirty before moving any further and listened for signs that it had been discovered.

The creaks and groans of movement sounded on the floor above, but the basement was empty. It hadn't been heard. It hadn't been dis-covered. It was time to move on to the next step.

It checked the extended magazine of the H&K MP7 A1, screwed a long suppressor onto the end of the gun's barrel, and activated the green reticle of the tactical scope. Then it moved toward the stairs to carry out the next part of its mission.

It was a guided missile. A bullet fired at a target. And its target was waiting patiently just above its head.

❖

Marcus took the corner at high speed, sending the big top-heavy Suburban leaning onto its right wheels as its rear end kicked sideways. The GPS unit on the dash showed a clear blue line toward their target, and a mechanical voice announced their next turn.

"Kaleb still isn't answering," Andrew said from the passenger seat.

"Try the precinct again. See if they can reach anyone on the scene."

Marcus veered in and out of traffic, their emergency lights reflecting off the surfaces of the other vehicles.

"Slow down," Andrew said. "I prefer not to die a fiery death."

"Just make the damn call!" Marcus yelled as the Suburban's tires screeched around the next turn

❖

It took the stairs with slow and calculated movements, hugging the side wall and being careful not to make a sound. It had memorized the layout of the house. The master had said that the police would focus on the room where the Dunham woman had died, so that was where the largest concentration of targets would congregate.

The master had said it should carefully choose the time to attack. Try to pick off isolated targets. Don't make your presence known until absolutely necessary. Like a lion stalking a group of gazelle. Pick off those that stray from the safety of the herd.

The door at the top of the stairs opened into a utility room. The overhead light was off. It could see the washer and dryer in the ambient light from the kitchen. It stepped into the shadows of the utility room and took up position beside the next door.

It listened, ever patient. There was no reason to hurry or be nervous. Bullets didn't get nervous. Inanimate objects didn't worry about consequences or death. They had no life to lose.

Someone was working in the kitchen. It could hear their shoes scraping across the linoleum as they searched for evidence.

It ran down the checklist from the master and felt that the moment for patience had passed. This was the moment to attack. It swung into the kitchen, aimed at the head of the figure standing across the linoleum, then squeezed the trigger.

The target fell over the counter and slumped to the floor. The target wore a strange white plastic jumpsuit and a mask covered its face. The killer had been prepared to see this. The master had mentioned something about the technicians being dressed in Tyvek jumpsuits. The master had told it not to be alarmed by this abnormality. The suits, designed to keep contamination from entering the crime scene, would also restrict the movements of the targets and make them easier prey.

But it didn't care about such things. It simply did as it was told. Easy or difficult had no meaning.

It heard more movement from the dining room. More targets. Its first strike had not alerted the others. It knew the master was watching and would be pleased. The others would fall easily.

But it had more instructions to carry out first. It dragged the body of the dead man into the laundry room and removed the white Tyvek jumpsuit.

❖

Kaleb had just lit his fourth cigarette when one of the uniformed officers who had been maintaining the police barricade ran up to him with a phone in his outstretched hand. "Detective, you have an important call."

He took the phone and said, "This is Duran."

"Kaleb, it's Andrew Garrison. Listen to me carefully. We're a few minutes out from your location, but we have reason to believe that the killer may still be on site."

Kaleb rolled his eyes. "Believe me. We checked that house multiple times from top to bottom. There's no one in—"

"The crawlspace, Duran. The killer had a specially made hiding spot in the crawlspace."

"We checked it."

"It's buried. Just get everyone out now and set up a perimeter."

"Okay, okay. I'll check it out."

Kaleb clicked off, sat the phone on the hood of the Buick, and took another long drag on his cigarette. Then he slid off the hood and started toward the house. He would do as he was told. He would check out the crawlspace, but he didn't expect to find anything and wasn't going to be in a hurry about it.

His attitude changed when a CSI technician in a white Tyvek jumpsuit ran out through the front door. A mask and goggles covered the tech's face and muffled a raspy high-pitched yell. "There's someone in the house! Someone attacked us!"

❖

Kaleb kicked through the front door, leading with his 9mm Beretta Px4 Storm pistol. Two techs were coming down the stairs on his right. "What's happening? We heard screaming!" one of the techs said.

"Get out now!"

Kaleb kept his weapon trained on the next room as the techs moved past him. The door was closed. It was a heavy oak door covered in a dark woodgrain. He couldn't hear anything from the other side. The door sat within a niche with no cover on either side. He would have to go in fast.

Taking a deep breath, he readied his weapon and kicked the door hard. It swung inward in a spray of splinters, the frame disintegrating. He rushed into the next room and dropped to one knee in a shooter's stance.

A man and a woman in Tyvek jumpsuits lay on the floor. Pools of blood forming around them. They had each been shot multiple times in the head and chest.

Kaleb's stomach churned from a surge of adrenaline. He fought the urge to retreat. He knew there was at least one more tech in the house.

He watched the kitchen door for movement. Then he heard footsteps coming from the front of the house, from the way he had just come. A uniformed officer joined him in the dining room. The officer cursed under his breath. Kaleb didn't speak but met the man's gaze and pointed toward the kitchen. The man nodded back, and they moved forward together. Kaleb felt much better having backup. Strength in numbers. Although that hadn't helped the techs.

They swept into the kitchen. Kaleb went low and right. The uniformed cop covered the utility room. The kitchen was empty, and they repeated the procedure for the utility room.

Inside, they found the last tech. He had been shoved into a corner like a discarded bag of trash. His Tyvek jumpsuit was missing.

It took a moment for Kaleb to register what that meant. When he did, he cursed himself for failing once again. To the uniformed cop, he said, "Watch the basement, but wait for me to come back. Anyone comes up those stairs, you shoot them."

Then Kaleb rushed back to the front of the house and out through the front door. The uniformed cops outside had set up a perimeter and were covering all the exits. Their guns swung toward him as he came out. He raised his hands in surrender. "Where did the techs go?" he said.

One of the the cops gestured to the other side of the street behind his car. Kaleb rushed over and found the two techs he had seen coming down the stairs. He asked, "Where's the other guy?"

They looked at him strangely and one replied, "We didn't see anyone else. We thought they were still in the house."

Kaleb's gaze darted around the neighborhood and checked the faces of the crowd on the other side of the barricades.

"Dammit!" he yelled.

The first tech who had come running and shouting from the house had disappeared. Only it hadn't been one of the techs at all. It had been their killer. And Kaleb had let the bastard run right past him.

CHAPTER THIRTY-THREE

"So NEITHER OF YOU SAW ANYTHING?" KALEB ASKED.

The first uniformed cop wouldn't make eye contact. He was young. A former military police officer who had done two tours in the Gulf. A black mustache hung over the older officer's mouth and a large scar cut across his face, turning up at his mouth's corners like a giant smile. Kaleb knew both men. Both good cops.

"I'm sorry," the older officer said. "When that tech came running out, he headed for the ME's van. We focused on the house."

The white panel van with *Jackson County Medical Examiner* stenciled on its side in big gold letters still sat against the opposite curb. Kaleb tapped his pen against the pad of paper in his hand. He hadn't written anything on it yet. "Give me something. Short, tall? Skin color?"

The younger officer shook his head. The older one said, "Short. Maybe five six, five seven. Skin looked dark, but everyone looks dark against the white of those suits. There was no light, and the face was pretty well covered up."

"Okay, guys. Don't worry about it. Just maintain the perimeter."

A vehicle screeched to a halt on the other side of the police barricade. It was a big black Suburban. Kaleb gritted his teeth as he marched over to meet Marcus Williams and Andrew Garrison. Instead of telling the officers to let them through, he stepped over the barrier and met them on the other side. Both men gave him strange looks, but Kaleb moved past them, heading for the Suburban. He didn't want to have this conversation with anyone else in earshot. "Let's go for a drive," he said.

He jumped up into the passenger seat and slammed the SUV's door behind him. Williams climbed up behind the wheel, and Garrison sat in the second row. "I'm assuming that he already got away," Williams said as he started up the engine and pulled away from the scene.

Kaleb slammed his fist against the dash. "Yeah, he got away. And killed three people in the process. I've known something was off about you two from the start. How the hell did you know he was still on scene? Who are you really?"

Williams meandered through traffic, driving slowly without saying a word. Finally, he said, "We're from the Department of Justice. Part of a think-tank specializing in the capture of serial murderers."

"Then why lie to us? Why the cover story?"

"We try to keep a low profile."

Kaleb laughed, but there was no humor behind it. "A low profile. What else haven't you told us? Have you been withholding evidence?"

From the back seat, Garrison said, "We have our orders, just like you."

"That's a load of—"

"You're right," Williams said. "We've been keeping things to ourselves." He went on to explain everything. A lead they followed that led to a man named Joe Colwell. The connection to Francis Ackerman Sr. The suspicion that there were actually two killers—a master and an apprentice. The woman they had found at the Colwell house.

When Williams was finished, Kaleb sat in silence for a moment. Then he said, "Take me to the station."

✦

The metro patrol station was a massive glass-faced structure covered in red brick and sandstone with a gray metal roof. In front of the station, a 25-foot decorative copper weather vane climbed into the sky. The display was named *Salute* for the two-dimensional figure of a police officer standing atop the weather vane. The silent sentinel turned when the wind blew as if it was saluting the surrounding community.

Kaleb jumped from the Suburban before it had come to a full stop in front of the station. He strode past the weather vane, beneath a red portico, and through the large glass front doors. He nodded at the desk sergeant and continued past him through the squad room, down a long white corridor, and into his mother's office.

He expected a stern dressing-down for barging in on her unannounced. Instead, Captain Maria Duran leaped from her leather chair, rounded her desk, and came toward him. He recoiled instinctively, as if she were going to attack him, but what she actually did shocked him even more than if she'd shot him on the spot.

She grabbed him around the waist and squeezed him tight against her body. "I heard what happened at the crime scene. I'm so glad that you're okay."

Kaleb didn't know how to react. The last hug he remembered from her had been when he was eleven. They hadn't even hugged at his father's funeral. He raised his arms but didn't wrap them around her. Her gesture was so alien and shocking that he forgot briefly why he was even there.

"I'm fine," he said as his mother pulled away and straightened her suit. "Are *you* okay?"

"Yeah, I just ... The thing with this Dunham boy and ... The way you ran into the Goodweather house to try and save those men. It was a very selfless and heroic thing to do."

"Really? I assumed that you'd tell me I was stupid, and I should have waited for backup."

"Oh, you were, and you should have. You could have gotten yourself and others killed. But that's beside the point. I guess I just saw something in you that I didn't know was there. I'm proud of you, Kaleb." Maria Duran stumbled over the words as if they didn't taste right in her mouth.

Kaleb was at a loss. Dumbfounded. Speechless. "Thank you," was all he could muster.

"What did you need to tell me?"

"Umm ... nothing. I was just going to tell you about the attack at the crime scene, but I guess you already know."

His mother nodded and sat back down at her desk, and the cold and distant exterior that Kaleb knew so well—and that now seemed almost comforting—settled back over her. He headed for the door, but she said, "Oh, and Brad Dunham is in Interrogation Room Three. He's been asking for you."

"For me? Why?"

"I don't know. Maybe he heard that the thing at the hospital was your idea and wants to thank you for trying. You'll have to ask him yourself. See if you can get him to open up. The FBI agents who were with him at his house said that he spoke to the killer alone on his wife's phone. And Mr. Dunham won't tell anyone what was said. But be gentle with him. He's been volatile. Which is understandable, considering the circumstances."

Kaleb gave a sympathetic nod. They were all on edge, but he couldn't begin to imagine what Brad Dunham must have been feeling at that moment.

CHAPTER THIRTY-FOUR

NONE OF THE CONTRACTORS WHO CAME WITH FAGAN HAD GIVEN THEIR NAMES, ALTHOUGH MAGGIE HAD HEARD FAGAN REFER TO THE BIG BLOND MAN AS MR. CRAIG. She had tried to introduce herself on two occasions when she'd found herself in the kitchen at the same time as one of the stern-faced operators. They hadn't necessarily been rude, but they also hadn't spoken more than one word at a time. She had given up on trying to learn their names and had started assigning them made-up monikers instead. Nothing too creative. Just a way of identifying them in her head. One man walked with a limp—she called him Festus after the character from *Gunsmoke*. One's head seemed to always be on a swivel—she called him Hoot Owl. She hadn't decided on names for the other two but was leaning toward Grumpy and Bashful.

Festus was the one who had come upstairs to tell Maggie that Ackerman had requested to speak with her. He and Bashful were on guard duty.

As she entered the room, she asked, "Has he had anything to eat or used the bathroom?"

"He hasn't asked."

Maggie walked over and pulled the black hood off Ackerman's head. He said, "Hello, little sister. How are things?"

"They said you wanted to talk to me, but I can barely stomach being in the same room with you, so talk fast. You have five about seconds to give me something useful."

"I thought of some aliases that father may be using. But you have to give me something in return."

She laughed. "What? You want to know my darkest fear? My most painful memory? No deal."

"Nothing quite so dramatic. I just want to know who the woman is that Marcus brought in."

"How do you know about her?"

"Thin walls and good ears."

"She's Marcus's former fiancée. Your father kidnapped her about a week ago. Now what are the aliases?"

"There's more to it. Why would father take her? Their relationship must have ended a long time ago."

"You can ask him all about it when he's in the cell next to yours. Aliases?"

Ackerman looked away, and his eyes moved back and forth from side to side as if he was processing a great deal of information. His normal cocky demeanor melted away, and his eyes filled with the anger that she knew dwelled just beneath his surface. "Did they have a son? Did Father take Marcus's boy?"

"How the hell did you know that?"

"It's the only thing that makes sense. You need to find him before he does to that boy what he did to me. I've tried hard to block out that part of my life, but I've been able to remember a few aliases that I heard Father use. And I think I may see a pattern in them. Criminals on the run will often use some kind of naming convention in order to make it easier to come up with an alias quickly and keep them straight. I think that Father used a first name from the Bible—which is humorous considering that he's an atheist—and a color for a last name. Moses Black. Noah Green. Isaiah Brown. It's not much, but it gives you a place to start. Then look at interests. Marcus said he's taping the killings. He may be a camera enthusiast. He's always been fascinated with human behavior and fear. He may be working as a counselor of some type. Holding clinics to overcome one's fears or something of that nature. And he's a very talented musician."

Maggie wrote it all down on a spiral flip-up notepad and then said, "Okay, we'll check it out."

As she headed for the door, Ackerman said, "And one more thing. I offer you this in the spirit of familial cooperation. Use it as you see fit. It's about your brother."

Maggie hesitated, her hand resting on the door knob. She swallowed hard and turned back to the killer. "Don't. Just don't."

"When I was in your computer systems, I didn't read only Marcus's file. I read yours as well. I have an insight about your brother's case that you may find useful."

"If you're playing with me, I swear to God in heaven I'll kill you right now."

"This isn't a game, little sister. But I won't speak of it again if you don't want to hear what I have to say."

"Tell me."

"The man who abducted your little brother."

"They call him The Taker."

"Yes, I had studied the case even before I knew of your involvement. On the anniversary of an abduction, he sends a care package to a victim's family that contains a small remnant of the abductee's clothing and a lock of their hair. He's obviously a sadist who derives pleasure from extending the grief and pain of the children's families."

"Get to the point."

"I just wonder why he sends only those two items. He has an interesting concept going, but it seems a bit restrained for a man of that type. If it were me, I'd send a finger one year, a toe the next, maybe a kidney after that. Clothing and hair seem a bit subdued. Why not go for the full shock value? Let them know the child is dead and bask in their grief. They've tested the hair and found that it's old, probably taken at the same time as the abduction."

"You better be going somewhere with this."

"What if he can't send body parts because he doesn't have the bodies? What if there are no bodies?"

"Meaning?"

"Maybe you're not dealing with a serial killer. Maybe he's a different animal altogether. Definitely a sadist and a psychopath, but one with a profession. One who puts his skills to use for a purpose. Like our CIA contractor friends here."

"I still don't get what you're telling me."

Ackerman shook his head. "Think, Maggie. The two items he sends. What do they have in common?"

She thought for a moment. Searched for the answer. "They could easily be kept as trophies?"

"Yes, but no."

Finally, Maggie's mind grasped at a spark of hope and an idea that she hesitated to even speak aloud. When she did speak, her tongue seemed fat and useless. "Hair and clothing could have been taken without hurting the abducted child."

"And why would that be important?"

"If it was against his orders to do any permanent damage to them. You think that the Taker is involved with human trafficking?"

"All the children were healthy and from good stock," Ackerman said. "All young enough not to remember their previous lives. People pay top-dollar for kids like that. And the serial-killer angle deflects suspicion. Other avenues of the investigation have been exhausted. This a new one to pursue."

"But that would mean ..."

"That your brother may still be alive. Food for thought, anyway." Smiling, Ackerman added, "But let's focus on catching one bad guy at a time. You have aliases to check out."

CHAPTER THIRTY-FIVE

MARCUS AND ANDREW STOOD IN THE LONG CORRIDOR THAT LED TO CAPTAIN DURAN'S OFFICE, WAITING TO SEE WHAT KIND OF DAMAGE KALEB HAD DONE TO THEM. Marcus saw several of the cops from the task force hurrying around the precinct. There was a palpable tension in the air. Everyone was killing themselves for a lead on the case, but they had nothing. No way to find the Dunham boy. At least, not while he was still in one piece.

He tried not to think of the other boy whom his father had also kidnapped. Dylan would be safe, relatively speaking. His father wouldn't kill his own grandson, but there were fates worse than death. Marcus tried to keep the boy from his thoughts and focus on the task at hand. The Dunham boy was the one in immediate danger. But it was hard not to think of Dylan. He was suffering for no reason other than that Marcus was his father. A father whom he'd never even known. He supposed the kid would have been better off never knowing.

"You shouldn't have told Kaleb all that," Andrew said.

"They needed to know. They need all the information. A kid's life's at stake."

"I know what's at stake. They didn't need to know about your father. Don't you know why Fagan wants to keep this secret?"

"Not really. We have a cover story. We've worked with other agencies before. They don't have to know about every time we bend the law."

"It has nothing to do with the Shepherd Organization itself. It has to do with you."

"What do you mean?"

"What do you think would happen if some reporter found out that Francis Ackerman Sr. was still alive and has another son? And that son just happens to be a member of a secret group in the government that hunts serial killers. You'd be a damn prime-time special. They'd expose the Shepherd Organization. They'd find out where all our skeletons are buried. We're small for a reason. Our budget isn't large enough to alert the bean counters on the Hill, and we stay out of the limelight. We don't draw attention to ourselves. If it gets out that you're the son of one serial killer and brother of another, it could be the end of the Shepherd Organization."

Marcus pushed hard against his temples. The pressure behind his eyes felt as though it would pop them out of his skull. "Great. One more death on my conscience."

"Not everything is your fault. And even if something is, who cares? All you can do is give it your all, and let the chips fall where they may. It doesn't matter what you've done or where you came from. What matters is what you do and where you're going."

"I tell myself that, but it doesn't make this feeling go away."

"You think you've cornered the market on guilt and regret? Sometime I'll tell you about what I did before this."

The Shepherd Organization had an unwritten don't ask, don't tell policy when it came to its agents' past sins. Each one of them had a story, and those stories were the reasons why they had been recruited. "I thought you were a deputy medical examiner?" Marcus asked.

"I was, and I also had a job on the side working at an abortion clinic. Lots of people have a lot to say on the subject, and they're welcome to their opinions, but I can tell you this: when I was the one doing the deed, it sure felt wrong. Plus, I ended up being targeted by a serial killer who murdered the kids of people who worked at the clinics. Not only was I taking the lives of unborn children, but I also lost my daughter because of it."

Marcus cursed and let out a long slow breath. "I don't even know what to say, Drew. That's awful. I'm sorry."

Andrew wiped away a stray tear. "The point is that we all have sad stories. We've all been through something. We all have regrets and mistakes that we wish we could take back. You can't change the past, but you don't have to let it define you."

The door to Captain Duran's office opened up, and Kaleb stepped out alone. He moved toward them, but he was looking past them, through them. As he walked past, he didn't make eye contact but said, "I have to speak to Mr. Dunham, but once that's done, we're going to talk some more."

"What did you tell your mother?" Andrew asked.

"Nothing yet. I'm going to let you do that."

Kaleb led the way past desks and cubicles and officers working vigilantly, making phone calls, chasing down leads. He showed them into the observation area connected to Interrogation Room 3 and shut them inside. Through the glass, they could see Brad Dunham. His eyes were bright red from crying, but they were also empty. As though the biggest part of him had already died.

When Kaleb entered the room, Brad barely acknowledged his presence. The father's eyes didn't move until Kaleb introduced himself. Upon hearing the name, Brad's head swiveled quickly in Kaleb's direction, as if he was surprised to find another person in the room.

"Captain Duran said that you were asking for me," Kaleb said. His voice sounded deeper as it resonated through the speakers in the observation room.

"Yes, I was. Before we talk, can I get these cuffs off and get something to drink?" Brad held up his manacled hands for emphasis.

"Oh, absolutely. I'm sorry. Why the hell did they put you in handcuffs?"

"I went a little crazy there. They had to restrain me. It's fine. I'm better now."

Kaleb removed the cuffs and then asked, "What would you like to drink?"

"Anything from a can. Pepsi, Coke, either one. Or coffee from a real coffee mug would work too."

Marcus wondered about Brad's request. He seemed pretty particular about his beverages. Maybe Brad had some obsessive compulsive tendencies that weren't listed in his files.

Kaleb seemed to wonder about the requests as well, but he didn't question the man. Brad had been through enough already. Kaleb left the room in search of Brad's beverage. Brad rubbed his wrists and stretched out his arms. Then he stood up from the table and paced the room. A moment ago, Brad Dunham had seemed to have one foot in the grave. Now he brimmed with nervous tension.

The door opened and Kaleb came in with a blue can of Pepsi, condensation dripping down its side as if it had come from a cooler. He handed the can to Brad and then sat down at the table. Brad remained standing. He didn't open the soda. He gripped it hard in his left hand and let it dangle at his side. His knuckles grew white from the pressure he was exerting on the can.

"Something's wrong," Marcus said.

Kaleb looked up at Brad and asked, "So what did you—"

"I'm sorry," Brad said.

Then he swung the fist containing the soda can hard against Kaleb's temple. Brad was a big man, strong from years of manual labor. The blow sent Kaleb falling backward in his chair. His face shot to the side and blood flew from his lips. It splattered across the observation glass.

Brad wasted no time. His movements were quick and practiced, as if he had replayed them over and over in his mind and knew exactly what to do. Kaleb seemed unconscious or at least dazed. Brad grabbed for something on Kaleb's belt and came up with a Beretta pistol.

Marcus rushed out of the observation room. Pulled his own gun. Shoes squeaking on freshly polished floors. Officers turning toward him in confusion.

He threw open the door to Interrogation Room 3. Raised his gun. Screamed for Brad to stop. And watched in horror as Brad Dunham fired the Beretta twice at the man lying on the floor.

Blood exploded against the white walls.

Marcus reacted on instinct. He leaped forward, slid over the gray metal table, and closed the distance between himself and Brad Dunham. He rammed the butt of his Sig Sauer pistol against the side of Brad's head. Then he twisted the Beretta from the man's grasp, jerked him around, and slammed him face-first onto the metal table.

Pulling out a pair of flex-cuffs from beneath his jacket, he restrained Brad before thinking of anything else. When he looked up, he saw Andrew standing in the doorway with a hand over his mouth. The look in his partner's eyes told Marcus that he didn't need to turn around and check on Kaleb.

Brad Dunham had succeeded in his mission. Kaleb Duran was dead.

Chapter Thirty-Six

MAGGIE HAD ALREADY GOTTEN TO WORK ON ACKERMAN'S LIST OF ALIASES WHEN SHE HEARD A KNOCK ON HER DOOR. She expected to find the Director and was surprised to see Claire standing on the other side. Maggie's own workout clothes hung loosely from Claire's small frame. Claire seemed like the kind of person who was thin not because she worked at it and ate right but had simply been blessed by genetics. Maggie didn't want to hate her. Claire had done nothing wrong. And neither had Marcus for that matter, not really. Maybe it was an evolutionary response or insecurity or human nature or all three, but she couldn't help but be suspicious and jealous of the woman.

"Did you need something?" Maggie said.

Claire looked at her shoes and said, "I just thought maybe we could talk for a minute."

"So talk."

"Can I come in?"

Maggie opened the door further and gestured toward the bed. She pulled over the desk chair. "What can I do for you?"

"I just wanted to ask how Marcus is doing. He doesn't seem well."

"He's fine."

"He seemed very ... depressed."

"He recently found out that his real brother and his real father are both serial killers. That's enough to mess with anyone's head."

"I didn't mean to imply that he was unhappy with ..."

"With what?"

Claire just nodded. "I'm sorry I bothered you. I'm sure you have a lot of work to do."

Maggie raised a hand to stop the woman and joined her on the bed. She felt silly for being so abrupt. Claire wasn't the enemy. She was just a frightened person dealing with an unimaginable situation and trying to make the best of it. Maggie knew that she was supposed to be the trained agent and able to deal with situations like this and the roller coaster of emotions that came with them. "I'm sorry," Maggie said. "I didn't mean to be short with you. We're all a little on edge right now."

Claire gave a half-smile. "The two of you are together."

"That's right."

"For how long?"

"Off and on for two years. What was he like when you knew him?"

"Marcus was a sensitive guy who covered that up with a lot of bravado and a smart-ass attitude. But he always had this adventurous energy about him. He loved being a cop, and he could never let anything go. One time we were down on the boardwalk at Coney Island. It was late, and we were some of the only people around. A guy came up to us and pulled a snub-nosed revolver, demanded Marcus's wallet. Marcus gave it to him. Not because he wanted to, I could feel the anger pulsing out from him, but I grabbed his arm and held him back. Anyway, the point is that Marcus couldn't let it go. He spent nearly every free moment for the next week tracking the guy down."

"And he found him?"

"Yeah."

"What did he do?"

Claire laughed. "I didn't see this part, but I can still picture it. He said he walked up to the guy's door, knocked, and when the guy answered he politely asked for his wallet back."

Maggie smiled. "Let me guess. The guy ran and then fought back and Marcus beat the crap out of him."

"No," Claire said. "The guy had his wife and two kids in the ratty little apartment. He begged Marcus not to tell them or arrest him. He said that the gun wasn't even loaded. He ended becoming an informant, and Marcus helped him turn his life around."

"Wow. We don't get many opportunities like that with what we do now."

"That's sad. Marcus has a good heart—or at least, he did. He cares about people. Wants to save them. I hate to see him in pain, and I'm sorry for the way things turned out between us."

Maggie nodded and looked down at the floor. Claire added quickly, "Not because of our relationship. I meant because of Dylan. Marcus and I were not exactly compatible."

"What do you mean?"

Claire said, "Let me tell you this, and I think you'll get the idea. I like elegant parties. The ballet. Classical music. Musical theatre. I hate going to the movies. I'm half-Jewish. I'm pro gun-control, and I always dreamed of a career in politics."

Maggie couldn't help but laugh. "How did you and Marcus make it past the first date? Hell, how did you make it past the appetizer on your first date?"

"I don't think either of us ever knew. We argued all the time, and I don't mean in a fun flirtatious way. I think the only thing that kept us together was a chemical attraction. Pheromones or whatever it is that makes two people who couldn't be more opposite attract. The point is that I knew that we couldn't build a life together with what he had. Marriage is hard enough without starting off with every obstacle imaginable in your path. I think we both knew that. But Marcus could never give up."

Maggie cradled Claire's hands in her own and said, "And he won't give up until he finds your son. Marcus will do whatever it takes."

Tears filled Claire's eyes, and she squeezed Maggie's hands. "I hope you're right."

CHAPTER THIRTY-SEVEN

MAGGIE SAT BY THE UPSTAIRS WINDOW OF THE OLD FARMHOUSE, TYPING NOTES ON HER KEYBOARD AND MAKING PHONE CALLS. She and Stan had taken the information that Ackerman had provided and had compiled a list of possible aliases. There were two thousand, six hundred proper names in the Bible. But most of those were strange and outdated. She didn't expect Ackerman Sr. to be using names like Meshach, Shadrach, or Abednego. They narrowed the list down to the fifty most common and most likely names still in use for a male. Then they tracked down every person within a hundred miles with one of those names and started cross-referencing by age group, race, and interests.

Maggie was on the phone, running down one of the men from the list, when Marcus entered the bedroom and dropped onto the bed. She hadn't even heard the Suburban pull up. She had been too wrapped up in her own work to notice.

"Ackerman gave us some possible aliases. Stan and I are ..."

Her voice trailed off as she looked back at Marcus. He stared off into nothing. His eyes were red and bloodshot. Even more so than usual. Then he broke down. He leaned forward, his head between his knees, and sobs shook his muscular frame.

She came over to the bed and helped him out of his leather jacket. Then she laid her head on his shoulder and wrapped her arms around him. "What happened?"

"The detective who was our liaison with the locals was killed today. Right in front of me. I should have seen that something was wrong. I could have saved him. He was just a kid."

"How did he die?"

"Brad Dunham killed him. My father must have given him Kaleb as a target."

"Why would your father target a junior detective?"

"His mother's the head of the homicide division. It makes sense. He just put the whole department on tilt."

"On tilt?"

"It's a poker term. When someone loses a big hand, their emotions take over, and they start making mistakes. Making calls that they wouldn't normally. They call it being on tilt."

"It seems like your father has it in for the KCPD."

Marcus sat up. "You're right. He does. Dammit, I should have seen this sooner. I need to talk to Ackerman."

❖

Marcus pulled the hood from his brother's head. Ackerman blinked his eyes at the sudden burst of light. He started to smile and say something, but Marcus cut him off. "How vindictive is our father?"

Ackerman laughed. "We were on the run from the police, and he still tracked our mother across the country and murdered her in the home of her new husband. Who happened to be a NYPD homicide detective."

"So he might be doing all this, the elaborate game, just to hurt the KCPD? He set traps for them at the Goodweather scene, and he just targeted a detective."

"I suppose so." Ackerman looked confused, but then he nodded. "Oh, I see. The initiating event. You're thinking that whatever changed the pattern of Father's behavior was due to the actions of the KCPD."

"Right. And, like you said, if we can identify that event, it could lead us back to him."

Marcus placed the hood back over Ackerman's head and started toward the door. His brother's muffled voice said, "You're welcome." Marcus ignored him, but then Ackerman added, "Be careful, brother. He brought you into this for a reason. It's only a matter of time before he comes for you as well."

CHAPTER THIRTY-EIGHT

MARCUS LEFT THE DINING ROOM, WHICH WAS NOW A MAKESHIFT PRISON, AND ENTERED THE LIVING ROOM, WHICH HAD BEEN CONVERTED INTO AN ARMORY AND BARRACKS BY THE GROUP OF MERCENARIES. Fagan was in a corner, talking on the phone and typing on a laptop. One operator clad in black tactical pants and a black T-shirt cleaned a Benelli M1014 shotgun at a small desk beside the front window. Another operator slept on a brown floral-printed couch along the south wall. Craig sat Indian-style on the floor, sharpening a long KA-BAR knife. The room smelled of musty furniture and gun oil.

Marcus asked Craig, "Have you seen the Director or Andrew?"

The blond mercenary didn't look up. He just pointed the knife toward the front porch and went back to his work. Marcus could see a sadistic glee in Craig's eyes as he worked the knife back and forth, as if he was picturing who he would cut with the blade next.

Marcus heard voices on the front porch as soon as he stepped into the entryway. The hardwood front door was open with only an old screen door held shut by a rusty spring separating the interior from the outside.

He heard Andrew say, "He's getting worse."

The Director asked, "The headaches?"

"It's more than that. I think he may need to be committed."

"Marcus isn't crazy. He's just struggling. He's had a lot thrown at him in a short amount of time."

"I'm not saying he's crazy. I just think he may need more counseling than he can get from us. And he could use a break from all this. Some time to clear his head. He's running on empty. If he doesn't come to grips with where he came from and who he is and find a way to separate the two, he's just going to keep slipping farther and farther down the rabbit hole."

The Director said, "I don't know. He's still—"

A gunshot echoed across the valley like the rolling of distant thunder, causing birds to abandon their perches on the surrounding telephone wires. Marcus watched in horror as blood splattered the wire mesh of the screen door.

Andrew jumped to his feet. Marcus pushed his way onto the porch.

The Director didn't scream. He just fell from his chair, a look of surprise on his face. His blood stained the dirty white boards of the porch crimson.

Marcus jumped forward, staying low to make himself less of a target. He hugged the exterior wall of the house and kicked the Director's chair out of the way. Then he grabbed the Director beneath his armpits and pulled him toward the safety of the house.

As the initial anesthetizing shock of the bullet's impact wore off, the Director screamed in agony. Blood poured from a wound in his shoulder. The slippery warm liquid soaked through the sleeve of Marcus's shirt.

"Get the door," Marcus yelled.

Andrew looked as though someone had just shaken him awake. He ran for the door and held it open from inside the house.

Another gunshot rang out. It struck the porch. High and to Marcus's left.

He ignored it and continued to pull the Director to safety. His feet slid in the blood, but he scrambled backward through the door and into the foyer, leaving a trail of blood across the floor in his wake.

The Director's breathing was fast and shallow. His eyes were wide and filled with fear. He seemed to be in shock.

As soon as they were out of the sniper's line of sight, Andrew pushed Marcus out of the way and went to work on the Director, applying pressure to his wound and shouting orders at the mercenaries who were watching from the dining room.

Marcus looked toward the stairs. Maggie was coming down so fast that she stumbled at the bottom. Marcus caught her and said, "Help Andrew." Then he asked everyone, "Where's Claire? Is she still in the bedroom?"

The CIA contractors had started to take action. They scrambled to the windows, staying low and watching the horizon with their weapons at the ready. One headed for the kitchen to make sure that no one crept up from the rear.

Kneeling beside one of the windows, Craig said, "The shots might have come from that patch of trees up there."

"I don't see anyone approaching," another contractor said.

"Where's Claire?" Marcus repeated.

Fagan cowered in a corner behind a large reclining chair. He said, "Last I saw, she was on the back porch."

Andrew was still trying to stop the bleeding from the Director's shoulder. Marcus asked, "Are you going to be—"

"Just go. Find Claire," Andrew snapped, all his attention on his wounded comrade.

Marcus rushed toward the back of the house. He bypassed the dining room. He didn't want one of Ackerman's guards to get an itchy trigger finger and shoot him accidentally. Instead, he circled around to the kitchen through a small room off the living room. A mercenary stood at a back door leading directly outside on the far right of the kitchen. The entrance to the back porch was on the opposite wall.

Marcus stepped out onto the screened-in porch. Old outdoor cushioned furniture sat atop bare wood 2x4s. Long vinyl shades covered most of the screens, shrouding the space in darkness.

"Claire?" Marcus said.

He heard the floorboards creak and saw her step from the shadows on his right. A big black pistol in her hand was aimed directly at him. He recognized it as one of the .45-caliber 1911s that the mercenaries used. Her hands shook, and her eyes were wet with tears.

"Don't move, Marcus," Claire said. "Take out your gun slowly and put it on the floor."

"What is this?"

"That gunshot was my signal. I'm supposed to deliver you to him. I'm sorry, Marcus. He has my boy."

"You know there's a good chance that turning me over to him still won't save Dylan."

"I know. But it's my only hope. I have to."

Marcus pulled his Sig Sauer from its holster and laid it gently on the floor. "I won't fight you. You're right. If there's any chance that it will save Dylan, then I'll gladly sacrifice myself."

More tears poured down her cheeks, but she swatted them away with her left hand. "Do you have the keys to that Suburban?" Claire asked.

"In my pocket. But my friends will come after us."

"That shooter out there will keep that from happening. We'll go out and circle around the house."

She gestured with the gun toward a screen door leading to a flight of concrete steps and into the backyard. Marcus pushed open the door and went down the steps.

One piece of him knew that he could easily overpower Claire and prevent her from taking him to his father. Another piece wondered if this was the purpose of his life—to die in exchange for his child's survival. And yet another piece knew this was the best chance he would have to catch the man who had murdered his parents, tortured his brother, and taken the lives of countless others. He just wasn't sure what it would cost him to make that happen.

CHAPTER THIRTY-NINE

MAGGIE'S HEAD JERKED UP AS SHE HEARD THE ROAR OF AN ENGINE AND THE SOUND OF TIRES CHURNING GRAVEL. She stood and looked through the front window. Field dust covered the pane of glass, but through the grime she saw the Suburban whipping around and veering down the field lane.

She cursed under her breath and ran toward the door. Bursting onto the porch, she watched the Suburban get smaller as it sped away from the house.

The rod-iron and glass porch light beside her head exploded from the impact of another bullet. Shards of glass shrapnel streaked out and ripped the skin of her face. She cried out and grabbed the side of her head. Another shot struck the wall nearby, driving her back into the house.

From the floor in front of her, Andrew screamed, "Maggie! What are you doing? Stay down and get over here."

She removed her hand and saw some blood, but nothing to worry about now. She shook off the shock and said, "What can I do?"

"I think the bullet punctured the subclavian artery in his shoulder," Andrew replied.

"What can we do about that?"

"I would recommend percutaneous endovascular repair by using a self-expandable stent graft. But since we don't have that, I need you to get me a tampon."

"What?"

"Just do it!"

She bounded up the stairs and into her and Marcus's bedroom. She wondered where the hell Marcus had been going. Was he rushing the shooter? Through the second-story window, she saw the Suburban reach the end of the lane that connected with the main road. The patch of trees that Craig had thought might hide the shooter lay to the left. Marcus went right.

"Maggie!" Andrew called from downstairs.

She refocused on the task at hand. A small bathroom connected their bedroom and the one that Claire was using. Maggie rushed inside and fumbled through the travel bag containing her make-up, haircare items, and feminine hygiene products. She pulled out a large plastic container which held a multitude of small pull-out compartments. She had organized the compartments alphabetically by their contents. Her finger traced a line down the Ts and pulled open the tiny drawer containing her tampons. She grabbed three of them, just in case. Then she rushed back down the stairs.

Handing one of the tampons to Andrew, she said, "What now?"

Andrew didn't reply. He just ripped the tampon out of its packaging and jammed it into the Director's shoulder. The Director cried out. His feet and head banged against the hardwood floor as he fought the pain. Andrew ripped off a strip of his shirt and wrapped it around the Director's shoulder.

He looked up at Maggie and said, "That should help with the bleeding, but we need to get him to a hospital soon. The wound's pretty clean, but he needs surgery to repair the artery."

Maggie turned to Fagan who was still crouching in a corner behind the large brown recliner. "Fagan! Where's your car?"

The bureaucrat replied, "It's a Lexus. I parked it in the barn so it would be out of the weather."

Craig said, "That's a hundred yards. Our van's over there too."

"And the Director's Buick," Andrew added.

"We could make a run for it," Maggie said.

Craig shook his head. "Even if you made it—which isn't likely—that sniper will be all over you while you're loading your friend into the car. You need to take the sniper out first."

"What about you guys? Aren't you supposed to be some kind of black-ops badasses?"

"No, we're hired mercenaries who are getting paid to capture and contain Ackerman. There's nothing in our contract about getting shot by snipers."

Maggie gritted her teeth and bit back a comment. "Fine. We'll just call in the locals and have them come at the sniper from behind."

Fagan stood up from his hiding spot and said, "Oh no, you won't. We can't get any local police involved in this."

"Why not?"

"Think about what you're saying. They might want to know why we're being attacked by some sniper, and then they may wonder why we're holding one of the country's most wanted fugitives in an old farmhouse. I won't allow this organization to be compromised. Not on my watch. Not for you, the Director, or anyone. That's a direct order."

Maggie's eyes narrowed as she stared at the little man. "And I don't intend to let anyone die on my watch," she said. "We have to get him to the hospital as quickly as possible. We're calling in backup." She pulled a cell phone from her pocket and started to dial.

Fagan said, "Mr. Craig, stop her. Shoot her if you have to."

Craig aimed his weapon at Maggie's chest and shrugged his shoulders. "You heard the man."

Maggie gripped the phone so tightly that she thought it would snap in half at any second. Her gaze lingered on Craig for a moment and then moved to Fagan. Reluctantly, she jammed the phone back in her pocket and stepped toward the window.

There had to be another way to get to the sniper.

If they had more time, they could wait for the cover of darkness to provide more options, but the Director didn't have that long.

The patch of trees was between a quarter of a mile and half a mile away. It rested on a hill not far from the field lane. A wide ditch, maybe three feet deep, ran the length of the lane.

But fifty yards of open ground lay between the ditch and the front of the house.

Maggie moved to the side window. A small brown and white shed covered with rotting wood siding sat to the south of the main house. The split-rail fence ran a few feet behind the shed, separating the yard from the empty field. The fence ran down to the lane.

If she could reach the shed, then she could reach the fence. If she reached the fence, she could use it as partial cover to crawl up to the ditch. If she could reach the ditch, she could crawl out to the sniper's nest and come at him from behind. If he didn't see her. If he stayed in one spot. If she didn't get shot between the house and the shed or between the ditch and the patch of trees.

She closed her eyes and shook her head. That was a hell of a lot of *ifs*.

But it was also the best shot they had.

She walked back to Andrew and said, "I think I can get to the sniper by crawling through the ditch that runs along the lane. But I need a distraction so that I can reach that old shed."

Andrew shook his head. "I should be the one going."

Maggie rolled her eyes. "Now's not the time for chivalry. I'm not a doctor. You need to stay with your patient."

"I've done everything I can for him right now."

"And what if his condition changes?"

Andrew said nothing. Maggie asked, "So what about that distraction?"

A voice called out from the next room. It was strong and confident despite being muffled by the layers of old wood and plaster. Maggie opened the solid oak door leading into the dining room. The two guards raised their shotguns in her direction, but she ignored them. Her feet creaked against the hardwood as she walked over to the killer. Pulling off his hood, she said, "What do you want?"

Ackerman replied, "I said send me. I'll be your distraction."

CHAPTER FORTY

B RAD DUNHAM STARED AT HIS HANDS AND ROCKED BACK AND FORTH. Four walls of gray concrete surrounded him, but his real prison was in his own mind. He had taken a man's life. The life of a good man. A cop who had been trying to help him find his family. He had bashed his face in and then shot him with his own gun.

How could he live with that? How could he ever explain the situation to his son?

Brad knew that, despite the extenuating circumstances, he would spend the rest of his life in a prison cell. He intended to plead guilty and throw himself on the mercy of the court. If the judge gave him life, then so be it. If the judgment was death, then that was fine too.

He thought of his son visiting him through the years. His hair going gray and falling out. An old man in an orange jumpsuit only having visitor's day to look forward to.

He supposed that was more of a life than he deserved. It was much more of a life than Detective Duran would ever have.

The solid metal door of his cell slid open, and an attractive yet stern-looking woman walked in. Her clothes looked expensive, but her hair was tousled and her eyes were blood-red and puffy. Brad didn't stand. He stayed on the floor, leaned back against the concrete.

"I'm Captain Maria Duran," she said. "I wanted to let you know that your son has been released. We received a 911 call from a payphone telling us his location. A pair of black and whites just picked him up. He's fine. A little disoriented, but he doesn't seem to remember much of what happened."

Brad closed his eyes as tears of joy started down his cheeks. "Thank God. Thank you for telling me."

"Don't thank me. Did you hear my name? It's Duran. As in the mother of the man you sacrificed for your son."

Brad raised his eyes to the woman. She held a black pistol in her right fist.

"I'm sorry," was all Brad could think to say. There wasn't much else he could say.

She stepped forward and placed the muzzle of the gun against his forehead. "I'll tell them you attacked me. It was self-defense."

Brad's gaze travelled along the black metal of the gun up to her face. "That would probably work. You should pull the trigger."

"He was just coming into his own. He had so much life left to live, and I had so much left to say. He was my baby boy. And I never ..."

The gun's barrel shook against Brad's forehead. He closed his eyes and said, "Do it. It's okay."

Maria Duran slapped the gun across his face, knocking him over on his side. As she walked out, she said, "No. You live with it."

CHAPTER FORTY-ONE

ACKERMAN STOOD AGAINST THE SIDE OF THE HOUSE, JUST OUT OF THE SNIPER'S LINE OF SIGHT. Craig stood five feet behind him, hugging the wooden siding, a shotgun at his shoulder. Another of the contractors held an additional shotgun, aimed at him from a raised vantage point through a side window.

Still, he suspected that he could be on Craig before the man could fire.

Ackerman pictured the events in his mind. Rush Craig, swiping the shotgun to the side. Simultaneously place a kick to the merc's knee, dropping him. Flip the shotgun over. Squeeze the trigger. A satisfying explosion of gunpowder, metal, and brain matter. Drop down. Fire at the window. The shooter there wouldn't have the angle to be much of a threat. His job was to ensure that Ackerman didn't run, not to guard against an attack. From there, Ackerman could deal with the others in the house or make a break for one of the cars.

"It's time," Craig said. "She should be in position. Now take a walk."

Ackerman was tempted to follow through on his internal musings or simply grab Craig and throw him out into the line of fire, but he resisted the urge. Instead, he walked calmly away from the wall and into the yard.

Each step was slow and leisurely. He felt no fear. He knew this wasn't the way he would die.

He counted as he walked.

Six, seven, eight.

A gunshot rang out, and the ground a few feet in front of him exploded into the air as a bullet struck the dirt.

He didn't flinch. He continued to move forward. He raised his arms out from his sides and enjoyed the cool breeze on his skin. He looked up at the azure sky and watched the clouds float lazily by.

Eleven, twelve, thirteen.

Another gunshot. Another bullet in the ground. This one closer.

He bent down, pulled a few blades of grass from the yard, and then released them to be carried on the breeze.

Sixteen, seventeen, eighteen.

He felt another bullet zip past his leg. A warm draft. Another small eruption of soil just behind him.

Twenty. He had reached the agreed limit. His job was done. At the same leisurely pace, he walked back to the side of the house.

Craig had lowered the shotgun and was staring at Ackerman as if he'd sprouted an extra limb. Ackerman knew he could use that shock to his advantage, but he decided against it.

He gave the mercenary a little bow and said, "Yea, though I walk through the valley of the shadow of death, I will fear no evil."

"You're insane."

Ackerman laughed. "Sanity is a matter of perspective."

CHAPTER FORTY-TWO

M AGGIE WAITED AT THE SIDE OF THE HOUSE OPPOSITE ACKERMAN. She checked her watch. It was almost time. They had agreed on a moment for Ackerman to step into the line of fire, and then she would wait five seconds to make sure that they had the sniper's attention before making a break for the shed. That should leave her fifteen seconds to cross the yard.

As she stood with knees bent and one hand on the farmhouse's siding, like a sprinter waiting for the baton, she realized that their plan relied on the fact that there was only one shooter. But, for all they knew, there could have been multiple assailants or one shooter and one spotter, like the way snipers worked in the military.

She checked her watch again. Too late to worry about it now.

She counted down the remaining seconds. Ackerman should have been drawing the sniper's attention away from her at that moment.

Five, four, three.

A part of her hoped that the sniper would put a bullet through Ackerman's skull, but she knew that probably wouldn't happen. Men like Ackerman were charmed in such ways.

Two, one.

Maggie dashed across the yard. The distance seemed to grow the moment she left cover. Funny how perception altered every experience. She tried not to think of the crosshairs that could have been focused on her head at that moment.

Marcus had taught her that—*concentrate on the task at hand*. But where was he now?

A gunshot rang out, and she thought for a moment that she had been shot. She stumbled from the sudden shock but kept moving. The bullet must not have been meant for her.

Another gunshot. Another instinctual reaction against which there was no defense.

But then she was there. She slid to the ground behind the old shed and leaned back against the cracked barn siding, trying to calm her pounding heart. She checked her body for bullet holes, just to be sure. All clear. She felt a strange stab of guilt for wishing that Ackerman would be shot. It seemed wrong somehow now that her wish might have come true. But she pushed that feeling away; he deserved whatever he got.

After a few seconds' rest, she moved to the end of the shed and army-crawled her way over to the fence. She tried to stay low, keeping the fence between her and the shooter. Her movements were slow and cautious. She didn't want to draw the sniper's attention through her own movements or those of any birds or other creatures that she might disturb along the way.

The going was slow and painful. The weeds were tall, which was good from a certain perspective. The overgrowth provided extra cover. But the briars also ripped against her skin in several places, and twice she saw the slithering tales of snakes moving out of her way.

Maggie forced herself to move carefully, even though she felt the pressing weight of time. The Director needed a hospital, and the longer they waited the lower his chances of survival. She was no doctor, but she knew that, when it came to gunshot wounds, the rapidity of treatment made all the difference.

Finally, she made it to a spot where she was close enough to move to the ditch. Once inside the muddy depression, she would be able to move faster, since she doubted that the sniper would be able to see her or get a shot at her from his position.

She waited, took several deep breaths, and then rolled three times to the side through the tall weeds. At the halfway point of the third roll, she dropped into the ditch with a wet slap, the mud splashing up into her face.

Keeping her butt down, Maggie crawled forward on elbows and knees, her fingers and the toes of her shoes squishing down into the muck. She felt like a soldier in basic training. A few times, the suction of the mud pulled her hands in like quicksand, and she had to be careful not to reveal herself as she pulled them free.

It was slow going. Every few moments, she would pop her head up and check her position. She focused on her goal: the patch of trees in the distance that kept growing closer with every furtive glance.

And then she was there. She had moved far enough so that she was past the trees and could swing around behind the shooter.

The next part of her journey would be the hardest. An open expanse of empty field lay between her and the sniper's nest. It was rutted, uneven ground littered with the brittle remnants of corn stalks. She couldn't move across the expanse as fast as she had traversed the space between the house and the shed. She would have to move more slowly, being careful of her footing. And if she had been spotted by the sniper at any point during her crawl, the hidden assailant could be waiting and could easily pick her off before she'd gone ten feet. If she stood now and started to run, she would have no cover. If she were caught in the open, it would be all or nothing. Either she pushed forward and reached the trees or scurried back to the cover of the ditch. There was nothing in between.

But there was really no choice. She had come this far, and she had been careful. She had done everything right, and this was the moment of truth.

Maggie took a calming breath and then leaped from the ditch. She pulled her gun and held it low and ready. The split-rail fence lay between her and the field. She placed her palm on the top rail and bounded over.

So far, so good.

And then a gunshot exploded from the patch of trees.

CHAPTER FORTY-THREE

A CHUNK OF WOOD FLEW FROM THE TOP OF THE FENCE WHERE THE BUL-
LET STRUCK. Maggie screamed involuntarily and ran back for
the cover of the ditch. She vaulted over the fence. This time her foot
caught on the rail, and she stumbled forward. She let her momentum carry her onward and rolled back into the ditch.

She had come all this way for nothing. She was pinned down,
just as she had been at the house. Only this time she was all alone.

Of course, the sniper couldn't watch the house and her at the
same time. Unless there were two of them, which seemed unlikely,
but she supposed that it was still possible.

Pulling out her cell phone, she dialed Andrew. He answered on
the second ring and said, "We heard another shot. Are you okay?"

"I'm pinned down in the mud. But maybe you can make it to the
car while his attention is on me."

"Unless there's two of them," Andrew replied.

"When did you think of that?"

"From the beginning."

"When were you going to tell me?"

"I didn't think it would help. Just freak you out more."

"So what are we going to do?"

She heard something happening in the background, and
Andrew said, "Hold on. Someone wants to speak with you."

There was a pause and then another voice came on the line.
"Hello, Maggie."

"What do you want?" she said to Ackerman.

"I want you to trust me for a moment."

"There's a better chance of you getting hit by a meteor than there is of you gaining my trust."

"He won't shoot you."

"What are you saying? He shot the Director."

"Yes, but that was just to get our attention. He shot him in the shoulder on purpose. Every other shot he's taken, he's missed on purpose. Think about it. He hit your Director from probably a third of a mile, but then he starts taking potshots at the side of the house. And then he knows that you're there, but he can't even hit you coming at him from a few hundred feet. It doesn't make any sense. Unless he's following orders. He's just supposed to keep us pinned down and occupied for as long as possible. If you stand up and rush him, you'll be fine."

Maggie was quiet for a moment. She hated to admit it, but Ackerman was making sense. Maybe that meant she was losing her mind? "That's quite a risk to take on nothing but a guess. Why would someone be out here only to keep us pinned down and occupied?"

"They found Marcus's gun on the back porch, and Claire's missing along with one of the mercenary's pistols."

She thought about the new information and gritted her teeth. That was why Marcus's father had led them to Claire. She was a Trojan horse. It was all part of his plan. And now, while everyone else was distracted, she had kidnapped Marcus right out from under their noses. The more she thought about it, the more sense it made. Marcus's father had her son, and a mother would do anything for her child. Even if that involved betrayal and deception.

"You're sure about this?" Maggie asked. "If you get me killed, Marcus will never forgive you."

"Don't worry, little sister. I just took a stroll out in the yard while you were running for the shed. He didn't even come close. Whoever's out there doesn't want us dead, just distracted."

"You better be right," she said as she hung up. Then she stood and headed for the trees.

She vaulted back over the fence, pulled her gun, and traced the same path as before. And as before, she heard the explosion of another gunshot. It echoed across the surrounding fields and hills and sent shivers down her back. But no bullet hit her.

It embedded itself in the fence like its predecessor.

Maggie continued forward, moving faster than she should have, almost losing her footing.

Another blast. Another miss.

She twisted her foot in a hole, but it didn't stop her forward progress.

Another shot. This one closer, but still a miss.

She had reached the halfway point. Her gun was up and aimed at the trees.

The boom of another shot startled her. At this distance, the blast from the high-powered rifle was deafening. A puff of dirt and a piece of a cornstalk exploded from the ground to her left.

Maggie centered herself and continued forward. "It's over," she yelled. "Come on out."

She half-expected another shot, but only silence greeted her. She slowed her pace as she drew closer to the trees. "Come out with your hands where I can see them," she said.

This time, the shooter listened. He stepped from the darkness of the clump of trees into the open expanse of the field. He held his rifle out at his side by its stock. His arms were spread wide in a gesture of surrender. He wore camouflage fatigues that blended perfectly with the foliage. If he hadn't revealed himself, she probably would have walked right up to him without even knowing he was there.

The man's face surprised her. He was old. In his sixties or seventies at least. His skin was deeply lined, and white hair poked out from beneath a military-style boonie hat.

Maggie kept her gun trained on his midsection and said, "Put down the rifle." He laid it lovingly on the ground, like a father tucking in his child. "Who are you? Why are you doing this?" she asked.

The old man's voice was gravelly and confident when he spoke. Maggie's grandfather had been a sailor during World War II. This man's demeanor reminded her of her grandfather's take-crap-from-no-one attitude. "Son of a bitch took my wife. Left me a video with instructions on what to do. I'm sorry. How's your friend? I was told specifically that my first shot shouldn't miss, but I tried to do as little damage as I could."

"We need to get him to the hospital, or he's going to die. Are you alone?"

The old man nodded. Maggie moved forward, ordered him down to his knees, and placed a pair of flex-cuffs on his wrists. Then she called Andrew and told him that it was safe to go for the car.

"On your feet," she said. He awkwardly complied, and she asked, "Do you know what happened to my other friend? The one in the Suburban."

"No, I was just shown a picture of the blonde woman and was told to let her and another guy get to the SUV. Then keep the rest of you pinned down. I swear I don't know anything more than that. I'm sorry. My wife's all I have. I can't lose her."

Maggie glanced down the road in the direction that Marcus and his kidnapper had driven. She knew exactly how the old man felt.

And then she realized something. Ackerman had told her that they had found Marcus's gun, but he hadn't mentioned finding Marcus's phone. Claire wasn't a professional criminal. She was just a scared woman who had been tortured and sent on an insane mission by a madman. She might not have thought about the phone. Even if she had been told to leave it behind, she might have forgotten.

Maggie grabbed her cell phone and clicked one of the numbers on speed dial. A husky voice answered. "Stan, the great and powerful. You have been granted three wishes."

"Good. My first wish is for you to track the GPS in Marcus's phone."

CHAPTER FORTY-FOUR

THE SUN WAS SETTING. Marcus watched the sky turn orange and red as the great star dropped below the horizon. Claire had given him an address for the meeting which he had plugged into the GPS unit mounted on the Suburban's dashboard. Then she had used his phone to call a number and inform the person on the other end that they were on their way. Claire tried again to say that she was sorry, but Marcus just told her that he would probably have done the same thing in her position. There wasn't anything else to say. In the end, this was his choice, no matter how she felt about it.

The GPS guided him up I-49, which merged into I-435. He kept his speed at seventy, not wanting to draw attention. He wove lazily in and out of traffic, just like any other commuter on their way home from a hard day's work. Neither of them spoke. Claire sobbed from time to time, but he didn't try to comfort her. The whole situation was like a dream. He felt numb.

Eventually, the electronic voice called for them to leave the major thoroughfares behind and guided them onto forgotten roads devoid of other motorists. Marcus steered the Suburban into an industrial park on the northeast side of Kansas City. Some of the buildings looked new and prosperous. Others were empty, with signs announcing foreclosure auctions.

Then their artificial navigator announced that they had arrived at their destination. The building looked new and unused. Marcus didn't see any for-sale signs out front, as if it had been purchased but the new owners hadn't moved in yet. Or maybe someone bought it because they needed to hide some money from the IRS. Either way, he hadn't seen another soul for several minutes, and it seemed like the perfect place for his father to conduct some business undisturbed.

Claire got out first, and he followed her to a side door. The inside of the building was wide-open space. Just metal walls, concrete floors, and support beams. He could picture the place filled with rows of high industrial shelving units and forklifts. It would make someone a nice warehouse. But right now, it only contained an older man sitting on the hood of a black S-type Jaguar. He wore a pair of black slacks and a gray polo shirt, as though he had just left his friends at the golf course.

The older man smiled at the newcomers and said, "Please toss the gun over, Claire."

Marcus had forgotten that she had the weapon. He hadn't even considered a way to turn the tables on his father. He felt strangely peaceful, as if by being resigned to his fate he had found a measure of serenity. He realized that he didn't care what happened to him. He just wanted Claire and Dylan to get out of this alive, and nothing else mattered.

Claire tossed the pistol onto the floor, and his father walked forward and retrieved it. "You look different," Marcus said.

The older man smiled, "Plastic surgery, my boy. I apologize for that. Believe it or not, you and I had quite a family resemblance going before I went under the knife."

"You seem pretty calm. You didn't even check to make sure that we didn't bring help. How do you know we don't have an army of cops waiting out there?"

The older man smiled. His eyes were a piercing blue. "I've been five steps ahead of you this whole time, Marcus. You knew that I wouldn't bring the boy here. If you were to try anything, the boy would die in a hole somewhere. You can't risk that. You know it, and I know it."

Claire stepped forward and yelled, "Where's my son? We had a deal!"

His father's piercing blue eyes, which had only a moment before seemed so calm and cordial, filled with a maniacal fury within the space of a blink. Marcus had once seen the same kind of change in the eyes of his brother.

"You will keep your mouth shut, whore! Say another word and I'll send that boy back to you in tiny pieces. Don't speak. Just nod if you understand."

Claire shook with rage. Her pale skin had gone red. But she nodded slowly.

Then the older man's gaze moved back to his son. He tossed over a pair of flex-cuffs and a strange collar. It was metal with a black box mounted on its side. It looked like a larger, more sophisticated version of a dog's shock collar. "Take off your clothes. Down to the underwear. Then put on the cuffs and the collar, and we'll talk."

Marcus did as he was told. He kicked off his shoes and slid off his leather jacket, shirt, and jeans. He strapped the collar around his neck and placed his wrists inside the plastic cuffs.

"On your knees."

Marcus complied, and his father walked over behind him. Claire stood facing away from him, shivering as if being in the older man's presence made her physically ill.

"Why are you doing all this after so many years?" Marcus asked. "Why now?"

"There comes a point in every person's life when they start to understand their own mortality and think of the legacy that they've left behind. When this is over, the world will remember."

"If this is about legacy, then why are you targeting the KCPD? Something happened to make you want revenge. That's all this is really about. Vengeance. Simple and petty."

"There's nothing simple about me, son. It's true that the KCPD has a role to play, but so do you. And you have played it beautifully every step of the way. I've always been fascinated by human nature and how people react to certain stimuli. I pull the strings and make people dance. And I've been in the game long enough to know exactly which strings to pull. But you are smarter than I gave you credit for. Unfortunately, you weren't smart enough to stop me."

His father's next movement was so fast and graceful that it took Marcus's brain a second to process what had just happened. A small blade appeared in the old man's hand. With two long strides, he was on top of Claire. Marcus screamed but could do nothing to help.

A flash of metal. A flick of the wrist. A twist of Claire's head. And it was over.

Claire didn't even seem to realize what had happened. Her face had just started to register something—shock or fear or both—when blood gushed forth, and she fell to the concrete floor, her throat slashed in a deep, precise cut from one ear to the other.

CHAPTER FORTY-FIVE

MAGGIE HAD COMMANDEERED THE DIRECTOR'S BUICK LACROSSE FROM THE BARN WHILE ANDREW RUSHED THE DIRECTOR TO THE HOSPITAL IN FAGAN'S CAR. She left the old man in the care of Fagan and his mercenaries. She supposed they'd just let him go. Fagan wouldn't allow him to be arrested. That would create a need for police reports and trials and depositions and all manner of entanglements that the bureaucrat wished to avoid.

Maggie didn't really care what happened to the old man one way or another. She only cared about the fate of one person at that moment.

"It looks like they've stopped at an industrial park on the north side of KC. Merge onto I-435," Stan said from the speakerphone.

She considered calling in backup from the local police. Fagan would order her not to and probably string her up later if she did, but she didn't care what Fagan said or what he thought about her. She only cared about Marcus, and right now, she could be the only thing standing between him and death.

"Stan," she said, "Contact the local police, give them the location, and have them meet me there. But tell them to stay quiet. No sirens, and no one goes in until I get there."

◈

Blood from Claire's wound splattered over Marcus's chest as she hit the concrete. He screamed and jumped to his feet to rush his father. His hands were bound, and he was going against a man with a deadly weapon and the know-how and will to use it, but Marcus didn't care. Rage eclipsed any rational or tactical thinking.

The old man didn't even flinch at the sight of his onrushing opponent. He simply pressed a button on a small device in his left hand. The device was oval-shaped with a couple of buttons and a red LED light. It looked homemade.

Marcus suddenly found himself on the ground writhing in agony. His body convulsed involuntarily as every muscle contracted and tensed. His eyes rolled to the back of his head, and he blacked out for a moment.

When he regained consciousness, the first things he saw were Claire's lifeless eyes. They were still red from all the tears she had cried recently. He had fallen beside her. He felt her blood pooling beneath him. It was still warm. Tears and blood. Both shed simply because of her connection to him. He knew that feeling responsible was irrational, but that realization didn't ease the weight of his guilt.

His thoughts were still scattered, but he surmised that the intense electric shock he had just experienced originated from the collar around his neck. It must have been some type of amped-up shock collar. The kind used to train a dog, but modified for his father's sadistic needs.

"Are you back with me, Marcus?" his father said.

Marcus's gaze didn't leave Claire. "What do you want from me?" he asked.

"Have you ever heard the story of Pandora's Box? The 'box' was actually a large jar which held all the scourges of the world. Pandora was told to never open the jar, but curiosity got the best of her, as it always does. So she released all the evils contained within it out into the world. The point I'm getting at is that once the evils were released, the only thing left in the jar was the spirit of hope. Pandora eventually released this into the world as well. Some would say that hope was in the jar because, without all the evils, the world didn't need hope. But I feel that hope was at the bottom of the jar because it is the worst scourge of all."

Marcus watched his father crouch down a few feet behind Claire's lifeless form. The old man twisted the blade in his hand. It was still coated in Claire's blood. "Some say that hell is all fire and torment for eternity," his father continued, "but—while I don't believe in such a place—if it did exist, there would have to be hope in hell. There would have to be some illusion of escape or freedom from the pain. Some glimmer of absolution that remains just out of reach. Because, you see, without hope, a person will start to accept their fate, even if that fate is a particularly terrible one. They will build up walls. They will achieve acceptance. They will transcend their circumstances. But if they cling to hope, their minds will forever be shackled to their circumstances. Hope is the bedfellow of torment."

The old man rose to his full height and circled around behind his son. Marcus felt a stabbing pain in his kidneys as his father kicked him. "Are you listening, boy? I'm doing you a great service, out of my love for you. Abandon all hope. This will go much easier for you if you accept your fate and seek transcendence. I'm going to share with you what's going to happen next because it is inevitable. You can hope that your friends will end your pain, but no one is coming. I'm going to start by breaking you physically. Then mentally, emotionally, and spiritually. Not necessarily in that order. I'm going to show you how to live without fear. And when we're done, I believe you'll thank me."

Marcus rolled over to face his father. "You have me now. You can let Dylan go. He's just a boy."

"Let him go? He's going to be my greatest pupil. I've learned a lot since the time I spent with your brother. I've analyzed my mistakes and won't make them again. We're all going to be together. Three generations of the Ackerman family. My legacy."

Marcus shot to his feet and charged again, and once more he felt the blinding white pain that blocked out the rest of the world. He convulsed for a moment, and then his mind shut down and the darkness took him.

❖

Maggie met three squad cars a block from their target behind one of the neighboring warehouses. She informed them of the situation and told them that they didn't have much time. They hit the building fast and hard, multiple units converging from multiple points of entry. They went on Maggie's signal and performed their tasks with utter professionalism.

Inside, they found a pile of clothing which concealed Marcus's cell phone. Claire's body lay a few feet from the pile. Her blood had spread out across the concrete, filling every fissure, tracing every crack. Maggie checked for a pulse. Not that she expected to find any, but it was procedure.

All units reported back that they had found nothing else at the warehouse. An all-points bulletin and a state-wide be-on-the-look-out announcement went out over the police channels. They were given descriptions of Marcus, Ackerman Sr., and Dylan Cassidy. Tire tread found at the scene was identified as that of an S-type Jaguar. Security camera footage from one of the neighboring buildings confirmed it. But that trail went cold when a similar vehicle was reported stolen the next morning.

Maggie and Andrew worked with the locals. They exhausted every avenue of the investigation. They searched for the initiating event. They ran down every mask-maker in the country. They checked companies that made the tools and supplies necessary to make such masks. They questioned workers at every store within a hundred miles that sold the type of high-end camera equipment that the techs believed the Coercion Killer used. They checked Ackerman Sr.'s interests and hobbies. They tracked down and vetted everyone with one of the suspected aliases.

They found nothing.

Marcus, his deranged father, and his estranged son had all simply vanished.

*P*ART *T*WO

CHAPTER FORTY-SIX

SIX MONTHS LATER

MAGGIE WOKE UP ON THE FLOOR OF MARCUS'S OFFICE IN ROSE HILL, VIRGINIA. An empty bottle of Scotch rolled away as she tried to stand. Her mouth felt as though she'd been eating sandpaper, and the room smelled of body odor. The smell made her stomach lurch. She leaped to her feet and ran to the bathroom. Flipped up the toilet lid and puked and dry heaved for a half-hour.

Then she walked back to Marcus's desk, popped two of his headache pills, and lay down on his old futon.

A ringing phone brought her out of her daze a few moments later. She answered with a rasping, "Hello?"

From the other end of the line, Andrew asked, "Maggie, where are you? You were supposed to meet me for lunch."

She checked her watch. It was two in the afternoon. "Sorry about that. I wasn't feeling well."

"Brown-bag flu?"

"Who are you, my mother?"

"That sounds like something Marcus would have said. I'm worried about you. He was my best friend, but you have to accept—"

"Mind your own business. I'm going to see Ackerman later today. I'll call you if he says anything new."

She hung up without saying goodbye and pulled herself up to a sitting position. The room felt like it was spinning, and she saw white spots in her vision. She closed her eyes and pressed a palm to her forehead. After a moment, she regained focus and stared down at the case files that littered the floor of the office.

Maggie grabbed up one of the files and started reading. Nearly every inch of the floor and desk were covered by the files. All of them organized according to her own system by the type of lead and then alphabetically. She had taken down Marcus's movie memorabilia and replaced them with whiteboards and maps. She had charted the disappearances of every missing person within fifty miles of Kansas City in the past two years, searching for some kind of pattern. She had contacted top geographic profilers to help create maps predicting the location of Ackerman Sr.'s home base. Nothing had proved fruitful.

She placed the case file neatly back in place atop its stack and straightened the row of files. A place for everything and everything in its place.

She checked the time again. Her meeting with Ackerman was in a few hours. She needed to get cleaned up and then undergo the CIA black site's insane security procedures. She didn't even know exactly where they were keeping Ackerman. All she knew was that he was at a secret site for high-value targets somewhere within an hour's drive of DC. Every time she visited, she had to be drugged and blindfolded. Maggie had undergone the process three times now, but she still held hope that this would be the time when Ackerman would provide some insight that would blow the case wide open.

She had to maintain hope. The alternative was unthinkable.

CHAPTER FORTY-SEVEN

THE ROBERT F. KENNEDY DEPARTMENT OF JUSTICE BUILDING SAT BETWEEN PENNSYLVANIA AND CONSTITUTION AVENUES IN THE HEART OF WASHINGTON DC. It was a neoclassical building similar to others in the Federal Triangle with its Indiana limestone facade, red-tile hip roof, and colonnades. An inscription on one side read, "Justice is founded in the rights bestowed by nature upon man. Liberty is maintained in security of justice." The sixth floor housed Trevor Fagan's office. The walls were a basic white. The fixtures were all of an art deco design. A picture of Bobby Kennedy hung on one wall. The Director didn't see any family pictures or anything of a personal nature. The whole place felt cold and generic.

As Fagan showed the Director to a leather chair in front of his desk, he said, "I never had a chance to apologize properly for everything that happened in Kansas City. I want you to understand that I'm very sorry for the loss of Special Agent Williams. He was a good man. And I'm glad that everything worked out with your gunshot wound. I hope you understand that I couldn't allow anything to jeopardize the Shepherd Organization. Looking back, I probably didn't handle the situation all that well."

"You're not a field agent, sir. It's nothing to be ashamed of," the Director said.

"I'm glad that you understand. The reason I asked you to come here today is that I wanted to tell you personally about Francis Ackerman Jr."

"Has something happened?"

"No, but he's put me in a bit of a compromising position. The facility that he's in is usually reserved for terrorists and prisoners held for reasons of national security. It's not a prison. Hell, it's a temporary holding facility with only six cells. The CIA has been all over me to get him out of there. He's costing the taxpayers a lot of money."

The Director sat forward in his chair. "You can't transfer him into a regular prison. We're not even supposed to have him in custody. I guess we could stage a capture and create a cover story, but where would we put him? He's escaped from some of the tightest security facilities in the country and killed who knows how many guards and personnel in the process. Innocent people, just doing their jobs."

Fagan sat back in his desk chair and steepled his fingers. "You're absolutely right. We've come to the same conclusions, and the decision's already been made. We can't keep him where he's at, and he's too dangerous to be transferred elsewhere."

"You're going to kill him," the Director said.

"Mr. Craig and his men are going to stage it to look like he's still free and attacked someone and was killed in the process. It will be clean."

"He can still be useful. He helped a lot in Kansas City. And Ackerman Sr. is still out there. We need him."

Fagan raised a hand. "This isn't a discussion. It's a notification. I know that Agent Carlisle is going to see him today. Let's hope she learns something useful, because this time tomorrow Francis Ackerman Jr. will be dead."

CHAPTER FORTY-EIGHT

AGGIE'S EYES ADJUSTED TO THE DIM LIGHTING AS THE GUARD PULLED OFF HER HOOD. She still had no idea where the facility was located, but it seemed industrial. Like a defunct manufacturing plant that had been repurposed. Ackerman's holding cell was a box within a box. The outer box was a tall concrete square with a catwalk along which a constantly circling guard armed with a futuristic-looking assault rifle patrolled and a lower level which held two guards armed with shotguns. In the center of the concrete box was a clear cube containing a cot, a blanket, a pillow, and a chair. There was nothing else inside other than Ackerman himself. He was allowed to read, but the book sat on a stand outside the clear cube. The guards would occasionally turn the page for their prisoner.

Ackerman had pulled up his chair in front of the reinforced glass or acrylic or whatever indestructible material composed his cell. He wore only a light cotton jumpsuit similar to the scrubs worn by hospital workers, but the fabric seemed less substantial. He gave Maggie a big smile. "It's good to see you, little sister," he said.

She wasted no time engaging him in small talk. She didn't want to be there any longer than necessary. "Your last request was denied."

He shook his head. The muscles in his jaw clenched. "How do they expect me to help you find Marcus without showing me all the evidence? We've wasted months playing this game, while Marcus is ..." His voice trailed off. He took a deep calming breath and shut his eyes. "If I don't have all the details, I'm of no use to you. I want to help, but your bosses have tied my hands. Literally and figuratively."

Maggie knew that every word was being recorded and reviewed by Fagan. He wouldn't like her sharing too many details with the killer. He had said that it was disrespectful to the victims to allow

Ackerman to "get off" on their deaths, and therefore he had refused to allow Ackerman to view nearly all the files and evidence.

"Fagan said that he won't allow you to watch the videos or see any pictures from the crime scenes. He said that it's not fair to the victims or their families."

"I'm sure you've watched them all many times. Did he say that you can't describe them to me?"

"Not specifically, but I've been over every aspect. There's nothing there."

"Humor me, little sister. There's always nothing there, until you realize that there is."

Maggie hesitated, but if there was any chance of Ackerman providing information that could lead to Marcus, she had to do it. She closed her eyes and tried to recount every horrific detail from the videos, the photos, and all the evidence.

When she had finished, Ackerman sat still as a statue for a long time. He seemed to be considering his next words very carefully and analyzing the new information. "You should have told me all this sooner. I think I may be able to help, but not from here. You need to get me out."

Maggie couldn't help but laugh. "You can't be serious."

"I'm deadly serious."

"Sure, I'll just sprinkle you with fairy dust, and we'll fly off to Neverland."

Ackerman leaned up against the glass. "If you want to save Marcus, then get me out of here. This isn't a game."

"Just tell me what you know!" She stood and slammed a fist against the clear barrier separating her from Ackerman. One of the guards rushed forward, but she stepped back and raised her hands in surrender. She sat back down.

Ackerman waited for the guard to back off and then said, "There's really nothing for me to tell you. I'm going off a vague memory. Just a ghost from my childhood. I can't tell you where to find him, but if I were there, looking at the streets, the shops, then I think I could find his old place."

"Find who?"

"My grandfather. Louis Ackerman."

CHAPTER FORTY-NINE

M AGGIE SLAMMED A FIST ON MARCUS'S DESK AND SWEPT A STACK OF FILES ONTO THE FLOOR. The papers scattered and flew into the air as an explosion of white. "You're not listening to me!" she screamed.

The Director stood up from his chair and said, "You need to calm down, Maggie."

"Ackerman said that his grandfather was a talented mask-maker in New Orleans. There's a big market for that kind of thing there, with Mardi Gras and costume balls. Ackerman says that his father always had a strained relationship with Louis, but that Louis might have been the one who showed Ackerman Sr. how to make the masks and could even be the one who's providing him with materials."

"I understand perfectly. If you can find where he's sending the raw materials for the masks, then you may be able to track that back to Ackerman Sr. and then to Marcus. If he's still even alive."

"Don't say that."

"It's something you may have to accept. And you also need to accept that Ackerman isn't going to be able to lead you anywhere."

"Dammit, sir. If I can't take him there, maybe we could set up some kind of video conferencing. That way he can help us without ever leaving his cell."

The Director walked over to Marcus's futon, navigating past the stacks of files, and dropped onto the makeshift bed. The metal supports creaked beneath his weight. He picked up a half-empty bottle of Scotch from beside the bed, popped the cork, and took a long swig. Maggie walked over and joined him. He handed her the bottle, and she took a swig of her own, the liquid burning her throat like cinnamon candy.

"What aren't you telling me?" she asked.

"They're going to kill Ackerman."

"What? When?"

"Tomorrow. They're too scared to transfer him, and they can't keep him at that black site forever."

"They can't do that."

"Sure they can. They'll make it look legitimate. It'll be clean. And I'm not even convinced that it's not the right thing to do."

"But what about Marcus? We're just going to abandon him?"

"Of course not, but let's face it—Marcus is probably dead ... or worse. We know that Ackerman Sr. has been brainwashing people, and he's already tampered with the brain of one of his sons. Even if we found him, the Marcus we got back might not be the same one that went in."

"I'm not giving up on him. Just find out where they're going to take Ackerman. I'll do the rest."

The Director ran a hand over his shaved scalp. "If you go down this road, you're walking it alone. I won't be able to help you."

"I know."

He took another swig of the Scotch and then headed for the door. He said, "I'll see what I can do."

CHAPTER FIFTY

DARKNESS. The black that surrounded him was so thick and heavy that he had nearly forgotten the light. He could barely recall the sensation of the sun's warmth on his skin. He could feel his memory slipping. And his memories were all that he had left.

In this place, there was no light. There was no comfort. No companionship. No mercy. No hope.

Marcus didn't even try to do a workout every day now. In the early days, he had done push-ups and presses upside down against the wall and had run in place. Now he couldn't find the energy to do even that much. He figured every other day or even a couple of times a week would be enough to keep his muscles from atrophying.

Although he had no concept of time. He didn't know what a day was. Or a week. He didn't even know how long he had been in this hole. It felt like an eternity, but time had little meaning in the darkness.

His father fed him the bare minimum to keep him alive and spoke to him through a speaker in the ceiling. The old man wouldn't respond to questions. Marcus wasn't even sure if it was a live broadcast or if his father had just recorded his insane ramblings and played them back for his son. They did repeat. Or at least, he thought they did. He couldn't be sure of much anymore. Beyond his father's occasional words, there was no stimulation. He couldn't hear anything from the world beyond. Which also meant that no one out there could hear him scream, either. The only sounds came from what he presumed to be other cells, but even those were sound-proofed enough so that he wouldn't be able to speak to anyone who was trapped with him. If there *was* anyone else. It could simply have been his imagination.

His mind had begun to question his existence. Marcus couldn't shake the feeling that he had died, and this was hell. He sometimes wondered if he had ever been alive at all. But then his father would initiate an electrical shock, and the agony would make him realize that if he could suffer, then he had to exist. But that still didn't rule out the possibility of hell.

He had tried to escape many times, but there was no way out. After he'd learned that, he had tried to kill himself. But he couldn't find a way out like that, either.

He had banged his head against the stone walls, but he had only succeeded in knocking himself out. He had tried to stop eating, but his father had just knocked him out and fed him intravenously for a few days. He had tried to bite into his own wrists, but his father had rushed in, treated his wounds, and punished him severely for the attempt. He had no clothes or bed sheets or blankets or anything to hang himself with. His only piece of clothing was the shock collar around his neck. The ceiling was about six feet high, but it was a large sheet of metal with holes drilled in it as points of access for his father's speaker and whatever else was on the actual ceiling— he presumed an overhead light and probably a night-vision camera documenting his descent into madness. His entire world was a stone floor, his father's monologues, and his memories.

Marcus was thinking about Maggie, trying to keep a perfect picture of her in his mind, when a voice cut through the darkness.

"Fear is truth. Fear is the only real emotion. Love, hatred, jealousy, loyalty, happiness. These are not real. They are merely the shadows of fear. Think of any emotion. At its core, you will find fear. Happiness. It is merely the absence of pain. Emotional pain is caused by fear. A person may be afraid that their spouse is cheating on them. Afraid that they'll lose their job. If these things are confirmed, they are afraid of how these changes will affect their lives. We hate what we fear. We love things that take away our fear. We may be afraid of being alone, so we seek companionship. We love the one who assuages that fear. There is no good or evil in the world. There is only fear. Fear of failure. Fear of consequences. Fear of your fellow man."

Marcus hated himself for the comfort he found in his father's talks. He hated it even more when he caught himself thinking that maybe his father was right.

"Think of the ultimate figure of evil in the world. The Devil. Satan. As the fairy tale goes, why did Lucifer rebel against God? Out of fear. He was jealous of God's other creations for fear of being replaced, of being forgotten. He was afraid that he wasn't loved anymore. This is why he tortures souls who turn from God. Because he fears them."

Marcus curled into the fetal position and tried to cover his ears, but the blaring sound of his father's voice couldn't be shut out.

"Fear is the only true emotion, but it is also what keeps us shackled to mediocrity and keeps us from realizing our potential. This is what I want for you, my son. To live without fear. This life is all that we have. The only chance we have to make a mark on the world. Don't be afraid to act upon your carnal desires and live out your deepest fantasies. That's what I do. Your desires may be different from mine, but the concept is the same. This is the secret of existence. A life without fear. A life without boundaries."

CHAPTER FIFTY-ONE

FRANCIS ACKERMAN JR. LISTENED TO THE HUM OF THE ROADWAY AND TRIED TO HEAR ANY SOUNDS OUTSIDE THE VAN THAT WOULD GIVE HIM AN IDEA OF HIS LOCATION. He couldn't hear anything specific, but he could make some extrapolations from the absence of certain sounds. He couldn't hear any other traffic. They hadn't stopped at any lights. He gauged their speed at a minimum of fifty-five miles an hour from the moment they'd pulled away from the gates of the holding facility. An isolated location in the countryside. Probably southwest of DC.

He was alone in the back of the van. For some reason, they had dressed him in jeans, a flannel shirt, and hiking boots. Then they had secured him to a metal chair bolted to the floor. He couldn't move at all, couldn't even turn his neck. And just to be thorough, they had also sedated him.

Unfortunately for them, Ackerman had been slowly building up his resistance to the sedatives and tranquilizers commonly used by prisons and mental institutions. He had started taking small doses and then had gradually built up a tolerance, specifically for situations like this. Drugs like Thorazine and sodium pentathol might have put most people under, but they were little more than recreational for him. Although he wasn't completely unaffected, he was far from unconscious.

Abandoning hope of hearing anything from outside the vehicle, he strained to hear the two men riding beyond the metal partition separating the front and back of the van. He heard Craig's voice. He couldn't understand every word, but he could fill in the rest. They were discussing a football game and women and then something about the drinking problem of one of their coworkers.

But then the second man said, "Are you sure about this plan?"

Craig replied, "This guy's a Gulf War veteran who's down on his luck. He uses his shotgun to kill Ackerman like he's a trespasser, and then he gets the reward money. It's simple. Clean."

"What if this guy tells someone that we were involved?"

"Who cares? What are they going to do? Post it on one of those crazy conspiracy websites? Besides, who cares what happens to Ackerman? They should give us medals for this."

Ackerman leaned back against the cold metal of his chair. That explained the change of clothes; they needed it to appear as if he was free, not a prisoner. He was offended that some random simpleton might get the credit for killing him. Everyone died, eventually. But he felt that his death should be in a blaze of glory. He wanted to go out with a bang, not a whimper.

The whole situation was unacceptable, and he intended to rectify that.

CHAPTER FIFTY-TWO

ACKERMAN FELT THE VAN ROLL TO A STOP AND THE ENGINE GROW QUIET. They had arrived. He lowered his head and went limp, as if he were sleeping.

Light flooded the back of the van. He could feel the change through the hood and through his eyelids. The air that washed over him was crisp and pure. He smelled moist ground, burning wood, trees, the sweet-and-sour scent of weeds. He heard birds and squirrels and the rushing of a stream somewhere in the distance. They had taken him to an isolated home in the woods. Which was perfect for him. All the better for his escape.

He heard the sound of another car and more voices. Four distinct voices. Two men to carry him out. Two to cover him with the shotguns. The contractors were thorough, but also predictable.

Craig gave the orders, and two sets of boots stepped up into the back of the van. The shock absorbers shifted and bounced under the added weight. He felt the men's hands cautiously undo the restraints holding him to the chair, and then they lifted him up and out of the van.

Ackerman kept his body limp, like a corpse. Like someone unconscious and defenseless.

His feet dragged over the path leading to the house. It was all dirt—no rock, no concrete, no asphalt. Definitely deep in the woods. Probably not the man's actual house. Maybe an isolated hunting cabin. He supposed that scenario made the most sense. They would make it look as though he had been hiding out in the unused cabin, and his killer had merely stumbled upon him during a hunting trip or a routine supply check. Maybe the guy came here every couple of weeks to make sure that kids hadn't vandalized the place or that raccoons hadn't found a way inside.

They dragged him up the steps. Definitely wooden. Definitely old. They banged on the door, and his designated executioner answered after only a few seconds. The man spoke with a southern drawl, and his words were slightly slurred. Ackerman guessed that his executioner had come to the cabin early and started drinking to build up the nerve for what came next. Amateurs—they always worried too much. When it came down to it, killing was easy. No different than a thousand other tasks performed every day. Like flushing the toilet or flipping a light switch. A simple cause and effect that required little effort to accomplish. The effect was just more permanent than most people were accustomed to.

They carried Ackerman inside the cabin and across the hardwood floor. He felt the uneven plane of the wood and heard the creaks. A fire crackled and popped in a fireplace against one wall. He gauged the space by the echoes and the sounds. An open layout. Maybe twenty-five by thirty. Probably a bedroom or two in the back. Definitely a hunting cabin.

They dropped him onto the wood floor. He didn't attempt to break his fall. He kept up the appearance of being completely unconscious. But when he struck the floor, he heard the rattle of hinges and a lock and the bouncing of a section of floor only a couple of feet from where he had landed. A trapdoor. Probably leading to an old cellar or crawlspace.

Ackerman heard the man with the slurred speech say, "Okay, guys, how do we do this? I've never shot anyone who wasn't shooting back before."

Craig replied, "Don't worry about it. This guy's a menace to society. He's a cold-blooded bastard. You're going to be a hero for this. We'll prop him up in a chair, and you shoot. He won't even know what hit him. Hell, it's more humane than a lethal injection."

"You're sure he's asleep?"

"He's out cold. Won't feel a thing."

"What about the restraints?"

"We'll leave them on him to be sure and then take them off after it's done. Just make sure you get him square in the chest. It'll be easy—just like a flipping a switch."

Ackerman wanted to laugh. Those were the words of a professional.

CHAPTER FIFTY-THREE

MAGGIE AND ANDREW WATCHED FROM A DISTANCE AS THE BLACK PANEL VAN AND DARK CROWN VICTORIA CAME TO A STOP AT THE ISOLATED CABIN. The Director had really come through for them. He had talked Fagan into discussing more details of the plan to get rid of Ackerman. Then Stan had taken the vague information that Fagan had reluctantly provided—a Gulf War veteran with a remote cabin in rural Virginia who had fallen on hard times—and worked his magic. Stan had narrowed the list of possibles down to three names. The first man was out of state. The second possibility was in the county lock-up for a drunk-and-disorderly. And the third man worked at a nearby cement plant and had taken the day off to spend some time at his cabin.

"You don't have to do this," Maggie said as she handed the binoculars over to Andrew.

"He's my best friend. If Ackerman knows something, then we have to take a chance."

"Chances are that Fagan will have us arrested for this. Or even killed. At the very least, it'll put an end to our careers."

Andrew shrugged. "It's no fun without Marcus, anyway. Besides, if we find Ackerman Sr. from this, Fagan will at least have to admit that he was wrong. After all, it's our jobs to bend the rules in order to catch the bad guys, right?"

"Yeah, but I don't think anyone wanted us bending the rules against our own people."

"These bastards aren't our people. They're more like Ackerman than they're like us. They're murderers."

"And what are we?"

"Now you sound like Marcus again. We both know that sometimes there's no other way, and I'm not sure that Ackerman doesn't deserve every bit of what they're about to give him, but there has to be a line somewhere. And we have to search our hearts and be objective enough to know what that line is and stop ourselves before we cross it. These guys *enjoy* crossing that line. They probably don't even *have* a line. We sometimes do bad things in order to protect good people. And then only if there's no other way. These guys are a different breed. You can see it in their eyes."

With a shake of her head, Maggie said, "I guess you're right." Then she pulled her Glock 19 pistol with her right hand and a two-shot TASER X2 with her left. "Let's do it."

They approached the house with ease. The mercenaries, not expecting any kind of attack, hadn't stationed a guard outside. Maggie ascended the front stairs of the cabin and took up position to the right of the door. It was a routine they had practiced over and over. Andrew would kick in the door. She would sweep in first with him at her heels. She'd take right. He'd take left. Simple, efficient, and effective.

Andrew didn't wait for any signal. They both knew they were as ready as they would ever be. He kicked the door with a smooth, practiced movement. The wood always gave at its weakest point, which in this instance was the casing. The door flew inward, and the rusty lock plate, which had just been torn from its housing, skittered across the floor with a thud and a rattle. Inside, they found the five targets and Ackerman. They were all gathered in a convenient circle around Ackerman, who seemed to be sitting unconscious in a battered wooden chair. Craig and one other dark-haired man stood to Ackerman's left. The two other mercenaries were on the killer's right. And standing in front of him was a short wiry-looking man with glassy eyes and a double-barreled shotgun in his hands.

"Nobody move!" Maggie yelled. Her focus was on the man with the double-barrel. He seemed scared and confused, the most immediate threat to them and Ackerman. "Everyone drop your weapons!"

"You're making a big mistake here," Craig said calmly.

"I said put them down!"

The man with the double-barrel shifted his gaze back and forth between Maggie and Craig. Each movement of his eyes grew more jerky and rapid. Then he swung the shotgun toward Maggie. She squeezed the trigger of the TASER X2. The barbs sliced through the air at high velocity and struck their target dead-center in the chest, sending a precision-shaped pulse of electrical energy into his body.

He convulsed, swung away from her, and involuntarily squeezed the trigger of the shotgun. It discharged into the face of the mercenary beside Craig. The man's skull exploded, splattering blood over the wall behind him and covering Craig's face.

Craig screamed and pulled his gun. Then all hell broke loose.

CHAPTER FIFTY-FOUR

MAGGIE SAW THE BIG BLACK PISTOL APPEAR IN CRAIG'S HAND. She recognized it as a Glock 18C with a huge extended magazine. She guessed the mag held thirty to forty shots. Only one reason for a magazine like that on a handgun. It was fully automatic. She had fired one like it at the range. It boasted a cyclic rate of 1300 rounds per minute, if your ammo could last that long. The classic Tommy gun and the modern AK47 both had a cyclic rate of about 400 rounds per minute. Which meant that the Glock 18C was like a chainsaw that could reach out and strike someone from a distance.

With a shout of rage, Craig unloaded an entire clip in their direction. But before he opened fire, Maggie and Andrew both dived for cover behind a sturdy brown leather couch near the door.

Maggie was closer. She made it to cover unscathed. Andrew wasn't so lucky. He fell on top of her with a cry of agony.

He sat up immediately and started pressing his hands against his legs. He had taken at least three hits to his thighs and calves. Blood flowed out from beneath his fingers as he pressed down on the wounds.

But Maggie had bigger problems than applying first aid. With his clip expended in only a few seconds, Craig was reloading. His men had dropped for cover. She popped up from behind the couch and returned fire to keep her adversaries from rushing them.

And she no longer saw Ackerman in the chair.

✦

When the shooting started, Ackerman let gravity drag him from the chair, still trying to maintain the illusion of unconsciousness. Although the mercenaries had more pressing concerns at the moment. He rolled beneath a nearby table while his captors took cover in the corners of the room or behind the furniture. The air was full of wood particles and couch stuffing and smelled of gunpowder.

With cautious glances, he analyzed each of the mercenaries. None of them were watching him. They were too busy exchanging fire with Maggie.

Ackerman crawled forward a few feet to the fireplace. Three split logs had recently been added to the fire. They still burned brightly. He crawled closer. He could feel the heat against his face. Then he reached into the fire and grabbed one of logs. The flames bit deep into the palm of his hand. White-hot electric tendrils of agony traveled up his arm through his nerves to his brain, but once there, his brain didn't interpret the sensation as pain. At least, not the type of pain that most people experienced. Maybe not pleasure. But somewhere in between. Perhaps both agony and ecstasy at the same time, melding together to create an experience incomprehensible to the mind of a normal person.

A large window was set in the same wall as the fireplace. Simple brown curtains hung at each side of the window. Ackerman pulled out the log and rolled it against the closest curtain. It took a few seconds for the fire to catch, but when it did, the flames licked up the side of the window with a primordial hunger.

He didn't waste any more time on the show. He rolled back to where he had felt the trapdoor. He pulled aside a large red rug. It was stiff with stains and dirt from years of abuse by hunters. It wouldn't roll up, but he was able to slide it to the side.

Beneath the rug, he found a three foot by three foot square cut in the boards of the floor. Hinges occupied the side opposite him with a slide bolt on the side closest. From its size, he guessed the trapdoor probably led to a crawl space rather than a cellar. He slid open the lock and dropped head first into the darkness below.

❖

When Maggie came back down from shooting over the top of the couch, Andrew was ripping off strips of his shirt and applying tourniquets to both his legs. His eyes looked glassy, as though he was about to pass out from pain or blood loss or a combination of both. He said, "I'll cover you. Go for the door."

"I'm not leaving you."

"You are. I can't walk, and you can't carry me. I'll buy you some time."

"But Ackerman—"

"Is on his own. We're no good to Marcus dead. Just go."

"I won't leave you!"

"You have to. I'll buy you some time, and then I'll surrender. I don't think they'll kill me. Let the Director know that they have me in custody."

Using his arms to pull himself across the floor, Andrew moved to the end of the couch opposite the door. Then he said, "Get ready."

Maggie didn't know what to do. Andrew was right, but leaving him behind felt so cowardly. She couldn't tell which was the right decision, and any hesitation now could mean the difference between life and death.

Andrew pulled himself out in the open at the end of the couch, raised his gun, and fired. Maggie ran for the door. It had swung back shut during the firefight, but there was no striker plate left for it to latch to. She lowered her shoulder and plowed through the obstruction. Bullets chewed into the wood around her, but none struck home.

She rushed down the steps but fell back against them as the dark Crown Victoria skidded to a halt right in front of her. The driver kicked the brake and spun the steering wheel to make the vehicle slide sideways, putting the passenger door directly facing her.

Ackerman reached across with his manacled hands, pushed open the passenger door, and said, "Get in."

CHAPTER FIFTY-FIVE

THE RESTRAINTS ON ACKERMAN'S WRISTS MADE DRIVING MORE DIFFICULT, BUT NOT UNMANAGEABLE. Plus, he had done it before. On several occasions, actually. He drove back down the lane leading away from the cabin and barely slowed as he took the turn onto the main road.

"Where are you going?" Maggie asked.

"Away from there. As fast as possible."

Ackerman already had his every move from this point on planned out. Although nothing ever went as planned. He could anticipate the variables, but in the end, improvisation and adaptation was key. Right then, he needed there to be another car on that road. If they didn't see another vehicle before reaching the next town, he would adapt, but it would complicate their escape. And he always liked to start things out right.

He got lucky. Two miles from the turn-off to the cabin, he saw a silver Subaru station wagon coming at them on the opposite side of the roadway. Giving no warning to Maggie, he slammed on the brakes and jerked the wheel. The car skidded to a halt in the middle of road, blocking both lanes.

"What are you doing?" Maggie yelled.

"Give me your gun."

"Did you get brain damage back there? Let's get one thing straight right now. You're my prisoner. Not my partner. You don't get a gun, and those restraints stay on."

Ackerman could already see that the driver of the Subaru was applying the brakes. He hoped the driver was a woman. He hated to stereotype, but women often complied with less application of force.

The Subaru would be on them in a few seconds. He didn't have time for a discussion with Maggie.

He glanced over at her. She had drawn her Glock 19 from its holster. "Keep driving," she said.

He growled deep in his throat. It was time to put her in her place. He supposed it was going to have to happen sooner or later. Might as well be sooner.

Before she could react further, he swung an elbow against the side of her head. Her skull bounced back against the passenger-side glass. Then he swept his hands over the gun and her wrist. With the proper amount of pressure at the right point, he easily wrenched it free from her grasp.

He pushed her face against the glass of the passenger door, stuck the muzzle of the gun into her ear, and said, "Don't think for one second that I'm some puppet whose strings can be pulled. I'm here because I want to be. Because I'm going to find my brother and my father. You can help me or you can get in my way. I would not recommend the latter."

The Subaru had come to a stop twenty feet ahead of them. The driver hadn't gotten out of the vehicle. If that was due to a lack of initiative, then it was a good sign. If it was because they were smart enough to know better, then they could pose a problem.

Ackerman released Maggie and stepped out of the car. A strong gust of wind pushed against him. There were no obstructions along the road to block the flow of air, just open fields. Which also meant that the driver of the car had nowhere to run. He could still smell the burned rubber from the Crown Vic's tires. He raised the gun and started toward the station wagon. His steps were small and jerky because of the chains around his ankles.

"Get out of the car!" he yelled.

A heavyset woman in her mid-forties exited the Subaru. Her hands were raised over her head, and she refused to make eye contact with Ackerman. He resisted the urge to smile. She was perfect.

He turned back to the Crown Vic and yelled to Maggie, "We're changing cars."

She complied, but her eyes were on fire. If he'd had a normal sense of fear, he might have found her threatening in that moment.

The heavyset woman still wouldn't meet his gaze. He walked closer, and she recoiled. He said, "What's your name?"

"Tammy," she replied with a whimper.

"Is your purse in the car?"

"Yes."

"Good, Tammy. We're going to play a little game. It's called Simon Says. Are you familiar with that game?"

She gave a rapid nod. Ackerman had the amusing thought that she was like a bobble-head doll only in reverse, a big body and a small head.

"Excellent, Tammy. The only difference between the way you may have played it before and my version is that, since I have your purse, I know where you live. I like to hurt people, Tammy. I can find you again and hurt you. I can hurt those you love. And if you don't do as Simon says, I'll do exactly that. Simon Says, nod if you understand?"

She bobble-headed in the affirmative.

"You're doing so well, Tammy. All you have to do is get in that Crown Victoria, turn the car around, and drive away. And don't stop driving until you see flashing police lights telling you to do so. If you do as Simon says, you won't get in any trouble, and you'll never see me again. It'll be a couple hours of your time. A minor inconvenience. Please don't turn this into more than that. Tell me you understand."

"I understand."

"Oh, Tammy... Simon didn't say." He stepped closer and pointed the gun at her head.

"No! Please!" she cried.

Ackerman couldn't help but smile. "Okay, my dear. Consider that your one and only do-over. Simon says, get in the Crown Vic and drive away."

Tammy hesitated for a few seconds as if she expected him to shoot her in the back once she turned. But then she shuffled off toward the dark car and sped away from them.

Ackerman turned to the station wagon and saw Maggie behind the wheel of the car. He walked around to the passenger side, got in, and placed Maggie's gun between them on the console. She grabbed it and jammed it back into her holster. The radio was blasting out a Jack Johnson song. He flipped it off. He hated that upbeat crap. It made his teeth hurt.

"Let's go, Maggie. We've wasted enough of our head-start already."

Maggie said, "You didn't have to scare her like that."

"I believe I did, little sister. She's our decoy. We need her to run in the direction opposite us as fast as she can for as long as she can. That's a government-issue vehicle. It'll be LoJacked. They'll track it down, and when they see it's still moving, they will hopefully think that we're still driving it. It won't be long before they catch her and start looking for this car instead. But, with any luck, it will be long enough. Don't forget, I'm the expert on evading manhunts. In order to escape, we're going to need to do four things: know their tactics, employ misdirection, do the unexpected, and be patient. That was misdirection."

"So what's next?"

"We're going camping."

CHAPTER FIFTY-SIX

ACKERMAN TOLD MAGGIE TO PULL THE SUBARU OVER AT A LONG WHITE AND BLUE PREFAB BUILDING. He had already scouted the business to make sure it carried the necessary supplies. He employed a similar procedure for every new city he visited. For him, preparedness meant the difference between freedom and life in a cage. The business was actually several small shops under one blue metal roof. Signs above three separate doors read: *C&M Grocer's and General Store, The Little Souvenir Shop,* and *Capt. Dave's Bait, Tackle, and Sporting Goods.* Ackerman only cared about the latter. They parked along the building's side behind a dumpster to conceal the vehicle from the road.

After taking a few minutes for Maggie to help him get free of his restraints, he said, "I need cash."

"Why? What are you doing?"

"Trust me. We need a few things. I'll need the gun too. Just in case."

"That's out of the question."

He met her gaze. He knew he could take it from her, but it wasn't vital and this was wasting valuable time. "Fine. Give me the cash."

She handed him two fifty-dollar bills, and he walked around the side of the building to the final door. It opened with a ding. A pretty young blonde wearing a tan baseball cap with a catfish motif looked up and flashed an obligatory smile. Ackerman returned the expression as he ran down his mental checklist of supplies.

He immediately bypassed the lures and reels and bait and moved to the back of the shop. Grabbing two green camping backpacks from a shelf, he stuffed one full of MRE—Meal, Ready-to-Eat—military field rations. The other he packed with bottles of water, two sleeping bags, nylon rope, and two Mylar thermal blankets. Then he grabbed two camouflage winter coats. He wanted to purchase a survival knife as well but didn't have enough cash, and he was just as deadly with his bare hands as with a knife anyway.

He had the supplies in hand and purchased and was back at the car in less than three minutes. He and Maggie switched positions, and he pulled out onto the two-lane and headed toward DC.

"Where are we going now?" Maggie asked.

"To find a drug dealer."

◆

Ackerman pulled the Subaru up next to a curb in a particularly bad area of Prince George's county, a suburb south of DC. The nearby houses had bars on all their windows. Many were covered in graffiti and looked abandoned. Two young black men in sideways hats and baggy jeans sat on a concrete retaining wall thirty feet ahead.

"Get out and grab the backpacks. Wait by the car," Ackerman said. Then he slipped on one of the camo coats and tossed the other to Maggie.

The two black youths eyed him suspiciously as he approached as if they couldn't decide if he was a cop, a potential customer, or a potential robbery victim.

Ackerman approached them with a smile, and gesturing back at the silver Subaru, he said, "See that car?"

"We ain't blind, son," the more muscular of the two youths said.

"Good. Then you can see a good deal when it crosses your path. I'll trade you that car for a switchblade knife."

The kid laughed. "If I want your piece-of-crap car, I'll just take it."

Ackerman let just a little predatory menace seep onto his features and said, "You could try. Or we could make a mutually beneficial trade like two businessmen."

The kid looked from him to the car. "Is it hot?"

"Yes, it is. Not a problem for your friendly neighborhood chop shop, though. It's quick cash."

The muscular kid pulled out a knife and pushed a button to expose the blade. "Sure, but I'll take everything in your pockets too."

Ackerman couldn't help himself. He laughed, loud and boisterous. The kid looked displeased. He glanced at his friend as if he couldn't believe the disrespect. Then, probably trying to retain his street cred, he thrust the knife toward Ackerman's gut.

The killer easily caught the thrust and then slammed his fist into the kid's throat. The kid released the knife, grabbed at his neck, and fell back on the concrete, gasping for air.

The scrawnier young man looked down at his friend and raised his hands as if to say he didn't want trouble. Ackerman tossed him the Subaru's keys. He caught them almost from reflex.

Ackerman said, "Nice doing business with you. I'd get rid of that car quickly."

Retracting the blade and sliding the knife into his pocket, Ackerman walked back to Maggie. He said, "Come on. We're five blocks from ten acres of woods."

Maggie didn't say a word. She just fell in step behind him. They walked the five blocks without being harassed, crossed a two-lane road, and entered a patch of timberland alongside the highway. They were a few hundred yards into the trees when Maggie said, "This is your plan. We're going to just hide in the woods. Those kids could be calling the cops right now."

"Our two friends back there were the go-between for a drug dealer. You walk up, place your order with them, and then you pick it up from another guy. They're not going to the police. The only way anyone is going to find us out here is with dogs, and how are they going to know where to look? Trust me. We're as good as vanished."

After another few minutes, Ackerman found their home for the next few days. The tree was perfect, tall with plenty of branches and foliage for concealment. "This is it. Now we climb."

Maggie looked up. "You can't be serious."

"As a heart attack. We can't just sit around where someone might spot us. We need concealment. What's the matter? You never climb a tree before?"

"Not since I was twelve. What about food and water?"

Ackerman pulled out an MRE and a water bottle.

"What about going to the bathroom?"

Ackerman cracked his neck and sighed. "You hang your ass over the edge and do what comes naturally. What's the problem?"

"How long are you planning on being out here?"

"At least three days. Should be longer to be safe, but three will do. After that they'll assume we've made it through their net."

"You expect me to live in a tree for three days eating nothing but those damn MREs?"

"I've survived ten times that long on nothing but bugs and berries and drinking from leaves. You'll be fine, little sister. Now climb."

CHAPTER FIFTY-SEVEN

MAGGIE WATCHED ACKERMAN SLEEP ACROSS FROM HER IN THE TREE. The nylon rope secured him in place. His eyes were closed, and his head rested on the bark at an angle. He looked so peaceful, so normal. But she knew what lay beneath those calm waters. She knew what kind of man he really was, and she considered, not for the first time, shooting him and shoving him out of the tree. But then where would that leave Marcus? Like or not, Ackerman was her best shot at finding him.

A branch snapped somewhere in the distance. It was a faint sound, barely even audible. Ackerman's eyes snapped open as if an alarm had sounded. He stared in the direction of the sound for a moment and then turned to Maggie. He said, "I should probably hold the gun."

"Not going to happen."

"What are you going to do if someone finds us out here? Are you going to use it?"

"No, and neither are you. We'll run."

"If we get caught out here, there's no running. Our only choice is to fight."

"You promised Marcus no killing," she said.

"I could shoot them in the leg. After all, it's better to give than to receive."

Maggie shook her head. "I don't think that's the right context."

"I feel it's applicable."

"You're not getting the gun, so drop it. And we're not hurting anyone. If we get caught and can't get away, then that'll be it."

Ackerman growled deep in his throat but leaned back and watched the forest for any more signs of movement. Then he took off his boot, pulled out a switchblade knife, and started cutting into the leather of the boot's toe.

Maggie said, "Where did you get that?"

"I took it off those nice young gentlemen when one of them tried to ram it into my midsection."

"I don't like you having that."

"We both know I could just as easily kill you or anyone else with my bare hands."

He continued his cutting until he had a small slit where the sole and the leather top of the boot joined. Curiosity getting the better of her, Maggie asked, "What are you doing?"

Ackerman didn't say a word, but he slipped the switchblade into the boot and placed it back on his foot. Then he raised his leg to show her, and with a small twitch of his ankle, the blade popped out of the front of his boot. He grinned with satisfaction, but Maggie just shook her head and looked away.

They sat in silence for another hour, and then Maggie commented, "It's so peaceful out here. It feels like we're the only people in the world."

"This isn't peaceful. You can still hear the highway and honking cars and the noise pollution marking the presence of the virus that is humanity. Not to mention all the chirping and buzzing and scratching of a million little creatures. You want peaceful? The ocean. A sailboat. That's been my dream for as long as I can remember. Just me and the wind and the waves. Not another person within a hundred miles. No temptation. No reminders. Just me and God."

"You really think God's forgiven you for all that you've done?"

Ackerman leaned his head back again and said, "Then I acknowledged my sin to you and did not cover up my iniquity. I said, 'I will confess my transgressions to the Lord.' And you forgave the guilt of my sin."

"The Bible?"

"Psalm 32. Written by David as one of the seven penitential Psalms. David was an adulterer and a murderer. Yet the Bible says that he was a man after God's own heart. Noah was a drunk. Jacob was a liar. Moses had a stuttering problem. Elijah was suicidal. Peter denied Christ. God doesn't choose perfect people. All people are flawed and stray from the path. I've just strayed further than most. And now I'm trying to make amends as best I can. Everything that's happened to me has been for a reason. We're the sum of our experiences. We can't change them, but we can learn from them and use those lessons and gifts born of hardship to make a difference."

"You really believe all that, don't you?"

"I have to. It's not easy for me, Maggie. Living in your world. The hunger is always there in the back of my mind. The darkness never sleeps. I see a building, and I want to burn it down. I see a group of smiling faces, and I want to see them twist in agony. I used to wish that I was normal, but now I know that I'm who I am for a reason. Pain is my nature, but I've chosen to transcend it. To use it. To be greater than the sum of my parts. George Bernard Shaw said that life isn't about finding yourself. It's about creating yourself. And that's what I'm trying to do. Create a better me."

Maggie didn't know what to say. She hated this man. He was a murderer and a danger to society, but she couldn't help but empathize with him and even feel inspired by his desire to become a better person. She pulled out one of the MREs and choked down a package labeled as BBQ chicken with black beans and potatoes. As she ate, she watched the sun rise over the trees—a beautiful halo of molten orange and purple, blue and yellow—and thought about Ackerman's words, her own mistakes and insecurities, and Marcus's struggles with finding himself. She couldn't help but wonder if the serial killer actually had himself together better than the rest of them.

CHAPTER FIFTY-EIGHT

CRAIG SHOOK WITH ANGER AS HE STARED INTO THE CRACKED MIRROR OF THE OLD GAS STATION. The business had shut down early on in the recession, and the company for which he worked had snatched up the facility for pennies on the dollar. He imagined that the reason the station had closed was because of how far off the beaten path it sat. That was also the reason they had picked it. No one nearby to hear the screams.

Craig washed his hands in the oil-stained sink, and blood flowed off his fingers and down the drain. Some of the blood had originated from tiny cuts on his knuckles, but most had spilled from his subject.

He looked deep into his own eyes through the grime of the gas-station mirror. He searched for any remnant of the kid from Nebraska who had played college football and briefly dated a goth chick just to drive his bible-thumping mother crazy. All that seemed like so long ago. Even the memories were alien to him. It seemed as if he had been implanted with the recollections of some other poor dead soul. The man staring back at him now was a warrior.

But even warriors had friends. Perhaps even friendships that ran deeper than those of most men because such friendships were forged in blood and mud and fear and pain and loneliness and putting your very existence in the hands of the man next to you.

Craig had lost someone like that today. A brother with a bond forged through fire that could only be broken by death. In that small cabin on a normally routine operation where they shouldn't have encountered any resistance, one of his brothers had been stolen from him. Maybe he could have accepted the death if it had occurred in combat in Iraq or Afghanistan or South America. But only a few miles from home, gunned down by a federal agent trying to liberate a serial killer? Craig couldn't wrap his mind around that. It didn't sit well with him. Someone needed to pay for it. In fact, more than one someone would pay for it. The man in the chair, whom he had been torturing for information, would be the first to suffer and die, but he wouldn't be the last.

Craig dried his hands and threw the towel at the reflection in the mirror. His phone sat on the edge of the sink, and its display lit up with a text message from his girlfriend, Julie. The message read, *Are you going to call later? I've had a hard day and wanted to hear your voice. Love you.* He felt a pang of guilt for always lying to her. Julie was a second-grade teacher at a Catholic school in Maryland, and she wouldn't exactly understand the true nature of his work. He considered, not for the first time, how he could take an instructor position closer to home and propose to Julie. But he just kept telling himself that he would look into it after completing one more mission. One more operation and then out. One more big payday. But one more never seemed to be enough.

Without responding to Julie's message, Craig walked back to where his subject, Andrew Garrison, was seated. White nylon rope secured Garrison's hands and feet to a metal chair. His face was a bloody mess. The pinky on his left hand had been broken and was still twisted at an odd angle. Bandages covered Garrison's legs where the mercenaries had patched up a few gunshot wounds—all clean pass-throughs or grazes—since Craig didn't want Garrison dying before the agent told him where to find Ackerman and Agent Carlisle. The whole room smelled of old oil and fresh feces. Garrison had defecated on himself during the interrogation. It was often involuntary, and Craig didn't fault the man for it. Garrison had actually maintained his defiance at a level that Craig hadn't expected. Still, he would break. They always did. And Craig hadn't even delved into his bag of tricks.

"Wake him up," Craig said to one of his men, a big black North Carolinian named Landry. The others were out pursuing other leads on Ackerman and Carlisle.

Landry looked down at Garrison and then back at Craig. "Are you sure about this, sir?"

Craig gritted his teeth but said, "Speak your mind."

Landry stood beside Garrison's unconscious form and pointed down at him. "This guy's a federal agent. I'll back your play, whatever that is, sir, but have you considered how much heat is going to come down on us for this?"

"He may be a federal agent. But an agent for an organization that's not even supposed to exist. And don't forget about Bobby."

"I know, but—"

Craig closed the gap between them within the space of a blink and wrapped his fingers around Landry's throat. The other mercenary didn't resist. "What did I tell you when I recruited you to this company? What were the two rules?"

In a choked voice, Landry replied, "We always get paid, and we protect our own."

"That's right. We have a code. You mess with one of us, you mess with all of us. Now wake him up." Craig shoved Landry roughly back toward the unconscious and bound Garrison.

"Yes, sir, but..." Landry hesitated. "What are we going to do with him after he talks?"

"Same thing they did to Bobby. We're going to kill him."

Chapter Fifty-Nine

DEEP BENEATH THE FLOORBOARDS OF THE THIRTEENTH FRET, THOMAS WHITE SAT OVER AN ALUMINUM WORKBENCH, A LARGE MAGNIFYING LENS AND LIGHT IN FRONT OF HIS FACE AND A SOLDERING IRON IN HIS HAND. With surgical precision, he applied the final touches to his newest toy, a device which could increase electrical voltage output based on the readings coming from an attached heart-rate monitor. He finished connecting the final wire and then leaned away from the lens. He placed the soldering iron on the aluminum surface of the workbench and rubbed his eyes.

The newly installed equipment looked out of place in the small room that he had converted into his workshop. The walls were old stone, and the space smelled musty and damp. It was March, but the snow had melted only a week ago, and the temperatures were still barely above freezing in Leavenworth. A space heater hummed in the corner to fight back the chill.

The basement of the Thirteenth Fret housed one of the largest examples of what had become known as the Leavenworth Underground—a series of tunnels and old storefronts and rooms that formed an underground city beneath the Kansas town. Thomas had heard much speculation on the true origins of the underground city. Some said that it dated back to the 1800s and had been used as part of the Underground Railroad. Others cited remnants of old business signs that still hung in front of many of the doorways and claimed that it had been simply a second level of commerce beneath the street or that the street level might have actually been raised at some point due to flooding and this original level had merely been forgotten. Some claimed that the underground city had housed speakeasies and dens of ill repute, which had been in use prior to and during Prohibition. Strangely, the academic community and researchers had largely ignored the presence of the underground city, and many feared that the secrets of the Underground had simply been lost to history.

Thomas White didn't really care about the original purpose of the tunnels and old stone rooms. He only cared about how well they suited his purposes in the modern day. He had converted the dilapidated old storefronts of the rotting structure into several soundproof chambers where his subjects could be monitored and housed during the course of his experiments.

He stifled a yawn and was about to head to his bedroom when he heard the creak of hinges and the sound of small feet padding against stone. Only one resident of his makeshift dungeon wasn't locked in his room, and so Thomas had no doubt about who was moving around. He noiselessly followed the sound of the footsteps and watched as his grandson Dylan entered one of the side rooms.

Thomas followed the boy, watching him from the shadows. He had always had the uncanny ability to sneak about and observe people without their knowledge. He enjoyed the feeling of power it gave him to watch someone who didn't know they were being watched. It could often be like seeing inside a person, beyond the masks they showed to the world, down deep to the real person beneath. It was an intimate experience whose impact could only be eclipsed by staring into the same person's eyes as the life drained from their body.

Thomas admired the familial traits evident in the boy's dark hair, naturally athletic frame, curious nature, and the intensely intelligent gleam in his eyes. The boy entered another room used mainly for storage and picked up a jar resting on a shelf. The thing that had caught his attention was a butterfly flitting back and forth inside the small glass prison.

Silently stepping up directly behind the boy, Thomas said, "What did you find?"

The boy gasped and dropped the jar. Anticipating the reaction, Thomas snatched the falling object from the air before it could shatter against the stone floor. He placed it back on the shelf.

Dylan said, "I'm sorry, Grandfather."

"Never apologize, my boy. Accept the consequences of your actions, but never be sorry for them. I'm glad you found this. I captured it for you."

A ghost of a smile crept across the boy's features. "For me?"

"Well, not as a pet, but as an illustration. How does it make you feel?" He handed the jar back to the boy. The monarch butterfly inside tapped against the glass as it tried to escape, its silky orange and brown wings striking an invisible barrier that its tiny insect brain couldn't comprehend.

"It's pretty," Dylan said.

"So it brings you joy?"

"I guess."

Thomas grabbed another jar from a higher shelf. "What about this?" he said, shoving the jar in front of Dylan's face.

The boy recoiled as the large wolf spider in the bottom of the jar scurried toward his face and leaped against the glass. "No! I don't like spiders."

"But why? Why are you afraid of something so small? It can bite, yes, but it can't truly hurt you. It's just a small animal following its instincts, same as the butterfly."

"I don't know. It's just ugly and scary-looking."

"Okay. Now, what if I asked you to kill one of them?"

"Why? I don't want to kill either one."

"But I need the jar back, and if we let either one outside right now, it will just freeze to death." A small lie, but Dylan wouldn't know any better.

Dylan seemed to consider this, his small brow furrowing. "I guess I'd kill the spider, then."

Thomas grabbed a cotton ball and tipped a bottle of ethyl acetate against it. He used a pair of tweezers to pick up the soaked ball and extended the tweezers, handle first, to the boy. "Go ahead. Drop this into the jar, and it will kill the spider."

Dylan hesitated but then took the tweezers, unscrewed the lid of the jar, and dropped the cotton ball inside. Thomas placed his hand over the air holes in the jar's lid and encouraged the boy to watch the show. The spider sensed the danger and flailed about the bottom of the jar, searching for an escape. It spasmed and fought but eventually succumbed to the toxic fumes and curled in on itself.

"Is it dead?" Dylan asked.

"Yes, you killed it. Does that make you sad?"

"No, it's just a bug."

"That's right, my boy. Its life was insignificant and so is its death. Go on to bed now. I'll come read you a story in a moment."

"Not another scary one?"

"I've told you. You have to master your fear. Like you did with the spider. But we'll see. Go on, now."

Thomas smiled as he watched the boy head down the hall toward the room he had fashioned for him. He looked back at the dead spider. The boy had easily put a value on one life over another. Thomas had been doing many small exercises such as this with Dylan over the past few months. All part of his education, or re-education. Once the concept of placing a value on life was established, it wasn't a huge jump to establish that no life had value. Dylan was well on his way, but there were still many lessons to come.

Thomas then turned his attention to the butterfly. He unscrewed the lid to its jar, reached inside, grabbed hold of the Monarch, and pulled off one of its wings. He stood there for a moment and watched it flap in a one-winged frenzy on the bottom of the jar. He cocked his head to the side and analyzed its death throes. Then he analyzed himself and why he had felt the urge to tear off the wing in the first place. He determined that it was more out of curiosity than pure malevolence. He had just wanted to watch it suffer and die. Simple as that.

CHAPTER SIXTY

THE DIRECTOR SAT AT A TABLE AGAINST THE BACK WALL IN A RESTAURANT NAMED ZATINYA ON 9TH STREET NW IN WASHINGTON DC. It served a unique blend of Turkish, Lebanese, and Greek cuisine. He was about to enjoy a late dinner of *garides saganaki*—sautéed shrimp with tomatoes, green onions, and *kefaloaviera* cheese—when he saw Trevor Fagan, dressed in an expensive pinstriped three-piece suit, enter and walk over to his table.

Fagan pulled out a chair, sat down across from him, and said, "Hello, Phillip. As you know, the Ackerman situation was about to resolve itself this afternoon."

"That's an interesting way of putting it."

Fagan ignored the comment and pushed on. "Unfortunately, I never received confirmation or any word from the team afterward. Naturally, any deviation regarding Ackerman is of immediate concern. So I sent out another team to the cabin. They found what appeared to be the aftermath of a shoot-out. Lots of expended rounds and blood."

This made the Director sit forward. "Did they—"

Fagan cut him off. "Then I sent a team to locate you and the members of your team who were involved with Ackerman, namely agents Carlisle and Garrison. Both of whom are missing, whereabouts unknown. Since you were the only other person aware of the operation, I assume that you tipped them off. I've already issued arrest warrants for Carlisle and Garrison. Can you give me any reason why I shouldn't have you put in chains as well?"

The Director tossed his napkin onto his plate and replied, "Not really."

"Why? Why would you interfere?"

"Ackerman still has information that could lead us to his father."

"And to your missing agent, who most likely died months ago."

"Marcus isn't dead. He's out there in a hole somewhere, undergoing the kind of torture that only the Devil could dream up. And he's waiting for us to save him. That hope might be the only thing keeping him alive. I won't give up on him."

"I admire your loyalty. I do, really. But I can't condone or allow this loose-cannon behavior. We have to have rules, Phillip. There are lines that shouldn't be crossed. Your actions have placed one of our country's most notorious fugitives back on the street."

"This was Maggie's play, and I trust her judgment."

"Her judgment is clouded. I need you to help make this right. Help me find her and Ackerman."

The Director frowned and asked, "Why do you say her and Ackerman? What about Andrew? There something you're not telling me?"

Fagan steepled his fingers and said, "I've received reports from someone inside Mr. Craig's company that he has Agent Garrison in custody and plans to extract information from him about where Maggie and Ackerman are headed."

Through gritted teeth, the Director said, "Extract? You mean torture. And you're going to 'condone' some mercenary revoking the civil rights of a federal agent?"

"Let's not get too dramatic, Phillip. We both step all over people's civil rights every day. The Shepherd Organization itself is a violation of those rights. But to answer your question, no, I'm not going to condone it. Unlike you, I insist on people beneath me following orders, and I don't allow them to go off half-cocked on their own personal crusades. That's why I'm here."

"I don't understand."

"I want you to come with me to collect your agent before Mr. Craig does something that we'll both regret. Then I want you to order him to tell us where to find Agent Carlisle and Mr. Ackerman."

"I get the sense that Craig won't give Andrew up easily, especially if one of his men was hurt during that gunfight you described. He seems the type to hold a grudge."

Fagan cocked his head to the side and said in his typical smug tone, "You have a gun, don't you?"

CHAPTER SIXTY-ONE

After tucking Dylan in and telling him a story about the Spanish Inquisition, Thomas White decided to check in on his son. He keyed up the feed from the night-vision surveillance equipment embedded in the ceiling above Marcus's head and stared at his youngest child. Marcus was naked and curled into the fetal position along one wall of his cell. Thomas pressed a button to initiate a violent electrical shock. He couldn't resist the urge to smile as Marcus's body convulsed. But once the initial shock stopped, Marcus didn't scream out in anger. He simply whimpered, curled back up into a ball, and tried to go back to sleep.

Thomas chuckled. He had physically broken the boy, but there was still much work to be done on his son's re-education. It would have been much easier to initiate the changes physically through surgery, as he had done with his apprentice, but those were invasive procedures, which produced the desired effects but also erased any trace of the person's identity. It had taken many subjects and years of experimentation to perfect that procedure, but his current apprentice had so far been an unmitigated success. He had started by operating on the temporal cortex, the part of the brain responsible for the storage of episodic memory, then he had moved on to precision scarring and removal of certain sections of the left and right medial temporal lobes, the amygdaloid complex, and the entorhinal cortex. It was a long and painstaking process, but the end result was the perfect soldier—never complaining, never questioning, but still retaining enough humanity to blend in and complete its objective. Once his current project was complete, he planned to share his research with the world over the Internet. He suspected that terrorist groups and governments alike would find his methods and data useful.

But he would need to take a different approach with Marcus. He wanted to give his son a gift—to show him a world without fear—not steal the essence of who he was. He wanted to set him free, not turn him into another automaton. He would break Marcus's mind, body, and soul. He would pour out all that he had learned and everything he was and recreate him in his father's image.

Thomas checked his watch and looked back at Marcus. It was time that they started the next phase of treatment. But for that, he would need another subject to be used as an illustration, in much the same way that he had used the butterfly and spider during his discussion with Dylan. In this case, however, the subject would require slightly more work to procure. Still, he had time to do so this evening and be ready to start phase two the following morning. He had grown accustomed to sending his apprentice out on errands such as this, but sometimes there was nothing quite as exhilarating as rolling up his sleeves and getting his own hands dirty.

He clicked off the monitor, grabbed his coat and keys, and locked Dylan's door on the way out. After all, the boy possessed his grandfather's insatiable curiosity, and Thomas couldn't have his grandson exploring unsupervised.

❖

Audrey Moynihan's eyes were red and puffy from crying. She still couldn't believe that Brad was leaving her. After all she had done for him. After all they'd been through. How could he just walk away as though it all meant nothing? She had supported him while he went back to school to earn his degree, working two jobs to help with his student loans. And now that he had finally gotten his dental practice off the ground and they were seeing a return on the substantial investment, he had decided that he "needed a break." She suspected that he planned to spend his "break" with the perky blond hygienist who had recently started in the office, but she had no proof of that. Maybe they had simply grown apart. Maybe—

Something struck the underside of her car as the wheels bounced over a large object in the road. Audrey locked up the brakes and let out an involuntary yelp. Her Hyundai Sonata skidded to a halt, and her gaze flew to the rearview mirror.

Her heart pounded, and her breathing became short and erratic. She searched the road for whatever she had hit. When she spotted it, she screwed her eyes shut and repeated, *This is not happening, this is not happening.* Then she said it to herself out loud like an incantation that when invoked would take back the last five minutes of her life.

It was a person. She had hit a person.

Audrey kept her eyes closed tight, not wanting to look again, not wanting to confirm her fears. Maybe it was a small deer? Or a large dog? Or anything else other than another flesh-and-blood human being. She cursed, not for the first time that day. This was Brad's fault. If she hadn't been distracted ...

There was no point in thinking such thoughts, she told herself. It made no difference. It was done and over. She forced herself to look again.

This time she was sure. She could see the clothes. The flesh. The undeniable, unmistakable shape of a person lying in the road. A person who wasn't moving. A person who was most assuredly dead. A person she had killed.

Her mind fought for a way out of the predicament, and a thousand different scenarios flipped through her head in the space of a few seconds. Maybe the person had already been dead? Maybe they were still alive and needed medical attention? Should she call 911?

And then the darker thoughts started to come. It was pitch black outside, and they were on a desolate country road. No cars or houses for miles. No witnesses. Audrey glanced at the ditches surrounding the roadway. They were deep and overrun with weeds and tall grass. She could easily drag the body into the ditch, and it could go undiscovered for weeks. It was probably some drunk who had wandered out and fallen asleep in the road. Why should her life be torn apart because of that person's stupidity?

But such thoughts evaporated nearly as quick as they had come. She was an honest person. Brad had wanted to siphon Internet access from their neighbor's unprotected network, and she couldn't even stand the thought of that. It had been worth it to her to pay the twenty bucks a month not to feel like she was a criminal each time she checked her e-mail. It would tear her up inside whether or not the incident had been her fault.

The decision made, Audrey opened her car door and walked back to where the crumpled form lay in the middle of the roadway. Each footstep seemed like a great labor, as if her limbs were covered in concrete.

Finally she reached the pale form and bent down to feel for a pulse. The body was turned away from her, and all she could see was a matted mop of brown hair. When her fingers touched the person's neck, her hand jerked back reflexively.

What the hell was going on here?

Audrey rolled the body over with her foot and gasped. The eyes were dead and wooden, but not because she had stolen the life from them. The eyes that stared back at her had never been alive.

It was a dummy. A very lifelike mannequin.

At first, relief and joy overwhelmed her. She hadn't killed anyone. She was off the hook. But as the moment stretched out, the feeling of relief turned to anger. Someone had done this to her on purpose. Someone had placed a dummy in the road as some kind of sick joke. She wondered what the hell was wrong with people these days.

She looked around, half-expecting to catch sight of a snickering group of teenagers in a nearby field, but there was no one there. Then she realized that there might have been some damage to her car. She gritted her teeth and fought back a scream of frustration. She would need to file a police report, but she could call that in once she got home.

Grabbing a leg of the dummy, Audrey dragged it off the road and returned to her car. Maybe the cops could find a fingerprint on the damn thing and teach the little punk who had done this a lesson. She slid in behind the wheel and pulled the door shut. She grabbed her seat belt with her left hand and clicked it into place.

And then she felt the presence.

It was like seeing a flitting shadow out of the corner of an eye or having that strange animal sense of being watched. But whatever it was, she knew that someone was there even before her attacker reached over her left shoulder and started to strangle her with her own seat belt.

She fought back with all her strength, trying to pull the nylon strap of the harness away from her neck, but it was of no use. Her mind quickly kicking into survival mode, she changed tactics. Maybe she could reach the steering column and get the car in drive?

A strange pinch and pressure bit into the side of her neck, and her extremities began to tingle and go numb.

Audrey's fingers raked against the handle that would throw the vehicle in gear. She stretched out and raged against the darkness creeping over her vision.

The man in the back seat spoke. His voice sounded deep and strange, as if he were a character in a movie being played in slow motion. In fact, the whole world was starting to feel slowed down somehow. And then Audrey realized the source of the pain in the side of her neck. She had been injected with something. She tried to reach out to the gear shifter again, but her arms were useless now. Her whole body had gone numb and cold.

"You know what I love about this, my dear," the deep slow-motion voice said. "It's the fact that I didn't stalk you or choose you. It was completely random chance that you were the one driving down this road tonight. It could have been anyone, but fate chose you. Fate chose you to die."

CHAPTER SIXTY-TWO

THE DIRECTOR PULLED THE SUBURBAN RIGHT UP TO THE FRONT DOOR OF THE DILAPIDATED FILLING STATION. Graffiti covered the front of the building, and weeds had taken over the lot. Vines snaked up the sides of the old gas pumps. An oval-shaped sign still stood on a large metal pole out front, but the logo of the business was gone with only the skeletal structure of the sign surviving. He could understand how the place had gone out of business. They were miles from a town or any houses on a road that was barely traveled.

He could see through the station's front window, and the light shining from the garage area betrayed the fact that although the building was not in service it was also not unoccupied. He pulled out his Beretta pistol and chambered a round.

From the passenger seat, Fagan said, "Let's try to reason with him first."

The Director nodded and put the Beretta back in its holster. "Of course. Just being prepared."

As they exited the Suburban and walked toward the entrance of the abandoned filling station, a cold breeze made the hairs on the back of the Director's neck stand at attention. He heard the clanging of a loose piece of sheet metal, and the rhythmic sound of metal on metal reminded him of the tolling of bells.

They entered through a small room that had served as the station's storefront. Now, it was empty except for some racks that had once contained rows of oil, a desk, and an ancient cash register. Fagan was first through the door to the garage. The Director followed at his heels. Although he didn't have his gun out, he still scanned the room in his mind in the same way he would have if they were breaching and clearing the building. Then his eyes focused on Andrew. Blood covered his friend's face, but the worst damage was a foot that appeared to have been smashed by a sledgehammer that the Director spotted sitting upright nearby. The sight of it made the Director's blood boil toward eruption.

Even in his ruined state, Andrew had enough presence of mind to think tactically. He caught the Director's eye and then looked toward a small oak door at the side of the garage. The Director placed his hand over his gun and was about to move toward the door when he heard a voice behind him say, "Don't. Take it out slowly. Two fingers and lay it on the ground."

He glanced back to see a large black man aiming a pistol at them. The man wore the same kind of dark tactical clothing that the mercenaries at the farmhouse had favored. He had apparently circled around the building to get the drop on them when he heard their vehicle pull up.

The Director complied with the man's demands and then said, "Where's Craig?"

"Right here," Craig answered as he emerged through the door that Andrew had indicated. His dark fatigues were pulled down around his waist, exposing a white tank top stretched tight across his thickly muscled chest. He held a blood-stained towel, using it to wipe one hand and then the other.

"What the hell do you think you're doing here, Craig?" Fagan asked.

"My job."

"I hired you to capture and contain Ackerman. Then you were ordered to eliminate him. You failed. Your job is complete. What would compel you to detain and torture one of my agents?"

The Director noticed the way that Fagan had taken ownership of Andrew as one of his men. Maybe there was hope for the bureaucrat yet.

Craig tossed the towel onto a nearby shelf. "I'm reacquiring the target, sir. And to be perfectly honest, the mission parameters changed the moment your agents decided to kill one of my men!"

Fagan shook his head and glanced over at the Director, accusation in his eyes. He said, "That's unfortunate, and a situation that will be dealt with internally. Your services are no longer needed, but you will, of course, be paid in full. With an added bonus for the loss of your man."

"Don't bother. I'll just take my payment in blood." Craig pulled a gun from the small of his back and pointed it at Andrew.

The Director stepped forward, but Fagan stopped him with a hand on the chest. Fagan said, "Mr. Craig, we're professionals here. Let's not be rash. I'm sure that we can come to some mutually beneficial arrangement."

"Can you bring back my friend?" Craig said, sighting down his gun's barrel at Andrew's bound form.

This time, the Director did step forward, placing himself between Craig and Andrew. He said, "You want vengeance? You want someone to blame? These are my people. Andrew's my friend, and I'm responsible for him. You want an eye for an eye? Blood for blood? Take mine. Kill me and let him go."

Craig stared at him for a long moment. The Director saw the barely contained rage bubbling just below the surface. Craig was only one step away from the men whom the Shepherd Organization hunted, and the Director wasn't sure if there was any way to reason with him. He could very well kill all three of them without a second thought.

Craig's finger tightened against the trigger, but then he lowered the gun and shoved it back into his belt. "Take him. He's already told me where the others are headed anyway. And you can keep your blood. I want Ackerman. He's the one who started all this. I want that bastard's head mounted on my wall." Craig gestured toward his man, and they gathered their things and left through the back of the station while keeping a cautious eye on the Director.

As they headed for the exit, the Director said, "Do what you feel is necessary with Ackerman. He can handle himself, and he probably deserves much worse than you can give. But if anything happens to Maggie, I'll hunt you to the ends of the Earth."

Craig didn't respond. He backed out of the room without another word. Once they were gone, the Director rushed to Andrew's side. As he worked at removing the bonds, he asked, "Are you okay, Andrew?"

Andrew looked at him as if the older man had lost his mind and replied in a rasping voice, "Not really."

Chapter Sixty-Three

THE SUDDEN ILLUMINATION PIERCED MARCUS'S EYES LIKE A MILLION TINY PINPRICKS. It took several moments for his vision to adjust beyond a white blur. When his eyes finally did start to focus, he saw the dark form of a person standing with him in the cell. He reflexively recoiled away from the shadowy form and retreated into a corner.

His father's voice—not the recording that had played over and over, but an actual voice coming directly from a real person—said, "Hello, son. It's time to play a little game."

It was the first human interaction beyond the beatings Marcus had experienced in months, and it took a moment for the implications of his father's words to sink in.

"Come with me, son."

Marcus hesitated but then pushed himself up on trembling legs. He still couldn't focus completely, but he saw the blurry figure gesture toward the door and say, "This way."

He headed toward the door, but once he was within range, he lunged at the blurry figure, going for the throat. He had no plan, hadn't thought it through. He doubted he had the strength to overpower his father, but he had to try. He had to do something.

A surge of pain spiraled down from his neck and reached his toes before he had come within three feet of his father. He dropped to the stone floor and convulsed in agony, the terrible spasms turning his whole world into all-encompassing pain.

After a moment, he lay there panting on the stone floor, the residual aching still causing his whole body to tremble. He smelled sizzling bacon but couldn't be sure if his senses were just out of whack from the jolt or if the smell was that of his own flesh cooking.

He had completely forgotten about the shock collar still secured around his neck. His father said, "If you've gotten that out of your system, let's try again."

This time, Marcus stood and followed directions. As he entered the hallway beyond his cell and caught sight of his surroundings for the first time, he tried to soak in all the details. But his vision still wasn't fully adjusted to being back in the light after so much time in the darkness, and what he could see wasn't of much help. It was just a long corridor with dirty stone walls. They were obviously underground, but he had surmised that already. Three more doors on the left side of the corridor appeared to lead off to more cells similar to his own.

His father directed him to the next cell down the line. Inside were two chairs facing each other with a strange home-made electrical device sitting between them. The contraption looked like a cross between a generator and the equipment that one would find in a hospital room. A woman was bound and gagged in the farthest chair. Black streaks of mascara covered her cheeks, and she wore a white sweater with jeans. She looked like a recent acquisition.

"Marcus, meet Audrey. She's volunteered to help us with a little experiment."

Marcus noted that wires and electrodes ran from the device in the center out to both chairs. The wires were already connected to Audrey. They snaked up her back and under her sweater and another pair connected to her temples.

"Have a seat, Marcus."

He didn't want to comply. He wanted to do anything that he could to defy his father, but another jolt of electricity knocking him to the floor wouldn't do anyone any good. So he sat down in the chair and looked deep into Audrey's eyes. He tried to tell her to have strength, and they'd get through this. But he didn't really believe that and was sure that seeing his emaciated form didn't instill much confidence.

"Place that belt around your chest." His father pointed at a black belt that looked similar to the kind found in gyms for lower back support. As the older man pointed, Marcus noticed the gun in his father's hand for the first time—a snub-nosed revolver, either a .357 or a .38.

Marcus secured the belt around his midsection, and his father said, "Excellent" as he bent down and started fiddling with the strange device. Marcus, his vision improving, examined the older man. His father wore a three-piece suit minus the jacket, and small round spectacles sat on his angular nose. His hair was the same brown color as Marcus's, but baldness had started to creep in.

After a few seconds, the device began to emit a familiar beeping sound that Marcus had often heard in hospital rooms coming from a heart-rate monitor. His father said, "I've always been fascinated with electricity. I guess it started when I saw Boris Karloff play Franken- stein when I was a small boy. I used to hook electrical current up to dead animals and watch them twitch, something first discovered in 1771 by Luigi Galvani. It was actually his experiments which led to the idea of reanimating dead tissue through electricity. Which obviously played a role in the birth of Frankenstein's monster. Such power—the power to give life or take it away. It's no wonder that our ancestors attributed lightning strikes to the actions of angry deities in the clouds. Now we know better. And through technology, we all have the ability to wield the power of gods."

His father pulled a black folding stool from a corner and sat on it between his two captives as if he were about to enjoy a show.

"What is all this?" Marcus asked.

Ackerman Sr. crossed his arms and pursed his lips. "Are you familiar with exposure therapy, Marcus? It involves a person sup- pressing a fear-triggering memory or stimulus by confronting their fears. It can be quite effective and therapeutic. We're going to attempt a form of that today. You have a deep-seated fear of failure. There's this compulsion to try and save everyone and a responsibility that you feel toward the safety of all the people around you. I guess I would call it a 'tragic hero complex.' And as I told you, I'm going to show you a world without fear."

Ackerman Sr. pressed a button on his device, and Audrey started screaming. "Audrey is now receiving a mild electrical shock due to an increase in your heart rate. You see, the natural physiological response to fear involves a lot of body processes. Accelerated breath- ing rate, constriction of the peripheral blood vessels, increased muscle tension including the muscles attached to each hair follicle which contract and cause what we commonly refer to as 'goose bumps,' sweating—"

Audrey's screaming intensified, and Marcus yelled, "Stop this! You're killing her."

His father ignored him, continuing with his lecture. "—increased blood glucose, increased serum calcium, increase in those white blood cells called neutrophilic leukocytes, alertness leading to sleep disturbance and 'butterflies in the stomach.' But, most importantly, it leads to a drastic increase in a person's heart rate. So you see, Marcus, I'm not killing her. *You* are. It's *your* fear that's killing her. The level of electrical current that she receives is tied directly to your heart rate. If you master your fear and control it, then you can stop her pain. If not, then she will slowly cook in her own skin."

Marcus reached up to pull the heart-rate monitor from his chest, but his father held up a small remote and said, "I wouldn't try that. I'll give you a shock of your own, and I can just imagine what that would do to your heart rate."

"You sadistic prick! I'm going to—"

Audrey's shaking increased, and she started to make gagging noises.

"Careful, son, anger is just fear in a different form, and it too increases your heart rate. And I tell you what, if you can learn to control your fear and keep her alive, then I'll let her go. You can save her, but only by playing the game."

Marcus fought to bring his mind into focus and his body under control. He tried to calm himself, to go to a happy place, to distance himself from the situation. But it was nearly impossible with the sounds of Audrey's agony echoing throughout the stone chamber. Her tortured screams pierced his soul, rattled through his brain. He couldn't block them out. He was failing her.

He grabbed hold of the thought and realized that his father was right. He felt responsible for everything, even things that were beyond his control or not his fault. He hadn't kidnapped Audrey and strapped her to the chair. Why did he feel responsible for her fate? Why was it his job to save her? He couldn't even save himself.

Still, he had to try.

He searched for a perfect memory to lose himself in completely, and finally, he found one. A memory of a perfect day with his father, his real father, John Williams. They had hiked into the woods of northern New York and found a small lake nestled between two hills. They had tried to fish but failed to catch any and had ended up eating beans from a can. They had laughed and joked and talked about silly, trivial things and most of all had just enjoyed each other's company.

When Marcus opened his eyes, Audrey was still sobbing and breathing hard, but her screaming had ceased. He looked at his father with a defiant look of triumph.

Ackerman Sr. smiled and said, "A good start." He pulled out a pair of pruning shears, the kind typically used in a garden. "But how would you feel if I cut off one of her fingers?"

❖

His father continued with his game for what felt like an eternity. He would torture Audrey, try to anger Marcus, manipulate him, distract him. It was a constant struggle for Marcus to keep himself calm, and he failed many times. But he was always able to bring himself back under control.

Eventually, he found that he had to make himself numb. He had to stop seeing Audrey as a person and start seeing her as an object. She was nothing to him. She was already dead. He repeated to himself that he didn't need to save her because she wasn't real, she wasn't a living breathing person, she was just a thing, as insubstantial and inconsequential as a character from a fairy tale.

When his father was finally satisfied, he reached down and clicked off the machine. The beeping of the heart-rate monitor stopped. He looked at Marcus with a smile and walked over behind Audrey. He said, "You did very well, son."

At first, Marcus thought that his father was going to untie her and keep his promise, but then the older man placed his gun against the side of her head and pulled the trigger. Her head erupted in a pink mist as the gunshot reverberated with a deafening thunder inside the small stone chamber.

Marcus screamed with fury, and before he realized what he was doing, he was on his feet and rushing toward Ackerman Sr. Then the pain shot through him again, and he dropped to the floor in another convulsive fit.

When it was done, Ackerman Sr. stood over him and said, "You can't save everyone, son. No matter how hard you try."

CHAPTER SIXTY-FOUR

AFTER STEALING ANOTHER VEHICLE—WHICH ACKERMAN ACCOMPLISHED WITH DISTURBING SKILL AND PRECISION—MAGGIE AND HER COMPANION WERE ON THEIR WAY TO NEW ORLEANS. *Over seventeen hours in a car with one of history's most notorious killers ... good times*, Maggie thought. She insisted on driving, and thankfully, Ackerman stayed quiet for most of the trip.

But as the hours stretched, she felt fatigue start to set in and her eyelids grow droopy. Needing a distraction, she asked the first question that came to mind. "So how long has it been?"

Ackerman glanced over and said, "Since we left DC?"

"Since you've killed someone."

A pregnant silence hung in the vehicle for a moment, and then he said, "Crowley was the last. And I don't really feel that a child molester should even count. Killing him was one step above stepping on a cockroach."

"Is that true? You haven't hurt anyone since then?"

"I told you that I wouldn't lie to you, little sister. It's been months. If I were in Alcoholics Anonymous, I would have received a gold coin by now, or whatever medal it is they give out for resisting a taste of one's desire."

"Do you miss it?"

"Yes, very much so."

"How do you resist the urge?"

"Have you seen the film *A Beautiful Mind*?"

"So now you're going to compare yourself to a Nobel Prize-winning genius?"

"I've never been tested, but I'm sure my IQ would qualify me as a genius. That's not the point. That film was loosely based on the life of mathematician John Forbes Nash, Jr. He struggled with mental illness and delusions. He described overcoming his delusional thinking as 'intellectually rejecting' such thoughts. That's what I'm doing. I'm intellectually rejecting my animal desires. And when I need some help, I self-mutilate."

Maggie slowly took her eyes off the road and looked over at the strange man in the passenger seat. "You cut yourself?"

"Cut, burn, whatever's handiest. I've found that I only feel alive when inflicting pain or experiencing it myself."

She fought back a wave of nausea, thinking of cutting or burning her own flesh. "I don't see the appeal."

"I don't see the appeal of living in an apartment, waking up every morning for a job that I hate, coming home, watching reality TV, going to bed, and getting up to repeat the same mediocrity the next day. But that doesn't negate the fact that many people find contentment and serenity in such activities. And I applaud them for that. I hope to find some measure of that contentment in my own life some day. Point being, to each his own."

They were quiet for another few moments, and then Ackerman sat forward and said abruptly, "Pull over at this truck stop."

"Why?"

"I need to use the little boys' room."

"Can't you hold it?"

"I could, but I hear that's not good for your bladder."

Maggie growled as she clicked on her turn signal and took the exit. Under her breath, she said, "Yeah, you're a picture of clean living."

The place Ackerman had chosen provided one-stop shopping for denizens of the road. As Maggie pulled up, she saw through the front windows that two fast-food chains had micro-eateries within the truck stop. Signs in the windows advertised showers and bunks and every other manner of amenity imaginable. She could see displays containing everything from souvenir knick-knacks to books and movies to replacement GPS units. There was even a sporting-goods section.

She flicked the gear shift into park and back to drive, repeated the procedure three times as her OCD dictated, and looked over at her companion. There was a thick black beard covering his cheeks after the days in the woods, but that wasn't much of a disguise. "Someone could recognize you."

"I am kind of a big deal."

"Be serious. We can't take the chance of you being spotted."

Ackerman grabbed some tissues from a box left on the passenger floorboard, wadded them up, and stuffed them between his teeth and gums. Then he rolled his neck and jutted out his chin. "How's this?" he said in a flawless Southern accent. They were all subtle changes, but Maggie had to admit that the way he did it was quite effective. Unless someone had just seen a picture of him or was specifically looking for or expecting him, he should be able to pass a casual inspection.

"See if you can find some reading glasses or something like that inside. Then, if you can keep from attacking any of the truck drivers, we should be good."

"No promises," he said, turning up the drawl on the Southern accent.

Maggie stepped out into the smell of diesel fuel and grease and decided to grab a burger for the road. She asked Ackerman if he wanted anything and told him to hurry up. They entered the truck stop and then parted ways. She figured that if he wanted to slip out the back and escape, there wasn't much she could do to stop him anyway, and she couldn't very well follow him into the men's room. So she jumped in line at one of the mini-restaurants and was picking out her meal and deciding if she wanted fries with it when she noticed that Ackerman hadn't headed for the bathroom but instead had moved toward the sporting-goods section.

She growled under her breath and followed him. Although she had little choice but to offer him some small measure of trust, she wasn't about to let her guard down completely.

She found him standing in front of a display case and speaking with a clerk, a bearded old man who looked like he'd just crawled off a shrimping boat after a three-day bender. "What are you doing?" she said as she approached, but as she drew closer, she saw what he was admiring and answered her own question. "Oh no. Absolutely not."

Ackerman twisted the enormous blade in his hands and seemed to revel in the way the light caught its surface. It was a massive knife with a silver hilt and a bone handle. Ackerman gave her an over-exaggerated frown and said in a whiny voice, "But Mom!"

She grabbed his arm and pulled him away from the counter. "Don't cause a scene. I may have to put up with your company in order to get this done, but I don't have to sit by and worry that at any moment you might plunge Paul Bunyan's knife into my gut."

"Actually, it's Jim Bowie's knife. Hence the name Bowie knife, but it's also referred to as an Arkansas Toothpick. Bowie was a fascinating character. The event that gained him and his knife fame was a duel where Bowie was shot and stabbed multiple times but still managed—"

Maggie closed her eyes and raised a hand to stop him. "I don't care if Jim Bowie single-handedly won the Revolutionary War and cured cancer at the same time. I—"

"Well, that's just silly."

"—don't want you armed."

Ackerman sighed, and his previously jovial demeanor melted away. He bent down and looked deep into her eyes. She shuddered and fought the animalistic instinct to run.

"If I wanted to harm you, Maggie, I could do so at any moment. I thought that I proved that in the car when I took your gun. I'm not some guard dog that you can teach to do tricks. You are alive because I allow it to be so. The only reason that I was in custody in the first place was because I allowed it. Because my brother asked it of me. I'm going to find Marcus, but my patience with your lack of respect is growing very thin."

"You wouldn't kill me. Marcus would hate you forever, and you couldn't stand to be without your beloved brother."

"You're right. I wouldn't kill you. I wouldn't harm a hair on your head. But that doesn't mean that I wouldn't gag you and make you ride the rest of the way to New Orleans in the trunk."

Maggie gritted her teeth. "You just try it."

From the look in his eyes, she could tell that he was tempted. But after a few seconds, he said, "This is getting us nowhere. We both need to be prepared to defend ourselves."

"From who? The only ones after us might be the cops, and I'll be damned if I let you—"

"Not the police, little sister. Mr. Craig and his band of merry men."

"What? You think Fagan will send that psycho after us?"

"No, I think he'll come all on his own. You killed one of his men, and I know Craig's type. His ego won't allow him to let that go. He'll demand vengeance."

"But Andrew..."

"Yes, I'm sure he's already tortured your friend to find out where we're headed. And torture is something that Craig excels at."

Maggie's face twisted in anger as tears formed in her eyes. "You're a real bastard, you know that." She tossed a fifty-dollar bill against his chest, said, "For your knife," and stormed out to the car. She suspected that Ackerman didn't even understand why she was upset, but she didn't care. Insanity didn't let him off the hook for being an asshole.

Chapter Sixty-Five

A CKERMAN HAD COME OUT OF THE STORE WITH A PLASTIC BAG FULL OF ITEMS, BUT MAGGIE HADN'T ASKED HIM ABOUT IT. She wasn't in the mood to talk anymore, and so she drove the last leg of their journey in silence. She thought about Marcus and whether or not he was even still alive. And if he was, what had he been through, what horrors had he seen, what torment had he endured? She thought about Andrew suffering at the hands of Craig and his mercenaries. She worried about the Director and what would happen to him and the Shepherd Organization because of her actions. In the end, she had no reason to believe that this trip would lead them to Marcus. She just chose to have faith and not let the other very real possibilities creep in.

Once they arrived in New Orleans, Ackerman told her to drive through the French Quarter until something sparked a memory. So they drove up and down streets that looked like the pockmarked face of a chronic acne sufferer with their rough surfaces and abundance of potholes, both patched and not. They passed nail salons, voodoo shops, cigar and coffee lounges, palm readers, art galleries, a multitude of bars, gumbo shops, bistros, and a wide range of small specialty boutiques. It seemed that nearly every building was of a Spanish or Creole type and many had wrought-iron balconies on the second stories adorned with ferns and other hanging plants. The buildings were all exuberantly colored—yellow, orange, red, baby blue. They met horse-drawn carriages as they clip-clopped down the uneven roadways. They saw a New Orleans-style funeral procession with a jazz band blowing out an upbeat version of *Just a Closer Walk with Thee*, players in black suits and white hats leading a marching group of somber mourners. Iridescent Mardi Gras beads hung from the cast-iron lampposts at each corner, even though Mardi Gras was a couple of weeks in the past.

"Anything?" Maggie asked.

"Not yet. Keep driving."

They rolled past Bourbon Street and Marie Laveau's House of Voodoo and turned onto St. Ann Street. They were coming up to a large pedestrian mall brimming with activity and street vendors in front of the St. Louis Cathedral and Jackson Square when Ackerman said, "Wait. Go around this block again."

Maggie circled around, and Ackerman told her to stop. They parked in a small garage operated by a big man in a black button-down shirt wearing a white fedora with a peacock feather poking up from it. They walked up and down one side of the street and then the other.

The whole time Ackerman had a disgusted snarl on his face. Maggie asked, "What's eating you?"

"I don't like New Orleans. It would make a good stomping ground for a serial killer, but it's not really my style."

"What do you mean? It's fun. Lots of parties and activities."

"Yes, it's so colorful and ... festive." His lips curled up at the word as if it tasted bitter on his tongue. "It makes me sick. Not to mention that the whole place reeks of urine and vomit."

"You're a real killjoy, you know that?"

"We're not here to partake in drunken revelry." He stopped, turned around, and pointed at a building up the street. "That's it. That's the shop my grandfather used to own."

"We've already passed that place twice."

"I wanted to be sure. Now I am."

"How do you know he doesn't still own it?"

"I don't. Let's find out."

A worn wooden sign over the door read Jezebel's Masks & More. A pair of white French doors, filled with small windows and flanked on both sides by solid oak shutter doors, opened into a newly remodeled showroom full of all types of masks. The air inside smelled of plastic and resin. Some of the masks were simple and elegant. Others were elaborate affairs, covered in jewels and feathers. Some covered only the eyes, while others hid the whole face. Still, these were props for costumes. None matched the detail or intricacy of the masks worn by the Coercion Killer.

Except one. It hung on the back wall behind the counter. It was incredibly detailed and showed the face of a smiling man with a thin mustache. It was a work of art and held a place of prominence among the others.

The clerk smiled and nodded as they entered but then returned his attention to the computer sitting on a table that served as the store's counter. He was a foreigner of some kind. Maggie guessed Armenian or something along those lines. A beard covered his face, all gray except below his nose and around his mouth, and his head was shaved. He wore a green untucked plaid shirt, black trousers that were two inches too short, and a pair of alligator-skin boots.

Ackerman didn't waste any time pretending to be a customer. He bellied up to the makeshift counter and said, "We're looking for a man named Louis Ackerman."

The clerk tensed but said in a slightly slurred accent, "Never heard of him."

"He used to own this place."

"Sorry I can't be of more help. I bought the shop from a friend."

"Who did he buy it from?"

"I don't know."

"Do you have your friend's contact info?"

The man was becoming more suspicious and perturbed with every question. "I can't just give out that information. What's your interest?"

"Personal."

"Well, I personally can't help you. I apologize."

"He made that mask hanging on your back wall."

The man didn't glance back at the intricate mask. "It came with the shop. If you're not going to buy anything, then I'd appreciate..." His voice trailed off, and his eyes went wide. Under his breath, he said, "You—"

Before he could finish his sentence, Ackerman slammed a palm against the clerk's throat. The man's hands flew up as he made a choking noise. Ackerman grabbed the top of his shaved head and slammed it down on the surface of the table. The keyboard he had been typing on shattered under the impact of his head. The man fell back against the floor in a daze.

Ackerman rounded the table in a blur of motion and grabbed the clerk in a chokehold. The man was already stunned and offered little resistance. Within a few seconds, he was unconscious, and Ackerman left him on the hardwood floor. He stood, looked into the back room, and said, "Close the front doors and flip the open sign."

Maggie was dumbfounded. She looked from Ackerman to the unconscious man and said, "What the hell?"

"He recognized me, and if he knows who I am, then he probably knows my grandfather as well."

"How do you figure that?"

"Think about it, Maggie. Out of all the books and TV programs that have featured myself or my father, none of them reveal anything about my grandfather except for a few vague details. We're not the first ones to come asking about Louis Ackerman and his family legacy. My guess is that this guy not only knows where he is, but has a deal with my grandfather not to send any reporters his way."

"So what now?"

"Now you shut the doors and go back to the car and retrieve the bag of goodies that I picked up at that truck stop. We're going to need a few of those items."

"I won't let you hurt this man."

Ackerman winked. "Don't worry, little sister. I'll be gentle."

CHAPTER SIXTY-SIX

THE BACK ROOM OF THE STORE HADN'T BEEN REMODELED. It was exposed brick and knotty pine floors, and it contained shelving filled with cardboard boxes, which Maggie guessed held more party masks. Tools and materials littered a small workstation used for making some of the more elaborate custom masks. An air-conditioner unit hummed in one window, and the muffled sounds of pedestrians carried in from the streets beyond. When Maggie returned with Ackerman's bag, she found that the killer had already suspended the unconscious clerk by his hands from an exposed rafter.

Maggie shook her head and instinctively placed her hand over the gun concealed beneath her leather jacket. "I won't let you torture this man."

"It won't come to that. I just need to scare him a bit."

She held out the bag. "Then why do you need this stuff?"

"All part of the show," Ackerman said as he snatched the bag from her grasp.

She watched him warily with her hand still on her gun as he moved to the workstation and turned on an old record player. The eerie melancholy of Billie Holliday singing *Strange Fruit* crackled out of the speaker. Ackerman reached into his bag and pulled out a bottle of lighter fluid and a Zippo lighter.

He popped open the squeeze bottle and sprayed it into the clerk's face. The man jolted to consciousness as he choked on the liquid. "What..." the man started, but then his gaze came to rest on Ackerman. He said, "Please don't hurt me. I have a family. I'll tell you whatever you want to know."

Ackerman said nothing. He just hummed along to the music and started spraying the man down with the lighter fluid. Maggie's grip tightened around her Glock. If Ackerman tried to set fire to the man, she would drop him. She made up her mind on it right then. She couldn't allow him to hurt an innocent, even if that meant that they never found Marcus. She would kill Ackerman and go on without him, if that was what it came to.

The clerk said, "Please! You don't have to do this. I'll tell you where Louis is."

Ackerman said, "I'm not really a big fan of the ambience of your fair city. But there are two things about New Orleans that I love. The jazz"—he gestured toward the record player—"and the history. One of my favorite stories is that of the Axeman of New Orleans. At least eight murders were attributed to him in 1918 and 1919, but he possibly killed many more. They never caught him or even determined his identity. But the best part of the story is that he sent a rather eloquent letter to the local papers stating that he would kill again at fifteen minutes past midnight on the night of March 19, the anniversary of which is later this week, but he would also spare the occupants of any place where a jazz band was playing. That night all of New Orleans's dance halls were filled to capacity. Every band around was booked, and there were parties at hundreds of private residences."

The clerk started spilling his guts, words falling from his mouth in rapid succession. "Louis lives out in Jefferson Parish. There's an old plantation house in the bayou. My cousin bought it, and I traded it to Louis for the shop. He didn't want it in his name because of the reporters and police looking for his son. He doesn't want any attention."

Ackerman didn't even acknowledge the confession. "Of course, not everyone complied with the Axeman's demands, but still, no murders occurred that night. It's a beautiful story, don't you think— the Axeman haunting the streets of New Orleans like the angel of death passing over the people of Egypt."

"That's all I know. I swear."

Ackerman flipped open the lighter but didn't strike the flame. The alcohol smell was thick in the air. Maggie pulled her gun and aimed it at Ackerman's back. "Don't move, Ackerman. I will shoot you."

He laughed and flipped the lighter closed. "Are you telling me the truth?" he asked the clerk.

"I swear."

"Directions?"

The man rattled off a series of directions to Louis Ackerman's home. Maggie committed the directions to memory and suspected Ackerman did the same. When the clerk was finished, Ackerman added, "And what happens if you try to warn Louis or call the police after we leave?"

"I'll tell no one!"

"But what happens if I walk out that door and you find courage enough to make a little phone call?"

The man swallowed hard and said, "You'll come back."

"And next time, I'll visit you at home. Do you believe me?"

"Yes."

"Good." The Bowie knife appeared in Ackerman's hand as it slid out from under the back of his shirt, and with a flick of his wrist, the rope was severed and the clerk dropped to the floor.

Ackerman gathered his things and headed for the front door. Maggie followed a few feet behind, her gun still at the ready. Once she was sure the encounter was over, she slipped the weapon back into her holster.

Back on the sidewalk along St. Ann Street, she caught up with him and said angrily, "You would have burned that man alive if I hadn't been there to stop you."

Ackerman didn't look at her but sighed and said, "Have some faith, little sister. It wasn't even lighter fluid."

"I could smell it."

"Yes, back at the gas station, I went into the bathroom, dumped out the lighter fluid, and filled the bottle with witch hazel. It's a type of rubbing alcohol that has enough of a smell to make someone think it's combustible. Even though it's only slightly more flammable than water."

"I don't believe you."

He stopped in the middle of the sidewalk and turned to her, the contempt clear on his face. Then he reached into the bag, pulled out the bottle, and sprayed some of its contents on his left hand. He dropped the bag and retrieved the lighter from his pocket. He lit it and held the flame against his fluid-soaked hand. He stared into Maggie's eyes as the flame licked at his skin. His arm didn't catch fire, but after a few seconds, she could smell his flesh burning.

"That's enough," she said in a whisper.

Without another word or showing any sign of pain, Ackerman flipped the lighter closed, picked up the bag, and headed toward the parking garage.

CHAPTER SIXTY-SEVEN

CRAIG LOVED NEW ORLEANS. He just wished that he was there under more amicable circumstances. He wouldn't even have a chance to enjoy himself on this trip, which made the people around him who *were* enjoying themselves all the more annoying. For the second time in the past hour, an inebriated man stumbled into him, this time spilling a beer on Craig's silk shirt. It took every bit of his self-control not to pistol-whip the drunken idiot. If he hadn't been on a surveillance op and trying not to draw attention to himself, he probably would have done just that. Instead, he choked back a scream and just nodded as the man apologized and went on his way.

Moving up St. Peter Street, he passed a shabby old building with peeling red paint. A sign read Reverend Zombie's House of Voodoo. He shook his head at the thought of all the poor rubes who bought into that crap. Another sign on the building advertised that the place also sold a variety of cigars. That sounded much better to him than the hocus-pocus trinkets.

His phone vibrated against his leg. He pulled it out of his shorts and recognized Landry's number. "Yeah," he said as a greeting.

"I just spotted them over on St. Ann."

It's about time, Craig thought. He had all six of his men walking up and down the streets of the French Quarter, based on the intel provided by Agent Garrison. They had specifically targeted the mask shops, but the type of business could have changed since the grandfather had owned the place, so they had been forced to cast a wide net and hope it paid off.

"Did they see you?"

"Negative."

"Are they still there? Can you maintain surveillance?"

"I'll do you one better," the big black man said. "I saw them leave a parking garage and slipped the guy at the door two hundred bucks to show me which car was theirs. We have a tracker on it."

Craig's face split into an uncharacteristic grin. "Good work. Text the others and tell them to meet back at the vehicles. We'll have this wrapped up and be back in DC before the weekend."

Chapter Sixty-Eight

HEATHER WOMACK EXITED THE ELEVATOR INTO THE PARKING GARAGE WITH A SPRING IN HER STEP, DESPITE THE DAMN HIGH HEELS THAT WERE PUTTING BLISTERS ON HER FEET. She hated the stupid things, but if she got this promotion, she supposed she'd have to buy a better pair because she'd be presenting to a lot more of the firm's power clients. She had just left a meeting with the primaries from a company in Tokyo that had approached the architectural firm she worked for about designing a series of new department stores here in the US. If they got the contract, it would mean millions for the firm, and she had been given the job of presenting the designs. It was her chance to prove herself, and she had come through in a big way. The clients had been extremely impressed, and while it wasn't yet time to pop open the champagne, it was a giant leap in the right direction. Before long, she could be earning more money and have a new title.

She pulled out her cell phone to tell her husband the good news, but she forgot that she never got any signal in the parking garage. The structure had been packed early in the day, but now it was only dotted with a few vehicles. In her excitement, she hadn't even realized how late it was and that the garage would be nearly deserted.

Ever since her cousin had told her a story about a coworker being raped while walking to her car after work, Heather had been frightened at the prospect of traversing the garage alone at night.

She heard a noise behind her but willed herself not to look. It was just her imagination.

But there it was again.

No, she told herself. It was a stupid cat or her own footsteps echoing off the concrete.

238 Father of Fear

But what if it wasn't? Had that rape victim heard something and told herself the same thing?

Making up her mind, Heather reached casually into her purse as if she were just retrieving her keys. But then she abruptly whirled around with a can of pepper-spray held in her outstretched hand like a talisman.

There was no one there. No attacker. Not even a cat.

She kept watch for a moment and then, shaking her head at her own silliness, headed toward her car.

Her cream-colored Toyota Corolla was only a few years old, but she had made up her mind that if she got this job then she would trade it in for something sportier, something with a little flash, something to tell the world that she'd made it. She smiled at the thought as she retrieved her keys from her purse and pushed the button to unlock the car.

Her fingers wrapped around the handle of the door, and she was about to pull it open when a terrible pain shot up from the heel of her foot into her leg.

Her leg could no longer hold any weight, and she started to fall. She caught herself on the door but was unable to stay upright. She looked down, and her heart froze in her chest as she saw a man's hand holding a bloody scalpel slide back under the car.

It only took a split second for her brain to process what had happened. Someone had been hiding under the car and had slit her Achilles tendon when she'd gone to open the door.

Heather tried to cry out but couldn't find her voice. She landed flat on the pavement, the air expelling from her lungs and making it impossible to scream.

The next few seconds were a blur of flailing limbs and overwhelming fear as she saw the dark figure beneath the vehicle and watched helplessly as powerful hands lunged forward, grabbed hold of her throat, and covered her mouth.

CHAPTER SIXTY-NINE

MAGGIE ALMOST MISSED THE TURNOFF TO THE PLANTATION HOUSE. It was a dirt lane overgrown with weeds and was barely visible from the main road. They followed the lane through the trees for a couple of miles, working their way deep into the bayou. Bald cypress, tupelo, and water elm trees flanked the one-lane path. A couple of spots were submerged under pools of water, and she wasn't convinced that their commandeered vehicle—a Chevy Malibu—would be able to plow through. Eventually, they made it up a rise and spotted the end of the line and their destination: an old raised Creole-style plantation house with an exposed basement and a main floor supported by brick pillars. Even in the waning light of dusk, she could see that it was good-sized, but definitely nothing luxurious. It was old and the white paint was peeling, but it looked like it had been kept up moderately well and was structurally sound if not aesthetically pleasing. A small yard surrounded the house but quickly gave way to wild vegetation and melded with the swamp. She could see a river or lake or some large body of water that butted up against the rear of the property. A closed-in boathouse hung over the water's edge.

Maggie stopped the car thirty yards from the main house and shut off the engine. She glanced over at Ackerman. He had a strange expression on his face. She said, "Any idea what to expect?"

"I only met my grandfather once when I was a boy. I know he and my father had a very strained relationship, but that's about all I know. I've never given him much thought over the years, but now that I know he's alive and we're here, I feel strangely..."

"Nervous? Excited?"

"I don't really know."

"Are you okay? I've never seen you like this."

"Of course." Ackerman seemed to shake off the momentary weakness and added, "He may not be very happy to see us. And he's not likely to want to cooperate with us finding my father—otherwise he would have helped law enforcement track him down years ago."

"You think we may have to dangle him over a pit filled with hungry alligators to get him to talk?"

Maggie was, of course, being sarcastic, but Ackerman didn't seem to grasp that. He just shook his head and replied, "We don't have time to dig a pit or lure in a bunch of alligators. Besides, I don't like working with animals. They're too unpredictable."

She raised her eyebrows and opened her door, saying, "Well, let's do this." Within ten seconds of leaving the car, she'd killed her first mosquito.

They ascended the front steps, and their noses were assaulted by the smell of dead fish. A trio of large catfish hung from the porch like macabre wind chimes. The tails had been sliced off, allowing the blood to drip down into buckets sitting beneath the hanging bodies.

Maggie knocked on the front door, but instead of someone answering from inside the house, the sound of a shotgun shell being jacked into a chamber answered from the front yard. An old man with snow-white hair and a bushy beard wearing a pair of bib overalls emerged from the shadows with a pump-action shotgun trained on them. "Get off my property," the old man said.

Ackerman turned around and moved halfway down the wooden steps. He said, "Hello, Grandfather. It's been a long time."

Louis Ackerman's eyes went wide, and the color drained from his face. He whispered, "You." Then he raised the shotgun to his shoulder and said, "I should kill you where you stand. Do the world a favor."

Ackerman moved slowly to the bottom of the steps and said, "Do it, then. Pull the trigger. But I guess you always knew what my father was, and you never had the balls to put a bullet in *his* brain when you had the chance."

Tears formed in the old man's eyes, but before he could say another word, Ackerman lunged forward and closed the distance between them. He grabbed the barrel of the shotgun and jerked it upward. The gun discharged into the air, and Ackerman slammed an elbow into the old man's temple, knocking him out cold. The killer bent down and checked his grandfather's pulse.

"Is he okay?" Maggie asked as she joined Ackerman in the yard.

"He's fine," Ackerman said. Then he glanced back at her and smiled. "Don't you just love family reunions?"

CHAPTER SEVENTY

THE INSIDE OF LOUIS ACKERMAN'S HOUSE WAS BEAUTIFUL BUT DATED AND CRUMBLING. The high ceilings had exposed beams, and the crown molding was elegant but decaying in spots. Scuffs and gouges from years of wear and abuse marred the hardwood floors. The whole house smelled of musty decay. They sat the unconscious old man at a French walnut table resting in what Maggie guessed to be the dining room, although the tabletop was covered with various types of tools apparently used in mask-making. A few unfinished examples and some raw materials rested beside the tools.

"Should we tie him up?" Maggie asked.

Ackerman was staring at some black and white photographs hanging on one wall. Without looking away from the pictures, he said, "He's an old man. I think we can handle him. Besides, I probably took the last bit of fight out of him."

"So what now?"

Ackerman walked over and picked up a small coffee cup sitting on the table. He sniffed the liquid inside and said, "We wake him up" as he tossed the contents of the cup into the old man's face. The liquid collected in his beard and dribbled down onto his shirt. He shook himself awake, and his eyes opened. He glanced around, orienting himself, and then his gaze shifted between Maggie and Ackerman and back again.

Maggie spoke first, figuring that there was no point in beating around the bush after the reception they'd been given. "We need to find your son."

Louis said, "I can't help you." His voice was soft and tinged with a slight accent that she couldn't place.

"I'm a federal agent, Mr. Ackerman. I work with your grandson." Louis looked at Ackerman, but Maggie added, "Not him. Your other grandson, Marcus. He's a good man. He helps people. But your son resurfaced and took Marcus. That was over six months ago. We...I need your help."

"I'm sorry about your friend Marcus, but I don't know where my son is."

Ackerman slammed his fist down on the table and screamed at the old man, "You're lying!"

Maggie said, "Ackerman, calm down. I'll handle this."

But Ackerman didn't listen. He grabbed the old man by the shoulders and said, "Tell me. Tell me why he did it."

Louis said, "I don't know what you mean."

Ackerman moved to a window and pulled back the curtain. He leaned a hand on the window frame and said, "I want you to tell me why. I know why I am who I am. I may not be able to justify it or easily quantify and categorize it, but I can trace back the roots of my psychosis and learn from it. But in the end, it all stems from him. He put the darkness in me, but how did it get into him in the first place? I need to understand why my father hated...why he did those things to me. Not just his psychobabble and his talk of research and understanding the minds of psychopaths. I want to know why he's broken, and why he insisted on breaking me."

Louis leaned forward and rested his forearms on his knees. His bearded face clenched up but small sobs escaped. Through the tears, he said, "I've asked myself that for years. Asked myself if I had done something differently could I have helped him, or at least stopped him. I really don't think it was one thing. No simple explanation or singular event, but a thousand little things. Death by a thousand cuts. I suppose you deserve the whole story."

The old man stood up and walked over to the wall of photos. He grabbed one off the wall and handed it to Maggie. "That's Marcus's grandmother. I guess it started with the day she died."

Louis dropped back into his chair and continued, "I was drunk that day. I was drunk most days back then. The three of us were in my old pickup truck, and I think something was in the road, although, to be honest, I can't even be sure if there was anything there or not. I might just have been too drunk to keep the damn thing between the ditches. Truck swerved and flipped. Landed on top of a guard rail. Thing rammed right through the passenger side of the truck. The crash knocked me unconscious and killed my wife on impact. Lord only knows how long I was out, but I do know that whole time my son was awake and staring into his mother's lifeless eyes. He was only four years old."

Maggie looked over at Ackerman. He slid down to the floor and stared off into space as his grandfather told his story. She thought that she saw moisture forming in his eyes.

"After that day," Louis said, "he didn't speak for nearly a month, and I could barely get him to eat or do anything. He screamed all the time. He would just sit there and shake and cry. I had one of those head doctors look at him, and they called it panphobia, the fear of everything. It was as if he thought that everyone and everything in the world was out to get him."

Maggie shook her head. "That's awful. Were they able to help him?"

"We tried all sorts of things, and some of them helped a little. At least they got him to the point where he wasn't screaming and crying all the time. But you could still see it in his eyes, the fear. That constant dread. It killed me seeing him like that, but we weren't rich. My shop was doing well, but the doctors were expensive. I started reading up on the treatments, studying the books. I thought that maybe I could treat him myself. And maybe that's where it all took a turn for the worse."

Louis ran his fingers through his snow-white hair and then tapped his fist on the table. "I had read that the most effective treatments involved forcing the person to confront their fears. So I started exposing him to things. Little things at first. Basically just forcing him to do all the normal things he didn't want to do. When that didn't seem to help, my methods got more extreme."

Maggie wasn't sure that she wanted to know what that meant, but she asked anyway. "What do you mean by 'extreme'?"

"All the details aren't important, but to give you an idea, I once locked him in a cedar trunk filled with snakes."

Maggie's left hand involuntarily covered her mouth at the thought of such abuse.

"I'm not proud of what I did, and I'm not trying to justify it, but to be honest, some of those things seemed to help him. But the biggest change came when I took him hunting up north. We killed a whitetail deer, and he helped me field dress it. I taught him how. He was scared to death at first, but by the end, he seemed to enjoy it. At the time, I thought it was a good thing. Until I started finding all kinds of other dead animals around. He would dissect anything he could get his hands on."

Maggie nodded her head in affirmation. The torture and murder of small animals was a major warning sign identifying those individuals with the potential to grow up to become murderers. Nearly all the great killers were proven to share that characteristic. Budding serial killers, it seemed, were the arch-nemeses of alley cats everywhere.

"I confronted him about it. He said that he was just curious. He wanted to understand how their insides worked. He became curious about lots of things, wanting to understand how they worked. Again, I thought these were all good things. If you can understand something, then maybe you're not afraid of it anymore. It seemed to work. He improved enough by junior high that he could start attending regular school, and he did well. He was a smart boy. Maybe too smart. I heard a lot of reports that he was a bit of a bully. The teachers said he liked to play with people's heads, turn kids against one another, see what they'd do. Kid stuff mostly. When he wanted to go to college to study psychology, I thought it was a natural next step."

Louis looked over at Ackerman. "I don't think he started killing people until your mother left him. I think that was when he finally snapped. But honestly, for all I know, that could have just been when he stopped hiding it. He could have graduated to dissecting people long before that."

Maggie asked, "So at that point you knew what he was doing to his son and to others? But you didn't do anything to stop him?"

"I didn't know what to do. He was my son. My flesh and blood. And I always knew deep down—I still know—that whatever he had become was because of me. I understand that he probably had some spark of insanity inside of him from the moment he was born, but I was the one who fanned those flames."

Maggie added, "And that's why you're still protecting him? Please help us to make this right. You know something. Please, help us find him. Marcus has a son. His name is Dylan. Your great-grandson. And your boy has taken him too."

Louis looked up into her eyes and swallowed hard. "I don't know where he is, but I may be able—"

Ackerman cut his grandfather short. "Quiet."

Maggie wanted to slap him. The old man had been about to open up. But when she saw the look on Ackerman's face, she knew that something was terribly wrong. "What is it?" she asked.

He got to his feet. "It's too quiet outside. The bugs have stopped their chirping."

"What does that mean?"

"We've got company."

And then the whole world exploded.

CHAPTER SEVENTY-ONE

MARCUS HAD SPENT THE HOURS AFTER AUDREY'S DEATH LYING AGAINST THE COLD STONE FLOOR AND SOBBING. He prayed for death. He thought about committing suicide by biting into his own wrists. His first attempt at that had been thwarted by his father's intervention, but the older Ackerman couldn't be watching at all moments. Maybe this time his efforts would be more successful?

The light once again burned his retinas, and the implication made his stomach harden into knots and the tears to fall anew. He couldn't watch helplessly as another innocent person died. He couldn't go on like this.

His father stepped into his cell and said, "Same drill as before, Marcus."

"No. If you want me to move, you'll have to drag me kicking and screaming."

"Okay," his father said. Then he initiated a shock so strong that Marcus's muscles were useless for several minutes. Ackerman Sr. dragged him into the next chamber, but Marcus didn't have the ability to do any kicking or screaming. After replacing the apparently expended battery in Marcus's large collar, Ackerman Sr. propped him up in another chair, but this time a metal table rested in front of him instead of the previous torture device.

Once his paralysis had worn off, Marcus saw a woman sitting across from him. She was apparently a very recent addition. She still wore a coat and an elegant pants suit. Marcus could still smell her perfume. It reminded him of an ocean breeze and was the first pleasant scent that had reached his nostrils in months. She had been crying, and her face was bruised and bloody. A thick gag covered her mouth. Her hands were bound, but they rested on the table in front of her.

"Marcus, meet Heather. You may exchange greetings if you wish, but neither of you should get too attached. At least one of you will be dead in a few moments."

Heather's terrified gaze darted toward her captor and then back to Marcus. Those beautiful green eyes pleaded with him, but he could offer her no comfort.

Ackerman Sr. then placed the .357 revolver he had used to kill Audrey on the table in front of Heather and pulled out a black Beretta Px4 Storm pistol, which he kept for himself. "Here's the game, Heather. All you have to do to win your freedom is to kill my son here. Pick up that gun and shoot him. Otherwise, I'll shoot you both. Simple enough, right? The best games always are." His father laid the pruning shears he had used previously on the table. "And before I kill you, Heather, I will separate all your little digits from your body. Starting with your left pinky. If I reach your right trigger finger, then you won't be able to pull the trigger, and I'll go ahead and shoot you."

Marcus could see the abject horror in Heather's eyes. His mind fought for something he could do to help her. Some way to escape. Some way to reason with his father. A way to save Heather. Anything at all.

He could devise no method of escape or way to stop what he was beginning to see as the inevitable. He could find no words to offer her comfort. He debated whether or not to speak at all. Maybe that was just playing into his father's hands. Maybe the best course of action was to do nothing. But he couldn't just sit idly by. It wasn't his nature.

"Don't do anything, Heather," Marcus said. "Neither one of us can escape this. But we don't have to play his game. We don't have to give him the satisfaction."

"He's trying to save himself, my dear. But you have the power here. If you choose to seize it. I picked you because you are a powerful person. A strong woman with a bright future. Don't throw that away. You can make it out of this. If you reach out and take hold of your own destiny. Shoot him. It doesn't make you a killer. I'm forcing your hand. I'm giving you no other choice. Back in the parking garage, I watched as you spun around with that can of pepper-spray.

Upon hearing a noise in that situation, most women would have started walking faster and tried to run from the problem. But not you. You turned to face it. You can do this. Shoot him."

Heather snatched up the gun and aimed at Marcus, sighting down the gun's barrel through the tears in her eyes.

"Don't give in to him, Heather," Marcus said, but he could see in her gaze that he had already lost her.

Her eyes seemed to say she was sorry, and Marcus closed his, making it easier for her and hoping that she was actually able to kill him. He heard the mechanisms of the gun as she pulled the trigger and the hammer fell. Then he heard a small explosion. He felt a wave of heat on his face, and some shrapnel struck his cheek.

He opened his eyes in time to see Heather gaping in horrified disbelief at a pair of bloody and charred stumps where her hands had been. She screamed beneath the gag. Thankfully, her suffering was short-lived as Ackerman Sr. used his gun on her and ended her shrieks.

Violent weeping shook Marcus's body, and he laid his face on the metal table. Whimpering, he said, "Why are you doing this? What the hell's the point?"

Ackerman Sr. laughed. "The point is that there is no point, Marcus. There's no reason for anything. There's no meaning to our lives. Heather's death was just as meaningful as anyone else's, in that it meant nothing. Thousands of women and children are being slaughtered over in some foreign land. Somewhere, right now, a mother is drowning her children. Is that part of a grand design? There is no higher power. There is no point to any of it. There's only right here and right now. And we can't waste the only precious moments that we have by being something that we're not. The only way to give meaning to our lives is by giving in to our desires and living a life without fear."

"I will never be like you. You can't make me become a killer. If that's what you're trying to do, then just put a bullet in me now. It won't work."

Ackerman Sr. laughed and shook his head. "You're still not getting it. I don't want to turn you into anything. I want to take away your fear so that your true self can shine through. A great sculptor once said that his creation was always there inside the rock, he just chipped away the extra pieces, the excess, to expose what was beneath. I'm not trying to *turn* you into a killer. I want you to be what your heart desires. But I also know that a killer *is* what you are. And I'm trying to chip away the excess, so that the beautiful murderer inside you can finally be set free."

CHAPTER SEVENTY-TWO

THE BRIGHT WHITE LIGHT FLOODED HIS EYES, THE SHRILL EXPLOSION FILLED HIS EARS WITH AN ALL-ENCOMPASSING RINGING, AND THE SMELL OF BURNED EXPLOSIVE ASSAULTED HIS NOSTRILS. Ackerman instantly knew the source of the attack on his senses—a flashbang grenade, probably multiple flashbangs. He cursed himself. He had allowed the story of his father's upbringing and the finding of his grandfather to temporarily break down his normal state of hyper-vigilance. He should have seen this coming. He should have been better prepared. But he had no contingency plans, no tricks up his sleeve. It made him feel naked and ignorant.

Within a few seconds, the mercenaries had stormed the room and had its three occupants on their knees near the back wall with their hands upon their heads. Ackerman's senses were slowly returning, and he saw the blurry form of Craig enter and pull up one of the chairs from the table. One of the other mercenaries, a wiry Hispanic man dressed in black tactical gear like all the others, searched them for weapons and confiscated what he found. The man specifically seemed to admire the Bowie knife he discovered on Ackerman and stuffed it into his own belt. Ackerman growled at the sight of it hanging at the man's side. In Ackerman's mind, stealing another man's knife was akin to groping his woman.

Craig waited a few moments for them to regain their faculties, probably reveling in his victory. Then he said, "I expected you to put up more of a fight, Ackerman. Further evidence that the stories about you are wild exaggerations. You just don't live up to the hype."

"How did you find us?" Maggie asked.

"Your friend Andrew told us where you were headed. After that, it was easy."

Maggie gritted her teeth. "Is Andrew okay?"

"He screamed like a little girl. But he didn't get anything compared with what I have in store for the two of you."

Maggie tried to get to her feet and make a lunge for Craig, but one of his men walking back and forth behind the prisoners pushed her back down. She spat at Craig, and then she rotated her head to face Ackerman. She said, "You know what I said about not killing anyone? These bastards might be an exception to that rule."

A grin spread across Ackerman's face, and he felt as though a terrible weight had been lifted. He felt light as air, almost exuberant. He moaned as if he had just tasted something exquisite and whispered, "Finally."

Then he twisted his foot to press the button on the switchblade concealed in his boot.

The six-inch blade slid out from the boot's toe. At the same time, he dropped his left palm to the floor, pivoted his weight on his arm, and spun his whole body up and toward the mercenary behind them. He drove the exposed switchblade into the man's crotch, doubling him over as the knife penetrated his flesh.

Using the momentum he had already built up, Ackerman rolled behind the injured mercenary and shot to his feet. The others raised their guns and opened fire.

Ackerman grabbed the injured man, using him as a shield, and back-pedaled toward the window behind them. The mercenary's body shook with the impacts of his comrades' bullets, but Ackerman kept pulling back, allowing his body to strike the window and fall through it into the yard.

He dropped to the ground on his back, the impact expelling the air from his lungs. The mercenary's now-lifeless body was still stuck in the window, half inside the house and half out. The others were scrambling to pull their dead friend out of the way to get a clear shot at their quarry.

Ackerman rolled quickly to his feet, dizzy from the lack of oxygen. He half-stumbled, half-ran toward the waiting shelter of the swamp.

Bullets tore into the yard at his feet. He felt the burn of one graze his thigh, but he kept his legs pumping and didn't stop as he entered the trees. Bullets slammed into the cypress and water elms that surrounded him, but he didn't look back. He needed to put distance between himself and his attackers.

He kept pushing—his muscles burning, but the pain feeling wonderful and refreshing—until he was a few hundred yards into the swamp. Then, in the moonlight, he spotted a large oak with easy handholds and a top hidden behind the foliage of the surrounding trees. He quickly scaled it to a height of twenty feet and waited. He pulled off his boot and retrieved the switchblade from inside, crouching high in the tree with the blade extending from his fist like a set of talons, a bird of prey waiting for a mouse to scurry beneath its perch.

CHAPTER SEVENTY-THREE

CRAIG YELLED FOR LANDRY TO STAY WITH THE PRISONERS AND THEN FOL-LOWED THE OTHERS OUT INTO THE YARD. HE FOUND THEM AT THE EDGE OF THE SWAMP, SHINING THEIR FLASHLIGHTS INTO THE DARKNESS BEYOND. He joined them at the edge of the trees and noticed immediately that something was wrong.

"Where the hell is Morales?" he asked the others.

Washburn, a thickly muscled former marine, replied, "The dumbass was first out. He ran into the swamp after Ackerman."

Craig shook his head and yelled Morales's name, not really expecting to hear a reply, which didn't mean that Morales was necessarily out of commission, just that he wouldn't want to give away his position.

Washburn asked, "Should we go after them?"

"Quiet," Craig said.

Then he heard what he was waiting for. A lone shot rang out in the distance, followed by a stifled yelp, and then nothing. Craig shook his head. Morales had walked right into Ackerman's hands. He didn't intend to make a similar mistake, and he refused to underestimate Ackerman again. They had the tactical advantage. They had the high ground and the numbers, even though Ackerman had already reduced his six-man fireteam to only four. Craig wasn't about to let Ackerman gain the upper hand by using guerrilla warfare.

"Everyone fall back to the house."

"What about Morales?"

"Morales is dead because he was stupid and didn't follow orders. I'm not about to go out there running around in a dark swamp so Ackerman can go Viet Cong on our asses. We take up defensive positions at the house and let him come to us. We control the engagement."

Washburn asked, "How do you know he won't just keep running?"

"He won't leave Agent Carlisle behind. Besides, this is what Ackerman lives for. He's a predator, and he loves a challenge. You don't follow a lion into the tall grass. You stake out a gazelle and let the lion come to you."

❖

Ackerman had trained himself long ago how to move silently through most environments by utilizing different techniques, including the ninjutsu concepts of balance and foot placement. He did this almost instinctively as he moved swiftly through the swamp, flitting among the dark shapes of the trees with eel grass and widgeon grass gently licking against his legs. He was hyper-aware of all the sounds of the swamp—the movement of animals, the chirping and buzzing of insects, the way the breeze moved through the vegetation. He studied these sounds for a disturbance in the natural order, an unknown and intrusive presence.

Falling comfortably into the role of predator, Ackerman cautiously made a wide circle around his prey. He suspected that Craig would hole up at the plantation house. It was the smart move, what he would have done if the roles had been reversed. After all, Craig had the numbers and the tactical advantage. That was, of course, only a temporary problem. One which Ackerman intended to rectify quickly.

As he moved among the shadows, his plan began to take form. If these men had been normal citizens or even local law enforcement, he would have relied heavily on fear and intimidation. He would have forced them into reckless actions and used their own natural instincts of self-preservation against them.

But these men were different and required a different approach. His opponents were well trained but lacked discipline. They were overzealous and overconfident. They were also heavily armed, but they would have to see him in order to shoot him.

The choice was obvious to him. He couldn't attack them head on, and so he would divide and conquer. A little misdirection, a little stealth. And it didn't hurt that the Hispanic man who had brazenly run after him into the darkness had provided him with a pistol, a flashlight, a lighter, and most importantly, his own Bowie knife.

Ackerman couldn't resist a smile. He hadn't felt this alive in months. It felt so good to be on the hunt again. This was going to be fun, and he intended to savor every moment.

❖

It didn't take Ackerman long to reach the dirt lane which led up from the main road. He followed it back to the plantation house, staying within the safety of the trees and thick foliage. Then he watched the house for signs of movement. The home's design made it an easily defensible position with its wrap-around porches and exposed basement.

He caught sight of one sentry on the front porch, assault rifle at the ready. A slight stirring of the shadows beside one of the exposed basement's pillars caused him to believe that another enemy lay in wait there.

He found a comfortable spot hidden beneath some groundsel trees and alligator weed and waited. Blending in with the natural landscape, he ignored the insects that crawled over his body and pierced his flesh for nourishment. He could have stayed in that spot without moving for days if the situation had warranted it. Fortunately, he would only have to wait a few hours.

The timing was important. He needed to wait long enough for the mercenaries to get into a rhythm and grow moderately complacent, yet not long enough for the sun to rise and steal the concealment of shadow. If he hadn't been concerned that Craig might have called in reinforcements, he would have watched the house for a day or two and let the mercenaries grow frustrated and angry.

As Ackerman waited and felt the tiny legs of the swamp's smallest residents dance across his flesh, the memory of his father locking him in a small concrete cell came back to him. Between the experiments and torture and pain, he would often be left alone for days in total darkness. He was never allowed friends, so he conjured some of his own. Some of them imaginary. He supposed the shrinks would call them delusions or hallucinations. He simply called it imagination. But other friends he made were the insects that not even his father could keep away from him.

A cockroach. A spider. Even a ladybug once. They all had names and stories to tell. He remembered them fondly, his childhood friends. To that day, he hesitated to squash an insect beneath his foot, even though taking a human life held great appeal.

There was no sport in taking a life so small and helpless. Plus, Ackerman admired their simplicity and their beauty. A spider didn't lie, cheat, or steal. It had no delusions of grandeur. It didn't judge him. It simply formed a symbiotic co-existence with its environment and fulfilled its small purpose without complaint.

Ackerman found nature to be beautiful, and people to be unnatural.

CHAPTER SEVENTY-FOUR

THE DOOR OF THE CELL OPENED AGAIN, LIGHT FLOODED IN, AND MARCUS FOUGHT THE URGE TO WEEP. HE COULD ENDURE HIS OWN PHYSICAL PAIN. He could persevere through torture, starvation, and psychological torment. But he could not stand to watch helpless as another human being suffered at his father's hands, and he knew that was what was coming: another of his father's "lessons."

Ackerman Sr. tossed a long black robe over to Marcus and said, "Put that on."

Knowing that disobedience was futile, Marcus slipped the robe over his shoulders and cinched the belt around his waist. The material was soft and silky against his skin. It was the first pleasant sensation that his body had felt in months. His father led him to the adjacent cell as he had done previously. This time, however, no other victim sat at the metal table. Still, that fact didn't fill him with any measure of hope; he knew better than to expect anything but malice from an interaction with his father.

Ackerman Sr. gestured toward Marcus's usual chair but then surprised him by saying, "Dylan has been asking about you, and so I figured that now was as good a time as any for you to meet your son."

"If you've hurt him, I'll—"

"You'll do what? Kill me? Please, let's dispense with the drama. I created you and Dylan. You wouldn't exist without me. I own you both, and I'll do with either of you what I please. However, I haven't harmed your son. Not yet, at least. I'm trying a different tactic with him. He's not really old enough to have much of a will of his own to break, and so I'm going to mold his pliable young mind in my own image. He's going to be my greatest apprentice. A true heir to our family's legacy."

"You don't need him. You can let him go. You have me. I'll be whatever you want me to be."

His father laughed. "I'm going to break you of that self-sacrificial nature, but I have to say that it *is* rather amusing watching you play the martyr card time and time again." Ackerman Sr. pulled out the chair at the opposite end of the table and continued, "I'm going to bring Dylan in now. He's been told that you are very sick and that's why you can't be with him yet. He knows that his mother has been killed and thinks that the bad men who did the deed are also after him. He believes that he's here for his own protection. If I have to hurt you in front of him, it would be very traumatic for the boy. Right now, he trusts me, and his current line of treatment hinges on that trust. If you try anything stupid, it may force me to re-evaluate the method of Dylan's education. Do we understand each other?"

As with every other time he was with his father, Marcus's mind searched for a solution, an escape, a plan of attack. And just like every other time, he could think of none, and so he simply replied, "Yes."

His father led Dylan through the metal door of the cell and directed him toward the chair at the opposite end of the table. The boy seemed nervous and afraid. He refused to make eye contact. Marcus was also afraid, but more than that, he experienced a warmth that he had never felt before. The boy was a stranger, and yet he seemed familiar, as though Marcus was looking at an old friend who had changed and aged but was still the same person whom he loved and trusted. He had Marcus's hair color, complexion, and eyes, but there were also undeniable traces of Claire. This was his son, a small human being who had come from him, who was part Marcus and part his mother and wholly his own person, a new creation. The joy Marcus felt was surreal, but he also felt ashamed and regretful. He hated the fact that his and Dylan's first meeting was tainted by these horrible circumstances. He hated the fact that his son would see him for the first time in this condition. He mourned all the years and experiences that he had missed.

The air seemed to brim with tension and potential. Marcus realized that he had been holding his breath and blurted, "Hello, Dylan."

"Hi," the boy whispered, still not taking his eyes off the floor. Then, with what seemed like great effort, his young eyes slowly traveled up to meet his father's. Dylan seemed to shrink away when their gazes met. Marcus hadn't seen himself in a mirror for months, but he could imagine what he looked like. "Grandpa says that you're sick."

Marcus couldn't resist a quick glance of hatred at his father, but he quickly recovered by saying, "That's right, but hopefully I'll be better soon."

"What's wrong with you?"

Marcus wasn't sure how to respond, and so he said the first thing that popped into his head. "It's my heart. There's a dead spot inside it."

"Does it hurt?"

"Sometimes."

"Grandpa says that you're my real dad."

"I'm your *biological* father, Dylan."

"What does that mean?"

"It means that your mother and I came together and each gave a piece of ourselves to make you. But your *real* dad is the man who's there for you. Who loves you and takes care of you and protects you. The one who teaches you to be a good person and how to be a man. Your grandfather here is my biological father, but my real dad was a man named John Williams. He raised me. Everything that's good about me came from him."

"So why didn't you want to be my real dad?"

Tears rolled down Marcus's cheeks. He reached across the metal table and placed his hand over his son's. "I wish I had been there for you. I wish that I was your real dad. And someday soon, we're going to get out of all this, and I'm going to make it up to you."

But even as he spoke the words, Marcus couldn't help but feel that he was making promises he could never keep and that neither one of them would ever see the light of day again.

CHAPTER SEVENTY-FIVE

ESTIMATING THE HOUR FROM HIS OWN INTERNAL CLOCK, ACKERMAN CONCLUDED THAT HE HAD WAITED LONG ENOUGH. It was time for the games to begin.

Luckily, Maggie had parked far enough away from the house for him to be able to crawl up beside the rear bumper of the Malibu without being seen. Tearing off a piece of his undershirt and flipping open the fuel door, he stuffed the cloth into the gas tank of the vehicle.

He checked the house for any sign that he had been spotted and analyzed his path away from the car for any obstacles. Once he set things in motion, he would need to be quick, and mental preparation could save valuable seconds.

Once he was satisfied, he struck the lighter he had taken from the fallen mercenary and lit the piece of his shirt, which he had converted into the makeshift fuse of a very large bomb designed by General Motors.

Then Ackerman bolted into the trees, skirting the yard and staying hidden within the foliage. Circling to the opposite side of the yard which he had exited from earlier, he reached the far side of the plantation house, the one closest to the water. He scanned the back porch, which slanted down at an angle due to structural decay, and examined the space below the house for watchers.

He saw a vague humanoid form among the shadows and waited for his distraction to kick in.

The wait was only a matter of seconds. The sound of the explosion echoed through the bayou, causing a stirring of animals in the undergrowth and birds to take flight from all the surrounding trees.

From his position, Ackerman saw the fireball and smoke and heard the roar of flame and the screech of metal.

Any doubt he had about the vague form that he'd seen faded when the sentry stepped forward into the yard and aimed his assault rifle back toward the front of the house. As Ackerman had planned, the explosion caused a split second's curiosity accompanied by a split second's vulnerability.

Ackerman rushed from the trees without hesitation and closed the distance to his opponent in the blink of an eye. The man still had his back to him. Ackerman leaped forward with the Bowie knife gripped in his right hand.

His weight and momentum struck the mercenary in the back at full force, driving the man toward the ground. But before they had even reached the moist soil of the yard, Ackerman had plunged the knife into the sweet spot at the back of the sentry's neck, severing his spinal cord. The man was dead before he landed.

Having no time to savor the kill, Ackerman dragged the body into the deep shadows beneath the house and collected the sentry's dropped M4A1 assault rifle. As he was about to head back to the trees, he noticed a bag of concrete mix leaning beside one of the pillars. His grandfather had probably planned to use the concrete to shore up his home's foundation. But Ackerman had another idea of how to put the bag of powdery material to use. He went back to the dead man and pulled off one of the mercenary's black tactical boots, deciding he would need that as well. With the M4A1 slung over one shoulder and the concrete mix over the other, Ackerman headed back into the swamp.

It had begun now. The time for waiting and caution was over. Now was the time to strike again while his enemy was still off balance.

❖

Craig stepped onto the front porch and looked out at the flaming wreckage of the car. Landry crouched at one corner of the porch, scanning the area surrounding the ruined vehicle. Craig keyed his radio and said, "It's started. Eyes open. Everyone check in now."

Each man rattled off his status. Craig waited a moment and then said, "Fitzpatrick, check in."

No answer came, and Craig swore under his breath.

❖

Ackerman was reminded of the words of Miyamoto Musashi, a great swordsman and tactician. *If the opponent expects the sea, give him the mountains. If he expects the mountains, give him the sea.*

Craig would expect a quick attack followed by a swift retreat. Ackerman intended to attack multiple times on multiple fronts in short order. Craig would expect him to use stealth and silence. He planned to make a lot of noise.

Only a moment after taking down the sentry, acquiring his assault rifle, and finding the bag of concrete mix, Ackerman had found a spot ten feet within the tree line that would be the perfect point from which to stage his next distraction. He propped up the bag of concrete mix in the crook of a water elm. Then he positioned the M4A1 assault rifle against the tree beneath the corner of the bag. Next, he took the dead mercenary's boot and wrapped one of the laces tightly around the trigger of the assault rifle.

Ackerman knew that the typical trigger pull on a rifle like this would be between five and a half and eight and a half pounds. Which meant that, if he did this right, he would have several seconds to get in position before the necessary weight was reached.

He checked that the safety on the rifle was off, and then he made a small puncture in the corner of the bag of concrete mix. The powdery material started raining down, and he adjusted the bag and the stolen piece of footwear so that the grainy stream landed directly inside the mercenary's boot. Eventually—hopefully once he was in position—the boot's weight would increase enough to pull the trigger of the rifle. The fully automatic weapon would discharge its full clip into the air, causing his enemies to think that he was in one spot firing at them, when in reality, he would be somewhere else entirely.

❖

Craig turned to Landry and was about to tell him to go cover Fitzpatrick's position—since the other man was probably dead—when the sound of rapid-fire shots from one of the assault rifles interrupted his orders. Landry's gaze shifted toward the source of the shots as well, and upon Craig's command, the remaining three mercenaries took up new positions in order to flank the shooter.

✦

By the time the boot had filled with enough of the powdery concrete mix to pull the assault rifle's trigger, Ackerman had darted across the backyard, staying low and hugging the water's edge, and had reached the trees on the opposite side of the house.

The wild shots pierced the air, and Ackerman watched as the mercenaries did as he had hoped and adjusted their positions to defend against what they thought was a new attack.

The shadows seemed less substantial with every moment, and Ackerman knew that the sun would be rising soon. He planned to have the situation resolved before that occurred.

The sentry who had been positioned beneath the front corner of the house had slowly rounded the porch, making himself a clear target. He was a big man with hair so blond it was nearly white. He held a tactical shotgun against his shoulder, aiming it toward the distraction.

Ackerman moved up behind the big man as noiselessly as if he were just another shadow stretching out from the darkness and invading the light. He slashed low with the Bowie knife, severing the muscles of the big man's knees, and then, as the mercenary fell, Ackerman caught his head and jammed the blade down into the side of his neck. The man's last words were nothing more than a wet gurgling sound.

Ackerman didn't bother to hide the body. They were approaching the end of this little dance, and the time for subterfuge was past. He simply dropped the corpse onto the ground and moved to the very back of the house where the old boathouse hung over the water.

He went inside and started planning how to finish off his next victim. What he saw sitting in the water at the end of the dock caused a wide grin to spread across his face.

CHAPTER SEVENTY-SIX

CRAIG AND LANDRY WATCHED THE TREES FROM THE COVER OF THE HOUSE, BUT NOTHING HAPPENED. What had caused someone to expend a whole magazine like that? Was it Ackerman or one of his guys firing at Ackerman? Why hadn't anyone reported in?

He keyed his mic and asked for a status report.

This time, no one answered.

Landry looked over at him and shook his head in disbelief. The big black man said, "I say we get the hell out of Dodge while we're still breathing."

"He's one guy."

"One guy who's taken down four of us already."

"I'm not going anywhere and neither are you. Pull yourself together. Here's the plan. We—"

The loud hum of a boat engine echoed out from the backyard. Landry shook his head and asked, "What now?"

Craig replied, "It's just another distraction. But it's about time we stopped dancing to his tune. Let's change the rules of this little game."

❖

Ackerman waited in the rafters of the boathouse for his prey to answer his call. He had a little trap rigged up, and he really hoped that only one of the two remaining mercenaries entered the building. If that happened, he had something very exciting planned.

Although, if they decided to stick together and rush him in force, he would be forced to use the pistol he had taken from the Hispanic man he had killed. That scenario wouldn't be nearly as much fun, but sometimes business had to take precedence over pleasure.

There were other possible outcomes and ways in which the mercenaries might react, but he felt that he had adequately accounted for the most likely results. And even if Craig went all out and tried to burn the boathouse to the ground, Ackerman knew that he could easily escape into the water and swim to safety.

Ackerman was running through the scenarios and mentally practicing his reactions—so that he could move instinctively and without thought when the moment came—when he heard Craig's voice call out to him from the backyard.

❖

Craig dragged Maggie down the steps of the back porch by her hair. Her hands and feet were bound, but she fought him every inch of the way. He was glad that she was fighting back. He liked it when they struggled.

Landry took cover beside him, his assault rifle trained on the boathouse.

Maggie said, "You look scared, Craig. Guess Ackerman lives up to the hype after all."

He kicked her in the side and said, "Shut up." Then he called out, "Ackerman! It's over. If you don't come out now, I'll put a bullet in Maggie's head."

There was no answer, and Craig added, "I'll give you ten seconds to surrender, and then she's dead."

Maggie said, "You think he gives a crap? He's not some hero. If you think—"

He kicked her again. "Quiet." He started counting out loud, waiting for Ackerman to emerge. When he reached three, his countdown slowed to a crawl. When he hit two, he stopped speaking altogether and just stood there, watching the boathouse.

Maggie laughed. "Guess he called your bluff."

Craig shook his head and cursed. He ran a hand through his blond hair and then looked over at Landry and pointed toward the boathouse.

Landry said, "Hell no."

"That's an order. Go check it out."

"If it's a distraction, then he's not even in there. Otherwise it's definitely a trap."

"I'm getting real sick of you questioning me. When I give an order, you follow it."

Landry's gaze went cold, and his lips curled back in a snarl like a junkyard dog's. "Maybe that would be true if we were soldiers. But we're not. We're contractors. Mercenaries. And mercs get paid. Nobody's paying me to go out there and get my ass killed because some psycho stepped on your toes and bruised your ego. I'm tired of—"

Craig shot Landry in the face. The big black man crumpled to the porch, his blood pooling and flowing down through the floor's cracks. Craig ripped off his tactical gear and tossed his guns onto the floor. He pulled off his black body armor and stripped down to the black tank top beneath. Stepping down into the yard, he yelled out, "It's just you and me now, Ackerman. You want a shot at the title? Think you're King Badass? Think you're so much better than me? Let's find out. Just you and me. To the death."

❖

Ackerman had watched through a crack in the boathouse wall as Craig threatened Maggie and killed his own man. He had known that Craig wouldn't kill Maggie—at least, he didn't think that he would—but he had been surprised to see that the mercenaries had turned on one another already. He assumed such reactions would have taken at least another day of psychological warfare. They must have been more unstable than he had thought.

Craig stepping down from the porch and challenging him to fight it out, on the other hand, hadn't been a surprise to him. He had hoped for such a result when the numbers dwindled to this point. He would, of course, accept the challenge, but it still made him sad that he hadn't been given the opportunity to kill anyone with his last trap.

It would have been glorious.

He stared back at the dock and the airboat idling beside it. He had used a cordless drill he had found among the boathouse tools to remove the back cover of the airboat's fan. The massive blades were now exposed and fully able to swallow up an entire person. That would have been a delicious sight, but with a sad heart, Ackerman accepted that one couldn't have it all. It would have been too perfect for him to get the opportunity to toss Craig into the blades of an airboat. He supposed that he would just have to take care of Craig the old-fashioned way, which would be almost as much fun. *Almost.*

CHAPTER SEVENTY-SEVEN

ACKERMAN STEPPED FROM THE RICKETY OLD BOATHOUSE WITH HIS PRO-
CURED PISTOL AIMED AT HIS OPPONENT, NOT TAKING ANY CHANCES NOR
TRUSTING THE MERCENARY TO BE AS GOOD AS HIS WORD. New daylight shone
across the water and through the water elms and cypress trees, cast-
ing shadows across the yard that resembled bony fingers. He said,
"All your weapons."

Craig held out his arms. "So you were in there the whole time.
How did you know I wouldn't kill Maggie?"

"Because you're not stupid. Killing her would eliminate your
only hold over me. If she were dead, I'd have little reason to stick
around. I could have just slipped away into the swamp and finished
you off six months from now when you were least expecting it. I
would have rather enjoyed that, actually."

The big blond man shrugged. "Fair enough. Are you ready?"

Ackerman repeated, "All your weapons. Then we dance."

Craig smiled. "Fine." He produced a concealed pistol from the
back of his waistband and tossed it back toward the house. Then he
pulled a KA-BAR knife from his boot and tossed it beside the pistol.

Ackerman dropped his pistol in the entryway of the boathouse
and stepped farther into the yard. He pulled the Bowie knife from its
sheath and threw it skillfully into a spot in the ground between him
and Craig. It twisted through the air and stuck into the earth with
the bone handle pointing toward the new morning sky.

"The legend goes," Ackerman said, "that Jim Bowie, the name-
sake of that knife, was a gambler and a bit of a rabble-rouser. In the
version I was told, if Bowie had a problem with someone, he would
take them out into the street, stick his signature knife into the mud,

and then they'd fight to the death with the first man who could pull the knife from the ground gaining a distinct tactical advantage. A little reminiscent of King Arthur and the sword in the stone, I suppose. Whether the legend is true or not, I find it to be a fitting conclusion to our relationship. Two killers, one knife. Two men enter, one man leaves. Just like in the days of—"

Craig had apparently heard enough because he took off in a sprint toward the knife, his gaze locked firmly on the prize. Unable to keep a small smile from spreading across his face, Ackerman followed suit and rushed forward to intercept the other man.

Apparently, Craig had never played this game. The knife was a distraction, a ruse. The inexperienced player would always go for the knife first in an effort to end the fight quickly, but their eagerness also opened them to attack. They always seemed to think that the other person would be going for the knife with equal fervor, instead of completely ignoring the knife and focusing on their assault.

The knife was off to the side, and so Ackerman took an angle that would allow him to intercept Craig's run. He dropped low and slid through the mud to sweep Craig's legs out from beneath him.

The large blond man landed on his stomach and, realizing his mistake, rolled to his feet and focused on his attacker. Ackerman rushed forward and sent a front kick toward his opponent. Craig dodged and came in close for a series of quick rabbit punches. Ackerman blocked them and matched him blow for blow, each man slapping and striking with open-palmed thrusts.

Craig landed a firm blow squarely against Ackerman's chest, causing the killer to stumble back. Ackerman rushed forward again, but Craig anticipated his enemy, dropped to one knee, and used Ackerman's momentum against him. Using a fireman's toss, Craig caught Ackerman's right wrist with his left hand and slid his right arm between Ackerman's legs. He then flipped him over and slammed him into the mud.

The ground was soft, but the slam still disoriented Ackerman. Craig didn't relent. He rolled onto Ackerman and starting bringing down fierce hammer-fisted blows, using the undersides of his fists and forearms to strike Ackerman's head and chest.

Ackerman twisted his hips and rolled Craig over. Each fought for position with neither gaining much ground. Ackerman tried to get a grip on Craig's arm and was almost in a position to snap the limb, but Craig's arm was by now slick with mud, and he was able to squirm free. They were a writhing mass of striking elbows and fists, but then they finally rolled away from one another and got back onto their feet.

They circled each other, each looking for an opportunity to attack. Craig said in a breathless voice, "Nice elbow technique. Brazilian jiu-jitsu?"

Ackerman offered a crooked half-grin. "Muay Thai, actually."

Craig moved in first, rushing forward and punching at Ackerman's head. Ackerman dodged but then realized that the attack had been disguised and wasn't a punch at all. He felt Craig's left hand ensnare his right wrist. The feigned punch then allowed Craig's right arm to slide over Ackerman's shoulder, gripping it with his elbow. Craig pushed down with his right arm to hold the shoulder and then jammed Ackerman's right arm behind his back in a move known as the standing kimura.

The move was fairly standard, but the technique was flawless. Ackerman felt the pressure wrench at the joints in his shoulder, the tendons bending to their limit. Craig followed with three violent knees to Ackerman's face.

Although dazed, Ackerman spun away from the attack and ripped his arm free of his opponent's grasp before Craig could snap the bone.

But instead of just breaking free and retreating, Ackerman reversed the move into a devastating scissor takedown, known in judo and other Japanese arts as the Kani basami. He placed one palm flat on the ground and threw his legs around Craig's knees, using his legs like a pair of scissors to cut the other man's legs out from under him.

Ackerman turned the momentum of Craig's falling body into a leg lock that snapped the limb at the knee with a sickening crunch. Craig screamed out in pain, but the sound soon died away as Ackerman rolled onto the blond man's chest and dug his fingers into his opponent's throat.

With a wet twist and squeeze, Ackerman ripped Craig's Adam's apple and throat from his body. Craig issued a tinny robotic-sounding rasp direct from his esophagus as he choked on his own blood. A crimson spray spurted out from the gaping hole in Craig's neck and covered Ackerman's face and chest.

Ackerman leaned over and looked into the dying man's eyes. Then he kissed Craig on the forehead and said, "Thank you. I enjoyed that immensely."

CHAPTER SEVENTY-EIGHT

WHILE ACKERMAN AND CRAIG HAD BEEN FIGHTING, MAGGIE HAD WORKED ON FREEING HERSELF USING CRAIG'S DISCARDED KA-BAR KNIFE. She was able to cut through the ropes in time to witness Craig's bloody death throes. She had to look away, bile rising in her throat. She had seen people die many times before and had visited the scenes of several brutal murders after the fact, but never before had she been physically present at the conclusion of such a violent and bloody struggle.

She looked away into the morning sky and tried to purge the images from her memory. Craig had brought it on himself, even asked for it, and would have done the same to Ackerman if he'd been given the chance. Still, she couldn't shake an irrational feeling of pity for the man.

She couldn't bring herself to look at Ackerman or at Craig's body, not now, not while it was all so fresh in her mind. So she went back into the house and freed Louis Ackerman from his bonds.

"They're all dead, aren't they?" he asked. "Those men. My grandson killed them all, didn't he?"

The memory of Ackerman straddling Craig and tearing out his throat flashed before Maggie's eyes. She couldn't find her voice, and so she just nodded in affirmation.

"Did he have any other option?"

She shook her head. "No, those men were killers in their own right. They probably would have killed all three of us. And if not us, then definitely him."

"So it was self-defense."

"I suppose."

"You don't believe that?"

"No, it was definitely self-defense. But he... It doesn't really matter."

"What, girl? What were you going to say?"

Maggie looked at a deep gouge in the hardwood floor as if the answers would appear from the swirls in the wood. "I guess it just bothers me how much he enjoyed it. Taking another life should never be that easy, even if it's justified and necessary."

The old man nodded. She could see the years of pain and guilt in his eyes. "You never did tell me why Francis is with a federal agent."

"I guess you could say that he's a special consultant. To be honest, I really believe that he wants to make some kind of amends for what he's done."

"So you think there's hope for him?"

"I don't know, but I do know that there's still hope for your other grandson. You said that you may be able to help us find your son. Please, you can still help make this right."

A single tear rolled down the old man's cheek. "I don't know if that's possible, but I'll do what I can."

CHAPTER SEVENTY-NINE

THE BUILDING LOOKED LIKE SANDPAPER, BUT THE APPRENTICE COULDN'T REMEMBER WHERE IT HAD EVER SEEN SANDPAPER. There was some hazy recollection of a man with dark hair and rough hands working on an old boat, sanding down the rough surfaces. It remembered using the coarse material to work beside the man. But it couldn't recall much more than that. It couldn't connect the man with itself. The memory was like a light bulb that had been pulled from its socket. Without the connection, it was useless.

It walked up to the service entrance of the sandpaper building and swiped the stolen keycard that had been given to it by the master. The master had stressed how to behave in this place. It replayed the words in its head.

The master had said, *People ignore and tolerate weird, but they pay attention to fake. In this politically correct world, if someone thinks you're strange, they immediately wonder if you have a disability. And it's repugnant to harass someone with a disability. So if anyone questions you, just stare at your shoes and mumble and say, "I'm sorry."*

Luckily, it was able to pass by security with ease while wearing the stolen janitor's uniform and pushing the trash cart. There was no need for staring or mumbling.

It entered the empty courtroom through a door that read 16th Judicial Circuit Court of Missouri. Then it moved to the hidden spot near the center of the room but close to where the judge would sit. It found the spot exactly as the master had described. It reached into its cart of supplies and retrieved the two liquids disguised as gallon jugs of cleaning fluids.

But it knew that these were not for cleaning. The master had used the words binary liquid and said that these were part of the bomb. It knew that word. Knew that a bomb was bad in some way. But it couldn't remember why.

CHAPTER EIGHTY

MARCUS HAD GROWN NUMB FROM THE EVENTS OF THE PAST FEW DAYS. He felt as though he was trapped in an eternal mist, some kind or purgatory or nightmare from which he would never awaken. Maybe this truly was hell. If so, then his own father was the devil.

This time, when the devil opened the door of his cell, he didn't fight back. He didn't even say a word. He just stood up on two shaky legs and stumbled into the adjacent torture chamber. The metal table and chairs were still there. Another woman sat at one end of the table. But this time Marcus didn't look at her. He kept his eyes on the stone floor and tried to disassociate himself from the situation. He had often read about people having a psychotic break with reality, and he hoped that would happen to him soon. But perhaps it already had. Perhaps none of this was real.

Ackerman Sr. took his place on Marcus's right. He wore a black dress shirt, gray slacks, and expensive shoes. He said, "Today's game is special. It's an intersection of my two pet projects at the moment. The re-education of my son, and the...let's say...lesson that I'm teaching the people of Kansas City, specifically the judicial and law enforcement communities."

Marcus scowled and said, "A lesson? That what you call it?"

"You don't approve?"

"Your killing spree isn't some kind of sermon you're preaching to them. It's more like the tantrum of a petulant child."

Ackerman Sr. laughed a deep throaty bellow that echoed across the stone. "That's good, Marcus. And you're right. It isn't meant to be a lesson or a sermon. And it's not truly vengeance, either. It's my magnum opus. It's a memorial, a tribute. I've brought that city to its knees because they stole my soulmate from me. But I'm not trying to avenge her death. I'm doing all this to honor her memory. It's my gift to her."

"How romantic."

"I think so. But as I was saying, today's experiment serves many masters. I get to strike a blow in one arena while continuing your treatment. Are you familiar with the trolley problem?"

Marcus said nothing. He continued to stare at the floor.

"I'll take that as a no. The trolley problem is a moral thought experiment involving sacrificing one for many. It's a question of human morality and an example of a philosophical view called consequentialism. This view says that morality is defined by the consequences of an action, and that the consequences are all that matter. The setup is that a trolley with five passengers is hurtling out of control and about to crash. Everyone on board will be killed. But you're in the unique position to flip the trolley onto an alternate track where everyone will be saved. However, a single innocent bystander is walking along that track and will be killed. Do you save five people and sacrifice the one?"

The woman at the table started to scream behind her gag. Marcus thought the muffled yells sounded like the word "help." Ackerman Sr. turned to her and said, "Please don't be rude, my dear. We'll be with you in a moment."

Then he continued his story. "So now think of the same setup. Only this time you don't just have to flip the switch to save the trolley. You're standing beside the man and can push him onto the tracks to save the others. Most people presented with the quandary say that the first is permissible and the second is forbidden. But what's the difference? Both examples end in the man's death. Why is there a distinction between actively killing someone and simply allowing them to die? They're still just as dead. It's a fascinating philosophical debate, don't you think?"

Ackerman Sr. leaned forward and placed his hands on the table. "Here's what I want to know, Marcus. If you were in either of those positions, what would you do? Would you divert the trolley? Would you push the man onto the tracks?"

"Neither. I'd throw myself in front of the trolley to save them," Marcus said.

His father chuckled. "Always the hero. Always the martyr. For the sake of argument, let's say that's not an option. What do you do then?"

"Who cares? It's just a stupid hypothetical problem."

"No, actually, it's not. You see, I've set up a real-world example of the trolley problem. My apprentice has planted a bomb in a courtroom within the Kansas City Municipal Building." Ackerman Sr. held up his cell phone. "It's activated by a cellular device and will kill at least five people, probably many more. But you can stop that. All you have to do is sacrifice this woman."

Marcus looked up at her for the first time. She had mocha-colored skin and full lips. She wore the scrubs of a nurse or hospital worker. He could detect that antiseptic hospital smell on her. She had kind eyes.

"If you ask me to, I will kill this woman and spare the others. I'll let the bomb go undetonated and tell the authorities where to find it. You'll save all those people. Just say the word."

"How do I even know that you're telling the truth? Maybe there is no bomb."

"You just have to take my word for it."

"Your word is worthless."

"I assure you that there is a bomb. And I will spare them. If you choose to kill for them."

"No matter what I do, it's not my choice. It's yours. You're the one responsible. I choose nothing. I won't play your game. I won't sacrifice a single innocent person. No matter what the consequences are."

"Interesting, but what if it was me? What if you could push me onto the tracks to save those people?"

Marcus looked deep into his father's eyes, his hatred shining bright. "I wouldn't hesitate to send you straight to hell."

"Of course you would. But, out of curiosity, how do you morally justify that?"

"I don't care. It doesn't matter to me what's 'morally justified' anymore. That's what my heart tells me. So that's what I'd do."

Ackerman Sr. smiled. "And you're not afraid to do what your heart tells you. That's excellent. We're making real progress, son. We still have a long journey ahead, but we're well on our way."

His father pressed a few buttons on his cell phone and said, "I just detonated the bomb." Then he raised his Beretta pistol and shot the nurse in the head.

PART THREE

CHAPTER EIGHTY-ONE

Driving a 1980s model GMC Sierra that they had borrowed from Louis Ackerman, Maggie had set off toward Kansas City in the hope that Stan, their IT guru, would be able to turn the new information provided by Louis Ackerman into a concrete lead. The eldest Ackerman had finally revealed that he had been in contact with his son a few years earlier. Francis Ackerman Sr. had shown up at his door one day and asked his father to complete his training in the ways of mask-making. Louis had apparently hoped the boy would take over his business one day and had begun his instruction when Francis was in high school. However, his son had never been passionate about it—his artistic talents leaned more toward music. Louis had given his son some advanced lessons, and Francis disappeared again. But not before leaving an address for Louis to send a monthly supply of raw mask-making materials, including silicone and vinyl chloride resin.

The address was that of an anonymous mail-forwarding service, which forwarded to yet another service, and then another. Under normal circumstances, law enforcement would have required three separate warrants to find out the final destinations of the forwarded mail. Luckily, the Shepherd Organization wasn't normal law enforcement, and one of Stan's specialties was breaking into secure computer systems without leaving a trace.

The MIT-grad had been reluctant to help at first—the Director had ordered him to report any contact he received from Maggie and offer no assistance—but she and Stan had always been close. He was like a big brother to her, and with a little bit of begging, he agreed to help.

Stan had already tracked Ackerman Sr.'s deliveries through two of the services and was now working on the third—and hopefully final—mail-forwarding company. With any luck, they would know an actual physical address soon.

Maggie hadn't said much to Ackerman during the drive, and he had been quiet as well. He just sat in the passenger seat with a satisfied look on his face, like the fat cat who had just eaten the canary. She noticed him raise his right hand to his nose and inhale deeply. She couldn't resist. "What are you doing?" she asked.

"I can still smell that metallic scent of blood on my fingers. I had forgotten how much I enjoy it."

"You're disgusting."

"Oh, come now, little sister. Are you truly angry with me for killing those men? Or are you just feeling guilty for having ordered their deaths?"

"I didn't order anything."

Ackerman said, "I seem to recall the situation differently. You wanted your little attack dog off its leash, but then you turned your nose up when it bit one of the neighbors. Not even you can fault me for what happened back in the swamp."

"You didn't have to be so..."

"What? Good at it?"

"Excited. But you know, it was for the best. You saved us. And there, for just a brief second, I almost started to think of you as a human being. So thank you for reminding me of the monster you really are."

Maggie expected some clever and twisted retort, but Ackerman said nothing. She briefly took her eyes off the road and looked over at him. He was staring straight out the window with a strange, distant look on his face. Then she thought she saw tears forming in his eyes, but that couldn't be. It must have just been a trick of the light. Ackerman didn't have feelings. Or did he?

Maggie was about to say something when her phone rang. She slid her finger across the display to answer the call and pressed the button to activate the speaker function. "Give me good news, Stan," she said.

"Your wish is my command. The last service is redirecting all mail to a PO box in Leavenworth, KS."

"Who owns the box?"

"It's actually registered to an LLC that doesn't do any business."

She slammed her fist on the steering wheel. "A dummy corporation."

"Exactly, like paranoid much? It's no wonder this guy has stayed under the radar all these years. Here's the thing, though. The shell corporation has a bank account in Belarus, which makes sense because their government doesn't like to play ball with our law enforcement. So I worked my magic, and I got the address from that account, which is linked to a building in Leavenworth."

"You hacked into a bank in Belarus?"

"Actually, no. I did this one the old-fashioned way. I got the bank's list of employees and then found one with some gambling debts. And, well, let's just say that our operating expenditures are going to be a little high this month. So... here's the part where you tell me I'm a genius."

Maggie laughed and said, "You're a genius, and I love you for it. What do we know about the building?"

"It's a music store called the Thirteenth Fret."

CHAPTER EIGHTY-TWO

As she pulled the Sierra up to the curb across the street from the Thirteenth Fret, Maggie couldn't resist the urge to slam her fist against the dashboard. Ackerman asked, "What was that all about?"

"I've been here before."

"What do you mean?"

"After Marcus was taken, I checked out everyone in a hundred miles with a name that could match the information you gave us. When that didn't pan out, I paid a personal visit to every music store or place that gave lessons within a hundred miles."

Ackerman added, "Also as I suggested."

"I remember coming here. I questioned a man that was the right age, but he didn't look anything like the pictures of your father I've seen."

"I suspect he's had multiple rounds of plastic surgery, plus it's been a lot of years. I may not even recognize him now."

"He gave me the owner's name, and Stan checked the property records. They matched up. I moved on. He was just so charming and personable. He reminded me of my grandpa. There was a kid in there getting a lesson, and the kid seemed to really enjoy learning from the guy. It just didn't match up with anything I knew about him. But now... that had to have been him. I was face to face with him. Hell, I could have been twenty feet from where Marcus is being held."

"Don't be too hard on yourself. You definitely aren't the first agent to stare a serial killer in the face and not know it." Ackerman gestured at the many people walking down the streets of Leavenworth. It looked like any other small Midwestern town. A group of teenage couples strolled hand in hand, joking and laughing. Men and women went about their daily business. Two kids who couldn't have been older than junior-high age entered a nearby restaurant.

He said, "All these people have been living and working beside him every day, and they didn't know it. The BTK Killer was president of the Congregation Council of Christ Lutheran Church and a Cub Scout leader. How are you supposed to pick him out from one interview? If the facts checked out, then you move on. It's all you could do."

"It doesn't feel like it."

"How do you want to handle this? Should we call in the police or some kind of backup?"

"We're wanted fugitives. We need to be sure. If we make a call like that, and he's not here, then we'll have blown our only shot. We can't even be completely sure that the older man I met was him. He could work here giving lessons on the side, or he might just be a customer or friend that knows the owner well enough to have some mail delivered here. We have to play this off like we're customers. See if the guy I met is here and then see how he reacts when he sees you. Besides, don't you think we can handle an old man?"

Maggie saw something in Ackerman's eyes that she never expected to witness. Fear.

He said, "Physically, yes. But you don't know my father. He's not a man you should ever underestimate. Compared to him, I'm practically cute and cuddly."

CHAPTER EIGHTY-THREE

THE DOOR OF MARCUS'S CELL CRACKED OPEN, AND HIS FATHER LAID A COMPUTER PRINTOUT ON THE FLOOR. With a smile, Ackerman Sr. said, "I just found that article on CNN.com. Our escapades are national news already. I'll leave the light on so you can read it. Think you'll find it intriguing. But just wait. That's a taste of what's to come. Merely a test of the binary explosive that I've acquired. The real show will be two days from now. My grand finale for the people of Kansas City. But don't worry, the three of us—you, me, and Dylan—will carry on somewhere else. Three generations of the Ackerman clan, together at last. Your education has only just begun, my boy."

The door clanged shut. Marcus heard the lock engage, but the lights stayed on. He dragged his pale, broken body over to the door and gathered up the two pieces of paper. The headline read, "Eight Die in Kansas City Courthouse Bombing."

He crumpled up the papers and threw them across the cell. The tears came fast and hard. His body shook, and he banged his head against the stone floor. He couldn't go on like this anymore. He wanted to stay strong and alive for Dylan, but his "education" was just giving his father an excuse to kill more and more innocent people. The death toll was rising, and Marcus could no longer bear so much blood on his hands. He was drowning in it. It was choking the light from his soul. A little piece of his humanity died with every one of his father's victims.

And worse yet, what if his father succeeded? Marcus knew he was capable of the same evil that possessed his father and brother. What if Ackerman Sr. was able to unleash that darkness in him? He couldn't let that happen.

Marcus looked down at his wrists. They were pale and thin, and he could see the veins through his ashen skin. His mind made up, he brought his forearm to his mouth and bit into his own flesh.

❖

Thomas White, the man formerly known as Francis Ackerman Sr., walked back toward his workshop and admired his masks that covered one whole wall. His skill was growing. Although he might never reach the level of ability that his father possessed, he definitely felt that he had captured the pain and torment of his subjects.

He grabbed one of the masks from its perch and admired it. The three-dimensional expression of death and agony was so vivid and alive, much better than any picture or video. The masks truly took him back to the moments of his victims' deaths and allowed him to relive their exquisite suffering over and over again. Reconnecting with his father and perfecting the craft was one of the best decisions he had made.

His cell phone rang, and he recognized it as the number of the music store. He had instructed the teenager he had hired to man the store not to disturb him unless absolutely necessary, and so he knew it must be important. Duty called.

"Yes?" he answered.

"Sorry to bother you, boss, but there's a couple up here who said they're thinking about purchasing a new sound system and a grand piano for their church. They wanted to speak to an expert, so I figured you would want to handle it."

Thomas thought about that. It was very fortuitous timing. He could definitely use some extra cash for his coming relocation. "I'll be up in just a moment."

❖

The kid manning the music store said, "The boss will be right up."

Ackerman nodded and ran his fingers over the strings of an expensive Martin guitar with intricate gold inlay. He had never learned how to play an instrument himself. He enjoyed music, but the thought of playing had never interested him. Still, he remembered lying on the floor of his cell as a boy and listening to the melancholy notes of his father's guitar on the other side of his door. He had always wondered how such beautiful and flawless music could come from a man with such an ugly and broken soul.

Ackerman heard movement from a back room and directed his gaze toward the wall behind the counter. A honey-colored door creaked on its hinges, and an older man stepped through. He wore a sweater over a white dress shirt and gray slacks. He looked like a professor. His eyes were bright with intelligence and madness. Ackerman felt his knees tremble upon seeing his father alive after so many years. The man who had tortured and molded him into a monster. The man who had stolen his childhood, his innocence, and any hope he had ever had of a normal life. And here he was, in the flesh.

His nose was different. The chin. The cheekbones. But not the eyes. He couldn't change the eyes. And those were the eyes that Ackerman had seen in his nightmares for as long as he could remember.

His father froze, recognition and understanding passing over his features like a creeping shadow, the mask he wore to the world fading away, the facade peeling back to reveal the killer beneath.

"Everything okay, Mr. White?" the kid behind the counter asked. "You look like you've seen a ghost."

From the corner of his eye, Ackerman saw Maggie go for her gun.

The man the teenager knew as Mr. White acted quickly and decisively before Maggie could bring her pistol to bear. If he had hesitated for just a fraction of a second, Maggie would have had him dead to rights, but Mr. White moved with a speed and assurance that surprised even Ackerman.

He spun the teenager around, using him as a shield and a distraction.

Ackerman ran forward, but it all happened so fast. There was nothing he could do.

Maggie fired. The bullets struck the honey-colored door as Mr. White shoved the teenager forward and slipped through to the other room, pushing the door shut behind him.

The kid fell onto Ackerman, but he shoved the teenager away and rushed through the door. The room beyond was a small storage room. Another door stood in the back left corner of the room. He tried the handle and found it locked.

But it was only a standard door. He braced his back against the rear wall and kicked the doorknob at an angle. It broke free as the housing snapped. Maggie joined him with her pistol at the ready. She nodded at the door, and Ackerman pulled it open as she aimed the gun into the darkness beyond.

There was a stairwell going down. They descended the set of old concrete steps into the bowels of the structure. At the bottom of the steps was another door. This one, however, was made of metal and looked as though it would take an explosion to open it. They tried the handle but found it locked as well.

Ackerman rammed his shoulder into it, trying to test the strength of the frame. People often placed a heavy security door into a frame that was one step above cardboard. That wasn't the case this time. He didn't feel it give in the slightest.

He slammed the side of his fist against it and screamed, "Dammit! It would take a tank to get through this thing."

"Could we pick it?"

"He probably has it braced from the other side. We'd have to drill the hinges to get through, and we definitely don't have time for that. He wouldn't have trapped himself in there. He has another way out."

Maggie said, "Then there must be another way in. Come on."

He followed her up the stairs and back into the main part of the store. The teenager was still there, lying on the floor and rubbing his ankle. Ackerman supposed the young man must have twisted it and had fallen when he'd shoved him away.

Maggie went to the boy and asked, "Is there another way into the basement?"

The kid seemed in shock from the whole situation, but he stammered, "I don't know. I'm never supposed to go down there. It's off limits."

"Think," Maggie said. "Is there an outside door? Another way in? Maybe some kind of cellar door in the back?"

The kid said, "I think Mr. White owns the building next door. He uses it as a warehouse. The basement there might be connected with this one. A lot of the old buildings here have these weird tunnels beneath them that connect. But most of the businesses have them sealed off from one another."

"Call 911 and tell the cops to get here asap. Tell them it's about the Coercion Killer."

The teenager's eyes registered his shock, but he nodded and started to stand.

Maggie ran out the front door at a sprint and halted in front of the neighboring building. It had a large display window that had been blacked out so that passersby couldn't see in. Ackerman watched as Maggie raised her gun and fired into the glass. The window cracked and shattered, revealing an old storefront now stacked with boxes and junk.

Ackerman was the first to leap through the window. The layout of the building's interior was similar to its neighbor, probably built at the same time by the same people. Seeing this, he concluded that the door to the basement would be in the same spot.

Racing to the back room, his suspicions were confirmed, and the pair bounded down the stairs.

The door at the bottom was unlocked, and they stepped into the darkness beyond.

CHAPTER EIGHTY-FOUR

THOMAS WHITE SHOVED HIS LAPTOP AND HIS BACKUP HARD DRIVES INTO A BACKPACK. Then he looked up at his exquisite masks. He would have to leave them behind. He had, of course, planned for such a contingency as this. He had an escape route, and there was nothing here that he couldn't live without. Still, now that the moment was upon him, it seemed like such a terrible waste. So much hard work. All that suffering captured so painstakingly and so beautifully, and now he was just abandoning them.

He supposed that was the nature of art. To create and then share with the world what your efforts had reaped. But these were never supposed to be on display. They were for his own enjoyment.

It couldn't be helped, he told himself. He just hoped that they found a good home somewhere and didn't just collect dust in an evidence room.

As he left his workshop, he patted the backpack that contained the hard drives and laptop. All his research and videos were contained in digital format on these devices. They were what was most important. With them, he could always recreate his mask collection.

There was only one other item that he would be taking with him during his escape. On his way to retrieve it, he passed the door to Marcus's cell. Unfortunately, like the masks, he would have to leave Marcus behind.

He regretted not being able to spend more time with his boy, but perhaps they could reconnect later.

He followed the corridor down and around a bend and opened another steel door. Inside was a room containing a bed, a desk, and a multitude of books and toys.

Dylan looked up from a seated position on the floor. He was surrounded by Lego blocks and was constructing a large pirate ship. "Do you like it, Grandpa?" he asked.

Thomas White ignored the boy's words and said, "Leave your things. We have to go now."

❖

Maggie led the way, and Ackerman followed close behind. She activated the flashlight function of her cell phone to light their path. The light revealed old stone walls that were stained from past water damage. The corridors smelled musty, but Ackerman detected another faint scent. It was the smell of decay, of rotting flesh and blood.

"This way," he said, following his nose through an archway and into another corridor. This one had rope lighting strung from the ceiling. It gave enough illumination to light the corridor but not to chase away the shadows. Soundproof foam tiles lined the ceiling.

They stayed quiet and moved cautiously

Several rooms lay along the stone corridors. The first was a workshop that contained a wide variety of tools and equipment. Ackerman recognized much of the material as bomb components, but he didn't voice his observations. The back wall of the workshop was a monument to suffering and featured the elaborate death masks of his father's victims.

Ackerman followed the smell of decay down to another corridor lined with newly installed metal doors. He opened one and found the body of a young woman in nurse's scrubs. She had died only recently and had been discarded in a corner like a piece of garbage to be disposed of later.

He listened for sounds of movement and thought that he heard footsteps on the stone floors deeper in the tunnels. He ignored the next door and moved toward the sounds.

Maggie, however, didn't follow. She removed a metal brace from the door and swung it open. The hinges protested with a groan and a scrape.

Ackerman was about to abandon her to check the other rooms when he heard her cry out for help. He whirled back and rushed to her.

Inside the room, he saw the crumpled form of a man in a growing pool of blood. He saw the blood seeping from wounds in the man's wrists. Maggie was cradling the body and rocking back and forth, wailing.

Ackerman couldn't see the man's face, and it took him a moment to make the connection. When he did, his heart sank. This pale, emaciated body had been his brother, Marcus.

"Go get help! Call an ambulance!" Maggie screamed.

Ackerman backed into the corridor and looked in one direction, then the other. He could still hear movement in the distance. If he hurried, he could probably catch his father. He could stop him before he escaped and hurt anyone else. He could rectify his earlier failure and put an end to the man who had caused so much pain. So much suffering. So much fear.

Marcus was probably dead already.

But he couldn't say that for sure. There was always hope.

Ackerman realized that he had reached a strange crossroads and would have to make a choice. Love or hate. Save the brother he loved. Or stop the father he hated.

He closed his eyes and made his decision.

He tore off two strips of his shirt and tossed them to Maggie. "Bind his wrists and stop the bleeding," he said. "I'll bring help."

CHAPTER EIGHTY-FIVE

HE DREAMED OF DROWNING IN BLOOD AND AWOKE TO THE SOUNDS OF LOW VOICES, THE BEEPING OF MACHINES, AND THE HUM OF FLUORESCENT LIGHTING. Marcus tried to open his eyes, but his vision was blurry and painful. It felt like he had sand in his eyes. Slowly adjusting, he took in his surroundings. A hospital room. Light blue walls. A TV facing him high on the wall. His throat was dry. The metallic smell and taste of blood still clung to him. Maggie held his hand to his right. Another man sat within the recess beside the window in the corner. He had a beard, glasses, and puffier cheeks—enough subtle changes to stand up to casual inspection—but Marcus still recognized his brother.

He smiled at Maggie and said, "I wish this was real."

She choked out, "It *is* real, baby. You're safe now. We got there just in time."

His voice didn't sound like his own, but he said, "It can't be. I was in hell. There's no coming back from there."

Maggie squeezed his hand, held it up to her cheek, and sobbed.

It took several more minutes for Marcus's faculties to return. When they did, his first thought was of his father. He pushed himself up in bed and said, "Ackerman Sr.? Did you get him?"

Ackerman hopped down from the window well and said, "No, he escaped through the tunnels."

"What about Dylan?"

"He must have taken him along. We only found you, a couple of dead bodies, and another victim still alive. She seems damn near catatonic. Maybe it's just shock."

Marcus tried to sit up farther but got dizzy and had to steady himself on the rail of the hospital bed. "Take it easy," Maggie said. "You're malnourished, dehydrated, and you've lost a lot of blood. But the doctors say that you'll be fine. You might need some physical therapy and things like that, but there's no reason you can't be back to your normal self in a couple of months."

He knew better. He knew that he would never be the same, but he said, "I don't have months. My father's planning his grand finale for... How long have I been out?"

"Since yesterday when we found you."

He looked at a clock on the wall. It read five thirty-seven. "Dammit. We have less than a day to find his next target. He's the one that bombed the courthouse here in KC. And he said that was just a test. He said something about explosives and that his grand finale against the city would be tomorrow."

Maggie said, "They found traces of PLX in his workshop. It's a liquid binary explosive invented during World War Two, originally designed to be sprayed over minefields and then detonated. Pretty nasty stuff. They're trying to trace back how he got his hands on it."

Ackerman added, "Father's a resourceful man."

"But that's not your problem anymore, Marcus," Maggie said firmly. "You need to focus on getting better. The police and FBI are tracking down Ackerman Sr."

Maggie briefly explained what the investigation had turned up so far about the man calling himself Thomas White. Then she filled him in on the last several days and how she and Andrew had rescued Ackerman from execution at the hands of Craig and his men. She described finding his grandfather, Louis Ackerman, and how that had led them to Leavenworth. She explained that, once they had located him, she had phoned the Director and learned that Andrew had been tortured but should recover.

"Give me your phone," Marcus said once she was finished.

"Why?"

"Because the police and FBI don't have our"—he gestured between himself and his brother—"first-hand knowledge of our father, and they also don't have Stan."

He grabbed the phone from Maggie and swiped through her contacts for Stan's number. Then he initiated a call and put it on speaker. Stan answered and expressed his relief at Marcus being alive. Once the pleasantries had been exchanged, Marcus said, "I need you to get me some information, Stan."

"It's what I do, boss. Just say the word."

"Now that we know Ackerman Sr. has been living as Thomas White I need you to find some correlation between a woman close to him, the Kansas City police department, and the judge or courtroom that was bombed. There has to be a connection somewhere. Dig deep. Not just news stories or police reports, but rumors and hearsay. Get me something. Maybe that will lead us to what his target could be."

"I'm on it. I'll call you back."

Stan hung up, and Marcus's mind continued to work at a thousand miles a minute. He had been a helpless victim for so long, unable to do anything to save himself or anyone else. But that had changed now. He felt free and alive. He was the hunter again.

He glanced over at Maggie, and the worry was written all over her face. She said, "Ackerman, could you step outside, please?"

"As you wish, little sister."

Once his brother had left the room, Marcus said, "You and Frank seem to be getting along."

"It's a long story, and I don't want to talk about him. I want to talk about *you*. You need to settle down. You're in no condition—"

"I'm fine."

"You almost died."

"I *did* die. A big part of me died down in that hole. Now I'm trying to revive a little of it. I was alone and helpless for so long. I need to do something."

"I know. It's just... I've been thinking a lot after you... And I want you to know that last year when you asked me to leave the Shepherd Organization behind and run away with you... To be normal. Start a new life. Well, saying no was the worst decision of my life. I was just scared. This life is all I've ever known. I don't know how to be normal. I don't think I'd be any good at it."

Marcus squeezed her hand. "This isn't just what we do. It's who we are. And I realize that now. I've spent so much time running from myself. Worrying about the kind of man I am and what I'm capable of. But I don't care about all that anymore. I'm tired of running. I just want to follow my heart and do the best I can with what I've been given. I think that's all anyone can do."

Maggie leaned up, kissed him, and laid her head on his chest. They didn't say anything else, just held each other, until her phone started to ring. She answered and put Stan on speaker. Ackerman must have heard the phone ring because he stepped back in from the hall so that he could hear.

"You were right about there being a connection," Stan said. "The woman who's on the deed for that music store is dead. She was allegedly killed by an intruder in her home, and a couple of KCPD officers found her body. That's the official line, anyway. I guess the facts in the case didn't add up. One of the officers involved was rumored to have been a drug addict, and he overdosed like a week later. Some said he was acting really unstable and depressed after finding the woman's body. A gun found nearby that was supposed to be the murder weapon didn't match up under ballistic scrutiny. There were a bunch of other things that made the whole thing suspect. Still, nothing was done. No evidence."

"If it never went to trial, then how does it line up with the bombing at the courthouse?"

"I didn't say it didn't go to trial. The woman's daughter filed a wrongful-death suit against the city, alleging that the officers were responsible for her mother's death. The judge killed in the bombing heard the case and ruled in favor of the city."

Maggie said, "So Thomas White's girlfriend was killed by the KCPD, and now he's out for revenge."

Marcus shook his head. "No, he said it wasn't vengeance. He called all this a tribute to her. A gift. He said she was his soulmate. Stan, is there anything suspicious in that woman's past? Anything that might indicate she's—"

"I'm way ahead of you, boss. At least two people close to her have died under suspicious circumstances. Her father when she was a teenager and then her husband. She was the prime suspect in both cases, but there wasn't enough evidence to move forward."

Maggie shook her head and laughed a humorless laugh. "So a couple of officers probably accidentally killed her and thought they'd taken out some nice older lady."

Marcus finished her thought. "When, in reality, they killed a serial murderer. I bet she and my father shared more than just a bed."

"Partners in crime. A regular Bonnie and Clyde story," Ackerman said.

Marcus considered the implications and tried to think what this could mean for the final target. He glanced up toward the TV mounted on the wall and caught sight of the name Thomas White. "Turn that up."

Maggie adjusted the set's volume, and Marcus watched a bit of the story. Then an image flashed on the screen of a woman who seemed strangely familiar. She was a beautiful black woman with high cheekbones and short, utilitarian hair. A vacant stare filled her eyes as police led her to a waiting ambulance.

"Who is that?" Marcus asked.

Maggie replied, "That's the woman who was being held captive along with you. They found her in the tunnel that your father used to escape. Apparently he had tried to take her with him, and she either fought back or was moving too slow because he sliced her and left her there. Did you ever see her?"

Marcus didn't answer. His synapses were firing, and an idea or memory danced along the edge of his consciousness, just out of reach. He knew that woman from somewhere. He closed his eyes and accessed his mental databanks. Using his eidetic memory, he recalled case files, video footage, crime scenes, missing-persons reports... He remembered the smiling faces in all those files he had reviewed at the start of the case. That woman had been one of the missing. Alanna Lewis.

But why did that matter? There was something else. Some other memory. Another place where he had seen her face.

He opened his eyes as it came back to him. The surveillance footage of the hospital where his father's apprentice had killed two police officers.

Alanna Lewis had been there. Then he remembered seeing her face at one of the crime scenes, posing as a CSI technician. Her presence had been completely overlooked, which made sense. There wasn't a demographic in the country less likely to be a serial murderer than a black female. She was practically invisible to the eyes of police and criminal profilers. And that was exactly why his father had chosen her.

"She wasn't just a prisoner. She's my father's apprentice," Marcus said. "We need to find Alanna Lewis, right now."

CHAPTER EIGHTY-SIX

THE PEOPLE IN THE AMBULANCE HAD ASKED IT FOR A NAME. It had been unsure for a moment and had replied honestly, "The master didn't give me a name for this mission." They had then taken it to the hospital just as the master had said they would when he'd rushed breathlessly into its room.

"I need you to be my distraction," he had said. "I'm going to slice your abdomen, nothing too deep, just enough to get the blood flowing. That way anyone following us through the tunnel will have to stop and tend to you. It could buy me the time I need to escape."

As they had moved into the tunnels, he had explained what it should do next. He explained that they would take it to the hospital and what it should do once it was there.

The master thought of everything. Knew everything. The people there had been nice to it, smiling like it was a real person. Treating it like it was a living thing. That made it feel strange, and it didn't remember how it should react. The police had tried to ask it some questions, but it had just stared at them. The master had said not to speak to the police. They were bad and wanted to cause it pain. And that was the only thing it cared about: keeping the pain away.

Following the master's instructions, it stayed quiet for a day so that everyone's guard would be lowered. When the nurse came to check the machines, the woman said, "Hello, Alanna. Are you feeling okay?"

It took a moment for it to realize that the woman was talking to it. Then it realized what she had called it. Alanna. Something was strangely familiar about that name. It seemed right somehow, but in the same vague and fuzzy way that the random images seemed to mean something. The name meant something, but the connection eluded it.

When the nurse turned her back, it struck her over the the head with the metal bedpan.

Then it asked the guard outside its door to come inside for a moment. The police officer was sitting in a chair in the hall, just as the master had said he would be. The man looked confused about what do. He looked up and down the hall and then entered the hospital room.

The master had said that the police wouldn't check its underwear, and so that was where he'd told it to hide the folding knife. It had already retrieved it and held it at its side when the police officer entered the room. Once the man was inside and clear of the door, it thrust the blade deep into his neck.

After the man stopped moving, it stripped the nurse and changed into her clothes. The master had then told it to leave the hospital and had said where it should go afterward. He had said that he still had another mission for it, and it didn't want to be late and disappoint the master. When the master was angry, the pain soon followed.

CHAPTER EIGHTY-SEVEN

MAGGIE HUNG UP THE PHONE AND LOOKED OVER AT THE EXPECTANT FACES OF THE TWO MEN. She had built a relationship with Maria Duran, the head of KCPD homicide, and had offered to call her to get some information on Alanna Lewis. During the months that Marcus had been missing, the two women had grown close through a bond of mutual loss and the shared goal of finding the man responsible—the killer who had ordered the death of Maria's son, Kaleb, and who had kidnapped Marcus.

"Alanna Lewis is right here in the hospital," Maggie said.

Marcus sat up in bed and swung his feet toward the floor. Maggie stepped forward and put a hand on his chest. "What the hell do you think you're doing?"

"We need to talk to her. She might have some insight into what the target may be."

Ackerman said, "Father may come after her. He has an obsessive dislike of loose ends and unfinished business. She may be in danger."

Marcus added, "Or she may just be dangerous. Either way, we—"

"Not *we*," Maggie said and pointed at Marcus. "*You're* staying in bed." Her finger swung toward Ackerman. "And you're keeping an eye on him. Plus, I don't want to take any unnecessary chances with someone recognizing you."

Marcus started to protest, but the look on Maggie's face must have made her point. He swung his legs back beneath the bed sheets and said, "See if she's well enough to come up here so I can talk to her."

"No promises," Maggie said as she walked from the room. She headed down a corridor of blue-speckled linoleum, weaving among nurses and visitors as she found the elevator. It was strange having Marcus back after so long. She had become accustomed to calling her own shots, instead of being told what to do by an overprotective superior.

The elevator doors dinged open on the fourth floor, and she stepped out into a hallway filled with rushing doctors and raised voices. Something had happened down the hall, and it was bringing a crowd. Maggie followed the sounds of murmurs and shouted orders until she reached the room that should have held Alanna Lewis. As she saw an officer—who had probably been assigned to guard Alanna—being rushed past on a hospital gurney, Maggie knew that the apprentice was gone.

She ran to the nurse's station and told the woman behind the desk, a heavyset black woman with a frightened and confused look on her face, to put her in touch with hospital security. Maybe they still had time to lock down the hospital before Alanna could escape.

♦

Once through the doors of the hospital and out on the sidewalk, it followed the master's instructions to the letter. It walked the four blocks until it saw the coffee shop on the corner. The car was there, just as the master had said it would be. The master knew everything. Saw everything. It found the key on top of one of the vehicle's front tires, unlocked the door, and dropped inside.

It started the engine of the beige Buick and then pulled out into traffic. It realized that it knew how to drive but still couldn't remember learning. There were ghosts of images, a man with a mustache sitting in the passenger seat with a clipboard, but those were just flickering illusions seen from the corner of its eye, no more substantial than a puff of smoke.

The master was real. The master was its anchor to the world, the only thing holding its fragile existence together. It had purpose because the master gave it purpose. It had a function. A mission. And maybe someday, if it did exactly as it was told, the master would give it an actual life. Maybe he would offer it a soul.

But, for now, it had its mission. It was to go to where the master was and help prepare for what he called "the grand finale."

CHAPTER EIGHTY-EIGHT

MANY HAD CALLED THE KAUFMAN CENTER FOR THE PERFORMING ARTS THE JEWEL OF THE KANSAS CITY SKYLINE, AND THOMAS WHITE DIDN'T DISAGREE. Fifteen years in the making and financed largely by the Kaufman pharmaceutical fortune, the three-hundred-and-sixty-six-million-dollar facility had been built on a hilltop and had an expansive glass lobby overlooking the city. It reminded Thomas White of that famous Australian landmark, the Sydney Opera House, but also evoked thoughts of Frank Lloyd Wright's Guggenheim Museum and the designs of Frank Gehry.

White had recently attended a performance there by the Los Angeles Philharmonic as they presented a program featuring Brahms's Symphony No. 2, a new work by Icelandic composer Daníel Bjarnason, and Rachmaninoff's Piano Concerto No. 3. He felt it would be a fitting site for the grand finale of his very own symphony of fear and suffering.

"First of all, Mr. Simmons, I want to thank you so much for your generous contributions to the center," their personal tour guide said to Thomas White. "Without private donors such as yourself, this beautiful facility couldn't even have been built." She was a perky blonde in a pink floral dress, and she had a beautifully tanned complexion, which would have been flawless if not for the scarring from what looked like a dog bite on one of her cheeks.

White nodded benevolently. "I'm honored to play a small part in bringing such beautiful music to our fine city."

"Well, I'm honored to have the chance to show you, both of you"—she nodded at his apprentice whom he had introduced as his assistant and who now stood beside him carrying a large black briefcase—"where some of your money will be going. Please follow me."

The guide led them through the pristine white halls, explaining this, pointing out that, describing the intricacies of the building's forty-eight thousand square feet of glass paneling, which made Kansas City home to the largest enclosed glass-and-cable structure in the world. He smiled and pretended to be impressed, but the whole time he was thinking more about the itchy tactical gear concealed beneath his tailored suit. He hoped it didn't make him look too bulky, but he supposed it didn't really make much difference. He was much more concerned about how hot the bulletproof vest and blue fatigues made him feel than whether or not the tour guide thought he looked fat.

As they walked through the interior of the massive glass facade, White couldn't help but stare out at the park occupying the space beyond the glass. It was one of the largest "green roof" structures in the United States, beneath which sat a one-thousand-car parking garage.

The perky blonde led them up a set of stairs and into the balcony of White's favorite part of the facility: Helzberg Hall. Richly stained wood the color of a dying sunset covered nearly the entire oval-shaped auditorium. It made White feel as if he had climbed inside a finely crafted cello. No seat in the house was more than one hundred feet from the stage. It smelled strangely like a forest, perhaps due to the finely regulated humidity. The stage had been constructed from a type of Alaskan cedar specifically designed to allow the performers to *feel* the vibrations of the music all around them as well as hear it.

Helzberg Hall possessed a certain ambience that White loved, and he wished, for just a brief moment, that he could have been there that day for pleasure and to enjoy a performance instead of for the business at hand. As things were, he would be the one performing.

He sat down in one of the seats in the front row of the hall and gestured for his apprentice and the guide to join him. They sat there for fifteen minutes before the guide looked at her watch and started to get anxious. He admired her dedication and patience. Finally, she said, "I'm so sorry, Mr. Simmons, but we're going to need to continue with the tour. We have a group from Archbishop O'Hara High School coming in for a private piano concert in another fifteen minutes."

White smiled and pressed the muzzle of his Beretta Px4 Storm pistol into her ribcage. "I'm perfectly aware of that."

The guide's eyes went wide, and she stammered, "Why do you need a gun?"

"Why, all the better to kidnap and murder with, my dear. Now, sit back and keep perfectly quiet or I will kill you. Don't speak, but nod your head if you believe me."

Trembling, she nodded her head up and down in a rapid staccato movement. Then she sat back and stayed quiet. White fought the urge to close his eyes and soak in the perfect energy of the place. He needed to be alert and ready, and this was no time for silent reflection. He regretted the fact that he would never again be able to enjoy a performance here.

◆

The freshman class from Archbishop O'Hara High School came in five minutes late for their private concert. The teacher and an usher directed the kids to their seats. The presence of three extra audience members went largely unnoticed, and those who noticed couldn't have cared less. Thomas White knew that the class would fill only eighty-one of the sixteen hundred available seats. A few extra people hardly made a difference.

But it wasn't the number of people that was important to him; it was the caliber of their familial connections. Sitting in the seats behind him now was an especially impressive freshman class for the private college prep school. It included the children of the mayor of Kansas City, as well as those of the chief of police, two state senators, five CEOs, and a handful of other movers and shakers in city government and business.

The pianist who had offered to perform for the kids that day also had a niece in attendance. The man took the stage and began to explain some of the unique features of Helzberg Hall. Then he sat down at the large black grand piano in the middle of the Alaskan-cedar stage.

Before he began to play, Thomas White stood from the front row and mounted the stage. He kept his gun in his pocket as he said, "I'm sorry for the interruption, but I have a very important announcement to make. What I am about to tell you is not a joke or a prank, and I need each and every one of you to remain seated and quiet." He paused to make sure that he had everyone's attention, and then he added, "There's a bomb in this room large enough to kill everyone here. If anyone gets out of their seat or tries to run, I will detonate this device."

Then he pulled his pistol and nodded at his apprentice who stood up with an H&K MP7 submachine gun in each hand, having retrieved them from beneath a hidden panel in the briefcase she carried. She joined White on the stage, aiming the impressive-looking black machine pistols at the crowd.

White directed the pianist to join the others and said, "If everyone stays calm and follows instructions, then there's no reason why we all can't walk out of here. If you test my resolve, you will all die." He leaned over to his apprentice and, loudly enough for everyone to hear, said, "Cover them. If anyone gets out of their seat, shoot them."

Then he made his way back out into the bright white halls of the structure until he found the unmarked room that he knew to be the security control center. He had already acquired the key-code for the door, which he used now to enter. Once inside, he shot the two security officers manning the control panels, kicked one of the dead men out of his chair, and started tapping keys. Within a moment, the words "Locks Engaged — Night Time Security Activated" flashed onto the screen in red letters.

As he made his way back to Helzberg Hall, he called 911 and said, "I've taken eighty-one students hostage at the Kaufman Center. I'm heavily armed and have Helzberg Hall wired to explode. If my demands are not met, I will begin executing hostages."

The operator, clearly not trained for this type of call, stammered out, "What are your demands?"

"I want twenty million dollars. I will give the account number for the transfer to the hostage negotiator. Have them contact me at this number when they're ready to talk."

Thomas White hung up the phone and chuckled to himself, wondering if they would actually try to get the money together. Not that he cared one way or the other. His motives were much purer than greed.

CHAPTER EIGHTY-NINE

MARCUS, MAGGIE, ACKERMAN, AND STAN HAD SPENT MOST OF THE NIGHT TRYING TO DETERMINE WHERE THOMAS WHITE MIGHT HAVE BEEN PLANNING TO STRIKE. When they saw the news story about a hostage situation, it rendered all their efforts pointless. Marcus was already out of bed, saying, "Get me some pants."

When they arrived on the scene, Marcus asked Ackerman to hang back at the truck and let them talk to the police. They had to park over a block away, since officers had cordoned off the streets surrounding Kaufman Center. But, from a tactical standpoint, the building was an island of its own with open space and parks surrounding it. Kansas City SWAT units had set up their mobile command center and the bulk of their forces in the most logical spot, the park right in front of the glass and steel lobby of the building. It was a large open area with a good view of the entire structure. Marcus imagined that they also had units stationed at all other points of ingress and egress, but this was the spot where those in charge of the situation would be bunkered down.

They showed their federal credentials to the uniformed cops manning the barricades and then made their way over to the massive black truck that housed the mobile command center. It looked like a cross between a semi truck, an RV, and an armored car and had the words "KCMO SWAT" stenciled on its side in three-foot-high yellow letters. Members of the tactical response team had taken up strategic positions all around, their rifles pointed at the massive silver structure. They were all clad in black tactical gear and assault helmets.

Marcus and Maggie entered the command center and were immediately stopped by one of the SWAT commanders who had been standing behind a group of six technicians working at computer terminals mounted along both sides of the trailer. They showed their credentials once again and explained that they were part of a federal task force that had been tracking the man involved in this.

The SWAT commander walked to the adjacent compartment, and after a moment, he returned and asked them to follow. Marcus knew that the next room was where the decisions about this operation would originate. Inside, they found a conference table filled with blueprints and maps, with a group of men and women standing around and pointing at different spots on the documents. Some of the people wore suits, others formal police uniforms, and others had donned the same type of tactical gear as the officers outside, minus the full body armor and helmets. The room smelled of strong coffee, cigarettes, and fear.

Marcus recognized the mayor, a stern-looking woman with glasses and short brown hair, and the chief of police, an older black man with gray and black stubble and a bald head. The mayor's eyes were red and puffy as if she had been doing a lot of crying. Marcus could understand why: her son was among the hostages.

The group didn't acknowledge the presence of the newcomers. They kept pointing at the blueprints and discussing options for breaching the building. The mayor said, "Maybe we should just give him the money?"

Marcus stepped up to the table and said, "Excuse me. I don't know what he's asked for, but the man in there doesn't care about money. And if you breach the building without being sure, you will get those kids killed. This man doesn't see others like we do. People are just pawns to be used for his purposes and then thrown away. He won't hesitate to kill every person in there just to spite you, if you let him dictate the rules of engagement."

The various faces around the gray-speckled conference table swiveled toward him. "And who are you?" the chief of police asked.

"I'm a federal agent on the task force that's been set up to capture this guy."

The mayor said, "It doesn't seem like you did a very good job, Agent ..."

"Williams."

The chief of police said, "You were the one who was his captive."

"That's correct."

"Just like that woman, Alanna Lewis, who killed one of my officers and is now in there helping perpetrate this kidnapping." There was a suspicious and accusatory tone to the statement.

"That's right. Which means that I know how he thinks better than anyone here."

The chief of police said, "We appreciate that, Mr. Williams, but I hardly think that, after your ordeal, you're in any state, physically or mentally, to help with this situation. Leave your cell number with the officers outside, and if the situation changes and we feel we need your insight, we'll be in contact."

Marcus started to protest, but the mayor chimed in with, "Mr. Williams, do you have any actual information about this situation that will help my son?"

He closed his eyes and replied, "No, ma'am."

"Then you're just in the way."

Marcus and Maggie left the room, gave their contact info to the SWAT commander, and then walked back to the truck. Maggie said, "You didn't put up much of a fight."

"I don't have much fight left," Marcus said. "Plus, I can't argue with them. We don't know anymore about this than they do, and we haven't done a very good job stopping him so far. He's been ahead of us at every turn. Maybe it's time we let someone else have a shot at him. We can't be everywhere. We can't save everyone."

"The Marcus I know wouldn't let that stop him from trying."

"I don't know if that Marcus exists anymore."

They reached the truck, and Ackerman jumped from the cab. "What did they say?"

"That they have the situation under control and don't need us," Marcus replied.

Ackerman cocked his head. "And you just accepted that?"

"What do you guys want me to do? Drive the truck right through the front glass of the building and go in with guns blazing like some half-cocked moron?"

Ackerman shook his head. "You're afraid of him."

"No, I'm afraid that I'll screw everything up again and get all those kids killed."

"Is that what he wants? To kill all those kids?"

"Maybe. He wants their parents to suffer. He wants the people of this city to live in fear. He wants to stage a grand spectacle."

"So we've been trying to determine where his target would be. Is this what you expected?"

"No, I thought that he would attack a police station or something along those lines. Hit them where they live. Show the whole city that their police can't protect them, that they can't even protect themselves."

Ackerman nodded. "But he didn't do that."

"No—he put a bomb in a room with a bunch of kids."

"The kids of the people he hates."

"Right," Marcus said. "But how did he get the bomb in there?"

"Father's a resourceful man. I'm sure he could find a way. That is, if his real target is the kids."

"But if not there..." Marcus looked back at the park where all the SWAT officers were stationed. Where the mobile command center was located. Where the mayor, the chief of police, and all the other top brass of the city were meeting and planning. Then Marcus looked down at the entrance to the parking garage beneath the park. It was a green-roof structure, so the police looked as though they had set up shop on solid ground. But in reality, there were many levels of a parking structure under their feet.

"Now you're getting it," Ackerman said softly.

Marcus continued his train of thought aloud. "He's lured everyone he hates, all of his real targets, into one spot. He's going to collapse the parking structure."

Maggie looked back at the park and added, "And kill half the cops in the city with it."

CHAPTER NINETY

THOMAS WHITE STOOD AT THE RAILING OF THE BALCONY OVERLOOKING THE MASSIVE GLASS LOBBY OF THE KAUFMAN CENTER FOR THE PERFORMING ARTS. He watched the SWAT teams scurrying about like the tiny insects they were. He was sure that sniper rifles were trained on him at that moment, but he didn't care. They knew that he had an accomplice watching the kids, and they wouldn't risk anything unless they could take both of them simultaneously. The police thought that they had him trapped, but in reality, he was the one who had set the trap. He imagined this was how the spider felt as it watched its next meal become caught and squirm to free itself from the web that would eventually serve as its grave. The police had so easily become entangled in his web.

He checked his watch. It was almost time.

His only regret was that the woman he had loved, Melanie, was not there to witness what he had done in her name. He had loved only two women in his life. One had left him and shattered his fragile world. Her betrayal was what had caused him to re-examine all he believed. The second had been stolen from him. He had killed the first, and he had killed *for* the second. And now he was about to take the lives of many more.

Thomas White didn't believe in heaven or hell or God or the devil. He was certain that only cold oblivion awaited human beings when they died and that people following their own carnal desires was the true meaning of existence. But that thought brought sadness, for he wished that Melanie could have been looking down on him and smiling with the same anticipation that he now felt.

Pulling out his phone, he pressed a button that activated a remote server and brought his new website online—which detailed why he had done all this and released evidence of this city's crimes.

The site also contained all his research. All the details about how he had created his apprentice and what he planned to do next. Although his current apprentice was a magnificent achievement, she still wasn't perfect. He eventually wanted to be able to do the same thing but while leaving more of the intelligence and personality intact. His apprentice was a wonderful tool with a variety of uses— soldier, suicide bomber, drone worker—but she was also completely dependent on him for detailed instructions.

He would eventually find a way to create a perfect biological robot, which would follow orders without question but could also function independently. He hoped that some observers would realize that he could never have achieved all this if he had been encumbered by outdated and pointless concepts like morality and abiding by the law. Perhaps that would spark a revolution of more freethinkers like himself. Or so he hoped.

He checked his watch again. The show was about to begin, and the anticipation was killing him.

CHAPTER NINETY-ONE

MARCUS HAD SENT MAGGIE TO WARN THE POLICE COMMANDERS WHILE HE AND ACKERMAN ENTERED THE GARAGE TO VERIFY THEIR THEORY. They passed a huge metal sign that read *Arts District Garage* and pulled up to the mechanical arm of the security station. A group of cops were now manning the station. Marcus flashed his credentials and was told that officers were already inside covering the garage exits. He explained that they wanted to check something else, and after verifying with their supervisor, the officers allowed him and Ackerman to pass.

The inside of the garage was different from any that Marcus had ever seen before. The same gray concrete composed the structure, but it was also clad in chrome, accented with neon lights, and included modern features such as charging stations for electric cars. Normally the garage was open to the public and provided parking not only for Kaufman Center but also for all the surrounding areas.

A disposable cell phone that they had picked up on the way from the hospital rang, and Marcus answered. "What did he say?"

Marcus had decided not to involve the top brass, who had already thrown them out and dismissed their help, but enlist instead the aid of the SWAT commander who had been monitoring the security feeds. In his experience, no SWAT team leader worth his salt would ignore any possible threat like this. The bureaucrats would be another story. On the other end of the line, Maggie said, "He grabbed us a copy of the blueprints and brought in his bomb expert, who says that he sees at least three spots you'd have to hit in order to take down the structure."

"Okay—guide me to the first one."

Within a moment, they had descended a level and were approaching the spot that Maggie had described. But the farther they went underground, the worse the cellular reception became. She was cutting in and out by the time they rounded the support pillar which marked the first location.

Marcus's heart sank as they saw a blue panel van in the space right beside the pillar. A part of him had hoped that their theory was wrong. In his mind, the van's presence confirmed things, but they still need definitive proof to be able to force an evacuation.

The two brothers stepped out of the truck at the same time, and Marcus reached for the handle of the van's rear door. Ackerman said quickly, "Don't touch that. It's probably locked anyway, but if not, it could be wired."

"So how can we tell if there's really a bomb in there?"

Ackerman tried to cup his hands and look through the tinted glass of the rear door, but he soon said, "The window's covered over. Give me your gun."

Marcus passed Ackerman the Sig Sauer that Maggie had acquired for him through Maria Duran. As he did so, he realized that before all this he would never have guessed in a million years that he would ever have been willingly handing his gun over to the likes of Francis Ackerman. But changing times and circumstances had a funny way of altering perspectives.

Ackerman held the gun by the barrel and slammed the butt of the weapon into the glass of the rear window. It shattered inward, and the pair peered inside. Two large blue barrels occupied the van's rear with all manner of plastic piping and electronic equipment hooked to each. Ackerman handed the gun back to Marcus and said, "That sure looks like binary liquid explosive to me."

Unlike in the movies, there were no flashing red numbers that indicated how much time they had before the van and everything around it would explode and transform into charred rubble. But Marcus knew that time had to be short. His father would want to wait only long enough to ensure that all his targets were in place.

He pulled out the disposable phone and redialed Maggie. The call connected, but he could only hear a garbled mishmash of unconnected syllables. He cursed and shoved the phone back into his jeans. "No signal," he said.

Ackerman looked at the van and said, "What do we do now? Father taught me about explosives when I was young, but compared with him, I'm only a novice. He gets obsessed with things like this and perfects his skills to the point of artistic creativity."

Marcus looked his brother in the eyes and said, "You can hot-wire a car, right?"

CHAPTER NINETY-TWO

MARCUS DIDN'T SLOW DOWN AS HE HIT THE RAMP LEADING UP FROM THE GARAGE AND BURST THROUGH THE MECHANICAL ARM BLOCKING HIS WAY TO THE STREET. Officers inside the small security booth ran out but could do little to stop him. Ackerman followed close behind his bumper in their grandfather's borrowed truck.

On the drive from the hospital, Marcus had seen a large vacant lot a few blocks away. His plan was simple. Get the bomb to a place where it hopefully wouldn't hurt anyone. The problem was that, if his father had come to the same conclusions as the SWAT team's bomb expert, then there were two other trucks loaded with explosives that could also go off at any moment.

He pressed the gas pedal all the way to the floor as he called Maggie and yelled out his plan. She screamed back something about him being out of his mind, but his attention was on the road as he swerved in and out of traffic.

The turn into the lot was blocked off with a chain-link fence, but he simply closed his eyes and slammed into the obstruction at full speed. It buckled and clanged off the front of the van, metal scraping and glass cracking.

The van bounced and jostled over the weeds and uneven terrain of the lot. He aimed for the center of the open space and skidded to a halt.

Marcus was about to step out and go back with Ackerman in the truck to retrieve the next explosive-filled vehicle when he heard a whirring and pumping sound emanating from the machinery in the back of the van.

His eyes went wide, and his aching and malnourished muscles nearly froze up.

Ackerman pulled the truck up beside the van's driver door, and Marcus didn't even bother to get into the cab with his brother. He simply vaulted over the side and into the truck bed, pounding on the rear glass and screaming, "Drive!"

The truck peeled away, and Marcus quickly dialed Maggie. As soon as the call connected, he yelled, "Get out of there now!"

The words had barely left his mouth when the van exploded into a brilliant ball of flame. The heat wave rushed over his body, licking at his exposed skin and scorching his hair. The pressure pounded inside his skull, and flaming debris struck the sides of the truck. The air was like hellfire, filled with the smells of a million molecules of different substances combusting at once.

Ackerman kept the truck barreling forward until Marcus felt the intensity of the heat recede. His relief at being alive was short-lived as he realized that the two other bombs had just gone off directly beneath Maggie's feet.

CHAPTER NINETY-THREE

WHEN MARCUS'S FIRST PHONE CALL CAME IN, MAGGIE WASTED NO TIME. She told the SWAT team leader who had been assisting them that the threat was very real and that they needed to evacuate immediately. He relayed the order over his radio. Then Maggie joined the rushing throng of police officers as they tried to escape the danger zone.

She was almost back to the entrance of the garage when Marcus called back a second time. She only needed to hear the tone of his voice to know what was coming next.

She tried to brace herself for the blast. She widened her stance as if she were standing on a boat and preparing for the rise and fall of an incoming wave.

Her efforts were pointless. When the bombs detonated, the ground jumped three feet toward the sky and then suddenly collapsed. It was as if she had been bounced up on a trampoline and then the trampoline had disappeared out from beneath her.

She slammed back down to the ground, which had dropped several feet. She couldn't breathe and confusion set in.

A cloud of concrete dust and dirt filled the air. Maggie heard screaming. She pulled herself to her feet. She heard men shouting orders but couldn't see through the fog of debris. It stung her eyes and burned her nostrils.

Moving in the direction she thought she had been going before, which was away from the blast, her shins knocked against a broken ledge of concrete, and she stumbled over another busted slab and landed on a sidewalk.

She ran out into the street and looked back toward the chaos. The haze wasn't as thick as it was inside, but she could still only see vague shadows in the fog. Geysers of water shot skyward in steady streams from broken pipes. The smell of sewage and burning metal hung in the air. The mobile command center and the sections closest to Kaufman Center had slid toward the collapsed center of the garage and disappeared, but it didn't seem as though the entire structure had fallen. Only certain sections had crumbled. Maybe the van that Marcus had removed had kept the chained explosions from having the intended effect or perhaps the structure had been built more sturdily than Thomas White had anticipated. Either way, the damage could have been much worse.

As Maggie looked around, she saw that the evacuation order had come just in time because a large number of officers were now stumbling out into the street, their black tactical gear covered in dust. She wanted to believe that every member of the KCPD was safe and accounted for but she knew there must have been some officers who wouldn't have been able to make it to safety in time. Still, the damage was nothing compared with what it could have been if they'd had no advance warning.

Then she realized that Marcus too must have been close to a blast of his own. She dialed the number of his cell phone and thankfully heard his voice a second later. "Thank God," he said. "I thought..."

"Me too."

"We're on our way back to you. What's happening there?"

"Chaos." A thought struck her, and she said, "Your father will use the confusion to escape. This isn't just an attack. It's his exit strategy."

Maggie scanned the faces of the SWAT team members nearby and spotted the man who had been helping them. "I've got to go, Marcus," she said and disconnected the call.

Then she ran over to the team leader, grabbed him by his tactical vest, and said, "We need to take the building now! We need to get those kids to safety."

The large dark-haired man looked around at the destruction and death surrounding them and then down at her. He gave a curt nod and started shouting orders to his men nearby who were trying to get their bearings.

CHAPTER NINETY-FOUR

THOMAS WHITE WATCHED THE GROUND HEAVE AND COLLAPSE. He felt the tremors shake the floor of the balcony and heard the glass front of the building protesting against the shock wave. The building's alarm systems began to sound. He steadied himself against the white metal railing and let out a shout of victory.

But as the smoke cleared, he noticed from his raised vantage point that the damage wasn't nearly as significant as he had predicted. That was a disappointment, for sure, but there was little he could do about it now, and the event would still make the significant statement he had hoped for.

He slammed a fist against the railing but quickly quelled his anger and headed back into the auditorium. Inside, the students were still in their seats, but most of them were crying now. That brought a smile to his face. They'd probably thought that the end had come when they felt the tremors from the explosions. He imagined they were probably overjoyed at being alive at that moment.

Crossing the stage, he joined his apprentice, who was still playing the role of the silent and dutiful sentry. He had one last job for his loyal robot. It would cover his escape by making sure that all additional focus would remain solely on this auditorium and not on his exit.

He leaned down to its ear and said, "Count to two hundred and then shoot as many of them as you can."

He imagined that, with a little luck, it could eliminate at least half of the hostages using the submachine guns. In a quick moment of self-analysis, he tried to determine if he felt anything at ordering the deaths of a group so young and innocent. Even a twinge of regret or guilt. He looked out at their terrified faces. And felt nothing but satisfaction.

Thomas White squeezed his apprentice's shoulder, the only gesture of affection that he had ever showed the thing. It had done well, and a part of him had grown attached to it. The same way that a person gave their car a name and achieved a level of familiarity and comfort with the vehicle. He could always go to the dealership and pick up another "car," but this one had served faithfully, and he hated to go to the trouble of acclimating himself to a newer model. But its face was known now, which meant that it had outlived its usefulness.

As he headed away from Helzberg Hall and down a service corridor leading to the front of the building, he peeled away his suit to reveal the black KCPD SWAT tactical gear beneath. From a pocket, he retrieved a black balaclava and slipped it over his face.

He only wished he could have been able to watch the moment when his apprentice opened fire. The hostages' screams would crescendo and echo throughout the grand auditorium, making beautiful music, the final notes of his very own symphony.

CHAPTER NINETY-FIVE

ACKERMAN STOPPED THE TRUCK A BLOCK FROM THEIR DESTINATION. Visibility was too low for them to continue in the vehicle. He and Marcus ran the rest of the way. Marcus was moving slowly and seemed extremely out of breath. Ackerman knew that his brother's body hadn't even begun to recover from the abuse of the past few months and now he was putting himself through the wringer again.

He put a hand on Marcus's shoulder and said, "Hold up. Let's think this through."

Marcus didn't have enough breath left to protest. He bent over with his hands on his knees and looked like he was ready to collapse. Ackerman knew it was a testament to his sibling's determination that he had been able to keep up the pace this long.

"If you were Father, how would you get out of this mess?" Ackerman asked.

Marcus, still gasping for air, replied, "I'd disguise myself as one of the SWAT team and just walk out."

Ackerman nodded. "Right, but you couldn't go out the back or sides. The officers there would, hopefully, remain at their posts even after the explosion."

"Okay, so he'd go right out the front," Marcus said. "Through the rubble, maybe along the outer edge, hidden by all this dust. Then he'd just slip down a side street and disappear. Probably has a car and a change of clothes waiting. By the time anyone realizes he's not still in the building, he's long gone."

"And your son will disappear with him."

Marcus pulled himself back up to his full height, a new determination in his eyes. "So let's find him before that happens."

The pair waded into the confusion, trying to spot anyone who was out of place or not trying to regroup with the others. Most of the officers were recovering quickly, either trying to maintain the perimeter and mount a counterattack or helping with the wounded.

Ackerman coughed on the dust still heavy in the air and shoved his way through the crowds. Other medical personnel and uniformed officers who had been stationed nearby had joined the fray in order to help, which made his and Marcus's job more difficult.

They had almost reached the next cross street when he spotted someone out of place. At first, he couldn't quite pinpoint what was different about this man. He wore the same tactical gear, and his face was covered. Ackerman had to smile when he realized what had caught his eye. This man's uniform was too clean. It was still dusty, but nothing compared with that of the officers who had been near the epicenter of the blast. This man had been inside the building when the explosion struck, so his uniform was still a dull shade of black. It gave Ackerman a small measure of satisfaction knowing that his father hadn't considered every detail. The old man was still fallible.

CHAPTER NINETY-SIX

MAGGIE HAD HER GLOCK DRAWN AND READY AS SHE AND THE KCPD TACTICAL RESPONSE TEAM BROKE THROUGH THE FRONT DOORS OF KAUFMAN CENTER. The once-beautiful glass facade of the building now looked like it had been hit by a sandstorm, but Maggie knew it was a credit to the designers that the building's massive glass-and-cable structure had withstood such trauma. The shock wave from the explosions had set off every alarm system within a mile, and so they didn't need to worry about the building's own security system working against them. They swept the lobby first and then converged on Helzberg Hall.

Snipers moved to the second floor in order to slip onto the balconies and hopefully get a clean shot. Maggie and the others gave them a moment to get in position and then entered the lower level.

There was no sign of Thomas White, but Alanna Lewis stood in the center of the stage, aiming two powerful machine pistols at the crowd. She didn't even seem to acknowledge the arrival of the tactical response team, as if attacking them or defending herself wasn't part of her mission parameters and was therefore to be ignored.

"Put it down!"

"On the ground, now!"

The SWAT officers screamed at Lewis, but the woman didn't respond or move. Maggie could see Alanna's lips moving as if she were whispering something to herself in her head, but it was in a steady rhythm as though she was counting down the seconds. Like a time bomb.

The response team moved closer, but Maggie held up a hand to stop them and pulled herself onto the stage.

"Alanna," Maggie said to the stone-faced woman, remembering the details of the file she had read. "Your name is Alanna Lewis." She saw Alanna twitch at the mention of her name. "Your parents are Bob and Ella. You grew up in Springfield, Missouri. You worked with animals. You were a veterinarian." She saw Alanna's aim lower just slightly, and the silent movement of her lips halted. "You have a younger brother named Eli. You're a good person. You don't have to do this. You're not his slave. You have a choice. He can't hurt you anymore. We're here to protect you from him."

Maggie closed within arm's length of Alanna, and then she reached out slowly and pushed the other woman's arms down. Alanna turned to Maggie and looked deep into her eyes. Maggie saw no malice there. Alanna cocked her head like a curious child and asked, "Am I alive? Is this real?"

CHAPTER NINETY-SEVEN

ACKERMAN GRABBED HIS BROTHER BY THE SHOULDER AND POINTED OUT THE TOO-CLEAN SWAT TEAM MEMBER. Marcus nodded, and fire filled his eyes. A look of understanding passed between the brothers. It was time that their father paid for his sins.

They pushed their way toward their target and watched as their father slipped into the front of a squat red-brick building with an orange and black for-sale sign hanging from its front.

Ackerman took off at a dead sprint, not about to allow his father, the man who had tortured and corrupted him, to escape. Marcus fell behind, but Ackerman didn't care. He didn't have a gun, but the Bowie knife was still in the sheath beneath his shirt. He would prefer to use that anyway.

Anger fueled his steps. Years of pain and hatred and guilt pushed him forward.

He ripped the door open and entered a small storefront with whitewashed walls and beige linoleum. A door was at the back of the room, and he barely slowed as he burst through it and into the empty warehouse beyond. The space was a large concrete room with loading docks along one wall. Another set of doors occupied the back wall, and the black-clad figure ahead of him was running toward them.

Ackerman imagined that they opened into an alleyway where his father had a car waiting, but he didn't intend to allow this foot pursuit to turn into a car chase.

The black-clad figure was aware of Ackerman's presence now and fired a few wild shots over his shoulder as he ran. Ackerman didn't slow his pace. His father had taken away his son's fear by scarring his brain, and now that lack of fear would be the old man's undoing.

His father fired again. This time Ackerman felt the bite of the bullet in his left arm. The pain invigorated him, gave him strength, made him run faster and harder.

His hand slipped beneath the back of his shirt, grasping the bone handle of the Bowie knife. Then he pulled the blade free, and with an underhanded throw, he sent the knife spinning through the air.

It twisted and caught the light as it closed the distance between them, faster than any man could run. The blade buried itself deep into his father's thigh, and the older man screamed and dropped to the concrete. As he landed flat on his chest and slid through the layer of dust that had collected on the floor of the disused warehouse, the black pistol flew from his grasp and skittered off into a corner.

Ackerman slowed his pace now, circling his prey at a distance. His father pulled off the black balaclava and looked up at his son with eyes full of hatred.

"You always did bring nothing but disappointment to me, junior. So what now? You going to kill me?"

"No, I am," a voice said from behind Ackerman. He looked back to see Marcus pointing his Sig Sauer at the wounded man. "Where's my son?"

"Marcus, I wish we could have spent more time together. You and Dylan. It could have been beautiful. Three generations of our family, together."

"You and I are *not* family." He kicked the old man in the ribs, but the movement caused Marcus to cough violently.

Ackerman said, "Are you okay?"

"I'm fine." Turning back to their father, Marcus screamed, "Where is my son?"

"I'd rather see him die today than live the rest of his life in a world where he's afraid to follow his true nature."

"What do you mean by that?"

"I could have showed you a world without fear, Marcus."

Marcus slammed the pistol against the side of the old man's head. "Do I look afraid? Where is he?"

"Anger is fear," their father said, wincing in pain. "Dylan will be dead soon. I didn't use all my PLX in the parking garage. I kept back a tiny bit as my fail-safe in case I didn't make it back to Dylan. If I don't disarm the device soon, your son will be set free one way or another. The arms of oblivion will carry him into the darkness."

Marcus pistol-whipped the old man over and over again, yelling something unintelligible. He only stopped when his muscles seemed to give out, and he collapsed to his knees. Ackerman rushed to his side and steadied him. Marcus fell against his brother's shoulder.

The old man spat blood onto the floor and laughed. "You have a choice to make. Let me go so I can disarm the bomb—or condemn Dylan to a fiery death."

Marcus pushed Ackerman away and raised the pistol to their father's head.

"Do it, Marcus," the old man said. "Give in to your desire."

Ackerman saw his brother's finger tighten against the trigger and surprised himself when he said, "Don't, Marcus. Don't kill him."

Through the tears, Marcus said, "Give me one good reason."

"Because we're better than him. He's just a terrified old man who's been afraid his whole life and needs to project that fear onto others to cope with the pain of existence. He has nothing. He *is* nothing. Don't let him have power over you. Don't let him turn you into something you're not."

"I've killed before."

"And you will again, but that doesn't mean that you're a murderer. You have a choice. We all do. Don't give him the satisfaction."

Marcus held the gun on target, his hand trembling and his eyes wild, but then he lowered the weapon and sank to the floor. He looked up at his brother and said, "What now?"

Ackerman turned to their father and placed the bottom of his boot against the bone handle of the Bowie knife that was still embedded in the old man's leg. He pressed it down, tearing the wound. The old man cried out, and Ackerman kicked him over. Then he searched through his father's pockets for anything useful. He found a wallet with a fake ID and credit cards matching the false name, a roll of cash, a set of car keys, a scalpel, and a hotel room swipe card with the Crowne Plaza logo on its face.

Ackerman showed the key card to Marcus and said, "This is where he's keeping your son."

"How can you know that for sure?"

"I don't know. Have any better ideas?"

Marcus tried to push himself to his feet but fell back down to the dusty concrete. "Help me up. We need to go. We need to get to the Crowne Plaza."

Ackerman placed a hand on his brother's shoulder and said, "Someone has to stay here, and you're in no condition to go anywhere. Guard our prisoner. I'll save Dylan."

"No, I—"

Ackerman leaned down close and whispered, "Let me do this. Let me be the hero for once. I'll bring your son back. I promise."

Marcus looked deep into his brother's eyes, and an understanding passed between them. Marcus pulled out his federal credentials and passed them to Ackerman while saying, "If you flash it quickly, most people won't look at the details."

With his father's car keys and the hotel room swipe card in hand, Ackerman sprinted toward the back door of the warehouse where he hoped to find his father's escape vehicle waiting and ready.

CHAPTER NINETY-EIGHT

THE LOBBY OF THE CROWNE PLAZA HOTEL WAS LINED WITH MODERN ART DECO FURNITURE AND COLORED IN EARTH TONES AND RED ACCENTS. Ackerman rushed up to the front desk and earned a looked of surprise from the short black man behind the counter. Ackerman knew that he looked like he had just been through a war zone, and in a manner of speaking, he had.

He quickly flashed Marcus's credentials and said to the black man, "I'm a federal agent, and I need your help. I'm sure you've heard about the explosion down at Kaufman Center."

The man barely glanced at the ID. "Yes, I—"

"I just came from there and have reason to believe that there may be another bomb in your hotel." He slapped the swipe card he had retrieved from his father's pocket down on the dark wood surface of the desk. "Tell me what room this card is for."

The man seemed momentarily dumbfounded. He looked at the card as though it was an alien artifact.

"Now!" Ackerman said. "Lives are at stake."

The attendant snatched up the card and went to work.

A few moments later, Ackerman was in the hallway on the seventh floor. He rushed down the brown and beige corridor, scanning the numbers on each door. When he reached room 717, he swiped the card through the reader and rushed inside.

He knew that his father would have allowed himself only a small margin of error before his failsafe was activated. Any deviation from the plan could have meant his capture, and so Ackerman guessed that after arguing with his father, trying to figure out Dylan's location, and waiting for the man at the front desk to read the room number from the card key, he had only a matter of seconds before the bomb detonated.

He had no idea what to expect inside. His mind conjured images of Dylan duct-taped to a chair with the bomb on his lap or locked in a closet or wearing a miniature version of a suicide bomber's vest. Ackerman, thinking of his own experiences as a boy, could easily imagine the kinds of atrocities that the grandfather could have committed against his grandson.

Instead, he found a healthy-looking little boy wearing a green collared shirt and playing with Legos. The boy looked up with wide eyes. Ackerman was a bit shocked to see Dylan in such a condition, but he shook that off and scanned the room for the bomb.

A briefcase sat on a desk in the corner. "Dylan, don't be afraid. I'm your Uncle Frank, and I'm here to help you."

Ackerman moved to the briefcase. He tried to pop the latches but found it locked. He was afraid to try and crack the case open, for fear of prematurely detonating the device. Judging by the size of the bomb, the effects of the explosion would probably be confined to that room, so Ackerman decided that he would just take Dylan to safety and then pull the fire alarm to get everyone clear of the potential blast radius and any residual damage to the building.

From inside the briefcase, he heard a mechanical whir and a sound like air being released from a balloon. His eyes went wide, and he acted on instinct.

Ackerman tossed the case on the floor beside the window and pushed the mattress off the bed, flipping it on its side and covering the bomb. Then he scooped Dylan up into his arms and ran for the hallway.

His hand grasped the handle and twisted. The heavy door swung open, and the bomb went off.

The blast was deafening in the small space. He cradled Dylan, shielding the boy with his own body.

He felt burning shrapnel pierce the flesh of his back and shoulders, and he was blown forward by the heat and concussive wave. He and Dylan slammed against the far wall, drywall crumbling and cracking around them. He felt something break and snap, and then the lights went out on Francis Ackerman Jr.'s world.

CHAPTER NINETY-NINE

ONE MONTH LATER

MARCUS DROPPED INTO A CHAIR AT ONE END OF A GRAY METAL TABLE INSIDE A SECURE CONTAINMENT FACILITY LOCATED IN BETHESDA, MD. The building was another black site on loan to the Shepherd Organization from the CIA. Fagan had arranged for Ackerman's temporary incarceration there while more permanent arrangements could be worked out. The bureaucrat had actually turned out to be a decent guy. He'd felt responsible for the actions of Mr. Craig, and so he'd allowed a bit of leeway to Maggie and Andrew for what they'd done. They were each suspended for three months without pay, and the whole group would remain on a tight leash for an indefinite probationary period, but at least the Shepherd Organization was still alive and kicking.

Ackerman's fate was still undecided and the subject of much debate. He had been deemed too dangerous and too much of an escape risk for a normal prison, and yet—given the help and insight he had provided in the capture of Thomas White and his apprentice and the lives he had saved—Ackerman had proved himself too useful to kill outright. Plus, Marcus had threatened to expose the entire organization if anyone harmed a hair on his brother's head, a move that had not earned him any friends and had probably even put his own life at risk. Against strong opposition, Marcus had argued that Ackerman could actually be a powerful asset to the Shepherd Organization. It was perhaps a crazy idea that would never be approved, but it was worth a shot. After all, their group was all about breaking the rules anyway.

The guards ushered Ackerman into the small gray chamber and shoved him down into the chair at the opposite end of the table. "Hi, Frank," Marcus said.

"You look good, little brother. You've actually been sleeping."

"Yeah, Emily Morgan came up with this crazy treatment idea that could help me to block out the world and get some rest. She has me spending time every day in a sensory-deprivation chamber. It's basically a big soundproof and lightproof tank full of salt water that's heated to body temp. You lie in there and feel like you're floating in space. It's pretty cool, and I was skeptical at first, but it helps. It's like turning off the world."

"Sounds wonderful. Emily's a very impressive and intriguing woman. You're lucky to have people like that in your corner."

"You have people in your corner too. I'm in your corner. Nobody's forgotten how you helped us."

"I'm sure that no one has forgotten anything else I've done, either."

"Our father scarred your brain. He's the monster, not you."

"We're both monsters. And I make no excuses. I can never make amends, only ask for grace and forgiveness."

"I'm working on something. Maybe a way for you to balance the scales a bit more."

Ackerman shrugged. "We'll see what happens."

"Please, do yourself and me a favor and behave yourself in here. I can't help you if you hurt anyone or try to escape."

Ackerman pursed his lips and bobbled his head back and forth as he seemed to consider the words. "Fine. But I'll provide you with a list of security flaws that I've noticed. It's best if I can avoid any temptation."

Marcus laughed and ran a hand through his hair. "I'm sure the CIA would appreciate that, Frank." Then his expression turned grave, and he said, "I tried to get our father into ADX Florence, but I had to settle for the Federal Correctional Complex in Terre Haute."

"I've heard that it's the most high-tech prison in the world."

Marcus pulled out a small piece of thin tissue paper and slid it across the table to his brother. Words were written across the paper's surface in red crayon. "He sent me that," Marcus said.

The note read: *I tried to show you a world without fear, but you rejected my gift. Perhaps because you don't yet truly understand the meaning of fear and the depths of despair. But I'll teach you.*

Marcus added, "If he ever gets out, he'll come for me and Dylan and everyone I love."

"Yes, he will. Father is obsessive about finishing what he starts. But that's *if* he can find a way out of the very impressive cage that we've put him in. Remember, he feeds on fear. Don't let him exert that power over you. Are you still having nightmares?"

"Only when I close my eyes."

"All that happened down in father's little basement of horrors is on his soul, not yours. You have to realize that."

"I know, but I still feel... tainted. I have the same darkness in me that's in the two of you. I've killed people. I would have killed my own father if you hadn't stopped me."

Ackerman took a deep breath and drummed his fingers on the metal surface of the table. "Are you familiar with the story of John Newton?"

"I don't think so. The name sounds familiar."

"He's the man who wrote the song *Amazing Grace*, arguably the most famous Christian hymn of all time. That song has brought comfort to millions in times of need and sorrow. But John Newton's story is much more complicated than that. He was the captain of several voyages on slave-trading ships. Those boats packed people in like cattle. They usually contained at least four hundred slaves, but often as many as seven hundred. The death rate was very high. Reaching twenty-five percent in the seventeenth and eighteenth centuries. So it could be argued that John Newton was responsible for the deaths of as many as one hundred and seventy-five people every time he sailed. If a man like that can change and go on to do wonderful things, then why not the two of us?"

Marcus smiled and gave a slow nod. "You know, Frank, you've been a horrible human being, but you're actually not half bad as a brother."

Ackerman chuckled. "How have you and Dylan been getting along?"

"Okay, I guess. It's been difficult, with everything that's happened. He misses his mom. It's lucky that Maggie and him have hit it off because I really have no idea how to be a father."

"You'll learn."

"You want to see how you do as an uncle?"

With a sincere smile, Ackerman said, "I'd like that."

Marcus stood, and the guard buzzed the door open. He stepped into the bright fluorescent lights of the hallway and waved his hand toward a young boy with dark hair and bright intelligent eyes who was sitting in a metal folding chair along the corridor, his feet dangling and swaying back and forth.

Dylan hopped up and joined his father. Marcus gestured toward the chair opposite Ackerman, and Dylan sat down reluctantly. His young eyes drank in his surroundings—the guards, the guns, the man in chains opposite him. He seemed nervous, but also curious.

"This is your Uncle Frank," Marcus said.

Dylan looked across the table and, without any greeting, said, "They say you're a bad guy."

Ackerman laughed and gave his nephew a wide grin. "My boy, as you grow older and wiser, you'll find that very few things in this world are merely black or white. Good and evil, like so many other lofty concepts, are often simply a matter of perspective."

ABOUT THE AUTHOR

ETHAN CROSS is the award-winning international bestselling author of *The Shepherd* (described by #1 bestselling author Andrew Gross as "A fast paced, all too real thriller with a villain right out of James Patterson and *Criminal Minds*."), *The Prophet* (described by bestselling author Jon Land as "The best book of its kind since Thomas Harris retired Hannibal Lecter"), *The Cage, Callsign: Knight, Blind Justice*, and his latest— *Father of Fear*.

In addition to writing and working in the publishing industry, Ethan has also served as the Chief Technology Officer for a national franchise, recorded albums and opened for national recording artists as lead singer and guitar player in a musical group, and been an active and involved member of the International Thriller Writers organization and Novelists Inc.

He lives and writes in Illinois with his wife, three kids, and two Shih Tzus.

Made in the USA
Middletown, DE
13 April 2021

37419343R00203